Elle E Evans

EXPLORING EDEN

Elle E. Evans

Cover design by: Elle E. Evans

Printed in the United States of America

This book is dedicated to my wonderful husband and children. Your support means the world to me. If no one else in the world believed in me but the four of you, it would be enough.

You are my heart.

Elle E. Evans

REGARDING EDEN

Writing this book has been part of the healing process for me as an abuse survivor. It was cathartic to write a world of fantasy fiction in which survivors of abuse become powerful in other ways, such as supernatural gifts, as they grow and heal from their trauma. Much of the abuse that Eden experiences in the book is very similar to abuse that I experienced myself. I addressed mental health issues that the characters and their family members experience based on experience with my own mental illness and experience as a nurse.

Your experience may vary from those portrayed in this work. It is important to note that this book contains discussion of mental illness, religious trauma, violence, abuse, sexual assault, child abuse, and mature themes including profanity and sexual content.

The setting of much of the book, Angelina, Texas, is a complete work of fiction. It is a hodgepodge of characteristics of several small towns in northern Texas. Several real towns and cities were mentioned in relative nature to its location.

TABLE OF CONTENTS

Prologue   1

Chapter One   3

Chapter Two   9

Chapter Three   15

Chapter Four   21

Chapter Five   27

Chapter Six   37

Chapter Seven   49

Chapter Eight   55

Chapter Nine   65

Chapter Ten   69

Chapter Eleven   73

Chapter Twelve   85

Chapter Thirteen   89

Chapter Fourteen   105

Chapter Fifteen   113

Chapter Sixteen   127

Chapter Seventeen   137

Chapter Eighteen   145

Chapter Nineteen   167

Chapter Twenty   179

Chapter Twenty-One   191

Chapter Twenty-Two   201

Chapter Twenty-Three   207

Chapter Twenty-Four   219

Chapter Twenty-Five   239

Chapter Twenty-Six   249

Chapter Twenty-Seven   257

Chapter Twenty-Eight   265

Chapter Twenty-Nine   271

Chapter Thirty   285

Chapter Thirty-One   291

Chapter Thirty-Two   307

Chapter Thirty-Three   313

Chapter Thirty-Four   321

Chapter Thirty-Five   335

Epilogue   339

Acknowledgements   345

About the Author   347

Elle E. Evans

PROLOGUE

E den Grace had never once considered herself crazy. Cursed? Maybe. A little troubled or even demon possessed had crossed her mind, but never insane. It was ironic to her, looking back, that the first time things began to make any sense to her was in the first few weeks of her confinement in the mental hospital. Over a year later, she clung to the three realizations she'd had in that time:

1. Eden was not insane, a touch broken for sure, but not insane.

2. Eden could see, hear, and speak to the dead.

3. Eden was not going back to where she came from.

CHAPTER ONE

E den jolted awake, blinking against the harsh, yet familiar fluorescent lighting. She wondered if the sounds of horrifying shrieks would ever stop startling her awake. Those screams jerked her out of a sound sleep daily. Her second thought to ponder: would her still pounding heart or her bladder fail her first?

She quickly assessed the familiar dorm room. From her recent television viewing experience, Eden thought the dorm was likely the love child of an office cubicle and a bunk house. Blue and grey partitions around each twin sized bed and nightstand gave the illusion of privacy. The partitions were shorter than Eden, who was just over five foot tall, giving the staff of North Texas State Mental Hospital access to monitor the teenage patients.

Eden sat up on her thin mattress and slid her feet into cheap flip flops. The floor was cold, but her footwear was more a preventive measure against foot fungus than anything.

Eden shuffled to the bathroom down beige tiled corridors while contemplating all the things that had led her to this point. The plain walls were likely intended to be soothing, but they bore the scars of past incidents with patients on their surface. For Eden, those scars felt physical. She focused on anything else but the emotions she picked up in this place. She turned into the bathroom. She imagined it was similar to a prison bathroom. No doors on the stalls, just thin off-white shower curtains. She pulled one back, hoping it was unoccupied. Finding it vacant, she closed the curtain behind herself.

While the idea of therapy and mental wellness appeals to most, staying in a mental hospital for a year isn't considered ideal. She knew that most of her roommates hated this place for one reason or another. For Eden, it was a living hell. The nurses smiled politely while firmly insisting on her taking a small pharmacy of medications meant for crazy people. Eden, however, was fairly certain that she wasn't actually crazy. *Of course, all insane people think that at one point or another, don't they? No one realizes the voices in their head are an illness at first,* she thought.

Despite the fact that Eden heard voices and saw people that others couldn't, she couldn't help but disagree with the diagnosis of juvenile onset schizophrenia. They claimed that due to the trauma of her childhood and some inherited traits, she had hallucinations and delusions. Psychiatrists promised the pills would help. And she thought they would; hoped even. Instead, the hallucinations grew worse. Eden still heard voices, no matter what medication they put her on. Without medication, it narrowed back down to one set of voices. The voices of the dead. Eden saw ghosts, visions, and some of her dreams had even come to life.

If Eden's parents had been normal, maybe they would have been accepting or tolerant of the things she experienced. Maybe normal parents would have tried to get her therapy. Not her mother and father.

Noah and Elisabeth Grace didn't believe in medications or illnesses, only demon possession and evil brought down upon oneself. Their beliefs were contrary to all sorts of science and health care. Sickness was a curse. Afflictions were caused by a moral failing. Suffering was a punishment from God. Her parents were extreme fanatics. Not content to simply be cult members, they were leaders. The Saints on Earth Cult, as it was known in the media, had always been the Saints on Earth Church, or simply 'the church' to Eden. The church was all Eden had ever known. Her whole life had been lived in the church's compound, until last year.

The rarely seen, never-heard daughter of Associate Pastor Noah and his wife Elisabeth hadn't watched television or been exposed to the outside world until the day Child Protective Services changed everything for her. She sighed as she looked at her own nearly unfamiliar reflection. Her cheeks were more rounded with regular meals. She had lost the ever-present dark shadows under her eyes. Not a trace of healing bruises or cuts. She had noted consistent freckles across the bridge of her nose and cheeks after the first month or so. She had been thin and fragile before, now she took on more womanly curves. Not to mention the change in her attire. Her assortment of donated clothes included shorts, jeans, and close-fitting t-shirts. Before she had only worn modest dresses. The girl she was before had disappeared. She wasn't sure who this new Eden was.

The memory of that day seemed almost like a dream now. She'd been allowed to go on mission work; delivering food while recruiting those families with food insecurity to come with them for the hope of stability and a simpler life. She'd kept her head down as she walked through the cluttered gas station to use the restroom. As she waited, a man approached with his eyes full of concern as he asked her if she was okay. She hadn't noticed her bruises were visible until he pointed them out. The concerned man and his wife questioned her in hushed tones about her safety. She'd tried to nicely brush them off quickly, but it was too late. Her father had seen her talking to strangers.

He jerked her out of line and shoved her back into the van. The couple tailed their van and called the police. Soon, they were pulled over to the side of the highway. Eden had felt a strange mixture of emotions, smug satisfaction and absolute terror at her father being handcuffed and forced into the back of a police cruiser. She would pay for this. The promise of it was in his dark eyes as Eden was led away to another car with a female officer. The rest of the van's passengers were questioned.

The series of events that day seemed to blur together. A cold exam room with a smiling nurse and a doctor who couldn't look her in the eyes but examined every inch of her body. She stayed silent throughout the entire exam. The female officer remained with her through it all. Eden heard their whispers. It was the first time she had heard the words "cult" and "abuse." Eden felt their shame, sorrow, and rage as they examined her physically. She felt the waves of pity roll off the sad eyed woman who introduced herself as a social worker. Their unending questions set her on edge. She answered as quickly and quietly as possible.

They asked questions about her mother and father, and about the church leadership. The social worker asked her so many questions about discipline. Eventually, their emotions became so overwhelming that Eden broke. She had shamefully hung her head as she told the police officer and social worker her secret: she believed she was demon-possessed. She was taught at home that she was inherently evil. That ungodly nature had plagued her with visions and apparitions. The fiend within her called out to spirits, pulling them to her. It had been the demon that lifted her parents' bed off the floor when she cried at night. Foul spirits had made her see visions of horrible beasts.

Eden had even stopped telling them when she saw things because she knew when she did, they would try to beat the spirits out of her. She had lost count of how many times they had held exorcisms with her tied to the bed. Every incident was followed by some new creative way to purge her of spirits. The social worker and officer gawked at her in horror then turned to each other in disbelief before calling in a psychiatrist to see her.

At the time Eden believed this was all her fault. Eden had tearfully confessed her sins to the psychiatrist. She had laid out all the failed attempts to cleanse her of this burden. She confessed that no matter how hard they tried, she, like her brother before her, had been born evil. The psychiatrist asked Eden about her brother. Eden confessed he had left when she was young. It felt like sinning, speaking of Adam. She wasn't allowed to discuss him. She wasn't allowed to discuss much at all. Eden told the psychiatrist that her brother had been even more wicked than her. He somehow attracted monstrous shadow creatures and set things on fire with the touch of his hand.

The psychiatrist grew more intrigued as she talked. Eden opened up more and more to this older, kind eyed man as he encouraged her. She didn't realize that her every word was recorded to lock her away.

Eden was disgusted with the docile naive girl she had been. The last year had been full of eye-opening lessons. She knew that some of the things she had learned clashed deeply with that little voice in her head telling her that it was wrong. Eden had learned the cost of trusting adults and to trust teenagers even less. Eden shook herself out of the dreary thoughts of her past, pulling herself back to the present.

She washed her face, determined to remain calm despite the fact that next week, she was supposed to go home. Home was such a foreign word. It wasn't the bedroom in the simple house that she grew up in. She didn't feel like she belonged in that world with her parents. Whatever her feelings were, they'd worked with the system to get her back. The family therapist encouraged her to embrace the changes they had made. He said that being a parent of a troubled child had been too difficult for ill-equipped religious parents. They had fooled him, but not her.

In their private visitation, her father scolded her for the medication and her new clothing. Her quiet, obedient mother had simply told her without any emotion or affection that she would not lose her like she had Eden's brother, as if Eden was property and not a person. Her brother Adam had run away seven years ago as soon as he was an adult. Eden only remembered him in vague memories. She recalled that Adam had seen things like Eden. However, evil followed Adam as if he was wielding it instead of being tormented by it.

She recalled hiding behind her mother's skirts as the pastor's suit caught fire while they were exorcising the demons from him. Her mother had rushed her from the room. She couldn't tell if she recalled it as a dream, or if he had actually spoken the words of the devil, creating horrible beasts that came to life and attacked their father. She recalled the next day how Adam ended up with a broken arm that Sister Hannah had to set with a splint and a sling. With Eden's parents though, you could never tell what was true and what was just a cover for their abuse.

The last year had opened Eden's eyes. She shook off the brainwashing of her childhood. She had learned a lot about herself, but mostly she had learned that her parents had lied to her. She had learned to keep her mouth shut at the right times. She learned to not acknowledge the spirits in the room. She learned that if she pretended to be normal and compliant with her medication regimen, adults would be more open and honest with her. They trusted her more when they saw her as sane and well-controlled. She'd developed some acting skills this past year compliments of the revolving door of compulsive liars and manipulators that graced her dorm. She had been so naive when she'd first come to the hospital; so appalled by the way other girls wielded emotions as weapons. It didn't take her long to pick up that habit of reading what others wanted from her and giving them the right response.

No matter how much she pretended, she still wasn't normal. She was self-aware enough to know that she was not the portrait of mental health. She still flinched when others raised their voices at her. A little therapy hadn't done away with all the trauma that was her childhood and all the deconstructing of her faith she had done had simply left her angry. She wasn't mentally unstable enough to merit hospitalization.

No, Eden wasn't certifiably insane, and after a year of watching television and talking with other people, she no longer believed she was demon possessed or cursed. She was almost certain that she was a medium. At least, that's what ghost hunting shows called them. The one thing she was absolutely certain of was that she didn't want to go home and get married off to whoever her father deemed suitable. She knew that future awaited her. Once the girls got married, it was almost impossible to leave the church. Most of the young guys turned eighteen and split, so Eden would probably get paired up with a thirty-something guy, who would treat her the same way her father had. He would consummate the marriage whether she wanted to or not, because once she was forced to marry him, she would be his property. That may as well be next week, since Eden looked old enough. The church didn't care if you were eighteen or not. If you were physically able to bear children, it was your duty as a woman to marry and start popping out babies. Eden didn't object to boys, or marriage in the future, but she was nowhere near ready for marriage, not at fifteen years old. Who would be? A year ago, she would have faced it with fear, but acceptance. The thought had her choking back the bile that rose in her throat. The Eden Grace who had walked in here timidly was not the same one who would leave here. She had watched quietly and learned to adapt.

Eden walked back to her room, trying desperately to ignore other voices she heard. The voices of the previous patients only rarely made sense. Now, all she heard were several of them muttering their crazy stream-of-consciousness speech patterns. She'd heard other patients speak this way when they came in; before they were medicated. She knew that the voices she heard now were of the truly deranged dead souls occupying this hallway.

Now that she'd been deemed well enough to go home, her parents had fooled these idiots into thinking they wouldn't hurt her anymore. *Screw that,* Eden thought to herself. Next week, she would run like hell when they gave her over to her mother and father. Sure, every other fifteen-year-old thought their parents sucked, but Eden's had given her ample reason to hate them. She walked into her dorm and tried to shake off the thoughts of her parents. Clearing her mind was a dangerous game, but she had to pick her poison and it was best not to start her day off in a rage over her parents.

As Eden grabbed her clothes for the day, she was bombarded by the voices of the dead around her. She had mentally catalogued this hospital as "uber-haunted". The buildings had been built in the 1930s before psychiatric medications were even developed. People died here, and badly. Even though it had been a long time ago, they were still unhappy about it. She did her best to ignore the sounds of a ghostly patient murdering the spirit of a nurse from some bygone era in the hospital. She was mostly successful and managed to not flinch. Eden wondered if this level of jadedness was healthy in the real world.

"Still pissed about going home, Eden?" asked her roommate Myra as Eden prepared to leave the room.

"Nothing I can do about it," Eden answered quietly as she looked straight ahead toward the window.

"Oh, you can do something, pretty girl. You can help me," The ghost of an old man said to Eden. He was strapped down to Myra's bed. No wonder she had nightmares.

"So, you are just going to go back and pretend everything is normal? What if they didn't change?" Myra asked. As long as she was awake, Myra never shut up.

"Like I said, Myra, there is nothing I can do about it. I got three more years there, then I can split like my brother did," Eden said as straight-faced as she could. She couldn't trust any of these people with her plan. She wouldn't risk it. Myra had made herself the biggest thorn in Eden's side for the last year, all while she constantly tried to become her best friend.

For the rest of the day, Eden went through the motions. Every weekday was the same: medications, classes, meals, and a little individual and group therapy time sprinkled in. This was her life for the last year. Eden didn't talk to anyone she wasn't supposed to see. She prayed to a god she wasn't sure existed that this week would fly by. Other people started fights; other girls told her they hated her for various shallow reasons. She ignored it along with a rumor that one of the boys wanted to be her new boyfriend. Not a single bit of it mattered. They could play sleep-away camp all they wanted; this place may as well have been a prison for Eden. Soon, she was going to get out, she reminded herself.

CHAPTER TWO

E den feigned boredom as she stared out the window of the hospital van. In the last two and a half hours they'd had made it just barely into Fort Worth. It looked busy enough here for her to get lost in a crowd. They wouldn't make it to Houston and to her parents for hours still, but Eden had no intention of going any further south than she needed to.

"I need to go to the bathroom." Eden muttered to Marcy, the designated staff member to escort her and the driver. Eden made a point to sound reluctant to bring it up.

"We can pull over in a few minutes." Marcy gave her a reassuring grin.

"Okay, but I need to go pretty effin' bad." Eden winced.

"I'm exiting." The driver called out as he glanced into the rear-view mirror. Eden didn't catch his name. He had an athletic build. All legs. Eden wondered if he was on this assignment because he could chase down anyone who ran. *Well, I've been working on my cardio, buddy, going to have to outlast me.* Eden thought. She glanced over at Marcy to size her up. Marcy was a middle-aged black woman. She seemed nice enough. Physically, Marcy was not thin, but not too overweight. She learned from other kids who tried to run away to not underestimate the "mom staff" when it came to tackling patients on the run. She'd need to try to out-smart Marcy.

"Marcy, I need my purse." Eden leaned in and whispered. "I think I started my period."

"Oh, okay honey." She nodded sympathetically. Eden's secret purpose was obtaining the cash in her purse. She'd worked at the laundry facility in the hospital and earned a whopping seventy-five bucks to take home with her. She stashed some tampons, a change of clothes and a few pilfered items in there as well. It was a nice big purse.

The driver pulled the van into a truck stop. Marcy walked Eden into the convenience store. Marcy surveyed the single toilet restroom and took up her post outside the door as Eden stepped in. It was time to break out the serious acting.

After a few seconds, Eden cursed loudly. She recalled the most embarrassing moments she could pull up, causing her face to flush. She poked her head out. "Marcy, I need some jeans and underwear from my bag. I bled through." Eden let emotion sway her voice toward tearful emotions.

Marcy sighed, "Is it that bad?" Eden cast her eyes to the floor and nodded shamefully. Marcy placed a reassuring hand on Eden's shoulder. Her voice softened, "You stay right here. I am going to run and grab your bag from the van."

"Where am I going to go with blood-soaked pants?" Eden whispered. She sighed as Marcy walked off towards the van. She was grateful Marcy hadn't made her show her any evidence.

As soon as Marcy was out the front door, Eden bolted down the hall to the fire exit. The door alarm sounded, and she knew she had seconds to get as far from here as possible. Behind the gas station, she rounded the corner behind two large blue dumpsters. As she headed up the street toward a block full of fast-food places and convenience stores, she spotted a bus stop peeking out just over the hill several blocks away. As she raced toward it, a bus was pulling up to it. Eden jumped on, startling the bus driver.

"Oh, thank God, I thought I was going to miss the bus." She hoped it made her running seem a little more normal. She paid her fare and took a seat as the bus doors closed with a hiss. Eden glanced out the back of the bus. No sign of them so far. She reached into her purse and pulled out a baseball cap and a hair band. She pulled back her thick curly red hair into a ponytail and adjusted the hat, so it stuck out the little hole in the back. Next, she pulled out a dark blue t-shirt and threw it over her pink tank top too. She glanced back. A little dark-haired woman eyed her suspiciously.

"Spilled coffee on my shirt on the way to the bus." Eden smiled and made a goofy face.

The woman smiled back, but cocked an eyebrow, "Shouldn't you be in school?"

Eden smiled what she hoped was a gracious smile. "Oh, I get that all the time. I graduated in May. I'm going up to A&M in a few months." After a year in the hospital, Eden had nearly become a professional at lying. Eden wiped the sweat from her flushed face. It was only early September in Texas, and the weather was still pretty warm. Sweat trickled down her back. She couldn't resist the urge to take another glance behind her. She rode the bus through the next few stops but was afraid it would be too easy to track her on the planned route. The next stop was a few blocks away. She would get off then and ask for directions to the greyhound station to get the hell out of this town and go to whatever destination she could afford. She was currently on the edge of Fort Worth, and she needed to leave the state if she could. She figured she was less likely to get picked up on a single bus than to try hitch hiking. Hitch hiking seemed suspicious.

Eden had been planning on a new name and a fake college story. She was pretty sure she could pull off being eighteen; her face had aged a little faster thanks to her stressful childhood. She was more likely to respond to a similar sounding name than something completely different. Instead of Eden Grace, her new identity would be Evelyn "Eva" Cross. Close enough to her name without being too close. She'd plotted this for the better part of a year.

The bus stopped and she bounced out the open doors. She asked a nearby stranger with a few small kids if she knew where the bus station was. Women with small children were safer than grown men. The woman pulled out her phone and looked up directions for Eden. She tried to memorize them.

When Eden finally made it to the bus station, she was physically and emotionally exhausted. She had gotten lost a few times in the few hours it had taken her to arrive at the station. Every time she passed a police car, she tried to casually duck into a store. She took stock of her situation and began looking up pricing at the self-service kiosk. The busy bus station had television screens everywhere broadcasting different news stations. She did a double take when her eyes saw a face, she hadn't seen in the mirror in the last year across a flat screen television. She glanced at the next one, and there she was. Several news outlets were broadcasting amber alerts with her picture and a description of what she was wearing when she went missing.

OH MY GOD! I didn't expect it to happen so quickly. I thought they would give me at least a full twenty-four hours. She fought with her panic. Because the Church was involved, theories about her reasons for running were the main topic of conversation. They showed pictures of Eden's father. Of course, they would discuss the charismatic associate pastor of the cult and the charges that had been dropped.

She needed to change her appearance. NOW. She formulated a quick plan. She casually turned and left the station. She glanced around for a cab. She walked over and asked him to take her to the nearest big box retail store.

"What do you need there?" He asked. Eden knew he was trying to make small talk, but she was too busy looking around and thinking through her plan to talk.

"Tampons and batteries." she said sarcastically. Mentioning feminine hygiene products ended most conversations with men in Texas. The ride wasn't too long, and only cost ten bucks. If she'd known where it was, she could have walked.

As she hurried through the automatic doors, Eden turned and located the hair products. She picked up black hair dye, some haircutting scissors and make-up. As soon as she was sure she was alone on the aisle and checked for cameras, she tossed them into her purse. *Yeah, stealing is bad, but going back into a cult with psycho parents is bad too,* she reassured her conscience.

She walked with a calm that she did not feel in her pounding heart over to the shoe department. She ditched her run-down white running shoes by shoving them under the shelf along with the tags from her new black and white hi-tops. Her next stop was the clothing department. She grabbed a casual dress that wouldn't clash with her hi-tops. She stuffed it in her purse when she was sure no one was looking. She walked around the store grabbing a few more things she might need here and there.

When she was finished with her "shopping" she headed into the restroom at the back labeled: "Family Restroom". It was equipped with a sink and a deadbolt lock on the door. After she locked the door behind her, she pulled off her hat and stashed it in her bag. She flipped her body forward and put her hair in a high ponytail on the top of her head. She reached into the bag and freed the scissors from their packaging. She cut the ponytail as close to the rubber band as possible. The effect was a short, slightly uneven layered bob. It didn't look half bad. She hoped her curls would cover the imperfections. She ripped into the box of hair dye and began following the instructions for how to mix it in the bottle. She let it sit for a moment while she scooped the hair into the toilet in small batches and flushed them. No need to leave any evidence of where she's been. After she disposed of all the hair, Eden peeled off her sweaty clothes and stowed them away in her purse while she pulled out the make-up. She pulled the crappy plastic gloves from her boxed dye onto her hands and rubbed the goopy solution into the roots of her hair with great care to avoid her pale skin around the hairline. A quick glance at the instructions revealed that it needed twenty minutes to color, and Eden made a silent prayer that no one needed this bathroom at that time.

As she opened the make-up, she attempted mouth breathing to avoid the acrid odor from the dye. As Eden applied the foundation, she struggled to blend and make it match. It was slightly darker than she should use, but not too far off. She needed to hide her freckles. She spackled it on all the way down into her cleavage. Using eyeliner and eyeshadow she was able to change the shape of her eyes. Thank you, YouTube tutorials. She took out a brown eyeliner pencil and added a small mole on her cheek, just to the left of her nose. She took out the brow gel kit that would match her new hair color and did her best to get them even without being too bushy. The contour came in handy to slim her slightly round face.

She examined the mirror and then reached into her bag for the items that were the hardest to stow away at the state hospital. A single nose ring she stole out of a staff member's purse when she changed them out, and a safety pin that she took off the back of a nurse's blouse while she cried on the nurse's shoulder about going back home. A small pang of guilt came with her full awareness that she had been a manipulative little shit, but she had to do what she had to do to get away. She stared herself down hard in the mirror and steadied herself by taking deep breaths. She put a thumb in her right nostril and pulled down a bit. While she held her breath, she pushed the pin through the side of her nose and tears welled in her eyes. She dabbed away the tears along with the small amount of blood on her nose. She took another steadying breath and replaced the pin with the nose ring. She shoved some toilet paper up her nose for any other blood. She finished up her makeup and checked her watch. She had about five more minutes before it was time to rinse. As she cleaned up the mess, a knock at the door startled her into a jump.

"Sorry, someone's in here." She called out.

"Can you hurry?" A female voice says on the other side.

"Not really." Her heart thundered in her chest. She reached for any good excuse. "I have the runs." Eden yelled through the door.

"Oh, sorry." The voice called back. Eden sighed in relief when she heard the footsteps retreat.

Eden reached into the trash can and shoved the hair dye stuff to the bottom. She stuffed all the open makeup back in her bag and placed all the wrappers and containers she didn't need under the mound of paper towels with her hair dye mess. Impatience and a need to flee pushed her to the sink and she started rinsing. Once the water came clear from her hair, she used her discarded shirt to dry it as much as possible. She scrunched it to get the curls to set a bit. She threw the black dress over her head. The sleeves were three quarter length and the fabric crisscrossed over her chest and cinched just below the bust before flaring back out. It accentuated the ample area that she'd spent younger years trying to cover. She couldn't help but think she actually looked pretty cute in the knee length dress, but it was so unlike anything she'd ever worn.

She was a far cry from the girl on display for the amber alert. On the news, Eden was clad in homemade modest dresses in plain patterns. In her amber alert, she looked around thirteen. The girl in the mirror looked at least nineteen or twenty. She picked up her purse and headed out of the bathroom.

Eden headed back toward the electronics area to make her most daunting purchase. She picked up the least expensive smartphone and a prepaid card with unlimited data for one month. If she was to find a job and a place to live, she needed to have a phone. She pulled out a stolen card from one of the staff members at the hospital and paid for it at a self-checkout terminal in separate transactions for each. She silently apologized to them as she hit the cashback option and took as much cash as it would allow. It was just a couple hundred dollars, but it could mean life or death for her in the near future, she reasoned. She walked out of the store hoping no one would stop her.

When she made it back to the bus terminal, she set up her new phone and started on her next step. She needed to find another city, one big enough for her to get lost in, where she would be able to find a job quickly making cash. She had already resolved that she would start waiting tables. She would take the first job that would hire her on the spot where she could make cash. Smaller businesses had less likelihood of running a background check, so small diners could earn Eden some cash quickly without raising red flags. Eden didn't want to chance it and get caught stealing. That would land her back with social services and back to her parents.

As the bus pulled away from the city, heading north, Eden finally relaxed enough to get a bit of sleep in the soft glow of the bus's interior lights in the dark night. Almost out of habit, she made a silent prayer to a God she wasn't sure existed. *If you are real, please, keep me safe. Help me when I get to Oklahoma City to find a place to lay low and find a job. Please, just help me find peace. And PLEASE for the love of all that is holy, do not let any visions come to me while I am sleeping on this bus.*

CHAPTER THREE

Three Years Later

E den dared to hope as she pulled into the driveway of a small older house. Before her was a one-bedroom house with off white asbestos siding on a corner lot. The paint looked new, and it had a nice wooden deck as a front porch. Paying the first month's rent and deposit on it would only make a tiny dent in her savings.

She had plotted it out over lunch. She'd get the house, then look for work. Things were going to be different this time. She breathed slowly to quiet her anxieties. This time she would get to be herself. No alias, no fake social security number that she'd hope wouldn't get flagged. Hell, this year she could even file a tax return. In fact, it all felt too good to be true. She frowned at the thought. A few weeks prior, two police officers had come knocking on her door. At the time, she worried she'd be sent back to the hospital or worse, back to the cult compound with her parents.

When they knocked on her door, she panicked. Her eighteenth birthday was over a month away. After several minutes of debate, and realizing she'd break an ankle trying to jump out of the garage apartment windows, she let them in. The officers inquired about her landlady's husband. Her landlady lived in the main house while Eden was in the garage apartment. The husband had been missing for a while, but only reported recently.

Eden knew exactly where he was. Not because of her involvement in his disappearance, but because his unresting spirit had woken her up multiple times per night since she had moved in. He would spout cryptic things like 'knife,' 'flower bed,' or 'in the yard'. Eden had simply rolled her eyes at his shimmering incorporeal form. Of course, he would say 'knife', he had a rather large kitchen knife sticking out of the massive wound in his chest. Eden was not qualified to judge anyone, but she figured he probably did something to deserve it. Her experience with men may have tainted her feelings.

Eden tentatively fed the officers the truth that she could tell. She explained that she had moved in right after he was last seen. She explained that she had never met him, only his wife. As it turned out, this was the exact reason they sought out Eden. Someone was suspicious of a young woman who moved in around the time of his disappearance who dealt only in cash and used burner-type cell phones. There had been an anonymous tip. Eden suspected her landlady was less benevolent than she had seemed when she took Eden's rent without a background check or signing a lease. Eden bet proverbial money that Mrs. Shaefer tipped the police off and was trying to pin all this on her.

"Oh, well, you see." She tucked a hair behind her ear and looked down to avoid eye contact. "I don't have any credit. When I met her at the diner, she said she needed extra income now that her husband was gone. She agreed to rent the garage apartment to me." She paused and debated whether she should add more. She looked up as if something had suddenly occurred to her. "One thing that was weird though, is that she had been gardening." Eden pointed out the window for effect. "That big flower bed over there was brand new when I moved in. I haven't seen her do anything back there since that first week. She doesn't even mow her yard, I do. That's part of the conditions of me living here. I mow and water the plants. She pays the utilities." Eden acted shocked and tearfully added, "You don't think she's got anything to do with it?" She'd been rehearsing this whole thing in her head in case the time came. She had been hoping for just a little more time.

The police wrote down her statement. "Now, what's your name, Miss?"

"Most people call me Elle. It's Ellen Grant." She smiled shyly.

"You got an ID, Miss Grant?" He smiled back. He had a friendly enough face.

"No sir. I left Oklahoma City with the clothes on my back and a little cash. I left a man who liked to swing at me." Eden stared down at the floor and flushed, allowing herself to feel her shame. That's how she had always explained coming into a town with next to nothing. Too bad it was true. She had left Cole over six months ago and had been hopping from town to town, from job to job, hoping for some stability. At least she was able to leave. He had allowed her to go without a fight and she couldn't decide even now if that hurt her worse than if he'd hit her that night. She still occasionally looked over her shoulder worried that he'd come for her.

"Alright. You did the right thing leavin' him." He nodded to Eden. He turned to his partner, "Okay, Dale, I'm gonna run this real quick. I'll be back up in a minute."

After he walked out, Eden glanced as casually as she could manage at the other officer and asked, "What's he got to run?"

"Oh, running your info: Name, birthdate, standard stuff. Just have to check and see if you got any warrants. Anything like that. What with you being a suspect and all." He smiled at her, not knowing that he had ruined her whole world. Eden could tell by the look on his face that her facade had started to crumble. She felt like the world was crumbling beneath her too.

"Okay. Then I better tell you something, because he's not going to find my name and birthdate together." A horrible feeling of dread spread through Eden, like a punch to the gut, it knocked the wind from her. Blood pounded in her ears. "My name's not Ellen Grant." She managed to say. "It's Eden Grace. I'm Noah and Elisabeth Grace's missing daughter. You know, the associate pastors at the Saints on Earth Church." She felt the sudden wet hot tears drip on her shirt as she struggled to keep her voice as even and steady as possible. "I've been running for almost three years. I want to come clean now, so I don't get in trouble for lying to an officer. I'm sure I'm in enough trouble as it is."

His jaw dropped. "Well, in that case, I guess, we need to call protective services then. Ma'am, will you come with us down to the station, or are you gonna fight me?"

"I'll go." Eden mumbled before she swallowed back the sob building in her throat. She silently resigned herself to going back just for a few months, just until she was eighteen. She sat in the back of the police cruiser promising herself that she would get out.

At the station, a woman with short black hair and an aged serious face sat across from Eden. She sighed and pulled out paperwork. "First of all, I need you to verify your date of birth." The social worker began. "Your parents gave us multiple birth dates from various years when you were hospitalized. By some accounts you were twelve, by others you were seventeen. We just need the official date, and we cannot get your parents on the phone to verify." Eden stared at her bewildered. "If you are legally an adult, this really isn't a child services case any longer." She glared at Eden as if giving her the right birthdate would result in them both getting out of there quicker.

As it happened, having been shady anti-government cultists, Eden's parents had never filed for her birth certificate, or for her social security number. She had been born in her parent's home on the grounds of the church's compound. On the day of Eden's disappearance, her parents were scheduled to meet with a social worker to sign and finalize the paperwork. When Eden had gone missing, her parents stopped talking to social services. Her father reportedly had stated Eden had too much of the devil in her to save. She was shocked to see it documented in her file. Eden read the reports as the social worker sat there looking impatient. Eden embraced this unforeseen grace and subtracted a few years from her year of birth. The overworked burned-out social worker never even questioned her on it. On paper, Eden had turned eighteen five months after she ran away. Legally, Eden would celebrate her twenty-first birthday in a matter of weeks. Only she and possibly her parents knew she was just shy of eighteen. Though, from the sound of it, they didn't even care to mark the date on a calendar. She could be older than she thought she was after all. They never celebrated birthdays.

The all too tired social worker wondered out loud why Eden had bothered to hide her identity this whole time. Eden pointed to her file and said simply, "Would you want them to find you?" The social worker gave a shrug as if to say, 'fair enough' and began her now much reduced paperwork. Once the paperwork was all squared away, Eden was free to go and Marla the social worker could be free of additional work and foster placement arrangements.

The police further investigated and had other neighbors to corroborate her story about the garden. Eden's landlady was arrested and the entire area she lived in was now a crime scene, so Eden was evicted. She told herself that at least she wasn't being packed off to the compound. The police allowed her to pack up her meager belongings quickly.

She tried to report to work the next morning after moving into a cheap motel room only to be told she no longer had a job. While Eden's employer sympathized to the point of not pressing any charges for falsifying information, due to company policies, she was no longer employed. Eden was used to being let go for this reason. She'd had a harder time of it when more mom-and-pop restaurants started using digital systems. She would have legit paperwork now. She did some small day labor type jobs, cleaning houses and the motel that she stayed at. She held out in this little town where everyone knew she was a liar and a fraud until she got her legitimate driver's license and proof of identity. Then she used some of her remaining savings to buy a car from a junkyard, loaded all her meager belongings in the back of it, and drove. She decided to go south, far enough that maybe no one would have casual contact with any of her former coworkers or acquaintances. Eden didn't really have friends. It was too risky to have friends. Having a boyfriend had been a disaster.

Over an hour later, she pulled into a little town, sat at a table of a sub-par Chinese buffet, and looked over the want-ads. Why she felt drawn to this little town, she couldn't say. She just felt it was right. She found the listing for the rent house she now sat in front of. She shook her head out of the daydreamy recollection of the last few weeks. The landlord was meant to be there any minute.

A late nineties model extended cab truck pulled up alongside Eden's car, out of habit she started to rehearse in her head what she would say and stopped short. *No rehearsing a new name!* Eden smiled to herself as she stepped out of her car, introduced herself as Eden Grace, and shook his hand. After a bit of small talk with the very Texan landlord, he gave her a quick tour of the house. Eden loved the simple charm of it. It had a living room separated from a bedroom by a set of folding closet type doors. On the wall to the right in the bedroom was a doorway with swinging saloon style doors into the kitchen. The kitchen was as big as the bedroom and living room combined. Plenty of room for a dining room table. The kitchen also had another door that led into a short hallway that connected the living-room, kitchen, and bathroom. There was also a walk-in closet with outlets and shelves inside it off the living room. The bathroom was so small, there was nowhere to hang shelving or cabinets, so the walk-in closet would pull double duty for linens as well. The bathroom had a small window that no human being could squeeze through. She paused momentarily to ponder if that would be a problem. Then, she remembered. *No more running.* Eden almost shook her head at herself. Freedom hadn't completely sunk in. She knew that it wasn't the best house, but it could be hers. The landlord threw a small snag in Eden's plan when he asked for proof of employment. He was not exactly happy with her current job situation, which was none.

"I have nearly eight grand in savings. I plan to apply to every job I can as soon as I am not living in a motel. In fact, as soon as I unload my car, I can apply to every open job in this town." Eden tried to give her best innocent smile.

"How about this? Since you are so set, we do a six-month lease. An' you can pay it upfront." He pulled out his phone and punched in the numbers into the calculator. "That's five a month for six months plus the deposit. It includes utilities. So, you got thirty-five hundred to put down, money bags?" He spit some chewing tobacco on the lawn.

Well, crap! I really don't want to sink nearly half my savings into this. What if I have to run? Oh wait. I don't have to run. I don't have to keep a backup plan backpack on me. Despite herself, Eden cracked a half smile.

"You mow the grass for all these properties?" She asked. He owned all the little houses down this street.

"You pay six months upfront; I'll mow yours." He gave her a 'put your money where your mouth is' kind of grin. He seemed gruff but based on the emotions he put off when she shook his hand, he was mostly honest and hardworking. A self-made man.

"Get me a lease and you got a deal." Eden delighted more than a little at the slight shock on his face. He gathered himself in a moment and asked if she had it in cash. After Eden's confirming nod, he is all business.

"Welcome to Angelina, Ms. Grace." He shook her hand. Eden fought the urge to screw up her face at his pronunciation of the town name. She'd never heard of Angelina before and had mentally said it like Angelina Jolie's name. He had definitely called it 'Angel-line-uh'. Must be a redneck thing like saying 'yallow' instead of 'yellow' or 'warsh' instead of 'wash'.

As white trash as he seemed, Eden was surprised when he pulled out a laptop from his truck and typed things into a program; Eden provided information as needed. When they were done, he excused himself for a minute and returned about fifteen minutes later, lease printed and ready to sign. *Damn, this redneck is efficient.* Eden thought to herself as she handed over the cash in hundreds from her lock box in exchange for the house keys. She glanced at the remaining amount warily. Working for almost three years and never buying anything that she couldn't get from a thrift store really added up, but she never felt secure. The house had a stove, fridge, heat, and air. She had an air mattress, so she technically was set. She smiled as she unloaded her belongings thinking about how she could have a REAL bed. *Hell, maybe this time I will go all out and get a couch or some nice lamps or something.*

After her belongings were safely inside the house, Eden pulled out her phone and started looking for online job listings. Her initial instinct was to apply to all the restaurants, then she realized she didn't have to wait tables anymore. She was very nearly giddy when she realized that she could get a job with some sort of benefits. Her bubble burst suddenly when she came back to the reality that her job options were very limited due to her lack of formal education. Eden hadn't even finished high school. Her only real education was conducted in the mental hospital. She had learned the basics of math, reading, and writing before that. She considered herself intelligent, she enjoyed learning and spent most of her time reading. Local library cards were easy to come by and library books were a free source of entertainment when you couldn't afford to make close friends.

Once she soothed her slightly bruised self-esteem by resolving to eventually take a graduation equivalency degree class and test, she applied to some motels, some factory work, and applied to a couple of retail places. Eden decided to go check out what the local thrift stores had to offer once she was done putting in applications. She made some wish lists, but old habits die hard and without solid employment, she couldn't bring herself to make a bunch of purchases.

CHAPTER FOUR

E den had surmounted a series of interviews, a drug screening, an orientation, and a mind-numbing amount of computer training modules to make it to her first real night of work at her new job. She arrived entirely too early. She sat in the breakroom, nervously picking at her nails as she waited to clock in. The night shift was understaffed and her willingness to stock on this shift gained her a quick onboarding process. Night shift was also given a small bump in pay. Her new employer was a corporate retailer, and Eden found herself giddy with excitement over access to health insurance. Her last checkup had been a free clinic for birth control when she started dating Cole. She had toughed it out anytime she got sick, which thankfully was not often or severe.

The cinderblock walls of the breakroom were stark white against the harsh overhead lighting. Safety reminders, corporate propaganda for teamwork, and the like adorned the upper portions of the vaulted break room walls. Corporate team spirit never appealed to Eden. It seemed too ritualistic, too much like the life she had known before she left the church.

A mass exodus from the break area occurred around a minute before ten in the evening. This too reminded her of the church. Eden followed the crowd to gather in a cluster of a line and swiped her badge.

Next to the timeclock stood a middle-aged copper skinned woman. Her hair was pulled into a ponytail and was the color of wet sand. She eyed the assembled crowd. "Everybody here?" She said to no one in particular.

"I don't see Sam." A male voice came from Eden's left. She turned to see two tall golden brown skinned men in their mid-twenties standing together. The one who spoke up had a furrowed brow and his lips were a thin line.

Obviously, this was a recurring problem with Sam. The other turned his warm brown colored eyes to Eden and smiled. She smiled back, blushing for some unknown reason. She averted her eyes to the ground and then looked back up to the woman as she spoke.

"Well, when we're done here, go out and see if he is asleep in his car again. And God help us, maybe he made friends with a bar of soap. You didn't hear me say that" said the boss lady. The annoyed guy nodded to her. He and the other man were tall and lean. Not overly muscular but fit looking. The one who spoke had longer hair, and they both had dark stubble on their chin. Eden turned her attention back to the woman leading their meeting.

"Okay everybody, we have a big truck tonight. They finally started getting us some help, so this is our new girl, Eden." She motioned to Eden. "Eden, you are going to go with Journey tonight." As she spoke, she nodded towards a tall twenty-something girl with long wavy strawberry blonde hair that was light on the strawberry. She did a 'what's up' head nod towards Eden.

The lady in charge gave assignments to areas with names that indicated what was sold there. Eden was to follow Journey in one of these departments. She learned that the men that stuck out to her were named Jayse and Kris. The woman called out other names and departments, but they had already blurred in her mind. She would need to learn people's names if she was going to work with them. As she came to the end of her list, she pointed lastly to a man wearing a cowboy hat and cowboy boots. "Dwayne, you get pets. Are we good? Alright, one, two, three."

"Work." Everyone droned out unenthusiastically. Eden tried to school her face into neutrality as if that wasn't entirely strange. She watched as everyone started grabbing trash bags and headed out of the back room. Sandy haired Boss-Lady stepped towards her.

"I'm Tessa." She smiled. "You need anything, ask Journey. If she ticks you off too bad let me know." She raised her eyebrows toward Journey. "If she does, you probably shouldn't work with us."

"Let's make that official, Tess." Journey laughed. "Trial by fire and whatnot." Journey was a solid ten inches or more taller than Eden. She was a thicker, curvier girl and carried it with full confidence. Her curls reached down to the middle of her back in her low ponytail. She wore thick plastic frames with slightly tinted orange lenses. She had clearly cut the neck band and cuffs off the sleeves of her navy t-shirt. The shirt had a white outline of a basketball on it and generically said BASKETBALL in all caps. No team affiliation or anything, just support of the sport of basketball. She carried herself with cool confidence as if she was fully aware of her status as a badass who was one hundred percent pure awesome.

Eden shrugged at Journey's suggestion of trial by fire, unsure of how to fit in with the cool kids. It was like being fifteen all over again. "I like your shirt."

Journey nodded. "Thanks. Alright, kid. Grab a trash bag. You got your box knife?" Eden affirmed her readiness, and the two headed to the front of the store. Eden followed Journey's lead and grabbed a shopping cart and tied her trash bag on it. She walked alongside Journey to the baby department. Journey explained to Eden how to stock. It was not difficult, just use the shipping tag on the box to determine what it is, look for it, see if it needs to be restocked and open it and restock it if applicable. Eden slowly picked her way through the first several boxes, locating the item on the shelf. It was frustratingly slow. Sensing her pain, Journey hand-picked some boxes that always needed stocked. Diapers mainly. They worked mostly in silence, with a few 'where is this?' and 'what the hell is a...' thrown in. A few hours passed and the guys named Kris and Jayse walked by and Journey set down the box she had just picked up.

"Break." Journey said casually. Apparently, after two hours, Eden got a paid fifteen-minute break. She bought some junk food from the vending machines in the break room and Journey pulled a soda out of a backpack. When the ladies sat down, the guys sat across from them.

"Eden, this is Jayse and Kris." Journey introduced them. Apparently, the guy who talked at the meeting was Jayse, and the other one, who was still smiling at her, was Kris.

"Where are you from, noob?" Jayse smiled.

"I moved around a lot. I grew up mostly around Houston. I lived in Wichita Falls for a bit, Tulsa, OKC, and Duncan. I just moved here about a week ago." Eden explained.

"So, why'd you move to our little backwards town? Why pick Angelina?" Kris said between bites of an apple. *The town really was called 'Angel-line-uh.' Huh.* She took a half a second to ponder the question. Should she tell the truth and just let it all out or should she give her normal left a bad guy answer? *Oh, what the hell,* she decided to give them half the truth.

"I lost my rent house in Duncan and my job in the same week, so I decided, screw it." She shrugged. "I'll just move. I drove south and picked up a want ad while I was eating lunch. Found my house and decided Angelina is as good as any place." Eden tried to be casual, cool, calm, and collected.

"You moved to the boonies, just because?" Journey asked, baffled.

"Yeah, why'd you move here?" Eden asked everyone at the table, now on the defensive.

"My parents moved here when I was seventeen to run an RV park." Journey looked at her slightly bewildered. "Grew up in upstate New York."

"We grew up here with our grandfather." Jayse said.

"You ARE brothers." Eden smiled.

"Nah, he's my mentally unstable clone." Kris laughed.

"I was born first, stupid. You'd be my defective clone." Jayse shot back.

"They're fraternal twins." Journey provided a straight answer while a few more insults flew back and forth between the brothers. Eden finished her snack and started to get up to go to the bathroom. "Where are you going? Break's not over for five minutes." Journey stopped her.

"Bathroom." Eden said.

"No, no. That's a rookie move. You always pee on the clock. Always. And that goes double for deuces." Jayse motioned toward the chair for Eden to sit back down.

"It always comes back to poop with you, man." Journey laughed. "We can't have one break without you talking about turds?" Journey sneered as Eden sat back down. Journey resumed her rant about Jayse's shitty topics of conversation. "I could be like, hey man I brought cupcakes, and you would tell me the frosting looks like crap. Or you'd have some cake related story that would involve a time when you took a dump. IT ALWAYS COMES BACK TO POOP!" She let out an exasperated breath.

Tessa strolled casually into the break room with a big bag of cheese puffs. She glanced around at the other tables. A guy that Eden assumed was Sam, mainly because he wasn't here during the meeting, was sleeping with his head propped against the wall. Tessa held out a cheese puff to Kris and whispered, "Stick it up his nose."

Eden found herself grinning as she thought that she may have lucked out and gotten the fun manager. Kris stood slowly and crept over stealthily. Ever so gingerly, he shoved it into Sam's left nostril. The dude didn't even flinch. Their table erupted with hushed laughter. Tessa was doubled over, laughing into her hands, as she tried to stifle the sound. She stood up and wiped tears from her eyes. "Oh, it's the small things that really make my life worth living." She pulled up a chair and offered cheese puffs to everyone.

"Whose nose was this in?" Journey inspected one.

"Mine." Tessa grinned a Cheshire cat smile.

With a shrug, Journey said, "Well in that case," and ate it whole. Eden hated how badly she wanted to be a part of this group, with their jokes and casual conversation.

"Going okay?" Tessa raised her eyebrows.

"Yeah. Going fine. I think once I figure out where everything goes, I'll be doing pretty good." Eden gave a small shrug.

"Journey hasn't threatened her with a box knife yet, so I'd say it's going pretty good." Jayse nodded approvingly.

"Don't make me cut you." Journey flashed her box knife to Jayse. Then, she glanced down at her watch. "Break's over." They all stood and started towards the exit.

Jayse and Kris yelled at Sam on their way out. He bolted upright, startled. He ran his hand over his face and found the cheese puff.

"Who the hell put this in my nose?" He looked pissed.

Kris pointed at Tessa, who was still seated and eating the snack in question.

"Tessa, really?!" Sam grumbled.

"Don't show up late and I won't shove food up your nose." Tessa's body language was casual, but her tone was serious. The group rounded the corner as Sam got up to leave.

"I'm gonna go pee, too. Your uterus is calling to mine for companionship." Journey motioned to the bathroom.

"What?!" Eden looked at her sidelong while smiling.

"That's why chicks have to pee in groups. The uterus calls out for company." Journey intoned her best documentary style voice. "The female homo sapien needs the companionship of the other uteruses in the nearby vicinity."

"If you say so." Eden chuckled.

They finished the baby department and headed over to housewares. Eden was grateful that their stock was mostly big boxes of pillows and plastic totes. They were able to knock out the whole department in half an hour and the ease of stocking made Eden feel more confident. After working their way tediously through the office supplies pallet, it was lunchtime. Eden clocked out and bought a microwavable meal from the frozen section. She ate quietly and listened to Jayse, Kris, and Journey chat idly about their plans for the weekend.

Eden and Journey finished their shift stocking the toy department. They shared the music they each enjoyed. They were excited to find that they had a similar interest in nineties grunge and alternative rock music. Eden hadn't had the influence of parents to guide her musical choices outside of singing hymns in the cult. What she did have those first years outside of home was the influence of line cooks who played their favorite music. Journey had older siblings who influenced her tastes. She confessed to Eden a secret love of Nickelback. Eden placed a hand over her heart and sarcastically swore a solemn oath to take this secret to her grave. Afterward, Eden confessed that she was a closet Matchbox20 fan. They found a common love for Billie Eilish and Lizzo as well. They both confused all the predictive features of their music apps on their phone. Would it be nineties grunge, top forty hits of the 2000s, or hip hop? The app never quite knew.

"I feel this moment has brought us closer." Eden said with feigned seriousness. She made a motion with her two fingers going back and forth between their eyes.

"I think we both have sufficient blackmail on each other to begin a friendship." Journey joked. Eden secretly hoped there was some sincerity in there. By seven in the morning, Eden was sore, and her arms bore the dust of several hundred boxes.

"See you tomorrow." Journey added as they walked out the front door to almost blinding early-morning sunlight. Eden squinted against the bright sunlight and said her goodbye to Journey. She resolved to buy black-out curtains and sunglasses as she swore at the sunlight. She found herself grinning, glad to have the first shift behind her.

CHAPTER FIVE

I t had been an easy three weeks of adjusting to her job. The work itself was simple if not a little physically demanding. Eden worked hard, talked to her coworkers when she could, but the tasks left time for her mind to wander at times. Occasionally she would encounter a spirit attached to a customer, but mostly, if she let them be, they didn't bother her. Only occasionally did she lock eyes with a ghost and feel the need to say something, but she would just breathe deeply and pretend she saw nothing. Only once did a ghost require her to say anything when it attached itself to her instead of the customer. She made an excuse to use the restroom and addressed the spirit quickly and rather forcefully about crossing over and leaving her the hell alone. Thankfully, it had obeyed.

Eden's retail stocking skill set expanded as she also learned to operate a couple of pieces of machinery. Tessa trained and licensed her on the powered jack, the walkie-stacker, the scissor lift, and the forklift. All it had taken was a few nights of watching videos, taking tests on the computer, and actual hands-on training, but she was officially a heavy machinery operator. Tessa had asked what Eden wanted to be trained on. Eden took advantage of free training and got licensed on it all. She knew the pride she held at being the only other licensed forklift operator on her shift beside Tessa was silly. It made her feel like a bad mama-jama. She made a mental note to never refer to herself as a bad mama-jama out loud to her coworkers. It didn't seem cool.

The forklift license was the reason Eden was working outside, all alone on this chill spring night. Tessa had been busy writing Sam up for yet another offense when a truck showed up to drop off lawn and garden pallets eight hours ahead of schedule. The weather was fine; it was a clear starry night. The moon was full. Eden delighted a bit in the calm breeze that blew around her.

One of the best things that had happened in the last three weeks was a lack of ghostly experiences. She'd had some dreams that seemed to be vaguely psychic but nothing horrible. She had been pleasantly surprised that her new home had no remnants of spirits left behind. A rare thing for an older home in her experience. She didn't want to jinx anything, but life was feeling fairly...normal.

The work of unloading the truck was tedious. Eden had to remove a pallet from each side of the flatbed trailer at a time. If it became too unbalanced, it could flip the trailer and damage the truck. She took her time unloading and stacking pallets, back and forth. The truck driver seemed convinced he could go faster. Eden thought she heard him mutter something about women drivers. She rolled her eyes.

When she approached him initially, he had asked if the forklift guy was coming. Eden tried to keep her voice even as she told him, "I'm the forklift guy," adding, "jackass" under her breath. When she finally got all twenty-four pallets unloaded, the driver asked to hitch a ride into the back to see the manager about his paperwork. "I can't give anyone a ride, or I can lose my job." Eden said flatly.

"But those other fellas give me rides." He complained in his New Jersian accent. Eden took a slow deep breath, trying to calm her annoyance. She gave him a look that said, "don't know what to tell ya" as she shrugged and drove back towards the parking spot for the lift.

As Eden entered the building Sam stormed past. "Screw this place and screw that bitch!" He paused and whirled to Eden. "Can you believe she told me that people don't think I keep up with my hygiene. Just 'cause I don't take a shower every freakin' day. And deodorant? That crap gives you cancer, man." He fumed. Eden screwed up her face as he got close. His stench was rather palpable today. Eden tried to breathe through her mouth without being noticeable. Eden thought that maybe, he might want to risk cancer if he ever wanted to get a date. He'd hit on her enough times in the last three weeks that she considered telling him as much.

Of course, Eden knew Tessa didn't fire him because of his smell. She fired him because this was his fourth serious write up. His write up from last week was due to him sleeping in the racks in the back of the store. This time, he had spewed profanities at a customer when they asked where a product was. He had yelled, "Do I look like I would fucking know?" Eden had stood there dumbfounded and horrified when it happened. They had been on the way to their first break. To no one's surprise, the customer had asked for a manager and Eden had to page Tessa.

"Dude, you cussed at a customer." Eden gave him an incredulous look. Most everything he had done in the last three weeks had made her very skeptical of anything Sam said. He mostly bummed food and cigarettes from other employees, yelled about conspiracy theories, and even said a few inappropriate things to Eden until Journey threatened him. That had been write-up number two.

"Screw him too. You should have told him you were the manager. You could have kept this from happening! You ratted me out, man. You know what?! Screw you too!" Sam made a rude gesture with both hands as he walked away.

"What was that?!" The truck driver exclaimed as he walked up behind Eden.

"That." Eden said calmly, "is not my problem. Just one less warm body on this shift. Maybe they'll replace him with someone who works... and bathes." The calm in her voice was an act. Her anger and frustration were on a very very short leash, ready to snap. Eden reached over the customer service desk towards the phone.

"You're a mouthy broad. You sure you ain't the manager?" The truck driver sneered.

Eden clenched her jaw as she grabbed the phone from the service desk and pushed the page button. "Tessa, service desk, please. A driver needs you." Eden dropped the phone into the cradle. She schooled her features into a false serenity, and icily said, "Now, you're not my problem anymore either. How's that for a mouthy broad." She forced herself to keep walking as he tried to reply.

As she approached the grocery department, she assessed the pallet load for the night. Several unworked towers of boxes faced her. It would be a long night in the land of dry goods for her. She focused her slowly diminishing anger into tossing boxes of cereal down from the pallet. The overhead speakers played various company-approved songs between ads. A female singer belted out her confessions of damaging her boyfriend's truck as a payback for his cheating. Eden felt that there really should've been a follow up song in response to it, one about how the singer got arrested for property damage. Or more likely, how he clearly saw her name carved into his seats and beat the hell out of her for her disrespect. Maybe Eden was just projecting from her experience, though. She shook the thought loose and continued to stock the shelves. She lost herself in the mindless activity, humming along with the music. It took an unfamiliar voice to pull her to reality again.

"Ma'am?" A deep thickly accented voice came from behind her as she reached up to the shelf above her eye level.

"What do you need?" Eden snapped and immediately winced. Silently, she hoped that this customer wouldn't snap back. As she placed the last box of cereal on the shelf, she donned her best customer service voice. "Sorry, can I help you?"

"Apologies, ma'am, but you're standing right in front of the peanut butter puffs." His voice drawled. She glanced down and right at her belt level was his cereal.

"Sorry about that." She muttered as she turned to hand him a box. Her eyes set on his outstretched hand and followed up past his tattooed arm. *Holy hell.* She thought. She glanced up to his full height. He had to be well over six foot tall by several inches.

He flashed a friendly half smile as he took the box from her hand. His toffee-colored eyes seemed to light up as his smile widened. With his other hand, he brushed his long jet-black hair out of his eyes. He was conventionally handsome, but there was something different about him. Hidden behind the glow of his eyes there seemed to be a mystery to unravel. Some sort of deeper puzzle she found herself wanting to unlock. *Or maybe it's hormones,* Eden reminded herself as she broke his gaze and returned his smile. His jawline was shaded with a bit of black stubble. It was defined but not too sharp, a perfect match to his high cheekbones. His black V-neck shirt hugged tight across his shoulders and chest but hung loose at the waist. He was inked with tattoos down both brown arms, but she found herself staring at his full sleeve with intricate patterns down to his right hand ending with two crossed hatchets with feathers hanging from them just as they approached his fingers. He wore faded jeans and black biker style boots. This was a much different customer than Eden was used to at night. He didn't reek of alcohol and wasn't wearing ratty pajamas. It was a pleasant surprise.

"You okay, ma'am?" He said politely.

Eden suddenly realized she was standing with her head slightly tilted and ogling this random customer. Her cheeks heated with embarrassment. She looked at the floor. "Sorry, sir. Just tired. I kind of spaced out." Eden murmured.

"I get that. You're new, right? I haven't really seen you around." His deep southern drawl was thick and rich, seemingly a perfect match to his rich brown skin.

"Yeah, I've only been working here for a few weeks. I've only been in town for a month." Eden tried to loosen her shoulders and relax into a casual tone. The night shift had its regulars, and she had carried out this conversation a few times already. If it meant a few more seconds of looking at him, she was okay with it. Her normal method of dealing with her usual night shift customers, mostly drug addicts and alcoholics, was to redirect or ignore them. This customer, he could ask her whatever he wanted. *Good lord, am I that desperate?* She pondered.

"I'm Anaiah." He gave his name casually. It sounded like An-neigh-yuh to Eden. She asked him how he spelled it. "A-N-A-I-A-H" He spelled out. "It's not exactly a common name." He laughed a bit.

"Oh, like in the Bible." The words were out without a thought, and she immediately regretted it.

"Yeah." He shrugged. Eden cringed internally when she revealed anything to do with her knowledge of Biblical teachings. It either brought up uncomfortable questions or led people to believe she was some sort of bible thumper.

"Sorry. It's one of those things that got drilled into my head as a kid." Eden rolled her eyes as she donned a smile, she knew accented the dimple on her right cheek, hoping a cute smile would play it off as casual. "I'm Eden." She offered her hand. "Nice to meet you." She noted how his large warm hand engulfed her tiny hand with his politely firm handshake.

"Now I remember that from the Bible. Heaven on Earth?" He tilted his head slightly and cracked another damn half smile at her. Her heart fluttered.

"Something like that." Eden's cheeks heated again with blush. "Can I help you find anything else?" *Look at me, asking questions like a day-shifter.* Eden resisted smirking. Amazing what hormones would do to a person. She could help him locate a date. *Calm the fuck down, Eden.* Her cute flirty smile faded into a more polite professional one as she thought, *you need another man like you need a black eye.* With her track record with men, she would get exactly that. His raised, interested brows lowered slightly, as if he had noted the shift in her as well.

"Nah, I think I got it, unless of course you want to go stand in front of the pop-tarts too?" He grinned wide. Eden suspected that he was possibly flirting. Or maybe he was just a genuinely nice person. *Maybe you don't know what normal men act like.*

"I'll pass this time. Gotta stay on top of the stocking or they'll can me." She looked back at the shelf.

"Then I wouldn't be able to bug you next time I need groceries." He inclined his head.

"That would be a shame." Her cheeks flushed again.

"Well, don't work too hard. See you around." Anaiah winked as he walked off.

Eden swore under her breath as Anaiah rounded the corner, and she went back to rotating stock. He was flirty and cute. Something about him just drew her in. She shook her head. Men had caused her nothing but problems. She still occasionally woke from nightmares of her last relationship. Some nights a shirt too tight around her throat as she slept turned to Cole's hand around her throat. She shuddered at the thought. She focused instead on the throwback tunes on the overhead speaker. She lost herself in the words and the work as she quietly sang along. After a good half hour or so, Journey appeared at the end of her aisle and signaled that it was lunch time with a jerk of her head toward the breakroom. Eden stood, dusted herself off and walked with her.

"Hey, you got a uterus?" Journey used their new code for needing to go to the bathroom.

"I got so much uterus; you'd think I had two." Eden said confidently.

"That's what I'm talkin' 'bout." Journey strutted toward the bathroom.

As they washed their hands afterward, Eden told her about the misogynistic truck driver and Sam's little outburst.

"Oh, that big baby can't take responsibility for his own mistakes. Doesn't believe in deodorant because it gives you cancer but he sure smokes plenty when someone lets him bum a cig. Did you know that idiot told me that yogurt sells so fast, it rotates itself?"

"Yeah. It rotates itself once the mold forms into legs and it develops sentience, though once that happens, we are all screwed." Eden laughed. They made their way to the time clock and punched out. They retrieved their lunch boxes and took up their spots at their regular table. Jayse nodded in greeting, his mouth already full. Kris smiled as Eden sat.

"Sup?" Eden said as she pulled out her lunch.

"So, who was that guy you were talking to?" Kris asked before he popped a pretzel in his mouth.

"Some random customer. I was blocking his cereal. Seemed to be a regular, knew I was new." Eden shrugged.

"What'd he look like?" Journey inquired as she freed her plastic wrap-covered sandwich.

"Like six foot-six with shoulder length dark hair...hot as hell." Eden picked the crust off her sandwich.

"Oh, that guy." Journey raised her eyebrows. "He comes in every couple of weeks to get his groceries. He's pretty nice and doesn't get in the way. What'd you talk about?"

"Just that I was new and whatnot." Eden responded casually.

"Heard you mention the bible, you weren't trying to share the good news with him or anything?" Kris smirked.

"No. His name is in the bible. I recognized it. I'm not worried about the state of our customer's souls." Eden shot back defensively.

"You're not some Latter Day Saint or anything like that are you?" Jayse asked, suddenly interested.

"No. I don't even go to church. My parents were the religious ones." Eden said between bites of her sandwich.

"Your parents run the Saints on Earth Cult, don't they?" Dwayne's drawl drifted over from another table.

Screw you Dwayne! Eden thought. Eden could feel her chest tighten as her heart started pounding. Her face flushed as she sat bolt upright, and her head swung toward him. She was just starting to develop some sort of working relationship with these guys and now he's going to throw her under the bus.

"You Google my name or something?" She worked hard, but not quite hard enough to keep from yelling. Half the damn crew was going to know, by the next shift, everyone would know.

"It sounded familiar. I looked it up." He shifted in his chair, seemingly excited to be part of the conversation. "Your parents took over the cult a few days ago. That other guy died. It was on the channel six news website. They even showed your picture in the story. They said you ran away." His nonchalant attitude and excitement in his eyes were a slap in the face. He was laying her entire life bare before everyone she knew, and he was excited about it. Her blood was pounding in her ears, and she could feel the heat burning there like the rising of the rage in her. Anger, embarrassment, and shame all boiling together through her like a cauldron.

"It's not really any of your business. Did the website tell you that?" Her face was burning with rage. Rage at the feelings she was fighting. It felt like a violation, like he was ripping out her heart in front of them all for their inspection. To weigh her worthiness for his personal curiosity. Her life's story was right on the news like she had given them permission to say anything. Beyond her control, hot angry tears rolled down her cheeks. *Christ! I hate crying in front of people. I hate Dwayne and his dumb curiosity.* She reached up to wipe her eyes the best she could without smearing her makeup and making it worse.

"Were they trying to make you be a child bride or something? Is that why you ran away?" Dwayne persisted, seemingly unaware of her tears, her anger, or her shame.

"Dwayne, you are a jackass, you know that?" Tessa's voice came from the break room door. "Did you ever think that she didn't tell anyone because she doesn't want to talk about it? No, because you don't use a single cell in your brain." Tessa looked furious on Eden's behalf.

"You can't talk to me like that!" Dwayne stood up, knocking the chair under him backwards in a clatter. "I'm calling Kenneth." Kenneth was their store's general manager. Eden had heard this threat before when Tessa challenged the people who didn't work diligently or acted inappropriately. Several people had threatened to tattle on Tessa. She was blunt and didn't tolerate people's crap.

"Call him. I'll just tell him how you just harassed another employee on some highly personal issues." Tessa replied flatly. Dwayne stormed out of the break room. Tessa followed.

"You alright, E?" Kris asked. Eden didn't even look at him. She was staring out after Dwayne with tears rolling down her stupid blushing cheeks.

"I'm fucking fine." Eden stood up quickly and walked briskly to the bathroom. *Dwayne could go to hell.* She stared herself down in the mirror. Her face was red and blotchy. Tear tracks ran down her cheeks and dark circles were smudged below both eyes. She turned on the water, using the hand soap and rough paper towels to wash her face and remove the make up the best she could. The door swung open, and Journey handed her some make-up wipes. Eden muttered her thanks, noting the damage the paper towels had already done; she looked even worse.

"I just want to get out of here, man." She looked at Journey through the mirror. "It's just so humiliating having that much personal stuff available to whoever wants it." She started to wipe away the make-up.

"Dwayne's an ass-hat." Journey said with a genuine look of concern.

"Thanks for not asking questions."

"I figure you'll tell me what you want when you want. I'm all about low pressure friendship." She gave Eden a small smile.

"That helps. Well, guess I'm going to finish lunch and face the crowd in the break room." Eden sighed. She wiped away the rest of her makeup.

"I already told them that you don't have to tell anyone anything, and I'll cut 'em if I have to." She chuckled, but Eden wondered if Journey wouldn't follow up on the physical threat.

"Thanks again, dude." Eden walked out with Journey trailing behind. The rest of lunch was quiet. People avoided eye contact. Eden's shame was their shame now.

At the end of their break, Tessa waited by the time clock. When Eden swiped her badge in, Tessa called her back to the office. As she closed the door behind her, Tessa turned to her and said in a calm professional voice, "Can you write up a statement about what transpired in the break room?" It was the most serious she had seen Tessa.

"Sure, why?" Eden crossed her arms.

"I'm facing disciplinary action." She gave Eden a sideways glance and made a lewd hand motion. There was the manager she came to know and love. "Just write the truth and sign and date." She handed Eden a piece of paper and a pen.

Eden wrote down the events as she recalled them. She added that she felt violated and humiliated in front of everyone. She didn't downplay the emotions she felt as she wrote them down and hoped that it would help Tessa get out of trouble.

When she was done Tessa read it over. She let out a heavy breath. "Sorry about all that, kid." She turned her brown sympathetic eyes on Eden.

"Did you know? Before tonight?" Eden forced her eyes to meet Tessa's and not stare at the floor.

"Yep. The runaway stuff and all that happened before came in with your background check. I didn't see you bragging about it, and figured it was none of my business." Eden blinked. Tessa knew. She knew that Eden hadn't just been a runaway kid from a cult. She had been a crazy runaway kid. She knew that Eden had spent a year in the mental hospital and had given her the benefit of doubt. She let Eden just be herself and let the others get to know her as she wanted them to. She had to break eye contact to keep the tears from forming in her eyes.

"I think you are the coolest manager I've ever had." Eden looked back up and gave a half grin. "Thanks for not judging me or bringing it up."

"Thanks, E." Tessa sighed. "I just hope I get to keep being your manager."

CHAPTER SIX

E den panted as she awoke covered in sweat. Her heart thundered in her chest as she turned on a light. She needed the physical reminder of where she was, that she was safe. She was shaking as she pulled the shirt that felt like a noose tightening around her neck from herself. She had dreamed of her ex-boyfriend. Dreamed that in a moment of anger, he had snapped like he had so many times before. She knew she was dreaming because the way he moved was inhuman. The strength he had to lift her off her feet as he choked her, it had to be a dream. That was her only comfort in the dream. She knew it couldn't be real. She had begged herself to wake up and return to her bedroom.

She made a beeline for her closet, flipping on all the lights, despite the daylight pouring in from the curtains in her living room. She pulled out a tank top when she reached the closet and made a note to buy more loose nightgowns and to wear more loose shirts and tank tops to bed. For a moment, in the dream, it had been like he was here, in her new home, not in the house they had shared in Oklahoma. She closed her eyes and took in slow deep breaths.

"It was just a dream. He won't come after you here. He let you leave. He let you go." She said out loud to herself. She walked back to her room to check the time. She had another hour until her alarm would sound, but now, there was no going back to sleep. She made herself a pot of coffee and picked up a book to distract herself. It shook in her hands, but after a while, she settled. She dressed for work and tried to put the dream behind her.

A week had passed since her incident with Dwayne. He hadn't spoken to her since and Journey gave him vaguely threatening looks when he even glanced Eden's way. Tessa had been given a formal write up for her handling of the situation, in addition to a complaint from Sam of all people, but it didn't seem to be as bad as she was anticipating.

While stocking, Eden couldn't help but grin when she noticed Anaiah as he approached her. He made a little small talk about the weather. She wanted to beam when he remembered her name. She had been practically giddy until he mentioned that his laundry soap seemed to be out on the shelf. Sudden, embarrassing realization hit her. He sought her out, not to chat idly, but because it was in fact, her job to know if they had more in the back. She hurriedly dashed off to check the backstock. She tried to use mind over matter to rid her cheeks of their blush as she made her way back out to the aisle to find him waiting for her return.

He flashed her a winning smile as she handed over the container of detergent. Of course, he wanted to talk to her. He needed something and it was her job to find it. He was polite enough to make small talk first. She kicked herself mentally at believing he would actually want to talk to her otherwise. He wished her well for the rest of her shift and she smiled and told him to enjoy his night off. The rest of the night passed with her carrying out her mind-numbing repetitive tasks. She avoided talking about it with Journey during her lunch and break.

As Eden walked toward the time clock, her work friends caught up with her.

"Are you coming out with us?" Kris raised his eyebrows.

"Out where?" Eden couldn't keep her sour mood from her voice.

"Pay-day breakfast." Jayse said as if she should have known.

"It's a pay-day tradition." Kris nudged her shoulder. Somehow the little nudge lifted her spirits just a bit.

"Does everyone go?" Eden looked up at Kris.

"No. God no. Just the cool people. Which is the three of us, and occasionally Tessa. Are you coming or not?" Kris laughed a bit.

"I mean, I am pretty cool. I guess I could make an appearance." Eden shrugged outwardly. Inside, she felt the warmth of her pride at her work friends deeming her worthy of an outside of work friendship. "Tessa coming?" She added casually.

"Manager meeting at eight. She can't." Journey added with a sour face.

Eden let the gloom of the night before settle into the background of her mind. She was actually making friends, not just acquaintances who were forced to befriend her due to proximity at work. She parked her car outside the restaurant and rubbed the bit of smudged eyeliner away from her under eye in the rearview mirror. She looked as tired as she felt. She shook off the dark cloud, refusing to allow her foul mood to creep back in. Her friends invited her out, she reminded herself. She plastered on a smile and hurried inside.

Journey, Kris, and Jayse were seated in a booth at the diner. They waved her over. The diner had a small breakfast buffet and the patrons at this hour were mostly senior citizens. The elderly customers didn't seem to appreciate their table's raucous laughter as the exhaustion of the night combined with the caffeine of the many cups of coffee made everything much more hilarious.

Kris told a rather funny story of a prank they pulled several years ago, when their grandfather was still alive. He claimed it would be even funnier if Eden had known his very proper British Indian grandfather. He modeled his accent. "Kristian, I expect better behavior from you. And Jayson, you are the eldest. Behave like it."

"Never mind that I am the eldest by ten minutes." Jayse laughed.

Eden wondered what it would have been like to have loving grandparents. Her father's parents had been very severe, closed off, unaffectionate older adults. They lived off the compound but still held most of the same beliefs as her parents, at least to her recollection. She'd never met her mother's parents. They never spoke of them. It wasn't as if they were a secret that no one would speak of; she'd never really had much interest in knowing them, as her father's parents didn't appeal to her. The concept of grandparents who doted on their grandchildren wasn't introduced to her until she saw it on television at the hospital. Eden felt the collective weight of the gazes of all her friends staring at her. She had been completely abandoned to thought.

"You okay there, Eden?" Kris' brow furrowed with concern.

"Yeah, sorry… just spaced out there." Eden shook her head.

"You didn't just space out, dude. You looked like someone just told you your dog had died. It was like all hope left your eyes." Journey added. Was that concern in her voice?

"Your RBF must be next level if that is your neutral off in space face." Jayse laughed.

"Were you thinking about what happened last week, with Dwayne?" Kris said quietly, face still screwed up with concern.

"Nah. I was just thinking of what hell it must have been to raise you two." Eden joked. She smiled when the tension seemed to break as Journey let out a chuckle.

"You have no idea." A smile bloomed across Jayse's face, "this idiot" Jayse pointed a fork with a stabbing motion in his brother's direction, "once hid in the dryer during a game of hide and seek… mid cycle."

"Our grandfather accidentally started it again." Kris raised his eyebrows for emphasis.

"A couple of thuds and some yelling had him stopping it again pretty quick, though." Jayse shrugs, "his brain damage was minimal." He smiled and winked toward his brother.

"Jackass." Kris muttered with a smile and tossed a biscuit at his head. Jayse caught it just before it struck and took a bite out of it. He started to laugh a bit and choked on the biscuit and started to cough uncontrollably. The table erupted with small giggles that quickly turned to full belly laughter as Jayse made a vulgar gesture at the entire table as he drank water to calm his coughing.

As the conversation wound down, they decided sleep was inevitable and should be taken up in a bed rather than a booth. Eden headed to the cash register at the front of the diner. She paid her tab and headed into the lady's restroom. Journey turned to follow. As Eden lowered herself onto the seat of the toilet a moment later, an apparition appeared before her. She recognized the spirit of the man she knew was Pastor Joseph from the Church.

"Devil's spawn. He slayed me with his black magic!" He exclaimed with his full hellfire and brimstone southern preacher voice.

This understandably startled Eden. She gasped out, "Holy hell!" She slapped a hand over her mouth.

"Devil's child. You gotta put an end to that spawn of hell and his forces of evil. He's got a legion of demons at his back." Eden was all too familiar with this rhetoric. He had once repeatedly baptized her in a manner she would recall as more water boarding and torture than actual exorcism. She had nearly drowned in the process, but he kept repeating it because he needed to 'wash away the devil's touch.'

"You alright in there, E?" Journey called out right before she flushed.

"I'm fine." Eden scrambled to think of an excuse quickly. "Fell asleep and almost fell in. It startled me." She heard Journey's giggles from the next stall. "I'm awake now." Eden forced a laugh as the sound of Journey washing her hands filled the lavatory.

"Okay, meet you out front." Journey chuckled her way out the door.

Pastor Joe just stood there, staring at Eden as he muttered to himself.

"Back off, Joseph. I don't want to help you. Cross the hell over and leave me alone." She said in a hushed tone. Worry curled in her gut.

"Satan's words fly from the demon child's mouth. But you will eat those words when Satan's spawn uses his black magic on you!" Joseph's unearthly voice rose in dramatic evangelical fervor. Eden flinched but remembered that this was a ghost. This spirit could not harm her. She scowled.

"Whatever. Okay, fine. The Devil's minions killed you. I'll get right on it. You can go." She rolled her eyes. His rotund grey-haired spirit dissipated and Eden dropped her head in her hands. She made herself take a few deep breaths and tried to focus on the task at hand. She finally was able to use the bathroom and hurried to wash her hands. She strolled out to the front of the diner to find Journey to say her goodbyes.

She spotted a red faced, seething Journey after a moment. "No. They can't do that! It's bullshit! Well, he can suck a... Fine. Fine! Okay, come to my place, Tess. Let's do that. See you there in about ten-fifteen minutes? Text the guys." Journey glared down at her phone as she hit the end call button. Eden took a step back as Journey's wrath filled expression turned on her.

"What's up?" Eden struggled to find a way of casually diffusing the situation.

"They are transferring Tessa to another store for 'retraining,'" Journey made air quotes on the last word. "They said she has fired too many people. They were worthless, but she was supposed to give them infinite chances! That and the whole Dwayne thing. Fuckin' Dwayne!"

"Oh...shit." Eden was struck with instant regret. Tessa had gotten in trouble, and had risked her job, for her.

"Yeah, and they are sending some day shift manager to watch over us until they get her replaced. She has to report in on Monday at Mineral Wells. We're giving her a proper send off at my place. You in?" Journey's expression smoothed out into a calm, calculating one. She cocked an eyebrow at Eden.

Eden barely hesitated. She was off work tonight anyway, sleep could wait, and she had the chance to hang out with friends. "You bet, I'm in. I'll follow you." Journey gave a Cheshire cat grin and walked Eden out to her car.

Eden pulled her car up behind Journey's parked just behind the main office of the RV park. Journey led her up a metal staircase with multiple peeling coats of white paint. Flecks of rust and paint sprinkled on the ground below them.

"I'm upstairs. Parental units live in the house behind the office." Journey pointed toward the house. Eden found herself wondering what Journey's parents were like... were they nice? As they reached the top of the stairs, Tessa pulled up beside the office. She hopped out and grabbed a couple of large grocery tote bags. Journey unlocked the door as a small SUV pulled up. She saw Kris emerge from the passenger side.

Kris and Jayse waved at her as they started unloading something from their car. Eden blinked as she watched them pull out a giant black plastic trash can with an assortment of items inside it. They began carrying it upstairs. When the twins reached the door, Eden hustled to move out of the way. Jayse called out a request to Journey to make some coffee.

After a few torturous minutes of waiting, the smell of rich fresh coffee drifted into the apartment. Eden joined Journey in the kitchen. Journey poured coffee and creamer into a mug. Then offered it to Eden. Eden took a long sip from her mug.

"Oh, that's good. It has kind of a smooth caramel flavor to it." Eden sighed at the comforting beverage.

"I'm a coffee snob. I don't brew cheap stuff in my baby." Journey stroked her very expensive looking coffee maker. "I buy that kind in the city. My other stuff I special order from Guatemala online. Between coffee and art supplies, I'll never be able to afford to move away from my parents." Eden followed Journey into the living room as she brought Jayse a mug as well.

Journey's living room was a hodgepodge of mismatched furniture and art. Much of her furniture had been painted in some way. The miss matched end tables had been painted over. They showed the same hillside covered in trees but with different seasons in each depiction. Each wall had canvases of various sizes of abstracts. The wall closest to the kitchen held a painting of a tree with blue leaves on it. Eden sat down on one of the couches and looked around. Across from her, there was a heavy looking large old-fashioned television. It was the style that was an entire cabinet and had big mechanical knobs for changing channels. It was being used as a television stand for Journey's smaller flat screen atop it. Someone had painted a landscape scene over the screen of the old cabinet television. Above the televisions, a painting depicted something Eden didn't expect to see in Journey's home. Amongst dark storm clouds, the painting portrayed in horrifying detail, a monstrous looking winged creature. The description of such a thing had been studied and spoken about by the church as Eden was growing up. It was a biblical angel with too many heads, too many eyes, and sharp features. Eden quickly looked away when she realized she had been staring at the painting for an unknown amount of time.

To each side of the television was a single door that led into what Eden assumed were bedrooms. The wall to her left, across from the kitchen door had another couch on it and two of the previously mentioned end tables. Kris took a seat next to Eden. She took a long sip of her coffee. They were rarely alone; she had suddenly realized. Always with his brother or Journey whenever they spoke. The others had walked back into the kitchen and were chatting. Still within earshot, she supposed. Anxiety still rose in her. She reminded herself that Kris was her friend. He had never been anything but nice to her. He wasn't a threat. He was her friend. Not a random stranger harassing her while she waited for the bus before her shift. Not a boyfriend expecting more than she wanted to give. *HER FRIEND.* She slowed her breathing. She sipped her coffee again and schooled her features into calm neutrality.

"Good stuff, huh?" He said quietly. Eden nodded as she swallowed. At that moment, Jayse walked into the room to start setting up the contents of the trash can.

"What is that?" Eden asks Jayse, hoping to avoid talking too much with Kris alone. She wasn't stupid. She could tell that Kris was attracted to her. It was what set her on edge. Plenty of men have been in the last couple of years. He was attractive enough, decent looking. His dark skin and smile were definitely pleasing to her eye, but she felt no spark there. She changed the subject and talked to Jayse instead. Why her gut deemed him safer, she had no clue.

"It's a kegerator. It's our homemade insulated keg holder and beer dispenser." Jayse's grin spread wide. He poured in bags of ice. "We homebrew beer. Our grandfather was a brew master. He taught us how."

"Your very proper grandfather taught you to brew beer at home?" Eden asked incredulously.

"He was very serious about the art of brewing. He said grandmother was too. They kept a garden for all their own ingredients. Did you know that traditionally, before men took over, women brewed the beer?" Kris said from beside her. "Then they made them out to be potion brewing witches if they tried to run their own brewhouses."

"Ah yes, feminist history lessons, the way to every young girl's heart." Tessa added from the doorway. "Come in here while they get it set up, I'll make you a drink." She smiled at Eden.

Tessa had set up a small bar in Journey's kitchen. Apparently, they were sending Tessa off with large amounts of alcohol. And now, with coffee in one hand and a shot of bourbon in another Eden was encouraged to down both so the real fun could begin. She shot the bourbon back, pretending to be a veteran drinker, but nearly choked as it burned its way down her throat. She chased it with coffee and was surprised to find that they went together beautifully. She smiled.

Tessa winked at her and said, "if you like that, I've got just the thing." She reached over and poured a milky brown liquid in her coffee. "Bourbon cream, and…" She grabbed a second bottle. "Amaretto. Try it." She swirled a spoon into the coffee.

Eden took a tentative sip and then immediately took another larger drink. "Oh my god. That is amazing." She took another and marveled at how sweet, yet dark and rich her coffee tasted. "You're going to turn me into an alcoholic. I'll need this every day before my shift." She smiled deviously over her cup to Tessa.

As she finished off her alcoholic coffee, her empty mug was replaced by a full glass of homebrewed ale. She had migrated back into the living room as Journey had walked out to get her own glass and Eden trailed her like a lost puppy. She took up her previous seat next to Kris who clinked glasses with her when he saw what she was drinking. Journey and Jayse migrated back to the kitchen while debating whether or not a certain song was good or terrible. Eden had never heard of it, so she remained out of the conversation. Eden realized she was sitting alone with Kris yet again. She tried to steady her nerves and be cool about it.

He looked over at her, contemplative, as if he was debating internally. "Mind if I ask you some personal questions?" Eden did mind, but then again, he could have chosen this moment to shoot his shot with her. For that restraint, she could humor him.

"Out with it, I guess." She shrugged as nonchalantly as she could muster. She took a sip of the beer. *Damn! Where has this nectar of the god's been my whole life?*

"Do you believe in God?" His question snapped her to attention. "After all the crap you've seen in that cult?" He didn't even attempt to make eye contact with her as she glanced over at him. His deadlocked gaze across the room told her that he'd known how uncomfortable this question was and still felt compelled to ask. She made a bit of a face but gathered her thoughts to answer.

"Start with the easy ones, huh?" She shook her head. "Sort of. I mean, I believe he or something like God exists. I just don't know what the right religion is. I know I don't believe in the fundamentalist shit my parents did." She shrugged. "I guess you can say, I believe, but I am not sure what. Agnostic of sorts."

"Huh." He swigged his beer casually as if the topic of conversation was not 'Eden deconstructs her faith'.

"Can we talk about something a little less 'crisis of faith' related?" She glanced at him as she drank.

"Sure. One more?" He gave her a small smile.

"I guess." Eden rolled her eyes. Why did men think that charm owed them the right to things she didn't want to give? *Ugh.*

"When you ran away, where did you go? How did you make it? You were just a kid with no place to go. How'd you do it?" He rattled off.

"You said one... that was like five." She took a big drink. "You really have to know?" The look on his face told her that he'd been dying to know for weeks. She let out an exasperated huff. "Okay, fine." She took in another big breath to prepare to ramble. "I changed my clothes, my hair, and pierced my nose. Then I took what little money I had and some I had stolen and hopped a bus and got a job waiting tables at the first place that would hire me on the spot. You get cash daily at a job like that." He eyed her with suspicion. She rolled her eyes and continued.

"I slept on city buses at first but found out that's a good way to get groped by other homeless people, then at truck stops. Not much better. But, for a little bit of money, they let you shower and sleep. I avoided shelters because they might have tried to turn me in. After I got enough money, I rented a room from some people I worked with." She paused for a beat wondering if his curiosity was satisfied. Then added, "That's one of the things that makes me believe there might be a God. Everything just kind of worked out for me. It was by no means perfect. Things happened that I am not proud of, but I came out alive. I don't know, maybe I'm lucky. You just do what you gotta do, every day to get by."

"I know you don't like talking about it, but it's a crazy story." Kris looked at her with wonder in his eyes.

"Don't look at me like I'm some sort of miracle, Kris. I did sketchy shit. Stuff I really don't like talking about. For the first time in three years, I've been able to actually let people get to know me. I've lied, stolen and cheated my way through life for a long time, dude. Honestly, I'm surprised that you guys even want to be friends with me." She finished her beer and walked across the room to pour another. She was emotionally done with the conversation. She wasn't in tears, but her skin was crawling with anxiety.

"But we are friends, right?" Kris asked quietly.

"Yeah." She gave him a small smile. Her chest was tight, and she took a few breaths to try to expand it. She walked past Kris into the kitchen with everyone else.

Tessa handed her a glass of some sort of frozen beverage despite having a glass full of beer in the other hand. "Amaretto-colada, drink up." Tessa took a sip of hers. Eden shrugged and tried it. Eden decided to be brave and do something that might embarrass herself.

"A toast," Eden held up a glass. "To the most awesome boss I've ever had."

"Here, here!" Jayse added as they drank. Kris walked in and took up a spot on the wall by Jayse. He smiled at Eden as he held up his glass, as if in apology. Eden nodded her head as if to tell him it was okay.

Tessa held up her glass and said, "As my Gran used to say, may those who love us, always love us, and as for those who don't love us, may God turn their hearts, and if he can't turn their hearts, may he turn their ankles, so we will know them from their limping."

"Damn Tess, the whole town is going to be limping around." Journey laughed.

At some point near noon, her coworkers called into work. They all claimed to have food poisoning. "Yeah, whatever I had; it's not sitting well. I'm pretty sure I'm going to hurl and then spend the night in bed." Journey was telling her half-truths to management over the phone. She had consumed enough alcohol to kill a man.

Eden counted herself lucky that it was already her night off. Journey hung up and walked back to the kitchen to check on the frozen pizzas in the oven. Something savory for drunk food.

"Come get some, bitches!" She yelled from the kitchen.

"You got bitches in there?" Jayse laughed from his spot on the couch. "Why didn't you tell me? I'll take two!" He headed into the kitchen. Eden followed close behind, swaying a bit on her feet. The full view of Journey bent over pulling out a pizza cutter from a drawer came into focus. Jayse, however, had no clue that Eden was also behind him. He looked at Journey like her ass was a complete work of art. Eden stifled a laugh. He averted his gaze nervously.

"What's so funny?" Journey looked up.

"Jayse. Jayse is hilarious." Eden giggled. She was delirious with exhaustion and drunkenness. She was crashing like a five-year-old after a birthday party. Jayse gave Journey a "I have no clue" sort of look and Journey shrugged it off.

Eden grabbed a plate off the counter and stood next to the stove impatiently. Journey served her up a few slices. Eden sat at the small table in the kitchen and blew aggressively on her pizza.

"Cool down! Imma eat your face." She muttered at it nonsensically. Her head swam. She tended to get silly and emotional when she was tired. Alcohol, it seemed, just added fuel to the fire. She tried a bite to see if it was cool enough to eat. *Pizza is the best thing on earth!* It had never tasted more delicious than right at this moment. Journey sat on her countertop eating her slice, as the twins sat down at the table next to Eden and dug in. For a while, the only sound was that of chewing noises.

"I gotta tinkle!" Eden announced to the now quiet room. Journey hopped down and showed her to the bathroom. One of the doors she had suspected as bedrooms did indeed lead to Journey's room, the other led to a room she used as an art studio. Between the two was a bathroom that opened to both rooms.

"Here ya go. Tinkle away." Journey gave her best mom voice.

"Thanks." Eden closed the door. She used the toilet and even stayed upright the entire time. She was proud of that accomplishment at this point. She washed her hands and stopped when she noted there was no towel or paper towels in sight. She shrugged and shook them off and headed out to the kitchen again.

Journey stood in the kitchen, talking with Tessa who had taken Eden's spot at the table. Eden walked up and for no logical reason, dried her hands on the back of Journey's shirt. Alcohol had taken away her personal boundaries.

Journey turned around laughing. "What the hell, man? Did you even wash your hands?"

"No." Eden lied with a giggle.

"You're a chick, how did you get your hands wet peeing?" Kris' face contorted with confusion.

"I played in it. Like a cat!" Eden cackled while making pawing motions in the air.

"God, I hope you are kidding." Journey chuckled.

"Nope." Eden brushed Journey's cheek with her still moist hand.

In a flash, Eden's vision was taken over by a waking dream. She saw Journey. She was younger... and standing with a young man. *Oh god no. Not now.* Journey spoke in the vision, "I just don't feel that way about you." Eden saw the shock and dismay of the young man flash across his face. He reached out to take her hand and Journey flinched back. A bright light flashed again, and the scene changed. The guy, a teenaged boy by the look of it, stood alone in a room. Under his feet was the seat of a chair. A heavy rope around his neck. He was crying. Eden tried to shake herself out of the vision as he kicked the chair. Tried to close her eyes as he dropped. Her vision flashed white, and her stomach turned slightly.

Eden found herself staring at Journey with her hand hanging in the air next to Journey's face. Eden could feel the wave of discomfort and unease pouring from Journey. Despite her unease, Journey playfully swatted Eden's hand away.

"Geez. Eden. You are like the queen of gay chicken. Just caressed her cheek and stared deeply into her eyes." Jayse chuckled. Eden attempted to play it off as intentional; shrugging as if it was no big deal. Grabbing the rest of her pizza, Eden hopped up on the counter where Journey had been. Journey hoisted herself next to Eden further down the countertop.

Conversation resumed. The rules of "gay chicken" were explained. Jayse explained that as a teen, the straight boys played this game where two people of the same sex pretend to have an intimate moment and the first one to break it, loses.

"But what if the other person is actually gay?" Eden blinked at the stupidity of the game.

"You coming out to us?" Kris asked.

"No. I'm straight." She shrugged and amended. "Well, mostly. I'm just asking."

"Well, we should get one thing straight." Tessa said coolly. "I'm not." She winked at Eden. "And I'm a little disappointed that you are." She grinned as she took another bite.

"We all know you have a crush on Journey, Tess. You don't have to pretend with us." Jayse said a little quietly.

"For the record, I prefer men in my sexual positions over me and women in my managerial positions over me." Journey proclaimed to no one in particular.

"Damn right." Tessa quietly added to Jayse. "Stop projecting. Just tell her." Jayse just shook his head.

Eventually, the lack of sleep and the abundance of food caught up to Eden. She felt nauseated. A full twenty-four hours had passed since she climbed out of bed the day before. She found an appealing spot on the living-room floor to lay down on. She closed her eyes for what seemed like seconds. When she opened them again, it was dark outside.

Tessa was passed out on the couch furthest from the kitchen. The couch next to the kitchen had been pulled out to a bed and the twins barely fit on it, sound asleep. Snoring was coming from Journey's room. Eden had chosen the spot in front of the door to the art studio room to pass out on. Her phone blared a ringtone from her pocket. She pulled it out and wanted to groan as she saw it was the number from work. She pulled herself up into a sitting position, her body protesting in the process. She was stiff and sore from her poor choice of sleeping location.

"Hello." She answered as quietly as possible.

"Hello, Eden? This is Loretta from work. Is there any way you can come in? We had a few people call in sick and we are really in a bind." Her cheerful southern voice rang harshly in Eden's ears. Eden's head throbbed in return.

"I think I'm sick too, Loretta. In fact, I think I'm going to puke. I'm going to let you go." Eden bolted for the bathroom and made it just in time to retch into the toilet. She regretted her choices.

"You okay?" a vaguely familiar voice said quietly from behind. When she looked, nobody was there. *Maybe I'm still sleepy. Or is there a ghost?* She cleaned up after herself and washed her face. There was an imprint of a carpet pattern on her face. She felt like she wanted to die.

"Are you alright?" She heard Kris say from the door.

"Yeah, work tried to call me in, woke me up." She said and turned toward him.

"Work makes you sick, huh?" He laughed.

"Yeah. Something like that. Excuse me." Her pounding head made her long for her pillow. She moved around him and gathered up her stuff. She was certain she was no longer drunk. No, this was a hangover. If she was going to die from it, she wanted to do it in the comfort of her own home. When she had gathered all her belongings, she made a halfhearted farewell to Kris and headed down the stairs. She mentally kicked herself for thinking this would just be a fun day; fun always had a price. Now she would pay it.

CHAPTER SEVEN

In the pitch black of her room, Eden silently made a vow to never drink like she had at Journey's ever again. She had spent her first day off sleeping away the effects of Tessa's send-off party. Sleeping, puking and bargaining with God to let her either die or quit throwing up was more like it. When she thought about it, Tessa's party had been less of a party and more of a gathering of people drinking and telling stories. Was that what parties were? Eden really didn't know.

On her second night off, she faced the thrilling chore of taking her clothes to the local laundromat and hauling them back home to put away. As Eden blasted music from her phone while hanging up clothes, she contemplated the need for more companions and friendships that involved more than mutual work experiences. How would she go about meeting new people apart from coworkers? She remembered how awkward she was around new people and decided that reading a few novels instead of being social was a better alternative. Maybe she'd meet a friend at the local library.

She was less than chipper when she clocked in on Sunday night, not knowing what to expect at work. Journey seemed to share her lack of enthusiasm. Though, this was hers and the twins' last day of work for the week. Eden and her workmates gathered in the usual loose circle for the shift meeting. With her over the top, big Texas hair unflinching, Loretta, the short manager from dayshift, strutted out of the office. Unlike Tessa, she wore business casual dress and was obviously intending to be managerial rather than functional for the night shift. Tessa had helped the crew when needed. Loretta's press-on nails didn't look up to the task of opening a single box, much less stacking freight. Loretta only looked prepared to gossip, do paperwork, and single-handedly keep Aqua net in business.

"Alright, Y'all. Go work where you normally do. Our truck is 1300 pieces, plus the grocery, frozen, and dairy trucks," She looked around. "You, Mrs. No Name Tag?" She pointed to Journey. Journey reached slowly to the bottom of her shirt and moved the name tag to the neckline all the while staring daggers at Loretta.

"Journey." Journey said in a too calm tone.

"Journey, why don't you lead us in the cheer?" Loretta said excitedly.

Eden was not familiar with 'the cheer'. She expected a "One, two, three, work" cheer like usual. With some groans, everyone around her started clapping slowly. Then the real cheer started. It felt ritualistic and forced. Everyone recited the letters spelling out the company name as Journey asked them to give her each letter. Then it wrapped up with a cheered affirmation that we want to be accident free. For Christ's sake there was even a squiggly in there. They indicated to Eden that you were supposed to shake your ass on that part. At least that's what Loretta did. Eden supposed that for the daytime crowd this was encouraging and formed camaraderie, but for the night shifters, it felt like their employer had just touched them inappropriately. At least, that was how Eden felt. *Dance and clap or else.*

As they walked away to work in their respective departments Eden said to Journey in a low voice, "Do you feel the need for a shower?"

"I'd laugh if it wasn't so true. Usually, managers become laid back on nights. I don't think this one is going to be. Get ready to do that cheer every single night until she rotates back to days." Journey said with quiet violence in her eyes.

While they stocked shampoo an hour or so later, Loretta came by to check on their progress. "Y'all need to be happier in your work. Makes you work faster. Y'all are acting like someone died." Loretta donned a fake smile and put her hands on her hips.

"Sorry, I recently lost a friend." Journey deadpanned. "We both did." Eden stared straight into the shelf she was stocking to keep from cracking a smile.

"Oh my, I am so sorry. I didn't know." Loretta displayed what Eden perceived as the first genuine bit of emotion she had seen from Loretta. "Y'all let me know if you need anything." She scuttled off, looking slightly ashamed.

"Didn't say anyone died. We both lost Tessa to that walking pile of southern belle bullshit." She cracked a half smile at Eden. God, Eden loved Journey's sense of humor. Dark, irreverent humor. They stocked while making idle conversation.

Finally, when the first break of the night was upon them, the ladies headed to the break room. They had just gotten settled in as Loretta strolled up to their table. Loretta started talking to them about freight and where to go next as if they weren't on break.

Journey held up a hand. "Talk to me on the clock. I'm on break."

"Well technically, you are on the clock, we give you these breaks." Loretta placed her hands on her abundance of hips.

"Well technically, I might spend my break time on the phone with the department of labor and see what they have to say about it." Journey added. Eden looked between them as the stare down continued.

"Enjoy your break, Y'all. Journey, after break, come to my office." Another fake as hell smile flashed across Loretta's face.

After Loretta walked away, Journey turned to Eden and said in a low but joking tone, "If I lose my job, wanna move in with me and help with the bills?" She batted her lashes.

"And put up with your snoring? Um, no thanks." Eden nudged her with an elbow.

"You could move in with us." Jayse offered as he sat down at the table across from them.

"You'd have to sleep in the garage though." Kris took his seat across from Eden.

"Well, I'm gonna go get fired just for that. Sounds glamorous." Journey rolled her eyes. "I don't know, Eden's probably less likely to drunkenly try to cuddle with me." She kicked Jayse's shoe. He stared down at the table, but Eden could have sworn he actually looked embarrassed.

"You're kidding! Cuddling is part of the deal, drunk or not!" Eden said, attempting to rescue Jayse from his embarrassment. She laughed softly.

"That's hot." Kris weighed in.

"I'm out then. I don't cuddle." Journey threw her hands up in fake exasperation.

"I can give you tips. It's pretty easy, really." Kris offered. Jayse gave him an odd warning look.

"Nope. I'm good." Journey shook her head.

When break was over, Journey headed back to the office. She joined Eden about twenty minutes later with rage radiating from her in waves.

"Want to wait around with me 'til eight after work?" Journey seethed.

"Sure." Eden shrugged. "What's up?"

"I'm contesting my write-up. She wrote me up for insubordination. If they want to get rid of Tessa for stupid complaints, I can do the same with Loretta." Journey seemed to be taking Tessa being reassigned as a personal affront.

As they moved on to the next department, across the aisle from the twins, Eden noted how Journey and Jayse seemed to watch each other in alternating turns. Every now and then they would awkwardly catch the other's eye and pretend to be looking for something. Eden rolled her eyes. It occurred to her that if they did become an item, she might be asked to double date with them and Kris. She hadn't realized the thought made her screw up her face until Journey spoke up.

"Did someone fart or something?" Journey eyed Eden with suspicion.

"Nah. Just had a weird random thought." Eden deflected.

When Eden turned back around, she caught Journey peeking at Jayse's ass as he bent over a pallet. Eden snapped her out of it when she whispered, "So you got a thing for him?"

"No." Journey lied. "Well... Shit." She sighed. "Yes. Keep your mouth shut and wipe that smile off your damn face." She scolded in whisper form.

"He checks you out too, you know. He was totally checking out your ass the other day." Eden whispered with a laugh.

"Yeah, but when can I ever see him when Kris isn't around. That's the deal. Kris is kind of a thorn in my side. Always there. Ready to commentate on me making any sort of move. Lost cause man. He probably doesn't like me like that. He's just a guy. He looks at butts and boobs and stuff. I've caught him looking at your rack more than once." She frowned.

"Really?!" Eden cocked her head to the side. "I've seen Kris do it once or twice when I bent over, but Jayse is usually looking at you." Eden smiled.

"So do you like Kris?" She asked while putting away diapers, glancing to the side at Eden. "Oh, there's that face. That 'it smells like farts in here' face." She giggled.

"He's not really my type, I guess. I just don't see him like that." Eden continued to frown as if someone had crop dusted the aisle. "Jayse either, really."

"What's your type?" Journey asked tentatively.

"Not sure really. I just know he's not it. He's decent looking and nice and all, but I just don't feel anything there." Eden said with a shrug and grabbed her next box. "I'm not exactly looking for a boyfriend or anything."

"Whatcha chatting about?" Loretta appeared around the corner.

"Dating prospects on the night shift." Eden said before thinking, then added, "Helps us keep up our spirits so we stock faster." She gave Loretta a big fake smile.

"Well, keep up the work girls." She smiled back.

"How can you not want to stab her?" Journey said to Eden in a barely audible tone.

"Oh, the urge to stab is there, but the need for a job is too. Just have to suppress the urges." Eden whispered back. "Being homeless and jobless is not a place I want to be in again."

Journey cocked a curious eyebrow.

"That's all I am saying about it." Eden crossed her arms.

"Take your time, your secrets will spill someday." Journey grinned a wicked half smile.

After an uneventful remainder of their shift, they wandered around the store for an hour after work, waiting for Kenneth to show up. When eight in the morning approached, they waited by the time clock. Kenneth strode in exactly on time. He carried himself with an odd confidence she wasn't used to seeing on older, slightly balding men. He was a nerdy looking guy in pinstripe blue slacks and a white button-down suit shirt with a blue tie. His corporate allegiance shone through his managerial wardrobe.

As he walked by, Journey said, "Kenneth, can I talk with you for a moment?"

"Sure, Journey. Is this about work?" He sounded bored already.

Journey dipped her head in a stern nod.

"Are you on the clock?" Ever the follower of corporate rules.

"No." she said.

"Clock in and meet me in my office." He smiled cordially.

"Will do." Journey mock saluted. As she walked off, Eden made her way over to the bakery department and picked up some donuts. She completed her purchase and sat in the break room full of strangers. She took a bite of her donut. God, she was tired.

"You work here?" An older lady asked her as if she was lost.

"Nah, I wear the blue shirt and name badge for fun." Eden said without making any huge effort to be friendly.

"Damn night shifters" she muttered as she left Eden alone at the table.

After finishing the donuts, Eden pulled out her phone and started reading an eBook on it. Journey walked back towards her with her menacing gait. Her face was as wrathful as it had been earlier in the shift.

"He won't take the write up off, because I was 'out of line' for speaking to her like that, but he will talk to her about policies regarding breaks." She huffed. "Let's blow this Popsicle stand."

As they parted ways in the parking lot, Eden considered how Journey was going to goad Loretta into screwing up. She seemed hellbent on Loretta's demise. Hating Loretta seemed to fill Journey with glorious purpose. Eden thought of trying to talk her down, but at the menacing glare in her eyes, Eden backed off. This was one ticking time bomb Eden was not going to be able to defuse.

CHAPTER EIGHT

fter a few weeks of back and forth, the war had fizzled between Loretta and Journey. Journey had received another write up and Loretta had gone to a management workshop on conflict resolution. Eden worried Journey might actually lose her job a few times over the last three weeks. A few days ago, Kenneth had come in to speak with the night shift. He had come to draw a line in the sand and crush any rebellion on the rise. He told them in no uncertain terms that his decisions about management were final. Any insubordination would be dealt with according to policy and that included termination.

Journey had set her jaw in determination, wild rage simmered in her eyes. Jayse miraculously had managed to talk her down. She had even allowed him to place a hand on her arm as he reassured her that Loretta would be a temporary problem. Management rotated every six months to work nights with them and Loretta was only riding out the last few weeks of Tessa's rotation. Eden had been a little bewitched by the way Journey's mood had shifted at Jayse's soft touch and calm reassuring words.

Additionally, Jayse had resorted to asking Loretta to explain things to him whenever she was condescending. That had resulted in Loretta only addressing Kris as if Jayse no longer existed apart from his brother. Journey and Jayse had been united in that. Loretta barely acknowledged either of them anymore. She had instead directed her attention to Eden and Kris. Eden was not thrilled by this.

As she prepared for her last shift of the week, Eden applied her make up and contemplated her 'weekend' ahead of her. She found herself loathing the thought of how she knew it would be spent: reading, streaming movies on her phone, and doing laundry. It was strange how she had grown used to spending time with other people. She found herself reducing her sleep hours on her friend's days off to do so. She hated to admit it, but her days off were a little lonely. She glanced around her little house. It was fully furnished now, thanks to help from her friends. Last week, the twins hauled the couch and loveseat in for her. She had spotted them on the way home sitting outside of a junk store and her friends had been more than happy to help her get them home in exchange for breakfast at the local waffle-based restaurant. Jayse and Kris had tied the smaller sofa to the top of Eden's car and the larger one to the twin's SUV. The SUV was on the smaller side though, so both cars looked a little ridiculous. She smiled at her full sized fluffy cushioned grey couch and matching loveseat before she threw her keys, wallet, phone, and a book in her crossbody bag.

On the uneventful drive to work, Eden sang along to the music on the radio. Her mood lifted when she recalled that her birthday was just over a week away. She knew that logically, it wasn't even her exact birthday. It hadn't been celebrated when she was a child. She began celebrating it after the hospital. A small rebellion that she sometimes went over the top with. If her parents had been at all truthful when she first got hospitalized, she would be eighteen sometime next week. On legal papers, and as far as anyone knew, she would be twenty-one. She'd already been drinking with her friends but having the ability to go out with them to drink or to buy her own drinks was appealing.

If Eden had any backbone at all, she would be brave enough to ask Anaiah out for her birthday. She had talked with him in the store every Thursday since her first encounter with him. Two months had gone by and he continued to shop every Thursday, just before midnight, every week. He always stopped and smiled that half smile that she had a love hate relationship with due to what it did to her hormones. He took time to talk with her as long as she could manage without getting in trouble. Topics ranged from small talk about the weather, how she was getting along in her new town, to what shows he or she was watching on their days off. She had hinted that she didn't have much company on her days off, hoping he'd take the bait. She'd come close to asking for his number, but she couldn't bring herself to actually ask him for it, much less ask him on a date. He was gorgeous, too nice to in-fact be human, and way out of her league, so of course he made her nervous as all hell when he was around. She'd changed tactics. She purchased a few new shirts that met the dress code of navy tops and jeans but had gotten ones that were more flattering and closer cut than her previous blue t-shirts and polos. She also chose jeans that showed off more of her curves. Those had become her Thursday outfits. Thirsty Thursdays as Journey had started referring to them.

Eden wondered if Anaiah thought she was dressing too provocatively in her tighter pants and lower cut blue shirts. She wondered if she was losing her mind. Then remembered where those thoughts came from. Her cheeks flushed with a small amount of anger at her internalized shame of her own body.

Modesty was a tenant of her parent's faith. She struggled with this every time she dressed in something with cleavage showing or in a shorter dress.

She wished she had the guts to make the first move. *It's been over eight months since I have even been kissed.* She thought in self-pity. *Well, if Journey can be a chicken about her crush so can I.* She stuck her tongue out at her own reflection in the car's mirror.

Eden parked next to Journey and stepped out of her car. Journey took one look at her shirt and shimmied her shoulders a bit. Eden gave a small mischievous grin as she looked down at her assets. The collared polo shirt was likely a little too small in the chest for Eden. She had worn a white tank top beneath it the last time she wore it to work. This time, edges of the black lace of her bra were visible. Her sizeable chest had come in handy with tips when she had waited tables. She was well aware of their effect on men.

"You going fishing?" Journey laughed.

"With these as bait, maybe I'll snag a date. Maybe you could bear some boob and get Jayse's attention." Eden jabbed.

"Shut it." Journey's eyes thinned to slits as she gave Eden a sideways glance. Her smile was gone.

After clocking in, they gathered around for the meeting with their coworkers. Eden noted that Loretta was decked out with a lot of big silver and turquoise jewelry today. Loretta grinned at them all. Her stenciled eyebrows were drawn so high she looked startled. Eden thought she looked like a living cartoon.

"Everyone knows where to go. It's a regular night, y'all. Tamara, you lead us in a cheer today. And don't forget the squiggly!" Loretta loved to watch them squirm, didn't she?

"I got your squiggly right here." Jayse muttered from behind Eden, but only loud enough for their little group to hear. She did her best to not crack up laughing at Jayse's comment. And in effect, accidentally looked enthused to be doing this thing for once. Loretta gave her a thumbs up. *Shit.* Eden thanked whatever God there was in the universe that Journey was behind her, and not seeing her face or she would never hear the end of it.

"Alright gang, get to work." Loretta swung her arm toward the store in enthusiasm.

"Well, now that we have offered our praise to our corporate deities, let us now honor them with our labor and our bodies." Journey said in her yoga instructor voice. In a rare moment of physical affection, she patted Eden on the back. The name KYLE rammed itself into Eden's brain. Eden stumbled for just a second but made herself walk on towards the health and beauty department.

As she stocked the conditioner, she noticed one of the bottles in the back was dusty. "Are we supposed to rotate shampoo and conditioner?" She wondered out loud.

"Hell, if I know...we never do." Journey called back.

"I know, but what if someone came in and the shelf was down to the one bottle way back on the shelf and they ended up with a five-year-old bottle of shampoo." Eden wondered.

"You can rotate if you want. I'm just here to shove it on the shelf." Journey sounded as bored as usual.

"Sounds sexy. Want me to shove it in your shelf baby?" Eden laughed. Journey made a few moaning noises while she stocked for a moment. As Eden grabbed the next box of shampoo another thought occurred to her.

"Why don't they make generic brand cars? Equate brand? Compare to Honda? Shoot, I'd buy one." Eden chuckled.

"They do. They're called Kia's." Journey laughed. Journey in-fact, drove one. "My car had to be sent into the shop two weeks after I bought it. The one I test drove before it broke down on the test drive. But they approved my credit for it, so I bought that sucker." She was laughing still as she brushed past Eden to get to the pallet.

At the graze of contact between them, an apparition slowly filled out a hazy existence trailing behind Journey. Eden recognized him as the young man from the vision Eden had seen when she was drinking at Journey's house. He turned a sullen look to Eden and then turned back to Journey. Eden resisted the urge to shake her head and scowl at the apparition. *Why can't I be normal? Why does my friend have a ghost haunting her?*

The spirit occasionally whispered things. Eden pieced together that his name was Kyle based on him whispering it along with Journey's name. He had become a permanent fixture throughout the night, not once dissipating as they worked. Journey hadn't even noticed when the spirit mustered enough power to pull out her chair for her at break. Eden watched, with a mask of calm plastered on her face as the ghost reached out to touch Journey's hand as she stood and pushed in the chair at the end of their break. Hope rallied for Eden as she saw him flicker for a moment. She nearly slumped with disappointment when he surged back stronger than before, more tangible and defined around the edges. Eden silently wished that this ghost would disappear on his own. Sometimes they did. Who knew why ghosts would just come and go and make themselves visible to her sometimes but not all the time?

Journey and Eden walked while chatting idly to the housewares department. As they worked, Journey's tag-a-long watched them uselessly. Eden wished she could just tell the spirit to either pick up boxes to help them or go away. Spirits were rarely helpful in her experience. They served their own purposes and stuck around for unfinished business that they expected the living to resolve for them. It seemed entitled and selfish to Eden. She was so wrapped in her thoughts about the spirit world that she barely noticed the movement at the end of the aisle.

"Hey Eden." Anaiah drawled as he came into view around the corner onto her aisle. She was stocking vacuums and unless he needed a new one, he must have come down this aisle to talk to her.

"Hi, Anaiah. It's your night off, huh?" She turned towards him, feeling instantly stupid for stating the obvious. She pulled out her box knife and broke down the oversized box she had just finished stocking.

"Every Thursday and Friday." He leaned casually over his shopping cart, resting his forearms on the handrail. Eden shoved the now flattened box into her cart with the others. She dusted off her hands on her jeans and turned to see his shining smile.

"Doing anything fun on your days off, besides the grocery run?" She smiled coyly as an attempt to flirt.

"Well, I'm talking to you." He smiled. "Makes shopping a lot less dull. Something to look forward to every week." He looked down for a moment at the cleavage and then brought his eyes back up. He blushed a bit when he saw that she noticed. "Nice shirt." His smile faltered for a moment and then stood up straight and looked over the shelf next to him.

"Thanks. I just grabbed whatever blue shirt was clean." Eden lied. She leaned onto the shelf to seem casual and cool, not the anxious mess she was inside.

"Looks nice." He said as he studied a bottle of carpet shampoo.

"Do you have anything planned for your days off?" She kicked herself mentally for asking the same question again. But he didn't seem to notice.

"I got a date with my laundry and maybe watch a movie. Nothing too big." He shrugged and Eden smiled, hoping this was it. She hoped that he would ask her out or at the very least, ask her a similar question so she could try to muster the courage to ask him out.

"Well, I guess, I'll see you later. I've gotta get these groceries home." His eyes didn't fall on her again before he walked away. It was like a punch in the gut. Eden glared at the floor willing herself not to cry at the unwanted shame she felt. Willing away the voices in her head and the names they called her.

Journey strolled back down the aisle; her ghostly buddy Kyle trailing behind. "That didn't go too well. You think he's scared of the ladies?" She nodded her head toward Eden's chest.

"Maybe he thinks I'm a whore." She reminded herself that not all guys like girls who show some skin. Familiar thoughts flood her mind. *Don't you have any self-respect?* She heard the voice of her ex-boyfriend echo in her thoughts. *They don't tip you because you're a good waitress, they think you're a whore and that if they give you enough cash, you'll go to bed with them. Who would want more from you than sex, dressed like a slut like that?* It set her on edge. "Can we talk about something else?"

"Sure. What do you wanna talk about?" Journey's voice was a little tense, echoing Eden's mood.

"I don't know." She muttered.

"There are other guys, you know." Journey tried to be encouraging.

Eden could feel the next thing she would say, 'guys like Kris.' And the mocking voice continued in her thoughts. *Not sure why he would want you either. You're a mess. You're damaged goods. You were lucky I wanted you at all. You don't deserve some knight in shining armor, that's for normal, nice girls.* Rage simmered in Eden's veins. She needed to walk away, to calm down. To shake off these thoughts.

"You mean like Jayse?" Eden said in a low voice while she glared hatefully at Journey.

"Walk it off, Boobs McGee!" Journey pointed towards another department. Her jaw set with determination as she motioned again.

Eden wanted to not care that she had pissed her only female friend off. She would never understand why she turned on people who cared about her when she was upset. Maybe it had something to do with teenage hormones. Maybe it had to do with the fact that she never learned to talk through her feelings with others. Maybe she was a terrible person who didn't deserve even one friend.

She walked over to the next department and started stocking goods from the pallet. She'd been fuming for a half an hour when, to her horror, Loretta approached her and asked to speak to her in private. Eden made the walk of shame back to the office, clamping down on her anger, her tongue.

"Have a seat." Her manager motioned toward the chair across from herself. "Let's talk about your shirt for a minute, hon." Internally, Eden rolled her eyes. Then, the actual fear of losing her job, losing her home, and being out on the street again hit her. She knew she needed this job and that deep down, she didn't want to be a jerk that everyone hated.

"I'm sorry. I usually wear an undershirt under it, and I didn't wash it in time. I promise it won't happen again." Eden's quiet calm voice didn't sound like her own. No, this voice was compliant and docile. It was the voice she used when she was younger. A voice she used to placate adults with extreme emotions. A voice that calmed threats. As much as she appreciated that her subconscious wanted to save her job, she hated the way she shut down like this.

"Hon, you are a cute girl. You don't need to go flashin' those things around to get the guys interested. I see you flirt with Kris all the time. Work ain't the place for that, now. This is a warning. Leave your relationships at the door and come in ready to work. You understand." Loretta gave her a pat on the hand as a sign of her concern. Eden felt it for the lie it was. Loretta didn't pity her. All Eden could feel from the moment of touch was annoyance and disgust.

"Yes, ma'am." Eden's voice was completely detached. Another voice within her was raging at Eden to jump across the table and scream in Loretta's face. For her assumption. For making her feel the shame she'd known before. For making her shrink the way she had so many times in the past.

Eden also wanted to yell at her that she had no interest in Kris, that it would be none of her business if she did. Her voice sounded so sweet and pliant as she heard herself say quietly, "I won't do it again. I promise. I'm sorry."

"You can go. If you can afford it, I'd like you to get an undershirt on your lunch break." As Eden walked out, the fog of self-preservation cleared, she rolled her eyes, but Loretta didn't see. *Screw her,* she thought, *I'll play the "I can't afford it" card. I'm not buying shit. Where was that attitude a minute ago? Why can't I tell the people I can't stand to bite me, but I can piss off my friends.* Eden realized why it was so easy to snap at Journey, but she couldn't bring herself to do the same with Loretta. Power and trust. She trusted Journey. The realization slapped her in the face. She trusted Journey and she had lashed out at her when she was upset.

She shoved her self-loathing down as she made the long walk back over to Journey. "Journ, I'm a jerk. You're a good friend. I shouldn't have talked to you that way. I'm sorry. Breakfast on me?" She looked at Journey with pleading eyes.

"Yeah. Don't tell people I am a good friend though. I don't want people to think I'm likable." She half grinned and nodded. "You can pay your penance in pancakes."

Eden grabbed the box in front of her. "Loretta told me my tits were too obviously out. And I need to quit flirting with Kris at work. I guess I flirt more than I thought I did, because I certainly wasn't doing it on purpose." Eden rolled her eyes and put the items on the shelf.

"She is such a meddling old hag. I can see why she thinks your boobs need to be holstered though. You might put out an eye or something." She laughed as Kyle looked at her wistfully. Maybe Eden could address this at breakfast. *Shit.* It would mean telling Journey what she could see. *Why not have yet another test of our friendship. She trusted Journey enough to lash out at her. Maybe she could trust her enough to open up a bit?* That sounded a bit like hell, but Eden resolved to try.

The last hour before lunch took forever. At last, Eden clocked out and turned to find the twins approaching the time clock behind her.

"Hey Eden. Nice shirt." Kris smiled at her with a hunger in his eyes. Even in his joking, she could see he liked what he saw. Eden remembered what Loretta had said about the flirting and her anger sparked again.

"Yeah, piss off." She snapped back and took her lunch bag to her seat.

"What the hell..." Jayse's head whipped towards her.

Journey cut in, "Loretta gave her a talk about it and thinks she wore it to impress Kris. Apparently, their flirting is just intolerable." Journey giggled while Eden fumed.

"Don't wear a shirt like that if you don't want guys to look." Kris snipped in annoyance.

"I didn't wear it for you to look at. But go ahead! Not like anyone else is. Sorry, I'm just in a bad mood." Eden blurted out.

"Her cleavage intimidated this guy she likes." Journey said to the brothers. "It's been a whirlwind of emotions today." Journey smiled at Eden's pissed expression.

Eden glared down at her sandwich and chips. She grabbed her soda from her lunch bag and twisted it open.

"If I wasn't such a fucking chicken, I'd ask him out instead of waiting on him to ask me." Eden muttered, her eyes still on the food. Her eyes rose to Kris as he responded.

"Maybe he's gay. If he didn't like your boobs, then he might be gay." Kris looked a little too hopeful for that outcome.

"Dude... don't be a homophobe..." Journey stared daggers at Kris.

"Not all guys are into slutty chicks." Eden blurted out defensively.

"Who called you slutty?" Kris quipped with a flash of anger across his eyes. Then he softened in a fraction of a second and asked, "Are you?" His eyebrows rose.

"No, but my outfit might say so." She shrugged.

"Screw him. You look good." Kris winked but underneath it she saw something defensive, protective even.

"Thanks." She mumbled. She wondered if he was flirting or just being nice. Maybe things would be easier if she gave him a chance. The idea made her frown.

"So, Journey, you got any shirts like that?" Kris grinned. Eden heard a muffled kicking sound from under the table. Whether the kick came from Journey or Jayse was unclear. Kris winced.

"I don't have the goods for a shirt like that." Journey sighed.

"It's not like you are flat chested...Jesus." Eden laughed. "Ya got boobs honey."

"Not like yours though. Yours are big for a skinny girl." Journey elbowed her lightly.

"Pssh, Skinny! I'm not one of those tiny girls." She laughed. She was average size as far as she could tell. Of course, with women's clothes you could be extra-large in some brands and a medium in others. She had curves but didn't consider herself big.

"Skinnier than me." Journey shot back.

"I used to exercise a lot. Rode a bike everywhere." She made excuses for her body out of reflex, internally cringing at the need she felt to justify just being herself. She looked up from her food to see that Kris was checking out her chest again. He hadn't noticed her returning his gaze. Eden slowly raised a vulgar gesture up from under the table to just between her breasts. When he blushed and looked away, she laughed. "Are they really that distracting?" Eden rolled her eyes.

"Sweetie, I noticed and I'm one hundred percent into dudes so..." Journey trailed off.

Eden tried to adjust her shirt to cover them up some more. It was not working. They just wiggled and caused a little laughter from Journey.

"Kris. Can I see you for a minute, please?" Loretta said with a sour face from the doorway.

"Sure." Kris's voice was polite, but his expression spoke volumes. He ran his hand over his frustrated features before he turned to follow her back to the office.

"Stop messing with them." Jayse laughed. "They bounce when you do that." He was losing it laughing. "Kris couldn't help but look."

"You can help it." Eden snipped. "You aren't gawking at me." She motioned towards him.

"I'm more discreet than my brother. Plus, sorry Eden, but I just don't see you like that. You're not really my type. Journey's right, you're too skinny." Journey smiled a little at that.

"Well, maybe Anaiah doesn't like skinny chicks either." She sighed. "I just gotta let it go." She threw her hands up in annoyance, accidentally brushing Journey's arm.

After a blinding flash, Eden found herself in complete darkness. Another vision was upon her. She heard a male voice in the darkness. "You're everything I want. You're all I want. Forever." Ice slithered down Eden's spine. Kyle's voice was so desperate.

In the darkness, Eden heard Journey's voice as she replied, "I'm sorry, I just don't feel the same."

The darkness was replaced by blinding light, causing Eden to blink and she was again in the breakroom. Jayse was giving her a concerned look.

She gave him a nervous smile and looked over at Journey. She was too busy eating to notice Eden's momentary lack of attention. Eden returned to her sandwich. Jayse thankfully didn't ask any questions. While finishing up her chips several minutes later, Kris walked in and tossed her a white cotton tank top.

"Cover 'em up before I get fucking fired." He grumbled as he sat back down.

"Did you just buy me an undershirt?" Eden blinked.

"If it means I never have to hear Loretta talk about natural desires ever again, it's worth every penny." He kept his eyes down.

"Oh, for fuck's sake!" Eden threw her hands up. "She is determined to just meddle in any way she can. She can go to hell. She won't though, she'll probably come back and haunt me after she dies." Eden threw her hand over her mouth. *Did I just say that out loud?* The silence was broken as everyone at the table erupted with laughter. *I am so out of touch with what is normal.* Eden shook her head and breathed a sigh of relief. She smiled at Kris, "Thanks for the shirt."

"Don't mention it." He grinned at her. His eyes drifted back down, he caught himself. "Sorry." Eden just rolled her eyes and walked to the bathroom to change.

CHAPTER NINE

After lunch, Eden decided that working in silence would bode better for her employment status than to keep bursting out as she had for the first half of her shift. She held to this sentiment as Loretta gave her a thumbs up when she saw her wardrobe change. Eden held back her response for fear she would deploy the wrong finger.

At long last, Journey and Eden clocked out and headed to Eden's car. They chatted idly as Eden drove to the restaurant. Once the comfort of a warm cup of coffee in her hand had settled in and breakfast foods had been ordered, Eden took a steadying breath and looked at Journey very seriously. Journey shifted in her seat at the gaze set on her.

"Do you believe in ghosts?" Eden asked in a quiet but serious tone.

"Yeah, I guess so. Are you into those ghost hunter shows? I kind of like the one with the cute dude bros that wear all the Ed Hardy shirts." Journey shrugged.

"Not really." She shifted her eyes to her coffee, "I am about to tell you something that I don't tell a lot of people...I sort of..." It was an effort to look at Journey's face, but she forced herself to do it. "I see ghosts." Eden said as matter-of-factly as she could. She prayed she didn't sound insane.

"You're messing with me, right?" Journey cracked a grin.

"No. I wish I was." Eden shifted in her seat uncomfortably. "That's why my parents and I have a bad history. I saw stuff...they thought I was demon possessed." Eden frowned without meaning to. She attempted to bring her expression back to neutrality.

"You're completely serious?" Journey sat her coffee cup down and stared at Eden incredulously. "Why are you telling me this?" She paused. "Do I need to tell you something super personal too? Are we...uh...bonding?" Journey looked about as uncomfortable as Eden had ever seen her.

"You don't have to tell me anything, but yes, I'm dead serious." Eden paused to find the right words. Were there right words for this? No, definitely no right words for being haunted by your ex-boyfriend. She still gave it a good effort. "You have a spirit that is attached to you. Every time you touch me or get close to me, I see stuff," Eden said carefully.

Journey turned a little red and if Eden was reading her emotions correctly, was a little pissed off. "Prove it." Journey shrugged and crossed her arms.

"Give me your hand." Eden said, offering her own. Journey stared at the outstretched hand before her like it was a snake. "I can prove it."

"Fine." She sighed as she very reluctantly placed her hand in Eden's hand every so lightly. "I'm not really into holding hands." She huffed. "It wouldn't matter if you were a six-foot-tall Indian man either, so leave him out of it." She muttered. Eden was overwhelmed by Journey's emotions. She was hating this.

"Shut up for a second." Eden saw Kyle and heard his voice. She closed her eyes and mentally pushed past him, into Journey's mind. She probed into her friend's feelings and memory. She saw flickers of memory and felt the emotions attached to them.

"Your parents are really into music. Your mom... oh wow, that's an unusual mix of emotions...anyway, your mom said you were named Journey because that's what she listened to during her pregnancy with you. You have an older sister named Janis after Janis Joplin and a brother named Hendrix. You are relieved that your mom didn't name you something like Ozzy or Bon Jovi. You try not to care about things that would tax you emotionally. Boyfriends, marriage, the prospect of having kids, this moment right now is filling you with panic... You REALLY have a thing for Jayse...but you are really afraid of touching him for some reason." Journey yanked her hand out of Eden's grasp.

"Okay." She nearly smacked herself in the chest as she ripped her hand back from Eden's grasp. "Fine, you are my psychic friend network." She crossed her arms. "How do I make Kyle go away?"

"You know about Kyle?" Eden furrowed her brows.

"Well, you said I have a spirit attached to me. Makes sense it would be the guy who killed himself when I broke up with him. We were sixteen. Declare his undying love. It was when I lived in Ithaca." Journey avoided eye contact. Eden could tell there was something here that Journey wasn't saying. She doubted Journey would let her touch her hand again. She struggled internally whether to pry further or not. Journey just stared at her coffee with her arms crossed, giving nothing else away. Eden made her best educated guess.

"It's not your fault. You didn't feel what he felt. He took his life; you have to let him own that." Eden reached out to touch her arm again.

"I don't know...I just feel a little guilty about how it turned out for him." Journey shifted back out of reach. "Like I could have stopped him. I should have seen it coming."

They paused their intense conversation as plates were delivered to them and coffee refilled. Eden took a bite of her pancake and swallowed. When the waitress was back out of view she motioned with her fork as she spoke, "You gotta let that go. That's number one." She took another bite and swallowed. "Number two, I need to talk to him. Like, out loud. It's going to be weird. He may not answer me, or it may be cryptic or nonsense. You probably won't see or hear anything from his side."

Journey rolled her eyes. She looked utterly annoyed by the prospect of speaking to spirits but started talking in a low voice. "Okay, Kyle, it's not my fault that I wasn't in love with you. I was a kid. You took your life. Not me." Kyle gazed at Journey with absolute teen angst and then glanced back to Eden.

"Kyle, what do you want? You need to cross over." Eden said evenly.

"I want her to be safe." Kyle responded in a near whisper.

"I will protect her." Eden said calmly like she was talking to a small child.

"You MUST protect her. I can't save her from the darkness coming," Kyle warned.

"What darkness?" Eden quirked her eyebrow.

"Darkness?" Journey's worried expression reminded Eden that she was out of the loop.

"A darkness falls upon all he touches." He said in a foreboding tone.

"Who?" Eden asked, ignoring Journey momentarily. She held up her finger to Journey as if to say, 'give me a second.'

"Promise me you will protect her. Do not let the fire consume her." He emphasized and leaned in closer. Eden felt a particular frustration with the cryptic ghosts. These spirits refused to give her specifics, as if they would be in trouble with their ghost boss if they gave you the real details. *Sure,* she thought. *I'll protect my friend as best I can. I can sure as hell do a better job than you.*

"Yes. I promise. I will protect her. Now, crossover." Eden commanded, "You don't belong here."

He looked wistfully at Journey again. Around the edges of his flimsy form, a faint glow started, slithering dark tendrils wrapped around him until he was gone.

"He's gone." Eden turned her eyes to a slightly horrified Journey.

"What was he saying?" She whispered. Journey rubbed her hands over her arms as if she was suddenly as cold as the grave.

"He said he was protecting you. He said darkness was coming and to not let the fire consume you. So, carry a flashlight and a fire extinguisher." Eden shrugged. "Ghosts say all sorts of shit. One wouldn't leave me alone for a few months because he was buried in the flowerbed next door." The waitress came and went with coffee refills. Journey continued to stare at her for a moment. Her expression shifted to that of pride for a moment.

"So, you just suggest to ghosts that they get over their shit and get them to cross over? Over to where?" She shook her head and dug into her food at last.

"I really don't know. I've picked up stuff from TV shows and a few books. Most of it seems like bullshit. I've always seen the ghosts but didn't really understand why. Once I got out of the church..." Eden cleared her throat and shook her head at Journey's curious glint to her eye. "I saw shows about mediums and stuff and realized that I was one of those. I read some books, watched a lot of reality TV, and then just started talking to them. Some respond, some don't. I don't always see them everywhere. Like, I didn't see yours until I touched you." Eden shrugged.

"That's weird." Journey said flatly, almost awkwardly.

"Yeah, I probably should know more about all this, but honestly, I spent too much time trying to work and save money and crap to take time to figure it out." Exhaustion and shame washed over Eden.

"Maybe that's something you need to figure out, dude." Journey suggested.

"Probably." Eden felt a little defeated. She avoided eye contact with Journey and ate her breakfast in silence.

By the time Eden finished her food, she was heavy with exhaustion. She made awkward small talk with Journey but didn't want to risk the conversation coming back to her "abilities" or shortcomings related to them. She drove silently back to the store to retrieve Journey's car.

Back at home, she visualized the warm water of her shower washing away her weariness. Cleansing her of her night of hard work and rejection. Whether Journey had been weirded out or not, at least Eden was able to help her with her ghost problem. She slipped on her night clothes and slid into bed, hoping that maybe next week will be better. She had a small spark of hope. She had a birthday coming. Maybe her new friends would celebrate with her.

CHAPTER TEN

E den tapped her foot in a nervous motion in the breakroom waiting for midnight to strike. Her friends would be taking their lunch break right as it rolled over into her birthday. It was her day off, and yet, she found herself at work because the only friends she had were through their mutual employment. The drawback to that was the staggered days off. Eden always worked two of her five shifts without her friends. She also now had a tendency to spend both those night shifts sleep deprived and get a few hours of hang-out time with her friends instead of sleeping.

Eden had been cordial with the rest of the team on nights, but none had taken her in like her little group. She couldn't quite decide if it was sad that this is how she chose to spend her birthday or not. She decided to give herself the gift of trying to be positive and not giving into self-pity for her birthday.

This was a milestone birthday. She felt a little self-conscious buying her own birthday cake, but the day had never really been celebrated by anyone else. Why would that change now? She purchased the biggest cheesecake sampler in the bakery section of her store along with several pints of ice cream. She sat awkwardly in the breakroom. She wore a casual black dress and just wearing regular clothes had her feeling a little out of place.

Her friends had asked if she wanted to celebrate with breakfast and she told them they could do both. They didn't know the true reason this day was such a big deal to her. They thought it was because she was turning twenty-one and that it should be celebrated with booze. Eden was able to purchase her own liquor now, but physically, on this day, Eden was actually eighteen, a legal adult. She had been pretending to be one for so long, that somehow, actually making it past that point seemed like such a weight off her shoulders. For her inner child who never got a real birthday, she wanted her favorite treats, cheesecake, and ice cream.

Having a day off was almost as joyous to her as her actual birthday. Eden wasn't sure why Loretta suddenly had taken a personal interest in her work and personal life, but she had been hounding Eden around the clock. She made remarks about Eden talking to Kris at break. She even suggested that their little group take lunch separately. When Loretta found out that their group went to breakfast together sometimes, she acted hurt that they didn't include her. Of course, she didn't bring this up to Jayse or Journey. No, she pulled Eden aside for a "little chat."

Eden had been biting her tongue and biding her time. Only two weeks remained of Loretta's stint on the nightshift. She had made Eden's one place of social interaction almost hostile. However, sitting at home alone on her birthday seemed just a little too sad and miserable to bear. Eden had decided before she left work the night before that she would spring for some desserts and hang out with the people who liked spending time with her. As her friends rounded the corner, Eden waved at them with a giant grin.

"Hey birthday girl!" Journey called out.

"Ooh, cheesecake sampler. Classy!" Jayse added.

"Happy Birthday." Kris smiled at her.

"Thanks." Eden grinned. "Here, pick one." She showed them the half dozen ice creams she had picked.

"Rocky Road!" Jayse grabbed his selection.

"Thanks." Kris pulled out the Chunky Monkey.

"Phish food? It's 'cause my parents are hippies isn't it." She smiled.

"It's because it's your favorite. Quit bitching and eat. It's my birthday and you will enjoy it." Eden sassed with a grin.

She grabbed the cookies and cream and shoved the extras she had gotten in case she guessed wrong on everyone's favorites back into the shopping bag. She opened her pint and pulled out a slice of cheesecake onto a napkin. She took turns savoring bites from the treats.

"What's the occasion?" Loretta walked in with three other workers.

"Eden's birthday." Journey said matter-of-factly, since Eden's mouth was full of ice cream.

"Happy Birthday. I didn't know we celebrated birthdays on this shift." Loretta eyed her with suspicion.

"I bought some stuff to share with my friends. It's my night off and I wanted to share my birthday with them." Eden said flatly.

"How do you think the ones who are being excluded on the shift feel about that?" Loretta said with a sour look on her face.

"They didn't bring me cheesecake on their birthday either." Eden shrugged. Loretta could piss right off.

"It's just not really fair to everyone." Loretta stared at her.

"This is a job. Not kindergarten. What we do on our off time doesn't have to be fair. I wanted to spend time today with my friends. So, I am here. I'm off the clock and so are they."

"Well, I just don't think it is very nice, why don't you celebrate at one of your breakfasts?" She snapped with an injured look in her eyes.

"Look, Loretta. I'm sorry, but we aren't friends." Eden shrugged and tried to let it go. She sighed. "Here, everyone, birthday cheesecake and ice cream, on me." Eden just wanted to enjoy a birthday for once. She stood up and set the extra cheesecake and ice creams out on the other table. The rest of the night shift team gave her small, "happy birthday" sentiments as they took some. Journey winked at Eden. Loretta turned her pink angry face toward the door and left the break room without another word.

When Loretta was out of earshot, Kris smiled at Eden and said, "Breakfast is at our place. Steak and Eggs with a side of beer?" He raised an eyebrow.

"Loretta can suck it. Don't let her ruin it for you." Jayse added with a soothing smile.

Journey elbowed Eden and said "Relax your angry eyebrows. She's not worth getting wrinkles over." Eden couldn't help but laugh at that. However, something about Loretta's need to be close to her just didn't sit well with her. Why was she suddenly obsessed with being Eden's friend and giving her advice on who to date?

Eden drove home after wishing her friends a quick and easy rest of their shift. She had a solid plan to spend the next four hours streaming some junk television. She stretched out on her cozy couch and propped herself up on a pillow with her laptop on her chest. She lost herself in episodes of a competitive cooking show. After the sun started to rise and glow through the windows, she realized she was running late for breakfast and cursed at herself. She stepped into the bedroom to grab her purse off her bed, and a figure moved out of the corner of her eye. *DAMN GHOSTS!* She slowly turned to see what flimsy pale spirit deigned to show up in her room. To her annoyance, in the middle of her room, stood Loretta.

"What am I doing here?" She looked confused.

"I was wondering the same thing." Eden stepped back, startled, and pissed off. *How did she get into my house?* Eden wondered to herself. Loretta walked towards the bed and then through it. *SHIT! No. No. No. When did she even die?* Eden's heart started to race. Eden didn't like Loretta, but she didn't want her dead.

"Loretta?" Eden spoke slowly as Loretta turned and looked at her. "What happened to you?"

"I don't know. I was going home, and I came here. I don't know."

"Loretta, cross over. Go home." Eden snapped, as she panicked.

"I can't." Loretta said with a worried look.

Eden put her head in her own hands and took a deep breath. She could feel the frustrating urge to cry welling up. Why was she so bad at this? This one thing she should know more about because it was her "gift". Why did this have to happen now? She breathed in slowly, resolutely. Loretta, even as a ghost, was not going to ruin her birthday. She could pretend she never saw her. She could deal with this later.

"Fine. Stay here. You are still not invited to breakfast." She picked up her purse and keys and headed out to the car. It was childish, she knew, but she couldn't help but feel like Loretta had somehow died on purpose to ruin her birthday. She tried to shake off the feeling of frustration with Loretta and get in a better mood as she drove across town to go to breakfast with her friends.

As she pulled up to the twin's house, she realized that no matter how old she was, she was always the actress, never truly getting to be herself even with her friends. She would always be pretending to be normal, to not know what she knew, to not see what she saw. *Well, happy birthday, Eden. The gift of the truth for yourself.* She thought sadly. She was going to get drunk. Very, very drunk.

CHAPTER ELEVEN

A t the very least, Kenneth's emotions were sincere as he led the meeting that night at work, "It's a tragic day for all of us. We lost a member of our family." Just this morning, Eden was celebrating her birthday. Reality had struck her almost as hard as her hangover. Her head throbbed with every sound wave and wave of emotion from the manager. *Nothing worse than hungover empath gifts.*

"This morning Loretta was in a fatal car accident. I understand this is going to be difficult for some of you. We must be strong and keep on going for Loretta's sake. She dedicated many years to this company. It would honor her memory for us to put on a brave face and continue to go above and beyond the way she did." Kenneth continued.

Oh my God. Eden thought. *Was he seriously telling them that Loretta would want them just to keep on doing their jobs because she loved telling them to get to work?* Her head throbbed, the annoyance at Kenneth's words was not helped by her hangover or the fact that Eden had not slept well with Loretta going bump in the night at her place. She supposed Loretta was technically 'going bump' in the day, as Eden was a night shifter. Loretta was in and out every few hours. On little sleep Eden could go from giddy to weepy to stabby, fairly quickly. Eden just needed to keep her head down and make it through the night.

"So, I would like you all to welcome Loretta's, um, successor. This is Scott Johnston. He just transferred here from Wichita Falls from manager training." Kenneth nodded to Scott.

"Guys, I am here to take over Loretta's position, but I know that I could never replace her." Eden swore she heard the collective sound of the night shift's eyes rolling in unison. "She was a great leader. I hope that I can pay proper respect to her by continuing her legacy." Scott appeared entirely too sincere. He truly thought they had lost a beloved manager. Was he delusional enough to believe that this shift revered managers? Tessa wasn't revered so much as respected and appreciated, and these types of managers had her transferred out.

"Now, everyone, if you could, please go around and introduce yourselves. Let's say your name and how long you've been with the company." Kenneth instructed.

Eden spaced out until it was her turn. She already knew everyone and didn't care how long they had worked here. When she said her name, Scott's eyes almost lit up. *Well, shit.* Eden's shoulders slumped. Kenneth and Scott ended the meeting with the corporate cheer before the crew split up to go to work.

"Eden, can I talk to you for a moment?" Scott followed alongside her.

"Sure, mind if we walk and talk? I don't want to put us behind." Eden hoped having others around would keep the conversation less personal. They were already behind as it was thanks to the thirty-minute meeting.

"Yeah, you're from south Texas, right?"

"Sort of." Eden sighed, stopped walking, and turned to face him. Might as well try to delicately tell him she had no interest in being asked personal questions. Eden looked at the clean shaven, blonde haired white man. If she had to guess, she'd say he was in his mid-thirties. He looked to be a few inches short of six feet. By the look on his face, he was giddy to unlock anything he could from her past and the cult she grew up in. She cut to the chase, "Scott, are you trying to ask me about the Saints on Earth Cult?"

"Well...Yeah." He shrugged and smiled as if this was not her life that they were discussing but some random group that has no bearing on her whatsoever.

"What do you want to know?" Everyone's incessant need to know about this part of her life was wearing on her. Never in the last three years had she discussed her real past. She guessed this would be the price she paid for getting to stay in one place and be herself.

"What was it like? I saw you on the news, but the photos they have aren't recent. What was it like having Noah Grace for a dad?" He said, a smile still plastered on his face.

"You know I ran away when CPS was giving me back to them, right?" Eden said seriously.

He nods his head but looks confused.

"Then you know that it was bad enough that they took me away from them. I chose to live on the streets just to stay away from them. I am not rushing back any time soon." She felt the tickle in the back of her throat as emotion built behind her eyes. "Look, do you want the gory details? Yes, they were abusive. Yes, I hated them. Yes, they believe that God wants them to treat kids like that." Her voice started to quiver. *I hate talking about my fucking family.*

At that moment, it dawned on Eden that she hadn't emotionally dealt with this topic for more than a few seconds when someone brought it up. She didn't talk it out. She didn't dwell on it. She hasn't really processed anything. Her last therapy session had been over three years ago, and, in that time, she hadn't addressed any of her issues with her parents. She just shoved those feelings down, sucked it up, and survived the last couple of years. The tears fell in earnest, and she choked back a sob.

"I am so sorry. I didn't realize this was such a sensitive topic for you." Scott reached out a hand to pat her on the shoulder.

Instinctively, her shoulder jerked away. "I just..." Eden sobbed, "need a few minutes." She rushed into the bathroom, feeling like an emotional fool. She stepped into the big stall in the back and slid the lock closed. She sunk her body down against the wall as far away from the toilet as she could get. Head in her hands, the full body sobs shook through her in waves. *My God. Why did I have to be there? With them. Why am I being punished for what they did? Why can't people just let me live my life and leave me alone? Why couldn't my parents just love me?* All the thoughts she hadn't wanted to think for the last several years flooded in.

The cold concrete floor was somehow a comfort. While her anger felt hot and abrasive, the floor was smooth and cool. It seemed to be the anti-venom to the hate within her. *Why can't I be cool, smooth, and solid?* She ran her hand slowly over the floor to her side back and forth for several minutes until her sobs slowed to every minute or so and the tears stopped. Her cool hand reached up and touched her face, and she closed her eyes. Her lungs slowly filled with air. Then she exhaled and blew out her anger. She let go of frustration. Maybe through osmosis, she could become cool and stony and unemotional in this moment. She recalled the grounding techniques she had used in the hospital. She walked herself through them until her breathing was even and her tears were gone.

She stood and walked to the sink. She ran cold water over her hands. And then over her face, wishing it was colder. Gently, she blotted the rough paper towels over her face. She glanced up at her reflection. With the red splotches, and blue-green eyes, there was Eden: short and not as thin as she would like, with her natural red-haired roots blending into an ombre of sorts with her darker red box dye ends of her hair. Her under eyes were dark with smeared eyeliner. She needed to change out nose rings or maybe dye her hair. She needed a change. *I'm me now, and this person in the mirror isn't exactly who I thought I would be.* Her hair was in long wavy curls. She'd wanted so much to look different from her old self for the last three years, she wasn't sure how she really wanted to look now. *So today is an existential crisis day.* Survival mode had caused her to live a constant life of running and hiding and now that she had some calm and normalcy, she wasn't quite sure what to do with it.

"Darkness is coming. The dark one did this to me." Loretta's familiar voice called from the first stall. *Well, not quite normal.* She couldn't even have a moment of emotional breakdown alone.

"Loretta, I will try to help you, but please leave me alone at work." Eden was immediately grateful that she was alone. At least, she was the only living person in the restroom. After what was likely a thirty-minute meltdown in the bathroom, Eden finally got herself together and headed out to work. Scott was waiting at the service desk for her.

"Are you alright?" Captain Caucasian asked. "I really should have thought that through. Clearly the last three years haven't been long enough for you to get over what happened." He was all confident and presumptuous. Eden wanted to tell him to go to hell. She chose a middle ground between telling him off and cowering in fear for her job.

"Scott, I would just prefer to leave my personal life...well, personal. At work, it doesn't matter that I grew up in some religious whack-job cult. What matters is that I do my job." Hoping that will be that she started to walk off.

"Right, then." He said from behind her. It was too good to get an awesome manager to begin with. Playing musical managers has not been fun since. *Isn't that how it always is? One good thing happens and then life shits on you to make up for it.*

Less than a half hour later, it was time for a break. Journey walked by and Eden followed her quietly.

"You okay tonight, man?" She gave Eden her standard sideways glance.

"Yeah. Just tired of having a meltdown every time someone mentions my family. I feel helpless. Crying makes me feel vulnerable and weak. It sucks."

"Who set it off this time?" Journey's jaw flexed.

"The managerial flavor of the week." Eden said quietly.

"Does he want to start out on my bad side?" Journey huffed.

"People are curious. They don't realize that just because it's cool to them doesn't mean I want to talk about it. They ask stupid things like 'what was it like?' as if it wasn't fucking horrible. And really, to me, they are saying 'your parents are awful, share something way too personal.' People don't mean to suck, they just do." Eden commented as they rounded the corner to the break room. Their group took their normal seats. "I don't know. Maybe I do need to talk about it."

"Not to be cliche, but you know, I am here if you need that." Journey said with a small smile.

"Have you been crying?" Kris asked as he sat down. His gaze was too intense with concern. Eden shifted in her seat.

"Yeah, a little." Eden said quietly.

"We all knew Loretta was working on being your new best friend, but we didn't realize it would hit you this hard, sweetie." Journey's sarcastically solemn tone lifted her spirits. Eden was thankful for the humor and helping her deflect personal questions.

"I didn't sleep well. I get weepy." Eden shrugged.

"Still your birthday for like an hour or so." Kris smiled. She felt too tired for his attempts to cheer her up.

"Yeah, I'm over celebrating" Eden laid her head on the table. She just needed to sleep.

"Your favorite customer was in here earlier with his coworkers." Journey added casually.

"Oh yeah?" Eden tried to sound casual as well, but she was glad he didn't run into her while she looked this depressed.

"Yeah, apparently the firehouse was low on supplies, and they needed to do a grocery run. He asked me about you. I told him I hadn't seen you since the shift started. Told him you may be lying low since you celebrated your birthday a little hard. He gave his sincerest condolences for Loretta." She rolled her eyes as Eden looked up at her from the table.

"He's a firefighter? That explains the muscles." She tried to smile.

"Nah, he's EMS...guess he could be both. He had the medic uniform on...You should see him in uniform. It would vaporize your panties, girl." She winked.

Kris cleared his throat, and Jayse asked, "New tech, self-vaporizing panties, huh?"

"Aww, the boys don't like girl talk, E." Journey smiled. "We should discuss how close we are to syncing cycles. Make them real uncomfy."

"Tampons or pads?" Eden sat up.

"So, I took a massive dump the other day..." Jayse interrupted.

"It always comes back to poop," sneered Journey. Eden felt her mood lift, even if it was ever so slightly.

"New rule. We don't do girl talk with the boys present...and Jayse keeps his shit talk to himself." Eden suggested.

"Deal." Kris agreed.

"I'm game," Journey shrugged.

"Traitors...all of you. Even my own brother. I am wounded. You wound me." Jayse clutched his heart. Eden smirked as a new tactic formed in her mind.

"Journey, what's the name of that actor that you told me about the other day? The one you said you would sell your soul to take to bed?" Eden stared at Jayse pointedly as she said it.

"Mmm. Rahul Kohli." She was apparently picking up what Eden was throwing down. Journey moaned softly. "So hot."

"Fucking fine." Jayse said with an exasperated sigh. The fact that this one mention of another man from Journey had him surrendering should be enough for the two of them to admit what they felt. Eden kept that thought to herself. She also didn't mention that the only reason he had come up in conversation was because Eden mentioned his resemblance to the twins when she saw him on a magazine cover near the registers one night. The new treaty was as good as sealed. Eden felt victorious.

As they filed out of the breakroom, Journey and Jayse continued a heated debate about which classic video game character was the best selection for some racing game and Kris came up alongside Eden.

"Good move back there." He said conspiratorially in a hushed tone.

"Are they ever going to get it together?" She whispered back.

He laughed. "I hope not. I'd have to find a new place to live. They are bad enough as friends. Can you imagine how loud they would be, on purpose, just to piss me off." Kris grinned broadly. "Did you drop Kohli's name intentionally? Because we've been told before that we look like him."

"Of course, I did. I'm surprised she doesn't flirt with you too." Eden grinned.

"Eh, don't say that. That's just weird. We've been friends for years, but they've only ever had a thing for each other. It's like, even though they aren't together...it would be like having a crush on my brother's girlfriend." His tone was joking, but Eden felt the undertone there. They were getting close to dangerous territory. She didn't want to have to turn down her friend and risk hurting his feelings.

"Journey, you got a uterus?" Eden called back.

"Yeah. Good point. Let's go before we stock the groceries." Journey waved at the twins as she deviated with Eden.

Eden avoided any talk of dating with Kris or the rest of their group for that matter for the rest of the night. At the end of the night, she told Journey a bit of what was said between them.

"Does everyone know?" Journey lamented as they walked toward the time clock at the end of their shift.

"Yeah, including you two. Just say something to him." Eden laughed.

"Mind your business, E." She gave her a warning glare.

"What's Eden getting nosy about now?" Jayse approached them from behind. Kris was with him.

"Girl talk is now over." Journey said in a matter-of-fact tone. Kris and Jayse easily caught up with them. Journey swiped her badge first as the others stood next to her in line for the time clock.

"Wanna get breakfast?" Kris looked toward Eden. She knew what he meant. She panicked.

"Journey, y'all up for breakfast?" Eden turned toward her and away from Kris. She gave her a 'help me' look.

"I could eat. Wanna ride with me, E?" Journey rescued her. Thank God. Eden turned to the twins and gave them a thumbs up.

"See you at Smiley's?" She looked from Kris to Jayse.

"Sure." Jayse said flatly. Was he in on it too? Or did he catch on to Kris asking just her? Eden needed to nip this in the bud. The thought made her stomach queasy.

"I'm going to have to just tell him, aren't I?" Eden crossed her arms. Journey drove them to the restaurant and Eden needed to brainstorm the best way to handle Kris without messing up their little group's dynamic.

"Would it be so terrible to let him down gently?" Journey played devil's advocate.

"You three are my ONLY friends. What if he gets upset and Jayse gets mad at me? Then you have to choose between them and me. It's obvious that you would have to pick them." Eden groaned.

"Whoa. Kris is a big boy. He can take some rejection. Trust me, I've seen it." Journey laughed.

"But did he stay friends with those people?" Eden ventured.

"No. But they weren't close anyway. I guess, I see your point. But he can suck it up and I'll tell Jayse as much too." Journey nodded. "I got your back, E."

"Thanks, dude." Eden sighed. "Now, all I need is a moment to talk to him alone and be nice about it." She shook her head. They parked at the restaurant and beat the boys there. She and Journey headed in to grab their usual table. She heard a group of men laughing loudly from the table next to their typical booth. Over the din she heard a familiar southern drawl.

"Don't get me started on that Sean. I've got more drunk O'Brien stories than you have on me." She glanced up to see Anaiah sitting at a table with a group of three other men. His eyes met hers and a smile bloomed on his face. She gave a little wave. He tipped his coffee cup towards her in acknowledgement.

"Stop staring at him," Journey said to her in a low voice. Eden averted her eyes and stared at the table they were headed for. After Journey sat in her regular spot, Eden slid in next to her. Her bench was facing Anaiah's and it was an effort to not look up at him. He was wearing a grey shirt with the local fire and rescue logos on it. Must have just come from work. She locked eyes with him again and realized, she was staring at him, again. He laughed quietly to himself and looked away.

"Talk to me dude, I'm just making fucking moon eyes over here." Eden whispered.

"Well, here comes the guy that wants to actually date you, so that should be a fun distraction." Journey laughed and waved the guys over. Eden swore under her breath.

"Truck needed gas. Sorry, it took a minute." Jayse said as he slid into the booth. "Been waiting long?

"Not long at all really." Eden said. "Waitress hasn't even brought us coffee yet. Oh, here she comes." The waitress brought them all cups of coffee and a lot of creamers for Eden, as was their usual order. The group ordered breakfast. The waitress could have placed the order already, it hardly ever changed. Journey's phone buzzed loudly from where it sat on the table.

"Well, shit." Journey said as she checked her messages. "Dad's taking mom to Red River today." She gave Jayse a meaningful look.

"Still not sleeping?" Jayse said quietly.

"We're on day three and the delirium hit bad apparently. He's going to check her in and let them get her meds adjusted." Journey ran a hand over her face.

Kris' eyes met Eden's. "Journey's mom has some issues." His face was a little grave.

"That's putting it a little lightly." Jayse said. "Sorry, Journ." He winced at the glare Journey gave.

"My parents were the recreational drug taking sort of hippies. My mom had a bad trip, early on in her pregnancy with me. Hasn't been the same." Journey's voice was quieter and more subdued than Eden had ever heard. "Actually, she's only gotten worse over the years, it's why I moved back here. Dad can't do everything."

"Oh. Red River is the other psych hospital in Wichita Falls, isn't it?" Eden said quietly, not wanting to reveal why she knew about the state-run psychiatric hospital.

"Yeah. And...just what we need, my siblings are coming to town." Journey sat her phone down and put her head in her hands.

"Great." Jayse rolled his eyes.

"This is bad?" Eden looked to Kris.

"Hendrix is a tool. And Janis is...special." Kris picked the last word carefully.

"My brother went complete one-eighty from my parents. He checks all the boxes: Conservative, evangelical, corporate douche. He tells my sister that her and her wife are living in sin. And Janis is no better on the other side of that. She will fill my parent's house with essential oil diffusers, probably do a sage cleansing and hide crystals everywhere. They are going to drive me nuts." Journey looked down at her coffee and made a face. "This should be whiskey if I am gonna have to deal with them later today. I haven't talked to Hendrix since Christmas."

"That still blows my mind." Kris shrugged. "I don't blame you. He's a jackass, but not being close to your siblings is a completely foreign concept."

"You two have your weird twin powers. You know what the other is thinking, and don't hate them for it. It's not natural to like your brother as much as you do." Journey shot back.

"Shit, I haven't seen my brother in a decade." Eden said without thinking.

"You have a brother?" Kris looked at her incredulously.

"Yeah. Weird how no one talks about how he ran away as soon as he could on the news coverage. But there was no child abuse stuff on record for him, I guess." Eden shrugged and shifted in her seat.

"He's older?" Kris asked tentatively.

"Yeah, I guess he'd be around like twenty-eight or thirty or something. We didn't celebrate birthdays. I just remember him getting the "you're gonna be a man soon" talk so I assumed he was eighteen when he left. Who knows? Haven't seen him since." Eden drank her coffee and desperately wanted to shift the conversation back to Journey. However, she noted that Journey seemed to be relieved it had changed as well. She could give her friend that comfort, she supposed. And maybe kill two birds with one stone. "I didn't really have a close relationship with him at all. You two are more like my big brothers than he is." She secured a mask of innocent contentment on her face. Like the thought of Kris being brotherly to her was a serene thought and that breaking it would be painful for her. She knew it was manipulative, but she didn't want to damage their friendship by being blatant about shutting him down.

"I'll accept that role, as long as I can tease you like a big brother." Jayse laughed.

"You already do. It's why she feels that way, dude." Kris gave his brother an elbow to the ribs.

"You guys have my back. I'd rather have you than Adam any day." She grinned.

"Adam and Eden? Why not name you Eve…it's like that close?" Jayse laughed.

"Avoiding original sin, I guess?" Eden shrugged. "I'm just glad I didn't get some other biblical name, like Dorcas or Gomer. My middle name is even biblical. It's Rachel."

"At least our mom got creative with the spelling on ours." Jayse laughed.

"You got some musical inspired middle name, Journ?" Eden smiled over at her friend.

"Nah, it's Leah. No idea where they got that one. Janis' middle name is Stevie and Hendrix's is Dylan. Like Stevie Nicks and Bob Dylan. I'll have to ask Dad what rock legend has the name Leah." Journey glanced down at her phone again with a worried look.

"Sorry you're dealing with that." Eden said softly. Another roar of laughter from the table behind the twins had Eden's head turning in Anaiah's direction again.

"Just go say hi, already. He keeps looking over at you anyway." Journey said in a low voice.

"Nah, I waved already. If he wants to talk to me, he can come say hi to me." Eden cleared her throat and shifted in her seat.

"Chicken." Jayse said pointedly.

"Are you the pot or kettle?" Eden raised an eyebrow at him. It was his turn to clear his throat and look uncomfortable. Kris turned to see who they were talking about. He rolled his eyes.

The food arrived and the twins launched into betting over which of Journey's siblings would get punched first. Eden bet on Hendrix as Journey seemed to like him least. Eden offered to let Journey sleep on her couch to avoid her brother if needed and Journey declined.

They finished their breakfast and found themselves leaving just behind Anaiah's table. He still hadn't said anything to her. Just smiled, waved, and continued talking with his friends. *He's just being nice. He doesn't like you.* She reminded herself that she should keep her expectations low. Kris seemed to stay in the friend and adopted brother lane since she dropped that on him. She was glad. She had to admit to herself that she really liked the idea of having the twins as older brothers. Some sort of family to replace the one she was born with would be nice. Eden approached the counter after her friends paid out.

"Yours was paid already, ma'am." The cashier smiled pleasantly at her. Eden shrugged and left a tip in cash for the waitress.

"Which one of you fuckers paid my tab? It's not my birthday anymore." Eden called out after her friends in the parking lot. Her friends looked at her with confused expressions.

"Happy late birthday." She heard Anaiah's voice call out from across the parking lot. She turned and he gave her that damn half smile as he climbed into the passenger side of a truck with one of his friends in silver aviator sunglasses driving. Anaiah waved at her and she returned the gesture, a little dumbfounded and blushing.

"See you Thursday." He gave her a mock salute.

"I think he does like you, dumbass. Take your own advice, and just say something to him." Journey said as Eden walked to the car in a daze. Maybe she was right. Maybe she would just have to make the first move.

Elle E. Evans

CHAPTER TWELVE

E den felt her luck was beginning to turn for the better. She hadn't seen Loretta's ghost for over a week. She was hopeful that the spirit was done waking her up to tell her that she couldn't cross over. As if Eden didn't know that just by being there, something was holding her to this world. She hadn't had a nightmare in days. In fact, today she had awoken from sweet wish fulfillment dreams. She didn't recall the dream in its entirety, but she did recall kissing a certain favorite customer and seeing his half grin just inches from hers just before she awoke. She had been so disappointed when her alarm went off, she had literally groaned at it. She couldn't shake that feeling of lightness. She marveled at the way the dream had made her feel. She decided to let the memory of that dream embolden her.

She had spotted Anaiah earlier but was helping another customer and couldn't talk to him. She had smiled at him, and he had waved back. She wanted to push the other customer aside when she saw him. She settled for quickly assisting the elderly woman to find the soup she claimed the store was out of, and to try to casually find her way to another aisle where he may be shopping. She had tried to be sneaky about looking to see where he was. She tried not to make a face as she looked all over the grocery section and he was nowhere to be found. She looked at her watch and left her stocking area a few minutes early for her first break.

She headed towards the cash registers in hopes that she would find him there before he left. After weeks of talking and flirting, Eden finally decided that she would need to ask him out if it was going to happen. She needed to know if he was just some nice polite guy who talked to her every Thursday at work, or if he had any interest in her. Nearly every Thursday for the last few months, he talked to her politely, sometimes asked about her plans for her days off, but never once asked her out. If she was going to dream about him, she could at the very least, find out if he was into her or not.

Eden bought a soda at the register. The cashiers knew that it was cheaper in the vending machine in the breakroom, so they were eyeing Eden suspiciously. Hell, Eden was acting suspiciously. Right as she was collecting her receipt, Anaiah pushed his cart up behind her. *Well, it's now or never,* she thought. *That's stupid. It's not now or never. It's now or try again next Thursday, dammit.* She smiled and turned around. *Don't be too upset if he says no,* she told herself. *He's just some really cute guy who happens to talk to you when he shops. It's no big deal if he doesn't want to go out with you.*

"Hey Eden." Anaiah cracked a small grin. *God, I would love to kiss those perfect lips.* He ran his hand through his black hair. It was a few inches longer than his chin length now. Eden wanted to run her hands through it too. She should shake herself and focus. He started talking again, "Didn't catch you earlier, thought maybe I missed you. Glad to see that I didn't." *That damn half a grin again.*

She returned the smile and reminded herself that it would be okay if he just wants to be friends. *I will not be crushed by his rejection.* "I was busy with another customer, but I wanted to ask you something."

He unloaded his groceries as she talked. "Go for it." He said, not looking up.

Eden rallied her nerves, "Would you like to go out sometime?" There it was. *Oh my God, don't show him you are upset.* She was already bracing for the blow to her self-esteem.

"Sure, I would love...."

"That's okay. We don't have to if...wait. What?" She stumbled out. *I'm a huge fucking idiot.* Her face flushed. He laughed. Eden wanted to shrink up and disappear.

"When are you off?" He asked as if she didn't make a fool of herself in front of him. *BLESS HIM. Good God, I'm such a fool.*

"Tomorrow and the next day." Sudden panic that maybe he was unavailable so soon rushed into her head, so she added, "Then the same days next week too." Eden said, while she looked at his green t-shirt instead of his face. She tried to banish the red from her cheeks with sheer force of will. It made it worse.

"Tomorrow's good." He pulled his phone from his back pocket and handed it to Eden while he paid for his groceries. "Here, put your number in. Six works for you?"

Eden punched in her information and nodded. After a moment, she finally gained the courage to look him in the eye again, his expression was relaxed, happy even.

He collected his bags and receipt and walked with Eden off to the side of the registers. "Dinner and drinks sound good?" He smiled at her, but his brows were furrowed. Eden tried to sense what that feeling was. Some sort of unease he was feeling about the date?

"Sounds great. I can't wait." She saw the furrow between his brows ease. "I should go back to work."

"I'll text you." He smiled.

Eden walked toward the breakroom, smiling like an idiot. She had made a total ass of herself, but he'd said yes. Maybe he really did like her. She was still blushing. She thought better of going to the breakroom for the last few minutes of break and decided instead to go back to work and try to calm herself down.

Eden mentally sorted through possible clothing options in her closet for the date as she worked quietly for the next two hours. Her heart soared when he texted her the details. He would pick her up from her place and take her to a Japanese hibachi grill. She was practically bouncing with excitement.

Journey walked by and said simply, "Lunch."

Eden joined her and walked towards the break room. Time was going by fast tonight with her wandering off into la-la land. "How's baby land tonight?" she asked Journey.

"Full of baby food bullshit. I hate rotating that crap, and you know dayshift isn't doing it so I'm fixing their mistakes. So where were you on your first break?" She looked at her with a sideways glance and a half smile. She must have heard from one of the cashiers already.

"I was talking to Anaiah," Eden said sheepishly. "Why? Did you miss me?" Her cheeks flushed again.

"Oh, you know it, baby." She said, "You're going out tomorrow?" Journey had obviously been filled in on her embarrassing exchange at the registers.

"Yeah, so you heard what I said to him too?" Eden rolled her eyes.

"It's okay, we don't have to...WHAAAAAT?" She said dramatically. Eden jokingly punched her arm.

"I'm lucky he said yes. I'm so stupid. Oh, and what am I going to wear?" Practically bounced on the balls of her feet.

"You could go with good old denim and blue. Ya know, stick with what you know...You got any more boobity shirts that you could wear? Wow him with those bad boys." She offered.

"I have a few. I do actually own nice clothes to wear when I am not serving our big box overlord." Eden shot back. "What would you wear on a date with Jayse?"

"I say this with love and light but shut your whore mouth." Journey gave her a small grin. Kris and Jayse met them at their usual table. Eden didn't bring up the date. No sense rubbing it in Kris' face. He hadn't asked her out again, but she didn't want to poke a sore subject.

Kris and Jayse launched into a discussion of the next beer they plan to brew and debated names to call it.

"It's a golden ale. Something heavenly seems appropriate." Kris brainstormed aloud. All their beers had names. Eden tried not to take offense to a red Irish ale they had named 'poor decisions' based on Kris' crazy ex-girlfriend being a redhead. Well, he had a type apparently. The beer Eden had tried at Tessa's sendoff had been a dark beer called "Guinness But Better." They all had names, not good ones, but they had them. They had turned Eden into a bit of a beer snob. They had ruined her for any of the normal beers you could buy at the local grocery store and instead, she had to drive to a liquor store the next town over to get new ones to try.

"Nectar of the Gods?" Eden suggested.

"That was the mead we made last summer. No repeats." Jayse shot her down.

"Smite Juice." Kris wondered. "Like the angels drink it while... no hearing it now, its dumb." He shot himself down.

"Ooh, What about 'Halo's off'?" Journey raised her eyebrows. Jayse pointed at her and his face lit up in encouragement.

"Halos Optional?" Eden built on Journey's suggestion.

"Yeeeeesssss." Kris drug the word out and held up a hand for a high five. Jayse and Journey nodded in agreement. "Good job, hive mind. Brew day is next Sunday if you all want to join. Eden, you are welcome to stop by before work. We will be drunk at that point, but you are welcome anyway."

"Sounds fun." Eden smiled. Her thoughts drifted to her Friday night plans and her smile grew. Kris grinned in return. *Shit.*

CHAPTER THIRTEEN

T he hazy halo of sunshine from around the blackout curtains greeted Eden after she silenced her alarm. She brewed herself some coffee and found herself nervously giddy as she sipped it. She contemplated outfits as she showered. She generously applied the leave-in conditioner to her curls afterward, taking time to scrunch them.

She went through half a dozen outfits. Some felt too dressed up, others felt too casual. She loved wearing heels but with all her dresses came nerves about what she might be showcasing, and she didn't need to feed the troll that was her own self-doubt. Eventually, she settled on some cute jeans and a low cut dark green top. She paired the outfit with black boots. The heel on the boots lent her five-foot two body a few more inches of height. She figured it couldn't hurt considering he was over a foot taller than her.

The color of her top brought out the hint of green in her mostly blue eyes. It complemented her coloring as well. It gave her freckles a golden glow and her hair was like spun strands of copper. The top criss-crossed over her chest. Drawing the fabric close at the top and leaving the rest of the fabric to flow down past the waistband of the jeans.

She selected a nose ring with an emerald, green gemstone adorning the stud and swapped it out for the black simple ring she had worn for the last couple of days. After she was satisfied that it matched the outfit well, she spent an embarrassingly long time on her make up, getting the shimmering earth tones just right over her eyelids. She added a slightly winged eyeliner and mascara. She pulled out her favorite lip-stain and applied it. It was a deep burgundy. She blew a kiss in the mirror. She had to admit, she looked hot. She winked at herself and headed to the living room.

Well shit, she thought to herself as she looked at the clock. Eden had been so nervous about being on time that she had an hour to spare. She plopped on the couch and sent Journey a selfie of her date look. She decided to scroll through the internet on her phone to waste time.

The sound of thuds and glass breaking from her bedroom had Eden flinching, then rushing to her feet. Was someone breaking into her house? *Who would break into this tiny house?* Attempting to be as quiet as possible, Eden slowly backed up to the wall beside her couch and crouched. She groped blindly behind the couch for the small baseball bat she left there, close to her front door for emergencies. She kept her eyes on the curtained French style doors as she grasped the bat and stood on shaking legs. She moved cautiously towards her room. She pulled the doors open in a swift motion, backing up to pull the bat into swinging position.

Eden's shoulders relaxed and she rolled her eyes as she beheld Loretta's ghost in the middle of the room. Loretta simply walked out of the room toward her, looking lost. Almost distressed. It was the same way she had looked the last couple of weeks.

"Why can't you leave me alone?" Eden said in a frustrated huff.

"Why am I here?" Loretta's ethereal yet southern voice grated on her. Eden opened her mouth to spew something sarcastic and full of obscenities but before she could answer the apparition disappeared.

To ruin my fucking evening, Eden thought irritably. *Why WAS she here? Why hasn't she moved on?* Eden realized that she was going to have to try to sleuth it out if Loretta was attached to her and not giving answers.

With a groan, Eden stormed into her room to turn on the lamp and locate her laptop. She found herself tripping over the antique floor lamp. *Dammit, Loretta. You had to break the GOOD lamp! She broke the one really nice thing in my house.* It was the first big ticket item Eden had purchased after three years of running. She had found it, like a hidden treasure in a junk shop on the day she was hired. Eden grunted in frustration as she picked herself up and turned on the bedside lamp.

"You couldn't destroy the ten-dollar lamp? You had to break the antique one with the glass shade, huh? Pain in my ass when you were alive, and now you gotta piss me off after you're dead." Eden turned around to yell at the apparition, despite the fact that she was gone. She muttered curse words about meddling spirits and being cursed herself as she cleaned up the glass and dropped the pieces gently into a bag, hoping her super glue skills could salvage it. If the spirit world was allowed to hound her at all times about their problems, it was going to listen to her curse and sass them a few more times before Anaiah showed up.

She ended up having plenty of time to clean up and salvage what she could of her lamp. Rage cleaning, it seemed, went much faster than normal cleaning. She swore at Loretta even more as she super glued pieces back together and turned the lampshade on the pole to make the mostly broken side face the wall. She checked her hair and makeup in the mirror to ensure they were unmarred by her supernaturally focused hissy fit. She glanced up and smiled at herself looking cute and dressed up again.

Anaiah's knock sounded through the house. She rushed to the door to answer, purse in hand. She found herself, not for the first time, marveling at him. His jet-black hair hung loose. He grinned his gorgeous half turned smile. Her eyes traced down his short sleeve black button-down shirt tucked into dark blue jeans. A black leather belt with a brushed nickel belt buckle ran along the waistband she wanted to grab ahold of, but she forced her hands to stay where they were as she finished looking him over, noting his black leather biker style boots. *Damn, he cleans up well,* she thought. She took in the smell of him: a hint of cologne and maybe of men's soap. From where she stood, just a foot and a half away from him, there was just enough trace of that mesmerizing scent, like a spell trying to lure her closer to him. The enchantment was working if it were true.

"You look really nice," his deep southern drawl pulled her gaze back to his face and that damn half grin. His accent always was an adorable surprise for her. It was pure country boy charm. His body, his tattoos, and the way he dressed said bad boy. She wondered which way he leaned deep down. He'd never been anything but charming to her, but damn did he look dangerous.

"You too." She managed to say. She swallowed. She felt entirely out of her depth. She looked cute, but he was a damn model from the pages in a magazine. Her insecurity told her to run, it was too good to be true, but another instinct told her to pull him in and start undoing buttons.

She tried to reign in her imagination when he said, "You ready?" She swallowed again and nodded. Not trusting what she might say. She grabbed her keys from her purse and locked the door behind her. He walked her down the driveway to his car, his hand lightly placed in the small of her back. It was distracting to the point that it took her a moment to realize that he drove a slightly newer version of her blue sedan.

She smiled, "Nice car," as they passed her car to get to his parked behind her in the driveway.

He laughed, "Guess we have similar tastes. Good gas mileage and they drive forever. And it was cheap."

"The blue is almost the same shade too. I think mine's just faded." She laughed a little.

He held open the passenger side door for her and she slid in. He closed the door and walked around. He had some manners. She liked that. She took the moment before he got in the car to take a deep breath and attempt to slow her racing heart.

"So, Journey told me you work for emergency services?" She said after a beat of silence. Her heart thudded hard enough in her chest that she wondered if he would hear it in the quiet.

"Yep, firefighter-paramedic." He started the car. *He could give me some mouth to mouth*, Eden thought with sudden embarrassment by the cheesy lines her internal monologue spouted. "Work the night shift. It can be cool. Mainly, I hang out at the firehouse with the crew until a call goes out." He backed them out of the driveway and onto the street.

"That's cool. Better than stocking for a living, I guess. Do you like working nights?" Eden asked. He reached his hand over to hers on the armrest and wrapped her hand in his easily. As if he'd been holding her hand for years. *Here come the butterflies.* She thought as warmth spread through her.

"Yeah. Always have. My whole circadian rhythm is just the opposite of everyone else. Night owl, sleep late. Though, it usually makes it hard to meet people and have a life outside of work. I guess I got lucky." He gave a little nod at their entwined hands. "What about you? You like working nights?"

"All the cool kids work nights." Eden said with a smile. She kept her voice steady to mask the fact that her heart was thundering and that she was dancing in her mind because he took her hand. She attempted to rationalize the warm fuzzy feelings swelling up in her. *It's just the daze of hormones from another person touching me. Don't get your hopes up.* Never mind that she felt like a cat stretching out to bask in the warm rays of sunshine in the dead of winter.

"You aren't from around here, but you never told me where you're from. Mind if I ask?" Anaiah said coolly with that Texan accent. She'd always hated the way most people in the south talked. The drawl had sounded uneducated to her ears. Too much like home and the fanaticism of the Saints. She'd worked to keep it out of her own voice. Though she slipped up from time to time, cringing to hear it come out sounding too much like her mother. When Anaiah spoke with that deep timbre of his voice, the accent sounded damn near sensual to her ears. She recalled he had asked her a question while she pondered the appeal of his voice.

"I moved here about four or five months ago from Oklahoma." Eden left off the part about her murderous landlady, or the boyfriend she left before that. All the ghosts of her past that could damage this little moment of happiness.

"An Okie? Oh no. Tell me you're not a Sooner fan." He gave her a smile as he glanced at her. "I'm just kiddin'."

"I'm not really a football fan at all." She raised her eyebrows. "Not really from Oklahoma either so not an Okie. I moved around a lot the last couple of years. I'm originally from the Houston area. My parents were missionaries." *Shit*, she flinched slightly at her mention of her parents. What was she thinking? What if he asked about them? Wanted to meet them eventually? *Calm down, idiot. It's a first date, not a marriage proposal.*

Anaiah shifted in his seat, noticing her wince and the way she tensed up. His thumb rubbed a light circle over her hand in a soothing gesture. She relaxed ever so slightly.

He asked tentatively, "Okay. So, missionaries...are you very religious?"

"Nah. I mean, I believe there's a God, but I'm not, like, religious. More spiritually inclined, you could say. Religion makes people do stupid things. My parents were crazy about their religion. Hardcore fundamentalists. I guess you could call me non-denominational. Or non-practicing...What about you?" She switched the focus back to him. Any topic besides religion would be welcome. Talking about it always set her on edge. It usually involved her falling into a black pit of despair when the memories of exorcisms, judgment, and the unpleasantness of her childhood.

"I'm not religious, per say. I mean, organized religion bogs things down, more like, I'm a believer...but you said your parents WERE fundamentalists? Did that change? Or are they..." He left it hanging for her to answer.

"Dead? No, I wish..." She threw her unoccupied hand over her mouth, and turned what she imagined was a very dark shade of red. *What am I saying? Have I lost my mind?* "Sorry, I don't have anything to do with them anymore. They kind of hate me." She cringed. She wanted to sink into her chair and possibly die. She never talked like this, what was it about him that made all her normal inhibitions and walls just drop.

"Sorry, I brought it up." His thumb circled on her hand again. He was giving her a worried glance, but it melted away into a calming small smile. "We don't have to talk about it. My parents weren't perfect either." He added gently. His eyes softened with the sympathetic look. He seemed genuinely sweet. She was rattling off whatever came to mind, blushing and cringing like a moron, and he was just going with it. Did he think she was some sort of idiot and was going on a pity date? Worry clenched her briefly.

"Thanks. You're really sweet," muttered Eden, not meeting his eye.

"I try. I'm glad we're going out tonight. Truth be told, I have been wanting to ask you out for a while, but I kept thinking you might just be nice to me because it's your job." He grinned. "Didn't want to take advantage or anything."

"Oh no." She felt herself relax a little. "I'm not that nice to customers. Sometimes I send them to the wrong department on purpose for talking to me." She joked. He chuckled at that.

"I like you, Anaiah. I enjoy chatting with you in the store. I..." She hesitated, "actually look forward to seeing you every week. It doesn't hurt at all that you're also really cute." She said sheepishly. Really cute was the understatement of the century. He was fucking hot, but she wasn't about to just say that. She felt vulnerable enough saying he was cute to his face.

The car came to a stop and Eden looked out the window to realize that he had pulled into a parking spot at the restaurant. She'd been so focused on the conversation and turning as red as an apple to notice they had already arrived.

Anaiah turned off the car and turned to look at her. He reached up and brushed the lock of hair that had fallen into her face back with his free hand. "I think you're beautiful, Eden."

Her heart thumped hard enough in her chest she was sure he could hear it, feel the reverberations through her whole body. She heard the blood in her ears. She felt the warmth in her chest expand as he leaned in.

"I've wanted to kiss you for a while." His breath was warm against her lips as she closed her eyes. The kiss was gentle and so brief, but so absolutely lovely. Those lips that she had thought about for weeks, were as soft and smooth as she imagined. His lips lingered on hers for just a few moments. She opened her eyes as he pulled back. He leaned back into his seat. His eyes were contemplative as if he was debating something.

"That was nice." She whispered. The breath had nearly been stolen out of her.

"Yeah," he said softly. As if breaking from a trance, his eyes cleared, and he looked back into hers as he asked. "Hungry? I'm starving." His hand dropped from hers as he unbuckled himself. The absence of its warmth left a small ache in her chest.

Okay, he is awkward after kisses, not that good at transitions. I'm the queen of awkward. This is fine. She thought to herself as he opened her door and took her hand. She looked down at their intertwined fingers. His hand was massive compared to hers. He gently guided her into the restaurant and spoke to the hostess. Eden was surprised that they were given a table right away despite the lines of waiting customers.

"Did you call ahead?" wondered Eden aloud.

"Nah, they just take care of public servants. You know, cops, EMS, fire fighters..." He winked. "The hostess is the sister of one of the guys at the station." He gave a conspirator's grin.

At his mischievous smile, Eden had to fight the urge to pull him closer and kiss him right on the corner of that upturned side of his mouth. Maybe he regretted the first kiss. Was that why he pulled away? *He's still holding your hand, idiot.* Her emotions were overpowering. Usually, she could get a read on someone without touching them. Touching them gave her insight to memories, emotions, and some random bits of thought. With her own brain bathed in hormones, she couldn't even tell if he was in a good mood. The more she thought about it, the more she found herself grateful for it. It made her feel somewhat normal. Well, as normal as she could be.

The hostess directed them to a table wrapped grill and sat two menus in front of two seats on one side; there were four other people in a group in front, clearly together by the way they laughed boisterously together. Across from them on the other side of the large rectangular grill, was a middle-aged man and woman. A married couple, she would guess, judging by their rings on their hands and the way they spoke quietly to one another with such ease. A slim waiter who looked to be around Eden's age was taking drink orders from the others as Anaiah pulled out her chair for her to sit. Eden glanced over the drink menu. She ordered beer she had tried with the twins and a glass of water. The beer was to calm her nerves, and the water she hoped would serve as a reminder to not nervously sip on alcohol only. Anaiah ordered the same dark beer. Eden didn't have to be psychic to know what the waiter asked for next. She was carded, but Anaiah was not. She expected as much and pulled out her driver's license to prove her age.

"Entrees?" The waiter asked after she flashed her ID.

"Hibachi beef, extra rice, soup, no salad." Anaiah rattled off. Clearly, he'd been here before.

"I'll do the same, without the extra rice." Eden said nervously. She wasn't a picky eater, and it saved her the nerve-racking moment of having to scour the menu to find what she liked. Anaiah ordered some sushi as an appetizer.

After the waiter moved on, Anaiah leaned in toward her, speaking into her ear so he could be heard over the din of the noisy restaurant. "I gotta confess, I'm glad to know you are old enough to drink. I was a little worried that you might be a little young for me. Didn't want to take advantage of a young lady. I should have asked you out sooner." The warmth of his breath on her neck gave her a warm tingly feeling just south of her stomach. Internally, Eden laughed nervously. Externally, she just smiled shyly and tucked her hair behind her ear as she turned to speak to him in return.

"Just turned twenty-one. If you'd asked me out a few weeks ago, I wouldn't have been able to order a beer. What about you?" She said quietly back into his ear.

"I'll be twenty-seven this summer." he said. "Not too old for you, right?" He pulled back to look into her eyes. His smile was easy, but Eden definitely picked up on his nerves. He wanted an earnest answer. She shook her head. *An adult was an adult, right? The number didn't really matter.* She thought. It wasn't as if he was more than double her age. That would have been the case if she had stayed in the church. She clamped down on the thought. Allowing it to go no further. No downward spirals for this date. She had already embarrassed herself in the car, she would not allow her past to chase her away from this, from him.

"You have a lovely neck by the way." He touched it softly and brushed her hair back. His gentle touch pulled her firmly from those thoughts of her past.

There go those damn tingles again. She had goosebumps down her entire arm. She turned her face to his, just inches away. He was smiling again. She leaned in this time and kissed him lightly on the lips.

The chef clanged his spatula and knife together and Eden started. Her attention snapped to the chef as he started flipping his spatulas around. Her unease fell from her shoulders. No threats, no need for fight or flight. Just dinner. She eased even further as Anaiah draped his arm around the back of her chair and gently touched her arm.

"Later." Anaiah whispered in her ear. She nearly melted not only from his warm breath against her neck but at that sweet promise of more. As the chef continued his show and began to cook the appetizers, their drinks arrived. Anaiah ordered sushi. Eden tried her best to pay attention to the show, but it was difficult with Anaiah's fingers drawing lazy circles on her arm. She drank her beer and prayed for steadier nerves or a slower heartbeat that had nothing to do with the knives and spatulas that flew around in rapid motion.

The chef served up their fried rice as they finished their miso soup. Anaiah's sushi arrived and Eden was surprised at how much she could eat, given that her stomach was full of butterflies.

Before she knew it, Eden had finished off two beers and started a third as the chef finished his show following the entree portion. Anaiah had stopped at one beer since he was driving but didn't seem to mind that she had more. They quietly chatted about food preferences as Anaiah ate sushi with more wasabi than Eden had ever seen anyone eat. Eden finished off her beer as she tried to tame the spiciness of the sushi roll. The waiter brought her a fourth and refilled her water.

"Sorry, this one is a little more tame." He said and turned the plate to hand her another piece of sushi, this one not covered in spicy mayo. "I like hot stuff." He gave her a wink and a half smile.

"Oh?" Eden raised her eyebrows and smiled. She played coy but she felt her cheeks flush anyway. His grin widened and she drank her beer nervously. "I'm stuffed." She pushed away her plate. Anaiah picked at the bits of her steak and mushrooms left on the plate.

"Tell me about your job. You said you and the guys hang at the station until the call goes out. What do you guys do?" Eden inquired as she drank.

"Paperwork, maintenance stuff for the rigs, restocking stuff, you know the boring side of fire and rescue. We also take turns cooking big family size meals, do some hobbies, and watch television, if time allows." He shrugged. "So, what about you? What sort of stuff do you do when you aren't restocking?"

"Lately I've been hanging out with my friends instead of sleeping. Their days off don't line up with mine." She giggled at his nod which seemed to say 'of course'. "I'm working my way through reading a fantasy series. I'm stuck.

The next book is checked out at the library, and I refuse to buy the fourth novel, since I don't own the rest. Pretty lame, right?"

"Not at all. I just finished a good set of audiobooks. I listen to them at work." Anaiah smiled and pulled up the app on his phone to show her the titles.

"I've read those!" Eden lit up. She found herself going off on a tangent about one of the characters and how she was misunderstood. She worried that she was rambling after she made her third point about the character's trauma driving her actions and stopped herself.

"Go on, I'm listenin'." He smiled and gave her an encouraging nod. He laid his arm over the back of her chair again.

"Sorry, I get...sort of crazy about books." She blushed.

"Don't apologize, you were making good points. You weren't acting crazy. Maybe a little loud," He chuckled, "but passionate would fit better than crazy, I think." When his gaze met hers, she blushed and had to look away from the earnestness there. It pulled at strings in her heart that she wasn't sure what to do with. She liked him, yes. Thought he was absolutely gorgeous as well, but she was a little scared of feeling more even if she wanted it. She felt his warm hand against her cheek as he gently tipped her head up to meet his smiling face.

"Don't be embarrassed." He said quietly. "I noticed it before in the store when we talked. I like when you get excited about things. It's beautiful to watch you light up when you get passionate about something." He chuckled. "Are you blushing more, now?"

"You're making it worse." She grinned but didn't break his stare. "I don't think I've ever blushed more in my life than I have tonight." Was it the alcohol buzzing through her or elation at this perfect moment? Eden didn't care. She was content to stay here forever. His thumb brushed lightly on her cheek. The movement sent warmth through her. She turned her lips towards his hand and kissed the thumb lightly then smiled back at him. He took in a slow breath as he stared into her eyes.

"You want to get out of here?" He said in a low voice that sent a thrill through her. She took a steadying breath to remind herself that she needed to control herself because she was in a crowded restaurant.

With much more calm than she felt, she said, "Gotta read my fortune first, right?" and nodded toward the two wrapped fortune cookies laying on top of the already paid check. His hand dropped from her face.

"Right. Can't leave without finding out what the cookies have in store for us." He held them out to allow her to choose one. She opened the crinkling plastic wrapper and snapped the cookie apart. She giggled tipsily at her fortune.

"Do not be intimidated by the eloquence of others." Eden donned her best serious voice of proclamation.

Anaiah added, "in bed. You always have to add that. It's a firehouse rule. Do not be intimidated by the eloquence of others…in bed. That's some solid advice from a cookie." He smiled and opened his. Eden laughed a little too loud. She tried to adjust her volume.

"If your desires are not extravagant, they will be granted," and then added on, "in bed." Eden giggled but blushed. His sideways grin appeared again.

"C'mon." He said as he helped her up out of her chair. He walked her out of the restaurant as she still giggled at the fortune cookies. She definitely had a slight buzz going.

"What next?" She turned to look up and ask him as he opened the car door for her. Anaiah's eyes drifted to her lips. She bit her lower lip following his line of thinking. Yes, that was his emotions, his desire she was feeling through their clasped hands. He wanted to kiss her as much as she wanted him to. She gave a subtle nod in confirmation and hoped he got the hint. He leaned into her and kissed her cheek; at the same moment, his hand slipped into her hair. He breathed in deeply and his mouth moved slowly down to her neck leaving a trail of kisses and goosebumps in its wake. Her arms instinctively wrapped around his head and shoulders pulling him in. She let out a soft sound and he stilled. She almost whimpered.

Anaiah whispered into her hair, "My place? We can watch a movie or something." He gently placed a few more small kisses up her neck. 'Or something' was sounding pretty damn good.

"That sounds good." She whispered back and wondered if he could hear her over the sound of her thundering heart. He continued his slow kisses, softly tracing a line up her neck to her lips. She put her hands in his hair where she had wanted to since she saw him. He leaned into her, and they backed against the side of the car. The hand in her hair began moving slowly down caressing her neck. The other found its way to her hip. Without a thought, she pulled him deeper into the kiss. Her mind was blurring, and she didn't care what happened next as long as it was with him.

Anaiah pulled back, and Eden came to her senses. She was about to wrap her legs around him in the middle of the parking lot. *Damn my teen-aged hormones!* His eyes had that cautious look again. He was still touching her, his breathing heavy, but watching her warily, like he was deciding something. All her insecurities started to bubble to the surface of her mind. She clamped down on those thoughts.

"Let's go to your place." Eden said in that soft placating tone and ran a hand down his jaw. She smiled sweetly at him. Instincts had kicked in. Calm whatever storm was brewing behind those eyes. He seemed to note the tone she used and let his hands fall. He backed up.

"Only if you want to." He said quietly.

"Trust me, I want to." She smiled a little more flirtatiously. He nodded and let her slide into the car. She kept herself from wrapping her arms around herself as she remembered where that instinct came from. He wasn't about to explode with rage. Why did her brain think he needed to be defused? Because he looked intense. He was huge, and even if she wanted him physically, part of her knew what sort of thing men his size were capable of doing to women like her. She shook off the thought and focused on the happier events so far this evening as he slid into his seat and drove them to his house. He drove silently for a bit. She felt the tension ease ever so slightly as he took her hand again.

Eden still felt a nervous need to break the silence. To ask what she did wrong, instead, she reached over and turned on the stereo. His phone connected to the Bluetooth and began playing an old Toadies song.

"I love this song." Eden beamed at him.

"Me too." he said, and gave her a small smile, "glad it wasn't on my guilty pleasures playlist."

"Ooo. I want to see that list." She teased. "I worked with a bunch of line cooks that introduced me to bands like this. Well, not so much introduced as blared constantly in the kitchen while I worked. It's weird to explain that my favorite music is from a decade I didn't even live through." Eden began to sing along, then remembering what the lyrics were about, she said, "This song has creepy lyrics. It's about a stalker breaking in and kidnapping his crush."

"Yeah, but it's such a good song." He added. "It's kind of hot to hear you sing it, though." He moved his hand from hers down to her thigh and rubbed his thumb lightly on her leg. "This okay?" He looked at her for confirmation that he hadn't crossed a line she didn't want to.

She nodded and smiled at him weakly. *If he only knew the lines that I wanted to cross.* She thought. They rode like this for a few more songs on the way to his place.

"Here we are." He pulled up to a small apartment complex and parked. She took the few seconds it took for him to walk around to check her phone and update Journey. *Date is going well. Going back to his place. I only accidentally have embarrassed myself about five or six times. He seems to like my awkwardness though. Text you when I get home.*

Anaiah took her hand again as she stepped out of the car. "I'm upstairs." He nodded toward the apartment up and to the right of the stairs.

"Lead the way, handsome." She grinned. His mischievous grin in response to her comment made her knees a little weak. Her legs thankfully still remembered how to work as he led her up the stairs. As he opened the door, he placed one hand behind her back to guide her in as he flipped a light switch with the other. Her heart sang at the small touch.

Eden pushed the door closed behind her as she glanced around the living room to see a black leather couch with a matching recliner, and a flat screen television. His place was tidy. *He must have been thinking we would come back here.*

"Nice place." She said quietly.

"Thanks." He smiled down at her. "Wanna sit?" She nodded. His hand was still resting on the small of her back. He gently led her to the couch and took up the seat at the end. She sat next to him in the middle of the couch. She was very aware of every point of contact between them. They sat with their knees touching and her shoulder brushed against him. She laid her hand on his thigh. It was like the calm before the storm, this almost electric current buzzing between them, waiting to strike. Anaiah wrapped his arm around her and playfully pulled her closer by her hip as he grinned down at her. She leaned into him, tipping her chin up to him in a silent request. He licked his bottom lip and she swallowed hard. She placed a hand on his chest. His heart pounded under her hand.

"Why aren't you kissing me, already?" Eden whispered playfully.

"Just marveling at how gorgeous you are. Sorry to keep you waiting." He leaned in and brushed his lips against hers. He seemed to have more patience than she did as he took his time gently kissing her before he traced her lips with the tip of his tongue. Eden's mouth parted and he grazed his teeth along her bottom lip, biting with such maddening gentleness, pulling it as he sucked on her lip before kissing her again. With each kiss Eden could feel his patience waning along with hers. She met his kindling fire with her own. She turned to face him, rising up on her knees on the couch to get closer to him. His broad warm hand fitted itself perfectly against the small of her back. As the heat within her rose and she found herself wanting more of that warm touch of his, to feel him pressed closer to her. She found herself moving over him, climbing into his lap as they kissed.

His mouth broke from hers in a nearly feral grin as he observed her there, straddling him on the couch. He traced along her neck with his fingers down to her collar bone. She leaned her head in response, offering it up to him. He pulled her closer with his other hand, still holding her across her back. And leaned his head to her and began kissing along the shadow of the line he traced. He gently sucked where her neck and shoulder met, and Eden inhaled sharply and let out a bit of a moan. His hand smoothly traced its way down her neckline to her breast. Her breath caught as he cupped it in his large hand. She had an overwhelming desire to have his mouth on hers. She grasped his chin and lifted his face back to hers. She kissed him deeply, tongues exploring each other. His hand groped hungrily at her breast while the other moved lower and gripped a handful of her ass. Her mind was blank except for the driving need within her for more of him. Her hands seemed to move of their own will as she unbuttoned his shirt. She slid them over the smooth toned muscle of his chest.

She pulled back and marveled at him. She noted the large tattoo on his right side of his chest. She recognized it as a mixture of firefighting and paramedic symbols with two fireman's axes crisscrossed behind it. She ran her hand over it and kissed him again. She shifted her hips into him out of some sort of primal need that was building in her. Dear god, she did want him.

He let out a low moan. Eden pulled back and gave him a playful satisfied smile and moved to kissing his neck, over his collarbone and back up the other side. She could feel his desire against her warm core, hot and firm as her hips continued in a slow dance against him. Her lips moved to find his again, with her hand in his hair.

Suddenly, he pulled back before she kissed him. His face became serious. Slowly, as if breaching the subject with the most care possible, he said. "Eden, you're not, um, drunk, are you?"

"What?" Eden stared at him confoundedly. Her hand dropped from his black mane. He placed his hand on the side of her face gently, his thumb making slow sweeping motions.

"Well, you had a few beers, and you were acting kind of tipsy." He said quietly, but seriously. "Don't want you to regret this later." *As if anyone would regret sleeping with him. Who the hell is this perfect guy?* He moved his hands to her now stationary hips.

"I'm a little buzzed, but I'm fine. Thank you for trying to protect my virtue." She giggled. "But that does remind me." Then she let out a long sigh, knowing she was about to annoy herself. She had told herself she would be better now. Less lying, more doing things the right way, that sort of thing. "Sorry. I'm not going to give it up on the first date." She sighed again. *Slow down. You like him. You want a possibility of more dates.*

He cocked an eyebrow as if he knew damn well that she wanted to. She almost threw caution to the wind and gave in to her desires.

"I don't mean to be a tease." She said with a small smile. "You're kind of irresistible." She added, rubbing her hands over his chest. *Good God, he is beautiful. Why am I not sleeping with him tonight? Oh right, things went so well for you last time you took things too fast with a guy. It's difficult to resist when I can feel him hard beneath me.* She gave another annoyed sigh.

"You are too." he said straight at her boobs. "I understand, though." He moved his eyes to hers. "We should go slow. Don't rush things." He gave her a brief kiss.

She gracelessly moved to sit next to him, adjusting her shirt back to where it was supposed to be. "Sorry. Hormones just sort of took over before I could think." She said quietly.

"Let's go with that. Hormones." Anaiah looked slightly embarrassed. "You want to watch something?" He adjusted his jeans and placed a throw pillow in his lap. His hand reached out to the side table and grabbed the remote.

"Sure." Eden said, pissed at herself for trying to do things right for a change. *Didn't I leave the morals behind with the overly religious parents? I like him though; I should take it slow.* Everything she felt physically was at war with her reasoning. She didn't want another guy who treated her like she was worthless because she was willing to sleep with him quickly. He didn't seem the type to do that. Then again, neither did Cole at first. The voice in her head told her, *get through the charming first couple of date phases, then see what he's really like.*

He turned on his television and picked The Princess Bride from his Netflix favorites. He wrapped his arm around her and tucked her against his chest as they watched the movie. She relaxed as he began quoting his favorite lines and she joined in. Occasionally, she would look up at him and he would give her one of those soft slow kisses.

As the movie came to an end, he whispered onto the top of her head with a little kiss. "I got work tomorrow, but I would love to call you. Would that be, okay?" His fingers gently ran down her arm.

"Yeah. I'd like that. Do you want to do this again sometime?" She almost held her breath hoping for a second date. "You promised to cook for me." She reminded him as she peeked up at him from her spot under his arm.

"That I did. Is next Friday good for you?" he asked with a smile. Eden had noted that Anaiah emoted through several different smiles. The one on his face now seemed hopeful.

"Sure." She nodded. She looked up at the clock and noticed it was well after two in the morning. "You wanna take me home?" She asked reluctantly.

"Not really, but okay." He laughed as they stood up off the couch. He grabbed his keys off the side table where he dropped them earlier. He turned to kiss her again. "Eden, I'm really glad you asked me out."

"I'm really glad you said yes." She said back as he buttoned his shirt back up. He took her hand and walked her back to the car. The drive home was quiet but not awkward. They held hands and listened to the music on the radio. He occasionally pulled their linked hands up to his lips and kissed the back of her hand. She enjoyed the comfortable silence.

When they arrived at her place, he walked her to the door. He delivered one hell of a good night kiss. It started as a soft affectionate lazy kiss and built up to her grabbing him by the belt to pull him into her and ended with her pressed up against her front door with both of them breathless. It briefly made her reconsider her ground rules she had set for herself. It took all her willpower to not invite him in. She stuck to her guns though. Before she let go of him, she told him to call her tomorrow.

With his adorable southern accent, he tipped his head to her and said, "yes, ma'am." She damn near melted. She couldn't watch him leave for fear that she would change her mind. She grinned like an idiot as she closed the door behind her. Next Friday couldn't come soon enough.

CHAPTER FOURTEEN

Eden smiled to herself every so often as she lay awake, trying to get her brain to wind down and sleep. She ended up buying the e-book of the novel she mentioned to Anaiah on her phone and read late into the early morning to finally get herself ready for sleep.

Hours later, Eden awoke to the familiar sound of her phone's ringtone. She panicked for a moment thinking she had overslept for work and grabbed it. Her face broke into a giddy smile when she saw Anaiah's name on the screen. She cleared her throat and answered,

"Hello?"

"Hello beautiful. I had a few minutes so I thought I would call. Were you sleeping?" Anaiah asked.

"Yeah, but I'll wake up for you." Eden rolled back on her pillows as she smiled to herself. She looked at her phone quickly for the time. *Oh. Damn. Just after ten at night.* "How's work?"

"We've been busy, mainly nursing home calls. Simple stuff. Mainly just put 'em on a stretcher and take 'em to the hospital, which is two blocks from there. They can't just wheel them over though." He laughed. After a short pause, "Is it too soon to say that I can't wait to see you again?" Eden's heart soared in her chest.

Eden fought the urge to do a victory dance. "I can't wait to see you either."

"Friday just seems too long to wait." He chuckled. "I guess I usually see you on Thursdays, though. Still seems so long to wait to see your gorgeous face." Eden felt her face warm with the compliment. It seemed he enjoyed their date as much as she had.

"Do you want to come by after work? We can go grab some breakfast." Eden suggested while she curled a strand of hair around her finger.

"That sounds great. What are you up to tonight after you get up?" Eden swore she could hear him smiling as he spoke.

"Laundry. Change my sheets. Maybe even spend some time with fictional characters in a book. Don't be too jealous." Eden responded playfully. She rolled over on the bed and turned on a light.

"Oh, that does sound like fun." He laughed. "Any book boyfriends I should be worried about?"

"I wouldn't worry much about Rhysand. He's fictional." Eden giggled. She'd disclosed her crushes on book characters in her tipsy state the night before. "I haven't even seen his tattoos in real life. Only in my imagination. I've touched yours." Her voice dropped lower with the tease.

"Mmm. It's not at all distracting to think about you touching me last night. I'm supposed to be saving lives, you know." He teased her back.

"Then definitely don't think about how much I want to kiss you again." Eden's face was still warm with the blush from the thought. She felt her nerves loosening as the conversation became easier the more, she knew him and knew that he thought of her.

"You're terrible." He laughed. "Torturing a poor public servant."

"No, torture was that goodnight kiss." Eden couldn't hardly remember her own name after. She giggled.

"I'll make it up to you." He said in a sweet low voice.

"Mmm." She considered what sort of straightening up she would need to do to get her place ready for him to come over and make it up to her. As she glanced around her room at the few pieces of clothing outside of her hamper, her eyes swept over the now slightly deformed lamp. She remembered her little run in with Loretta's ghost. A voice came through the phone that sounded like a CB radio.

"Well, that's a call out from dispatch. I have to go. Want me to pick you up a little after seven?" Anaiah said.

"Yeah, I'll be ready. See you then." Eden said as she rose from the bed.

"See you then, Eden." He said over the rush of voices in the background.

Eden made her first stop into the bathroom, then headed straight for her coffee maker. Once she had a cup of coffee in her hand, she plopped on the couch and pulled the browser window up on her laptop. Her fingers typed swiftly over the keys and searched for the online edition of the news for the article about Loretta's accident. She read over the details each news site gave about the crash while she drank her coffee.

According to the articles, Loretta had fallen asleep at the wheel around seven-thirty in the morning on her way home from work. She'd entered oncoming traffic and was hit head-on by an eighteen-wheeler. She was pronounced dead at the scene of the accident. The picture of the wreckage was gruesome. There were no bodies in the photos, just a twisted and charred frame from what was once her Lincoln Town Car. Eden continued to scroll, setting her mug on the coffee table once it was empty. The accident hadn't been featured in major news outlets in the area, just the smaller local papers and television stations. The articles were all nearly identical. Eden heard a thud as her coffee mug hit the floor. She wasn't surprised to see Loretta's flimsy looking form standing before her. Loretta no longer looked lost. She looked...angry. Verging on pissed off.

"Was it really an accident?" Eden pursed her lips.

"He did this on purpose. Because of you. I can't move on until you surrender." The spirit had the audacity to place a hand on her hip and glare menacingly at Eden. As if this really was Eden's fault.

"What? Who did this to you?" Eden knew it was stupid to hope for a name, or any sort of straight answer. Instead of giving any answers or insight to what Eden could do to help, Loretta simply dissipated again. Eden threw her hands up in frustration and made a vulgar gesture to the empty space where the ghost had been a moment before. She made a frustrated growling noise before she forced herself to breathe slowly and calm the irritation with Loretta. She needed to think through all of it. Her irritation would not help her figure out this nuisance.

Loretta was haunting her because something about her death linked her to Eden. Who would hurt someone Eden worked with just to get at her? Especially a manager she didn't particularly like? And why did ghosts speak in cryptic bullshit riddles? *Just say it! Just say 'This is it; this is why I'm here!'* Her shoulders tensed with her flair of emotion. She felt a headache slowly building. She rolled her neck and shoulders and tried to think of anything that would link her to Loretta besides work.

Eden spent the next several hours between loads of laundry on dead end internet research, mainly just Google searches. She pondered the possibility that someone at work could have killed Loretta. If so, why would Loretta think they had done it because of Eden? She felt a small temptation to get background checks on all the men she worked with since Loretta had said "he" had done this to her. However, she wasn't so tempted to do the background checks when she saw how much she would have to pay for them. She vacuumed her small house and tidied it up a bit, changing out the sheets and duvet cover while she mulled over everything she knew about her coworkers. Which outside of her little circle, was mostly nothing. Just their names. After more dead ends from scouring Loretta's social media for clues, Eden decided she had enough theorizing about Loretta's death for one night.

She checked her phone for the time. She noted the notification on her texts and read the message from Journey. She laughed out loud at the response to Eden's news that she had already secured a second date. *Paramedic ass with a side of pancakes, huh?*

She fired a message back. *No ass was promised, but pancakes are on the menu. How's your night going?* She wouldn't get an answer right away, knowing Journey. She'd check her phone at break. She pushed herself up off the couch, set her phone down and headed to her closet to find something that was fitting for a breakfast date. She pulled on a clean pair of black leggings and a simple grey cotton tunic length top. Simple, but comfortable. She scrunched curl cream into her hair and let it do its natural curly thing. Her hair in its curled state nearly passed the middle of her back now. It was even longer straight ironed or when it was wet.

She swapped out the emerald-green stud in her nostril for a simple silver ring. She changed out the accessory often enough, it was part of her pre-make up routine. She took her time perfecting her makeup before she plopped onto the couch to scroll on her phone until seven rolled around. Journey had responded. *This job is slowly sucking away the last remnants of my soul like a dementor. Scott tripped over his shoelace today after the meeting and I felt the thrill of joy in my shriveled heart once again, if only for a fleeting moment in time.*

Eden giggled and responded. *Bribe Phil into letting you into the surveillance room to back up the footage and record that moment for me. I need to feel alive again too.*

Journey's response was swift. *You have a date to make you feel alive again.* Eden kept herself from typing a response that brought up how Journey could also have a date if she would speak up and ask Jayse out. She considered an alternative message for a moment before responding. *That's true, but I need to laugh with my best friend about Scott. It's a bonding experience.*

Journey's response lit up the screen with the notification. *Aww, I made it to bestie status. Eden and Journey: BFF's and Bad-Ass Bitches.*

Waiting without checking the window for Anaiah was a practice in patience. It grated on her nerves to keep herself from peeking through the blinds. It was ten after seven and she had nothing to do with her nervous energy. She stood to go check anyway, and a knock at the door sounded. She jumped at the sudden noise.

When she opened the door, Anaiah was still wearing his EMS uniform. She fought the urge to lick her lips. His hair was tied back out of his face, and he had a black bag in his hand.

"So, I hate to ask, but do you mind if I grab a quick shower and change before we go? I would have run home, but your place is closer, and it has an Eden." He winked at her.

"Sure." Her mind wandered to more flirtatious responses. She resisted the urge to ask if he needed a hand in the shower. As he walked by her into her house, he planted a quick kiss on the top of her head. She showed him where the bathroom was. She sat on the couch and texted Journey. *'I should be commended for the restraint I am showing. He's naked, in my bathroom, in the shower and I am being an innocent angel on the couch.'*

When he emerged fully dressed in jeans and black brushed cotton Henley a few minutes later, his hair was still damp. He pulled it back with a hair elastic and tied it up as he walked toward her. She watched his grin spread as she realized she was staring at him open-mouthed as he stalked straight for her. She closed her mouth and averted her eyes. He gently took Eden's hand in his and pulled her up from the couch for a quick kiss. He held her against his chest and kissed the top of her head.

"Mmm. You smell good." She felt the words vibrate in his chest as he held her close and sniffed the top of her hair. "But bacon is calling my name. I am starving." He smiled down at her. "Let's go eat."

Their local waffle restaurant was busy. Maybe that was a good thing. Eden somehow managed to get through breakfast without succumbing to the temptation to latch herself onto Anaiah's face. It was a struggle. They chatted about his night and her laundry. He told her about the new "kid" that was driving him nuts that he was training. She observed the way he talked about his job; she could tell he loved it. She could see the joy in every smile and laugh while telling her stories about his buddies at the station.

She gave him a run-down of their small group of friends at work, their regular after work breakfast hangouts and the occasional hang out at Journey's place before or after work. None of her work friends had her same day off, so they each took turns sacrificing sleep to hang out. Occasionally she would note the way he smiled when her eyes met his, like she was something special, something to be admired and appreciated. It filled her with a drunk sort of giddiness. At least she blushed less this time around.

After breakfast it occurred to Eden that she could ask him if he knew anything about Loretta Rodgers death. He might have even been there at the crash site. She cleared her throat as they walked out of the restaurant and into the parking lot towards his car.

"Can I ask you about an accident a few weeks ago? My manager was in a bad wreck, and she died." Eden blurted out.

"Oh yeah, Loretta Rodgers. I heard she worked at your store, but I didn't know she was your manager. Were you close?" Anaiah's heart of gold, sympathetic expression made her almost lie and say that she was.

"Well, no, not really close. Just curious about the details. Can you tell me what happened?" She tried to sound sweet and caring.

"It was really bad. When we got there, the semi had run head on into her and the car was completely burned out. From the lack of skid marks, we figured she fell asleep at the wheel. Her body was torched, almost completely gone in the wreckage. The weird thing about it though, was that the semi driver wasn't wearing a seatbelt and the crash killed him too. Doesn't happen often. He was thrown from the semi and broke his neck. Usually, semi drivers don't get injured unless they roll over. He was just unlucky I guess." Anaiah seemed to realize that he might have over-shared or been too detailed in his information. He eyed her with concern.

"They didn't say anything about the driver in the article I read." Eden did her best to look more affected. Some ghosts walked around with brain matter hanging out, so she was less sensitive about death than most.

"Hmm, Yeah, young guy, out of Oklahoma. Cole Sparks, was the name, I think." As Anaiah said the name, it was as if someone had punched her in the gut. The breath went out of her, and her chest tightened. His name was one that haunted her. One of the frequent faces in her nightmares. *But dead?* And just miles from where she lived? She couldn't breathe, could barely keep one foot in front of the other as she felt the world spinning.

She heard Anaiah's voice, distant as if from another world, asking if she was okay. Asking if she needed to sit down. The world continued to blur and spin around her as she tried in vain to breathe deeply and calm that ache in her chest from the absolute dread filling her.

She would have thought that after the crappy relationship she and Cole had, hearing that the bastard was dead would be a relief. Instead, it had sent her reeling. "Cole Sparks, from Mustang, Oklahoma?" Eden gasped. She wondered for a moment if she might be hyperventilating. The edges of her vision blurred.

"Yeah, how'd you..." Eden barely heard him through the pounding of her own blood in her ears. She couldn't breathe. Her chest felt like a crushing weight was squeezing her. Her body felt too hot, but at the same time she felt like her blood was chilling. She reached out to grab onto anything to keep her from falling.

"Eden?" Anaiah was standing in front of her. His worried face the last thing she saw as the darkness at the edge of her vision closed in and she fell.

Eden could feel the hard ground beneath her. Her head swam still as she pressed her eyes tighter shut against the too bright sun.

She heard Anaiah's voice, "She's okay. Give her some room, she needs air."

She blinked open her eyes and saw his face above hers. At the edges of her vision, she saw the blurry shapes of what must have been other people gathered around.

"Eden, can you tell me how many fingers I'm holding up?" He said in a steady-even tone. All business, then. Eden blinked a couple of times, and her eyes came into focus on his hand before her.

"Three." She started to sit up, and Anaiah laid a very large hand on her shoulder to stop her. There were several people gathered around her in the parking lot.

"Eden, just stay down for a minute. You hyperventilated and passed out. I am just gonna check to see if you hurt yourself. Now here, follow the light with your eyes." He must have retrieved his bag from the car. He felt with his fingers through her hair, checking her scalp for any bumps or open wounds. After Eden passed his battery of tests, he decided that she was okay to sit up. He assured the others that he had her under control now and they dispersed.

"I take it you knew Cole Sparks, huh?" Anaiah asked, still crouched down beside her on the pavement. His expression was less neutral and professional than before. Something like disappointment lined his features.

"My ex-boyfriend." She said softly, hugging her knees to her chest and not wanting to meet his gaze.

"I was 'fraid of that." He let out a long breath. She looked to him, but his gaze didn't meet hers as he stood up. "Let me take you home." His voice wasn't unkind, but it was flat. Subdued from the bright cheerful tone it had been earlier.

"Ok, I guess." She said, resigned. "What a way to end a second date. I am the most awesome date ever." She muttered sarcastically.

"You keep me on my toes, hon. C'mon," he said as he helped her up. He wrapped his arm around her shoulders to keep her steady as he walked her to the car. He drove her home in silence. His expression was unreadable. She felt like crying. She looked out the window to avoid him seeing it if she did. When he pulled up to the house, she opened her door first and headed up the stairs. He followed but didn't kiss her goodbye. She waited to see if he would, but instead he told her to get some rest and gave her a small hug. She didn't watch him leave.

She closed the door behind herself and sank onto the floor. *Well, I probably ruined that.* She thought to herself as she cried.

CHAPTER FIFTEEN

E den got through the next few days by working and sleeping. Journey and the twins were off work when Eden returned so she hadn't even talked to anyone. It was reminiscent of life before she moved here, cold but familiar. She'd never been close with her coworkers before. She'd had a few casual friends, but no one who really knew her. Especially not after the fallout with Cole. She'd not entertained friends in her home before either. She fell back on old habits. She stuck her nose in a book at break and pretended that she didn't care that Anaiah didn't text or call her for two days. She hadn't texted him either. *What could I say? 'Sorry I ruined everything?'*

Her friends returned to work as scheduled that evening, but she hadn't spoken to them yet. She had been too embarrassed to text Journey about how her date ended. Now, despite her embarrassment, she found herself looking forward to talking with Journey about it. Work began with the same meaningless meeting. Everyone knew where to go and what to stock, but for some reason, a meeting was necessary. Jayse and Journey were standing side by side with a "we aren't together" sized gap between them. Eden wondered which of them would crack first. She was vaguely aware of Scott speaking about where they needed to work first.

Eden was less worried about Scott's directions. What concerned her now was the apparition standing behind him, staring at her expectantly. She wondered why no one else ever saw them. She glanced around at all the bored faces of her coworkers. None of them showed any sign of seeing this figure from the great beyond. Eden also wondered why Loretta didn't wait until the end of the meeting when Eden might be able to acknowledge her. As it stood, Eden attempted to not look insane or show any response to Loretta's intense staring as she walked around the circle of people. The ghost paused at Journey and Jayse, and then looked to Eden pointedly.

"Help them." Loretta said, making a desperately pleading face before dissipating. *Of course, she would be stupidly dramatic in death as she had been in life.*

Journey gave Eden a look that seemed to say, "You're weirding me out, why are you staring at me?" Eden gave the slightest shrug.

Last week, Eden had informed Journey that she was seeing Loretta around. Journey laughed and joked about working in hell. Now Journey continued to make puzzled looks at Eden and even mouthed the word, "What?" at her.

Eden shook her head and mouthed the word "later" to her. What did Loretta want her to do? Help them say what they want to say to each other? Was Loretta sticking around to play matchmaker? *That tracked with her meddling before she died. Can't a spirit for once be straightforward and just tell me what's up?* As Eden began a rant in her mind about the bullshit of the afterlife, she heard Scott say her name. *Oh Shit. What was he saying?*

Eden noticed that, to her horror, not just Scott, but the entire room was looking at her expectantly. She quickly looked to Journey for some clue. Journey mouthed a word that Eden could not decipher. Seconds ticked by awkwardly as everyone waited. Journey saved her when she started to clap, and the others joined in. It dawned on Eden that she was asked to do the stupid cheer.

Eden stumbled her way through the cheer while she turned a deep shade of red. Journey shook her head at her and stifled laughter. Despite the thorough teasing Eden would get from Journey, she knew that Journey was a good friend. She had her back. Maybe she could help her by playing matchmaker and set Journey and Jayse up.

After the cheer, they split up into their areas. Journey caught up with Eden. She could tell that Journey wanted an explanation. Thankfully, she waited until they were out of everyone's earshot.

"Are you losing it or did you decide that daydreaming during a meeting was a good idea?" She quipped. "'Cause I personally loved it when you turned to stare at me for a good five minutes. You did it so noticeably that Scott called you out by asking you to lead the cheer."

Eden groaned. Then threw back her best sarcastic remark. "Really? I'm glad you enjoyed it. Did it just for you." Then added with more sincerity, "Thanks for saving my ass."

"Oh no prob. Just helpin' my hoe. See, if I do these things, over time, you lose the ability to function without me, and I become forever embedded in your life. I grow on ya. Like a fungus." Eden loved how Journey took the pressure off their friendship by turning everything she did graciously into a seemingly selfish act. She also had a habit of never taking anything too seriously. She once told Eden not to pay her back for picking up a breakfast tab, because one day when she snapped she'd need Eden to help hide a body.

She'd said that Eden would think back on all the breakfasts she had bought and think, 'yeah, I owe her.' Eden smiled at the memory.

"So really, what happened?" Journey asked.

"Loretta." Eden said flatly.

"Dedicated beyond her years, Loretta still makes the shift meetings." Journey placed a hand over her heart in mock reverence.

"Let's rock out some housewares." Eden attempted to be encouraging, but really, all she wanted to do was send a bunch of cringe worthy text messages to Anaiah to make sure that she hadn't ruined her chances completely. They worked their way through pallets of goods. The first hour was also spent giving a recap of her first two dates with Anaiah. She finally finished her story, explaining how he had just hugged her and left at the end.

"You hyperventilated and passed out? Dude, I want to be on your next date to see what happens." She laughed.

"Ha ha ha. It's fucking hilarious." Eden said humorlessly. She resisted the urge to grind her teeth. "I had a panic attack. It sucked. He took me home and left. I just hope he calls me again." She was feeling less hopeful each day. Would he avoid her when he came in on Thursday?

"If he doesn't it's his loss. For all your kooky weird shit, you're a decent person, E. Fuck him if he can't deal with your shit. Everyone has baggage. If they say they don't, they are lying." Journey sounded legitimately offended on her behalf.

"Journey, was that genuine and heartfelt? Are you sick?" Eden gave a half smile.

"Don't get used to it." Journey said, bumping her shoulder as she walked by with a smile on her face.

"What did you do on your days off?" Eden asked.

"Jayce came over and helped me with some stuff my parents needed us to do at the park. Eh, no… I see the bright hope in your eyes. My dad paid him to help me. He's getting too old for all the physical labor. And my mom is… well, my mom." She shrugged. "I mean, it was cool getting to hang with him, but it was work stuff." Journey avoided eye contact.

Eden's pocket made a small musical tone. She pulled her phone out expectantly and was delighted and nervous to see the notification for a text from Anaiah. *Been a busy couple of days, but I've been thinking about you. How about a do-over breakfast in the morning?* His message read.

"Oh, sweet baby Jesus…That poor gorgeous idiot really likes you." Journey said, reading over Eden's shoulder.

"Thanks, bitch." Eden said in a high defensive tone. *Should I wait to text him back? So, I don't look desperate?* She stood in the middle of the aisle staring at her phone debating her next move. She typed out a message, then deleted it. She felt like chucking the phone as far as she could while also wanting to text him back immediately, accepting his offer. She made a face.

"Sweetie, you got him all hot and bothered and then just...cuddled with him. Then you ruined any chance of second date sex by freaking out when you heard your ex died. He may have been disappointed. Don't take this the wrong way, but you might let him take a crack at it just for pain and suffering." Journey weighed in.

It wasn't as if Eden had set a specific rule on when her 'business district' opened, but the third date seemed about right. Sex was one thing she was willing to admit she wanted from him, but really, truly, she liked him. She liked the connection they had. Liked how conversation with him flowed easily enough that they could chat for hours. Had he wanted more on the first date than he let on? Maybe he was bummed out that he had to tend to her post-panic attack instead of getting to move forward with her physically. Or maybe he was a decent guy and was giving her space to process things. He certainly seemed like it. Why was she hesitating?

She shrugged to herself. A plan formulated in her head. Her lip twitched up with a small sneaky smile. She shot Anaiah a text back asking if he cared if she brought along a couple of work friends, sort of a double date. Maybe they could be a bit of a buffer for her weirdness. He responded with a thumb's up emoji. She headed to the backroom of the store to the baler to dump her empty boxes.

She spotted the guy she was looking for on her way there and stopped near the electronics. "Hey Jayse."

"What's up?" He stood up from the pallet he was working on.

"Hey, so, my, um, guy I'm seeing." She fumbled for the right word.

"Your boyfriend, what about him?" Jayse looked uncomfortable.

"I guess...my boyfriend, whatever. But anyway, he and I are going to breakfast in the morning. I was wondering if you might wanna go with us and bring Journey." She finally rambled out. She raised her eyebrows hoping he understood her meaning.

"Why would I bring Journey, can't she ride with you?" He looked confused.

Eden gave him a pointed look. Realization hit him. "Unless she wants me to go with her. Does she?" His eyebrows perked up with anticipation.

Eden lied, "yeah, she does. She just, uh, didn't wanna ask, in case you said no...since it's like a double date and all. You know, 'cause you guys are friends she's afraid it'd be weird if you didn't want to." Eden knew it was close to the truth. She got a knot in her stomach at the twist of the truth. She had never been happy with all the lies she told, but she usually was better at it than this.

"Yeah, we could do that. Waffle Casa, or Smiley's?" He looked excited. Eden was relieved that it was this easy.

"Let's do Smiley's." Eden said.

"You're dating that tall guy that comes in every week?" He said with remarkably less interest than he had shown a moment before.

"Yeah. Anaiah's pretty cool." She started to walk off. "I'll tell Journey it's a date."

"Sounds good! See ya at break." He gave her a nod.

When she returned to the hardware department, Journey was working her way through the pallet. Eden cleared her throat. "So, I stopped to talk to Jayse for a second."

"What was that about?" She said without looking up.

"You and Jayse are going to breakfast with Anaiah and me. We're doing a double date." Eden said with a smile.

"What?!" Journey stilled. She slowly rose and stared Eden down with an expression that had Eden backing up a step.

"I... he said yes, said he wanted to go on the date with you." Eden said in a small voice.

"You set me up? Without asking me?!" Journey's voice rose. She shot Eden a dangerous look. Eden felt real fear of Journey for the first time. She stepped back again.

"You would have said no. So, I did it. And he said yes, so you could thank me instead of kicking my ass." Eden kept her voice steady, trying to bring the humor back to Journey's expression.

"Thanks...bitch. Don't pull that shit again or I'll...." Her face was red with anger. She shook her head. Something twisted in Eden. Why should she be afraid of Journey? She was tall and intimidating but she was her friend. Was she angry that Eden had taken away her excuse to pine after Jayse and not actually do anything about it?

"Be eternally grateful that you are finally going out with Jayse?" Eden blurted out quickly. Eden could tell Journey was very pissed but trying to calm down.

Journey shook her head. "That's a very junior high move, Eden. We're not a bunch of children, okay? What if he said no? Huh? What then? Then I am stuck looking like a teenager with a crush. As it is, he probably thinks I resorted to this bullshit because I am too afraid to ask him myself. So, thanks for the push, but I'll take it from here. K, punkin?" Journey snipped.

It stung like a slap in the face. It was an 'I'm not mad, I'm disappointed.' The tone raked down her nerves. At first Eden was embarrassed, and then her shame turned to anger.

"Oh, what the fuck ever! I did it because you didn't have the balls to. So fine, I won't help you anymore. See you at breakfast, cookie." Eden turned around and stalked to the automotive department to work alone. She'd let Journey stew for a while.

Was this just how Eden was with people? Never doing the right thing. Always screwing it up. She realized while she worked in silence, she wasn't mad at Journey. She was mad at herself. She'd nearly blown it with Anaiah and now here she was again, lashing out at her best friend just because she happened to be upset with her. Journey had been right to be upset. It was childish and stupid, but she wanted them to be happy.

Journey didn't come to find her when their first break rolled around, but when Eden caught up with her, they both muttered quiet apologies. Jayse sat down beside Journey, which took up Eden's usual spot. She sat down next to Kris.

"Hey Journ, you think we could take your car to breakfast so Kris can take the truck home?" Jayse asked. Kris perked up.

"Sure, so where are we going, Eden?" She stared pointedly at Eden and didn't spare a glance at Jayse. Eden thought for a second that Journey was still mad, but no. Was the tough as nails Journey that she knew...blushing?

"Smiley's" Eden said as she texted Anaiah.

"Texting your boyfriend?" Kris asked like a twelve-year-old boy dragging the word boyfriend out. He chuckled. Eden nodded.

"Oh, he has been elevated to boyfriend status now?" Journey said with a cocked eyebrow while grinning. She knew how bad that last date had gone in the end.

"Yeah. Sure. He's a guy I'm dating. Whatever. What would you call it?" Eden snapped defensively while keeping her eyes on her phone.

"Geez, I'm just messing with you. Chill." Journey said, putting her hands up in surrender.

"Sorry." Eden muttered. She toyed with the ring through the right side of her nose absentmindedly.

"He's a night shifter too?" Kris asked.

"Nah, I'm just texting him at midnight to keep things interesting." Eden responded with their usual snark. Her mouth quirked to the side with a small grin. Why was Kris so interested in Anaiah suddenly? *Guess he feels like the fifth wheel now that people are coupled off.* Jayse thankfully changed the subject by telling them about his customer interaction so far that evening. Apparently, a customer had told him earlier that he was asking him about a particular computer because "his people" worked in I.T. Eden noted the wrath stirring in Journey's expression as Jayse and Kris rolled their eyes at the ignorance of their usual customers.

Their truce was tenuous, Eden could tell. Journey wasn't angry with her, but she didn't talk much for the rest of the shift. The night seemed to drag on.

She felt the tension break in herself as she finally was able to clock out and head to Anaiah's apartment. She texted him that she had arrived.

He took the stairs down two at a time with a big grin plastered on his face. She felt the butterflies awaken in her stomach. He slid into the car and to her surprise, he leaned in and planted a soft kiss on her lips.

"Hi." he said with his face still inches from hers.

"Good morning." She said with a small smile. He leaned in for another kiss, this one lingering. As he pulled back, his lips parted into a grin.

"I'm starving." As he spoke, his stomach grumbled loudly.

"Does being that tall and muscular require constant food?" Eden giggled.

"No, it's the other way around. I work out because I love food." He buckled his seatbelt. "But it was a busy night, I hardly got to eat, and I am wasting away to nothing." He winked.

"Can't have that." Eden pulled the car out of the parking lot.

"Not that I mind, but why the group date with your friends from work?" he asked casually. Eden glanced sideways at him. He didn't seem upset. "Feel like we need a chaperone?" A slight upturn at the corner of his mouth.

"Journey and Jayse...I sort of set them up to double with us. Played matchmaker." She made an awkward face. "They have been friends for a few years. They like each other but they were both just waiting for the other to make a move. I hope you don't mind." She gave him another glance when they stopped at the red light. He shrugged and made a face as if to say, 'fair enough'.

"It's cool. I'm just glad to be here with you." He took her free hand. "Maybe we can hang out a little after breakfast." Eden smiled but wished she had showered and changed after working all night.

"I'd like that." She said and he kissed the back of her hand intertwined with hers. She sighed a little.

"So...are you okay? After the other day...I should have checked on you. Sorry." He said in a quiet voice.

"I was just in a bit of a shock. I'm okay now. Glad it didn't freak you out too much." She kept her eyes on the road ahead.

"Takes quite a bit to freak me out." He seemed to hesitate. "I just didn't want to be too pushy if you were grieving."

"I've shed far too many tears over Cole already." She muttered to herself mostly. She pulled into the parking lot. She turned to look at him. Worry creased his brow.

"How about we don't talk about my ex for a while?" She said quietly.

"Okay." He gave her an encouraging smile. She sighed contentedly. Her expression melted into a happy glowing smile as he reached out and touched her cheek with his thumb, cupping her face in his palm.

"I missed seeing that smile." Anaiah said quietly. She blinked. Had he missed her? "Mmm. You're gorgeous." He said reverently before leaning into her and brushing a soft kiss against her lips. His stomach bellowed its discontent with them.

She giggled, "come on, you're obviously wasting away."

He took her hand as they walked into the restaurant. Eden spotted Jayse and Journey sitting on one side of a booth and beelined toward them. As she approached, she noted that their hands were intertwined. Eden wiggled her eyebrows at Journey. Journey gave her a deathly glare and mouthed the words, "shut it".

"Jayse and Journey this is Anaiah; Anaiah, Jayse and Journey." Eden made motions back and forth with her hands and slid into the booth.

"Nice to meet you." Anaiah nodded to them as he slid in beside her.

"So, you're Eden's boyfriend?" Journey grinned ferally.

Well, I guess, I'm not entirely forgiven. Eden thought as she gave Journey a scowl that told her she was a traitor. Journey matched it.

"Am I?" Anaiah looked to Eden for confirmation with raised eyebrows. Eden shrugged and nodded, trying to act like it wasn't a big deal. Even if it was a huge deal to her. "Yeah, I guess I am." he put his arm around her shoulders and kissed the top of her head.

Eden sighed internally. All was well with him even if she had screwed up before. She was tempted to stick her tongue out at Journey.

The waitress came up to take drink orders. Coffee was ordered all around. They all studied the menu for their breakfast selection studiously. Eden decided that she had a physical need for butterscotch chip pancakes. Not a mere desire. She was certain she might die without them. She closed her menu and asked Anaiah what he was having.

"Don't know yet. You?" he said without looking up.

"Butterscotch chip pancakes. If I go into a sugar coma afterward, you can revive me, right?" She said before thinking and then cringed internally.

"Nah, I'm off the clock. I'd call it into the guys though. An' send you flowers in the hospital o'course." His grin spread wide. He never once looked up from his menu. *Guess we are to the point of joking about it now.*

"Of course." Eden nodded.

"I think I will have bacon, eggs, and... crepes. Wonder if they come with a side of pancakes too." He wondered out loud.

"It's Smiley's, a glass of water comes with a side of two fluffy buttermilk pancakes." Jayse laughed.

After they ordered, Anaiah inquired if Jayse played video games. And Eden learned he did. The men flew into their own conversation about some first-person shooter game. Journey rolled her eyes and smiled at Eden. Seated across from each other, they easily started up a conversation.

Journey informed Eden about her new obsession with a reality show about becoming a model. She watched all the episodes on her day off. Eden confessed that she didn't even own a television and shocked everyone at the table into silence.

"You don't have a TV? At all?" Anaiah said dubiously.

"No, I sleep all day, and work all night. I mean, I have a laptop and internet. I watch stuff on it." Eden said. "Besides, there are these things...called books. They are really entertaining. I don't know, I just haven't talked myself into buying one yet."

"Weirdo," Journey laughed. "You gotta come over and watch this with me then. It's so funny to watch those pretty bitches fight."

"Sure." Eden shrugged.

The waitress arrived with their food. Eden immediately grabbed the butter pecan syrup and drowned her pancakes. If heaven existed, they served these fluffy syrupy delights there every day.

"Quit bogarting the butter pecan" Jayse reached for it.

"Get your own," Eden slapped his hand jokingly. Journey kicked her shin lightly and Eden relinquished it.

"I've changed my mind, the two of you on the same team is unfair." Eden glared at Jayse.

"Too late." He said with a wide smile. Journey tucked her hair behind her ear and blushed. Eden marveled at that. Anaiah removed his arm from around her to eat, but leaned over again to kiss her cheek before digging in.

The table fell into a void of conversation as they ate. As Eden's stomach filled with carbohydrates, she felt the heaviness of her night's work and lack of sleep. She gulped down more coffee and leaned on Anaiah's arm. He wrapped his arm around her again, and her heart soared in her chest. *C'mon caffeine, don't let me down.* She wished on her cup of coffee.

"Other than swearing at strangers online while you shoot them in game, what else do you do for fun, Jayse?" Eden asked.

"Watch movies on my TV, like a normal fucking person. And brew beer with my brother. Now, maybe I'll start going out and leaving the house more." He glanced over at Journey. "Though, I'm not sure I can handle the sunshine." Jayse placed his hand on Journey's on the table. Journey smiled. Eden mentally did a small victory dance.

"Maybe Jayse can watch America's Next Top Model with you, Journey." Eden suggested.

"Not likely." Jayse fake whispered.

"Journey knows how to curse like a sailor with Tourette syndrome. Maybe she can play games too." Eden giggled.

"You could play with me sometime." Anaiah suggested to Eden. She looked up at his smile.

"Nah. I would need to work on my trash talk." She giggled. "I swear a lot, but I don't think my skills would match Jayse's."

"You're doing that thing you do when you're tired. You know, the thing when you won't shut up." Journey informed her. "Turn the crazy down a little, cookie." she made a hand motion like she's turning a knob.

"Sorry." She turned to look at Anaiah. "Am I being too chatty?"

He grinned at her as her eyelids drooped. "Not for me, but let me drive you home, sleeping beauty." She handed over her keys.

"Fine." She wondered to herself about the logistics of him getting home, but her eyes were betraying her, and she wanted to sleep desperately. Anaiah slid out of the booth and pulled out some cash.

"I got yours, Eden." He put some bills on the table before placing his hand on the small of her back.

"My hero." She turned and wished her friends well before she headed out with Anaiah leading her by the small of her back. She glanced back at them as she walked out the door and was surprised to see them making out.

"You look exhausted." Anaiah said as she slid into the passenger seat of her car. "You'd fall asleep at the wheel." He walked around to the driver's side and opened the door.

"I'm just a little sleepy. We could still hang out." She said as he fiddled with the seat to adjust it for his height. He clicked it all the way back and climbed into the driver's seat.

"I guess we will see if you can keep your eyes open." He laughed.

She managed to not nod off all the way home. When he killed the car, Eden decided to make her move before he had a chance to deem her too tired for her own good. She leaned into him with a passionate kiss. She slid a hand into his hair. His lips parted as she slid her tongue past them, claiming his mouth with hers. His hands pulled her into him hungrily and sent a rush of adrenaline through her. She was definitely awake now. Warmth filled her chest and she felt other parts of her come awake too. She slowly ran her hand down his chest, stomach and then, lower. Her mouth ravenous on his. When she felt him harden beneath her touch she gasped. He moaned in response onto her lips.

She whispered, her mouth hovering over his lips, "Come inside." She kissed him lightly, teasingly on the lips. Then she backed away and opened her door. He hesitated only for a second but was quick to catch up. He followed her up to her door and handed her keys to unlock the door when she held out her hand.

As she led him by the hand into her room, he stopped and said, "Eden, we don't have to..." She cut him off with a kiss and pulled him to sit on the bed. He pulled her closer to him and she climbed into his lap, straddling him. He kissed her deeply, his hands in her hair and gripping her around her hips. She broke the kiss for a moment, as she peeled away his shirt and discarded it. His mouth was on hers half a second later. She ran her hands over his smooth chest and wrapped them around to his muscular back. If she had any reservations about sleeping with him, they were long gone now. His hands stilled and he pulled back.

"Sugar, stop for a sec." He said as she leaned back in to kiss him again.

"What?" She said in a soft voice. She leaned away from him so she could see his face. He was looking her over with that serious face. Hearing him call her "sugar" with that deep southern drawl was not slowing things down for her. Her heart pounded.

"Why? I'm not drunk or too tired to make sense. I know what I want." She whispered in his ear as she tried to guess what could be wrong. "I want this. I want you." *Was she reading him all wrong? Did he not want her too?*

"That's fine, darlin'." He whispered back and kissed her cheek softly. He ran a soothing hand down her arm. "I want you too. But...I'm not, you know, prepared." He winced. And it dawned on her that he meant protection. *Where on earth did this great guy come from? Had he just wanted to spend time with her after breakfast? Not have sex?* Guilt stabbed through her. She had pounced on him without a thought for what he wanted.

"I'm sorry, I thought this was what you wanted. I just sort of threw myself at you." She whispered. Trying to keep her emotion from her voice.

He kissed her neck gently. "I do. Believe me, I would have stopped you if I didn't. But we can wait, right?" he said softly against the nape of her neck.

She turned her face to his and brushed the hair back from his face before she kissed his forehead. He stared up at her with pleading in his eyes.

"You really are a good guy, aren't you?" As she said it, he looked confused. She answered the question there. "You pay for meals. You try to protect me from drunken sex that I'll regret. You gave me space..." She didn't finish that thought. She didn't want to think about Cole right now. She went on, "You feel responsible about bringing and using condoms. You even hold doors for me. I didn't think guys like you existed." She looked at him with amazement. "How'd I get so lucky?"

He smiled. "Baby, I just try. I try to do the right things and be a better man. I don't know why women date those jackasses. Sometimes I think it's 'cause they don't know anything better. I grew up around guys like that. I never wanted to be like them." He sighed. "Did you want me to be a jackass?" He laughed a bit.

"No...I like you. I like this. Talking with you, laughing with you." She laid her forehead against his. "Seems too good to be real, if I am honest."

"I am holding a gorgeous woman in my arms who wants to have her way with me, tell me which one of us is dreamin' here, sugar." He kissed her collarbone.

She lifted his chin up and kissed him lightly. He moved his hands up to her face and neck and kissed her passionately. Feelings burned in her heart and in other, more worldly places too. Eden put her hands in his hair and returned his passion with her own. He traced a line of kisses down her neck.

"God, I want you." He whispered as he kissed her neck. "But it's not going to hurt to wait a bit, honey. You just decided I'm yours today and believe me, I want to be. I don't just want to be some guy you sleep with. I want more." He worshiped her with kisses across one shoulder, across the collar bones and up the other side of her neck. And Eden couldn't hold back the tear that rolled down her cheek. *I don't deserve this.* She thought to herself. *He's too perfect... too good.*

Anaiah looked up at her and noticed the tear. With a small swipe of his thumb, he wiped it away and planted a small kiss where it had been.

"I don't deserve a guy like you." Eden didn't mean to let it escape her thoughts, but it had in a whisper.

"What kind of men made you believe that?" He searched her face with his compassionate eyes. "I could tell someone hurt you." He caressed her face with his hand. "What happened the other day, at first, I thought you might still have had feelings for him. I wanted to give you space. But I just realized that just saying his name... it filled you with panic. That's what happened wasn't it?" She didn't meet his eye, just nodded her head. "Baby, you don't deserve a guy like that. Why would you ever think you do?" He caressed her against him in an embrace. Cradling her in his arms. Something icy cracked in her heart. As if the warmth of his embrace, his words, was melting its way into parts of her heart that she had shut away from everyone. Frozen in time from when it had been shattered before.

She couldn't bring herself to answer his questions. He was too good, too kind. She felt ashamed that she couldn't say that she'd always been a good person. How could she tell him that until now, she only believed that guys who were good and kind to women like this existed only in fiction like in movies and books. Her whole life, she never allowed herself to hope that someone would hold her like this and care about what she felt. So, she just let him hold her in silence, gently stroking her hair.

"Baby, you need sleep." he whispered with his face full of concern.

"Stay with me?" she tried to keep her voice from wavering.

"Yeah. I'll stay." He kissed the top of her head as she laid her cheek against his chest. They settled into bed, Eden snuggled up under his arm, tucked into his side. She breathed him in and laid her arm across his chest. Sleep came so easily with him holding her like this.

Eden was running, terrified. *How did he find me?* Her thoughts raced as fast as her heart pounded. She was outside, down the block from her house. Her only thoughts became a mantra repeating in her head: make it home, lock the doors, call for help. She repeated the words in cadence with her feet thudding on the pavement. She knew it wouldn't stop him from trying to get to her. He would keep trying to get in. Her lungs ached and her legs burned from running. *I'm not going to make it.* She reached the front door, finding it locked. *KEYS! Where are my keys?* There was no time for her to think. She took off running down the block. It was pitch black between the streetlights. No moon illuminating the streets before her. She could hear the thump of her blood thrumming in her ears. Her heart was racing. She heard her sneakers slapping the pavement as she ran and the heavy huff that was her breathing. She turned down Greenwood Street toward the hospital. *If I can make it to the emergency room, they can help me.* She heard the heavy rhythmic footfalls behind her. He was catching up to her. Fear made the hairs on her arms stand up. She pushed her legs as fast as they would go. She was almost there. Twenty yards or so. Ten yards. FIVE. She pushed herself as the automatic doors opened so slowly and she slid through them. She panted and tried to yell, "Help me. Help me. He's trying to kill me." The waiting room was empty, no one was at the glass windows to assist her. She tried the doors to the main hospital, but they were locked. She beat on them and cried and begged for help.

"EDEN!" Her name broke the dream and she gasped for air as she opened her eyes. Anaiah was crouched over her in her room with a worried look. "Are you okay?"

She felt the tears roll down her face as she reached out to him, and he hugged her to himself. *Thank God, it was a dream.*

"Eden, honey, are you alright? Talk to me." He stroked her hair as she held him silently. "What were you dreaming? You were crying and you kept saying 'help me.'"

"I was being chased." She whispered. "I'll be okay. It was just a nightmare." Her voice broke when she said, "I'm so glad you are here." She wiped her face and breathed in slowly. She felt like an idiot; She was just starting to date this guy and here she was clinging to him because of a nightmare. "I'm so sorry. This is too much, isn't it?" She shook her head.

He looked her in the eyes and touched her cheek. "No. It's okay. Really. I understand. When you see some of the things I've seen, you have some pretty bad ones. Are you sure you're okay? You're still shaking sweetheart." His sweet southern accent put her a little more at ease.

"I'll be okay. I'm sorry I woke you up." She said softly.

"Don't be. It's almost time for you to take me home anyway." He brushed her hair back and kissed her gently. He held her for a little while longer, until the shaking and tears had stopped completely. He gave her another sweet soft kiss before she slid out of the bed to dress for work. She quickly cleaned her face and applied a small amount of makeup. He watched her carefully as she drove him home. When she pulled up to his apartment, he invited her in to keep him company while he got ready for work. She didn't want to admit that she wasn't quite ready to be out of his steady, calm presence yet. She agreed to come in for a chat with him.

"You want to talk about it?" He asked from his room while putting on his uniform. She sipped coffee from the kitchen island just on the other side of the door. She was still pretty shaken up about the dream, but she really didn't want to pull him into her drama. She was surprised he hadn't bailed on her bullshit yet.

"No. It was just a dream. Sorry, I should have warned you about that. It's been a minute since I had someone in my bed when that happened." She sipped her coffee at the implication and made a face she was glad he couldn't see conveying her thoughts. *A minute? More like a year! Damn! No wonder you are throwing yourself at him.*

"You have them a lot?" He stepped into the doorway, buttoning up his shirt and giving her a look, she had decided was now his "worried about the crazy girlfriend look." She shifted her expression to neutral.

"Yeah. I didn't have a pleasant childhood," She paused to consider, "Well, adulthood hasn't been great, either; I have nightmares sometimes." She watched him as he put all the pieces of his uniform together. He placed his radio on his belt and pulled the cord around to clip the speaker part to his shoulder. He stepped over to her perch on his barstool.

"Oh, Eden, I'm sorry. I know what that's like." He touched her cheek and kissed her softly. "I'm here if that helps."

"It does." She smiled. "I just don't want to burden you with my crap. If I cried about every crappy thing that happened to me, I'd just be a puddle of tears. I'd rather just be happy with how things are going now. Here. With you."

"I'm happy I'm here with you too." He kissed her again. "But if we don't leave soon, I am going to be late." He walked her to her car. "Have a good night at work. Text me on your lunch." He called out after her.

CHAPTER SIXTEEN

T he last two weeks had been filled with sweet text messages and phone calls between Eden and Anaiah. She now woke every day to his charming drawl via phone call. Even though she woke up every day smiling, she hadn't invited him to spend the night again and he hadn't asked. They were taking it slow, building something real.

He'd been busy with work, and she had distracted herself by starting some research in occult books. She read anything online that had some sort of credibility and checked out a couple of books from the local library.

They hadn't been able to see each other except for his weekly grocery run. It had been tortuously chaste as he didn't want her to get into trouble at work. He had stolen one too brief kiss in the parking lot before her shift three days prior, and Eden had been longing for more since. He had sent her a few shirtless pictures that drove her a little crazy but nothing wilder than that. Selfies of him in uniform were almost as hot. She'd kept her own selfies she sent to him relatively mild as well. Only a little cleavage here and there.

They usually shared Friday nights off, but Anaiah had worked overtime last Friday due to wildfires. Springtime in Texas meant lightning, wind, and dry grass. This apparently was a perfect formula for raging fires. Work had been brutally busy for him. For the last several days, he seemed to only work, sleep, and eat. He sent her pictures of the sunset, of himself in the rig, and texted or called her when he could. Friday had come yet again, and Anaiah informed her that he was taking the night off and had plans for them.

Eden dressed for the warm April evening in a white cotton handkerchief dress covered in blue flowers. As she finished up her makeup, a text notification from Journey lit her phone. Journey wanted Eden's opinion. '*Too early to sleep over at Jayse's place?*'

Eden texted, '*Sexy time with him yet?*' No matter the response she received, Eden would answer the same. She was just being nosy and using this as an excuse to ask.

Her phone dinged again, '*Not yet...no judging, hoe. Considering sleeping there in the morning but I don't know if we are gonna fool around or not.*'

Eden considered. '*Do what you want, man. Anaiah slept after breakfast a few weeks ago, but still no sex. Maybe tonight? I'm no expert. I've had three boyfriends, counting him.*'

'*Well, when it comes to guys, I'm just as clueless as you.*' Journey texted back.

Eden startled at the knock on the door. Out of habit, she peeked out the blinds to see who it was, despite knowing Anaiah was coming.

"Hey, gorgeous." Anaiah drawled as she opened the door. She sighed internally. When she was with him it was as if she could finally breathe suddenly, even though she never knew she was holding in a breath. Some ever present ache was soothed by that sweet southern drawl.

She tiptoed in her flats to kiss him. His hands steadied her by bracing her hips. He leaned in to meet her, kissing her with a slow but passionate determination. Was it her imagination that he was holding back something; like he's afraid she was going to shatter if he held her too tight? She pulled back and whispered, "Are we going to do this all night, because I could."

"We could try, but I don't think I could keep up my strength. I'm starving."

"You're always starving." She laughed. "There are starving children in Africa who say they are hungry less than you." He laughed as she closed and locked the door.

"One of these days it's going to catch up to me. I need to hit the gym more." He patted his flat stomach.

"Where are we eating?" She asked as she slid into his car.

"It's a surprise." His eyes glistened as he raised his eyebrows as if to say, 'are you impressed?' He drove toward the edge of town. She wondered if they were headed to the next town over, but instead he turned down the road toward the lake. He continued past the public areas of the lake and turned onto a private drive.

"Are you taking me into the woods to murder me and ditch my body?" She joked.

"Not today." He winked and explained, "One of my buddies at the station, his family owns this property. He let me use the place." He said in his calm, deep drawl. Sunset approached as they pulled up to a gazebo. There were candles lit on a table and on the ledges in the gazebo. The view is breathtaking and yet simple. The sun was setting over the lake and they had a perfect view from this cliff edge. She noted the wine bottle on ice, two glasses, and music playing softly from a little wireless speaker. She pulled out her phone to take a photo of the beautiful landscape. She snapped the photo.

"Here." Anaiah grinned as took her phone from her hand. He turned them around with the Sunset behind them. He pulled her back close to his chest and kissed the top of her head before snapping a picture of the two of them in front of the vibrant sky. "Gorgeous." He looked down at the photo on her phone when he handed it back.

"Yeah, that view is breathtaking." Eden said as she tucked her phone back in her purse.

Anaiah shrugged. "Sunset is nice, but you are the most breathtaking thing in the picture." Anaiah led her by the small of her back to her chair. He pulled it out for her. *Always the perfect gentleman.* He poured her a glass of wine before he reached into an insulated bag. From it, he pulled a covered tray of appetizers. He set them on the table and took the seat across from her. She was speechless. She could hardly take her eyes off him even to look out at the colors of the sunset reflecting off the glass-like top of the lake.

"I... I don't know what to say." She sighed.

"Well, let's say grace, 'cause I wanna eat, honey." He laughed. She bit into one of the savory tarts. He confessed that the appetizers were store bought. While he could cook and had prepared the rest of the meal, mini quiche was outside of his wheelhouse. He also admitted to eating a quarter of the appetizers after he had warmed them in the oven. The sweet wine was almost too easy to drink. *Dangerous.*

"What is this?" She asked and took another sip. "You should know that if it's not some cheap wine from my store, I wouldn't recognize it. I like this, it's fruity."

"I remembered you said you like craft beer and sweet wines. So, I got some from the local vineyard. This is a blackberry one." He showed her the label. "Got a peach white wine too."

"Okay, other than the fact that you could cost me millions in groceries, what's the drawback with you?" She wondered and swirled the wine in her glass. She knew there had to be a catch somewhere.

"I'm no angel." He shrugged with an easy smile. "I just try. And I love to see you smile." His face drew up into a serious expression, "I talk in my sleep. That's one thing." He winked at her and drank from his glass. She giggled.

He brought out the main dish of rosemary lamb chops with a side of roasted potatoes and carrots. The meat melted in her mouth. It was an effort not to gorge herself, because he'd promised that there was dessert.

"I'm impressed. You're a great cook. I usually throw veggies with whatever meat I have in the oven with some seasonings and olive oil. You actually know how to cook like a real adult." She giggled.

"Well, I am a real adult." He smiled at her. "I cook a lot for the guys at the station."

"I've been on my own for three years now and I still don't always feel like a real adult." She laughed. The thought flooded in, *it's because you've pretended this whole time. It's just now that you are an actual adult.* And she stared down at her plate.

"What's wrong, sugar?" He noticed her fallen expression.

"Nothing." She realized what was really bothering her, she told him, "It's just...my life has never been this good. Good things usually come with a pretty big price, and as happy as I am right now, I am just sort of waiting for the other shoe to drop." She noted his furrowed brow. "I don't just mean you. I have a decent place, a decent job, friends, and you..." She stared at him, half filled with desire and half filled with terror that something terrible was going to come along and rip him away from her. *Is this what falling in love feels like? Like I'd be incomplete without him somehow?*

"Sweetheart, you know you can tell me about it? About whatever made you so scared to be happy. I promise that I am not going to hurt you." He set his glass down. "At least, I can promise that I will try not to hurt you."

"I know." She sighed and ate a carrot. "Maybe later. I just want to enjoy being happy with you right now."

"Me too." He took a bite and smiled at her. As they ate, he recounted his busy week. He'd had to work in the surrounding counties too. There have been a lot of accidents, wildfires, and the like. It wasn't unusual with the weather warming up, but it had meant long shifts for him. Sometimes he worked twenty-four to thirty-six hours straight.

Eden found herself wondering if all the horrors he saw at work would allow him to handle all the supernatural hell surrounding her. If he could fall in love with her and actually know all of it. And despite knowing, if they could talk about his day like this for years to come. If they could be like a normal couple who talk about work and make each other dinner and joke about little things that only the two of them laughed at. As much as she has run from life, she found herself wondering if he could be what she ran to.

He brought out the dessert, which was a chocolate mousse. He proudly declared that he made it from scratch. She made a small noise that made him quirk an eyebrow when she tasted it. She blushed at his mischievous grin. After dessert, he opened another bottle of wine and held her hand across the table. He listened to her complain about the week's crazy customers and talk about her friends at work. He listened to details about Journey and Jayse's new relationship and smiled at her like she was some sort of treasure.

The song changed on the speaker. Anaiah stood up and pulled her to her feet. "Dance with me darlin'." He pulled her close to him and she took in the scent of him: cedar, rosemary, and sandalwood. In her flats, her head rested in the middle of his chest as he danced with her. He leaned down and kissed the top of her head as he swayed her back and forth in the little gazebo. She could hear his heartbeat strong and fast in his chest. *Could he possibly be nervous?* He pulled her back and spun her a bit like a little ballerina before he pulled her back into his arms. The sun was set, and the candlelight from the table glowed softly in their little bubble of happiness. The tealights had already guttered. The starlight alone left the night dim under the new moon. She lifted her chin to meet his gaze as he smiled down at her.

"Getting chilly?" he rubbed his hands down the goose bumps on her arms.

"Yeah." She whispered.

"Wanna go someplace warm and cozy?" His eyes held a flirtatious promise. Intrigued, she nodded. He lifted a candle from the table and took her hand in his. He led her through a small patch of woods. The walk wasn't too difficult through the low grasses in her flats, but Anaiah handled it with much more agility than she did. She tripped once or twice, but Anaiah would pull her close, steadying her.

The woods cleared and the candlelight illuminated the front of a small cabin. Anaiah pulled a key from his pocket and guided her into the living room. He lit glass lanterns on the mantle and built a small fire in the fireplace. Eden set her small purse down next to the couch as she watched him in awe.

"Is that better?" He said as he pulled her close to him. She nodded. She had no words. All this, for her. He whispered in her ear, "It's been hell to keep my hands off you. You are so beautiful." He leaned in and brushed his mouth against hers. His slow but determined kisses built with passion.

"Do you know how much I've wanted to do this for the last two weeks?" She whispered back to him. Her hand went to his hair and his hands started moving from the small of her back out to her hips and up toward her breast. She wrapped her arms around his neck and back, pulling him closer as she felt the desire in her stir.

Their mouths roved over each other hungrily as his hands were sweeping under her dress and up under her legs. He picked her up effortlessly, holding her close to him and carried her as he sat on the large sofa across from the fireplace. He hadn't stopped kissing her neck and lips the whole time as she straddled his lap on the sofa. She unbuttoned his shirt and slid the fabric open to smooth her hands over the warm soft skin and hard muscle of his chest. She marveled at the firelight flickering off his tattoos and glowing in his warm light brown eyes. She leaned in and kissed the tattoo on his chest as his hands slid over her body under her dress. She kissed her way up his neck and meeting his mouth, he devoured hers. His hands grabbed greedily at her ass, tracing her panty line with his fingers. He moved one hand up deftly between the fabric of the dress and her skin where he found the clasp of her bra.

"Yes." She whispered in response to the question in his eyes. His large hand conquered it immediately and his hands grazed over her skin toward his prize. Impatiently, she pulled her dress and bra over her head, discarding them on the floor. In the soft light of the fire and lanterns, Anaiah surveyed her near nakedness. She worried briefly about what he might have seen in this light. What scars would have been visible to him? What flaws could be found with her form that would make her too broken for him?

After a moment of staring at her in awe, he looked her in the eyes and breathed, "God, you're perfect." He pulled her mouth back to his. He slowly kissed his way down her neck to her chest. His tongue grazed over her nipple and noises beyond her control escaped her lips. She ground her hips forward into him. She felt him there, solid against her. The barrier of his pants and her underwear were the only thing between them. All she wanted in that moment was to remove those barriers, to show him how much she wanted him. All of him. She wanted every part of this perfect man. *And my god, that was terrifying.*

She slipped his blue button-down shirt off his shoulders and down his arms. She gave him a few more kisses on the lips then pushed herself away to stand. She slipped her shoes off and slid down her last remaining piece of clothing. She saw the desire in his eyes as they roved over her bare body before him. He kept his gaze locked on her, as his hands deftly unclasped his belt and unbuttoned his pants. She dropped to her knees and helped him pull his pants off. He kicked his clothing aside.

"Come here, baby." he whispered as she knelt before him. She reached up to him from where she knelt between his legs. He took her hand in his and kissed it. He started to pull her gently toward his face and she shook her head teasingly as she bit her lip.

"I want to taste you first." She said quietly. She gave him a playful glance. "Would you like that?" Her eyes fell to the considerable length of him. There was nothing small about him from his towering height to his massive warm hands, to his rippling muscles, and now, she saw that he was indeed proportional in this aspect too. She licked her lips in anticipation.

"Baby...yes. Yes, I would." His breath seemed to hitch at her gaze over him. She leaned over his lap. With delicate flicks of her tongue, she licked the tip of his member. He let out a moan. She grasped him in her hand and slid her mouth over the tip of him, sucking gently. She stroked him as she sucked and licked.

"Eden, that feels amazing." he watched her, running his hand over her hair. He caressed her face. She stared straight into his eyes as she took him deeper into her mouth while she stroked him with her hand. A low growl-like moan rumbled through him. He encouraged her, told her what he liked, told her she was gorgeous, and that she made him feel incredible. He said all of this between his moans of pleasure. She felt for once like a goddess to be worshiped and he was giving her due praise.

His growling moans echoed in her. Desire overwhelmed her. She couldn't bear the ache between her thighs, which threatened to consume her. She needed him. As she climbed up into his lap, his hands and mouth roved over her. She reached for him to finally slide him into the place she wanted him most, but he grabbed her wrist before she guided him in. Her eyes shot to his. She found his face soft, but his eyes pleading.

"In my pocket," He whispered. She nodded in understanding. She bent over and grabbed the tiny packet and opened it. She slid it over him, feeling his throbbing desire in her grasp. He swore as she swiped her hand over him, and he licked at her throat. Slowly, she guided him into her core. He let her set the pace, taking him into her slowly. His breathing was ragged as she slowly raised and lowered herself onto him, allowing herself to open to him a little more with every single slide back into her. Until he was fully seated into her. He kissed her passionately as he held her hips there for a moment and she savored every sweet inch of him filling her.

"You feel so perfect." His fingers trembled as he gripped her hips.

"God, I can feel every inch of you. I want every inch of you." She breathed out as she began to move her hips again. Her breath caught. He was patient, attentive. He waited for her to move with him. Her emotions were intense, but she could feel his desire, his affection radiating from him. She'd never felt it before, someone else so intense with emotion like this. It was beautiful and warm. His hands on her body, his mouth on hers, him moving within her, all of it pulsing with his intent. His every stroke was like a declaration of his affection and adoration. His touch spoke of his absolute rapture and joy. She felt compelled to cry, to sing, to shout out everything she was feeling, but all that came from her was a deep cry of ecstasy. Their faces separated only by a breadth of a whisper, he kissed her softly, sweetly between thrusts. When she cried out her pleasure as she rode him, he smiled that wonderful, charming smile.

"You're so sexy when you do that." he whispered to her.

"It just feels so...so...OH MY GOD...amazing." She moaned back. They moved together, his hands guiding her body in sync with his. "Oh, Anaiah. Oh, God." Then she lost the ability to form words, just breathy syllables. He took her over the top and she was screaming in pleasure.

He kissed her deeply again after her climax and she responded by passionately pulling him into it and further into her, as she drove her hips into him. He slowed their pace and moved his kiss down to her collar bone. He had very nearly stopped what he was doing.

"Is something wrong?" She whispered in response to his change.

"No," he sighed. Then, he laughed softly. "I don't want this to end just yet, and what you did just then almost put me over the top." He whispered in her ear.

"Ah." She said quietly. She kissed his lips lightly. Then she traced his lips with her tongue. He kissed her impatiently. He wrapped his arms around her and moved to lay her gently on the couch. He repositioned himself over her, taking time to kiss her all over her breasts. Licking, sucking and driving her utterly mad until she was very nearly ready to come again. He slid himself slowly back inside of her keeping the pace slow and deliberate. She savored every inch with each thrust as he ran his hands over her.

His voice was low and husky as he stared into her eyes, "Your eyes are gorgeous." He panted. He ran his hand over her body again, "I love the way your skin feels. So soft. So warm. Especially here," He licked that spot at the nape of her neck then kissed it. He opened his mouth over her neck again and bit down softly, sucking gently and then kissing it again. She cried out at that. He stared into her eyes intently as he continued to move in her, pulling her closer to that edge. "I could stare into your eyes for eternity." He breathed out.

She pulled him into a kiss so deep it nearly hurt. She could feel the fullness within her building again. He placed his large warm hands under her shoulders. He held her close to his body as she felt him quicken his movements. As the dam of pressure within her was about to burst again, he moaned into her ear that he was about to explode as well. They rocked as they reached the peak together both crying out. She shivered with ecstasy as she felt the throbbing pulse of him within her. He stayed still over her, kissed her gently as they panted and waited for their hearts to stop racing.

"That was incredible." he breathed heavily. He rested his forehead against hers with his eyes closed.

"You are amazing." She whispered.

"No, you." he said, cradling her. "You were amazing."

"You set the bar pretty high for the first time." She giggled. She pushed back the hair that clung to the perspiration on his face.

"I aim to please, sweetheart." He kissed her forehead. "And you..." He kissed again. "What you can do with that mouth. I wasn't sure I was going to be able to hold off much longer." He mumbled with his mouth still against her forehead and kissed it again.

"I'm glad you liked it, but isn't that pretty much a given?" She tipped her chin up and pecked him on the lips.

"What? That all men like getting blown? Probably so." He chuckled.

"I mean, isn't getting that pretty much a given?" She raised an eyebrow. He looked at her with confusion.

"No," he said. "Baby, you don't have to do that if you don't want to. I don't expect it."

"Oh." She said softly. *He really is a different kind of guy.* His brow was furrowed with worry. "I wanted to." Her voice was soft as she took in his wary expression in his eyes. "I wanted to make you feel good." She smiled. "Seemed like you really enjoyed it." Her eyes glittered.

"Mmm, you did good, sugar." He brushed her hair back from her neck and placed a few more kisses there.

"Is there a powder room in this cabin?" She wondered aloud, as nature's call made itself known.

"Yeah, the whole place has electricity and plumbing, but I thought this would set the mood." He laughed.

"Ooh...up for a shower?" She wiggled her eyebrows at him.

"Sure. I may walk like a newborn deer though." He laughed as he sat up and she rolled off the couch to her feet.

She located the bathroom in the direction he pointed out. A few minutes later, she had the shower running and he joined her in the steamy water. They started getting each other clean, but quickly started getting dirty again. Eventually, when the warm water started running low, they abandoned the shower. They found the towels and Eden started looking for her clothes to get dressed again.

"I've got the cabin for the night, if you want to stay with me." His eyes were so hopeful it made her chest ache.

She smiled at him and said, "I didn't bring anything to sleep in."

"Well, I'm sure we can work something out." He stepped closer to her with a towel wrapped around his waist.

They spent the rest of the night kissing and fooling around. She sent Journey a proof of life text message and told her where she was staying. She fell asleep in his arms sometime that night and awoke the next day, alone in bed. It was a jarring feeling waking up alone, naked in a strange place. She had forgotten where her dress had ended up the night before. In the daylight, strutting about a strange place naked in search of Anaiah seemed odd, so she wrapped the sheet around herself. She checked the bathroom, living room, and kitchen. As she started up the small flight of stairs to the loft in the pitched part of the ceiling, she heard Anaiah's deep voice in a hushed tone. She peeked up over the landing. She heard Anaiah's voice clearer.

"Father, please." He whispered. "Let her be the one. Let her love me like I love her. Give me the strength to be the man she needs. And help me show her your love through my love. Amen."

Her heart hammered in her chest as panic settled in. She didn't want him to see her spying on him there. She slunk back down the steps, into the bedroom. She was unsure if she should be happy that he talked to God about her, and said he loved her, or if she should run screaming. The fact that he was religious at all made her feel trapped and scared. He had told her he was spiritual, but she had not fully grasped what he meant.

She ducked back under the covers in the bedroom. Unsure of what to say, if she needed to say anything. Eden decided in the end to pretend she had just woken up when he came in with coffee a few minutes later.

Anaiah had been so perfect. Too perfect. She sipped the coffee and wondered if this was the catch. The one thing she didn't know how to talk to him about. Well, not the ONE thing. She had a whole lifetime of things she was hiding from him because she was too afraid to show him all the terrible, ugly things about herself. Eden the liar, Eden the thief, Eden who made excuses for all the terrible things she had done to escape her life. She smiled at him over her coffee. He could keep this secret until he was ready to share it. She couldn't say when she would be able to share her secrets. Or if she ever would be.

CHAPTER SEVENTEEN

E den had to wait three agonizing days to talk to Journey face to face at work. Texting all the thoughts in her head was daunting. Instead, she spilled the details of her date with Anaiah while stocking housewares. She told Journey about how it had been perfect. How he was seemingly perfect. So perfect that she didn't trust it.

"Generally, life tends to suck for most people." Journey told her. "Yours, apparently, more than most, but no, Eden, happiness does not have to come at a cost."

Eden shook her head. "It's not supposed to, but it always does. There always seems to be this trade off. What's the catch?"

Journey thought for a moment before telling her, "This guy really seems like a great guy. You've given him ample opportunity to bolt. Maybe the clincher is that if you really care about him, you are going to have to tell him everything. He has had the decency not to google your name yet. I'd get that shit out in the open before he finds it."

Eden's utter disapproval was plain on her face, and Journey, being the friend she was, laughed out loud at it. Eden debated internally about telling her about the prayer the next morning. *Nah. I'll save it.*

"Journey, the sex was…" Eden paused to find the words. She struggled to find a way to describe it without sounding sappy and stupid.

"Oh, was it horrible?" She stopped stocking and stared at Eden with an amused look on her face.

"No." Eden made a surprised face. "It was awesome. Not just good. Like…crazy intimate and passionate and like…" Eden marveled at this thing she never knew sex could be. Hot, powerful, fun, yes. But not like this.

Journey's giggle stirred her from her thoughts as she said, "So it was like really making love? Like because you love someone, not just getting your rocks off?" She continued to giggle at Eden's annoyed expression.

"Okay, fuck you. My ex sucked. And sex was..." Reflexively her eyes started to tear up. "Not always fun..." Her shoulders slumped. "Sometimes it was good...but I've never felt like that." She looked away and tried to dry her eyes.

"Oh damn." Journey's expression shifted to concern. "Now I see why you are so scared of this stuff. This guy cares about you, E. Maybe he's someone you can trust to know all of you. You know?" Journey offered a hopeful shrug.

Journey spent the rest of the night trying to quietly tell Eden some details of her and Jayse's relationship. They'd been friends for a while, so they are taking things sort of slow to work out exactly what they want.

"You guys slept in the same bed that night though?" Eden asked. Journey blushed, a lot. Eden hid her smirk and stared at Journey. Journey did not blush, Journey deflected. And lately, Journey had blushed ever so slightly around Jayse, but this. This full-face redness? This was not her friend's norm.

"What happened, Journ?" The smirk creeped into her voice anyway.

"Ok, I didn't want to have it compared to your night of romance and wonderful love making." She stared straight at her task at hand, stocking diligently. "I was going to tell you it happened a different time."

"So, was it...good?" Eden Inquired carefully, as if picking her way through landmines. Journey probably wanted to stab her. Journey sighed.

"Oh my god..." she breathed out quietly. "It was the best fucking thing on earth." She said in an excited whisper and turned to smile at Eden. "Dude, Jayse is cute and all with all his clothes on. He's not built like your himbo boyfriend, but he does it for me. Damn, with clothes off, the man is the most delicious piece of meat on the planet. And it makes me feel so fucking weak, because dammit all...I would do anything he asked me to in bed." She whispered. "I am letting a man steal my power from my vagina. Just like my mother said they would." She only seemed to be half joking.

"Journey, what the hell are you talking about?" Eden screwed up her face in confusion.

"Ya girl is a badass, we all know it. Jayse knows it. Says it is sexy...But in that bed, I am his delicate flower. He touches me and it all melts away and I let him call the shots. E, I teared up when he saw me naked and told me I was lovely. I don't fucking cry. I called him pet names. He makes me feel pretty and delicate and I fucking love it...but I don't want anyone else to know it. Okay." Journey's eyes stared in pleading for understanding.

"We are so fucked up." Eden giggled.

"Yep. Too broken little peas in a pod." She grinned.

The topic of conversation veered away from amazing experiences in bed and toward plans for the next hang out at Journey's place in a few weeks. During their breaks, it was a concerted effort on Eden's part to look Jayse in the eye and not wiggle her eyebrows at him to tease about what she knew. She knew their teasing had limits and Journey might punch her if she crossed them so soon. Eden bit her tongue and let Kris steer the conversation to brewing supplies.

After the shift ended and Eden approached her front door, she noticed the card and flowers on her doorstep. It was a simple arrangement of sunset roses in a small vase. He had remembered her favorite flower. They had had that conversation weeks ago in the store. She grinned like a love-struck fool as she picked up the flowers and unlocked her door. She placed them on the coffee table.

She peeled open the eggshell-colored envelope and removed the card. A squirrel with a goofy grin was on the front with the caption 'I'd be nuts without you' underneath the picture.

Handwritten inside was a note from Anaiah: "I know people don't normally send thank you cards for an evening of intimacy, but when it was that mind blowing, I couldn't stop myself. I can't wait to see you again and to hold you in my arms. -Anaiah Parker"

Eden was floored by this gesture. Not just the flowers and the card or even the thought behind them. She'd mentioned the roses in passing while he picked out flowers for the wife of his station chief. It had been that woman's birthday. She had helped him select a completely different bouquet that night, but he had remembered her preference. He was either the most thoughtful man on earth or he knew how to keep the head coming. Maybe it was both. She smiled at herself as she stripped off her clothes and stepped into the bathroom for a shower.

"Hey babe," a dark, familiar voice called out casually from behind her. *No.* She froze at the sound. As recognition of that voice calling her 'babe' again hit, her stomach dropped. She hadn't heard it in so very long. Only in her dreams. Her heart all at once filled with agony, terror, and anger. Her chest heaved with irregular breaths. One word had pulled at memories she had buried. Buried as he should have been because Eden knew for a fact that he was dead.

She wrapped a towel around herself and turned to face him. *Fucking ghosts.* Only, as she eyed him, she realized that he wasn't the normal flimsy looking ghost. He looked alive and well. He stared at her with an icy glare down the hallway. He regarded her with a cool calm. The calm before the storm that usually ended in him over the top of her with violence promised.

"Cole." She said quietly and walked toward where he stood in the living room.

"Miss me?" He smirked. His appearance made her more uneasy by the second. She glanced at the couch next to him. To her phone laying there on top of her purse. But who would she call for help? Cole couldn't be arrested for breaking in. He was dead. He followed her gaze and his smile spread, realizing the conclusion she'd come to. *That fucking smile.* Only Cole could grin in a way that sent chills through her blood.

"Not really...Why are you here?" She said shakily.

"Oh, didn't you hear? I died, babe." His voice was low and seething with disdain as he looked her up and down.

"I heard. You don't look dead." She said slowly, backing away instinctively. Something was off. This didn't feel like a usual ghostly encounter. Interactions were much less direct with spirits. *He's dead. Anaiah told you he was dead. He can't be here unless he's a ghost.*

She took a steadying breath. Ghosts had never been able to harm her. Their touch was like ice but passed through her. Spirits could occasionally nudge objects but couldn't really affect her in any way. Why did this one fill her with terror? Because of their history?

"Ah. Confused?" His smirk remained plastered on. Like he had every advantage in the situation, like he always had when they were together. She nodded. "Thought so." He walked across the living room and stood a few feet from her. "You haven't got a clue. Oblivious to what is happening around you. No idea what I am or who I am...hell, you don't even know WHAT you are." The disappointment and veiled anger in his tone was so reminiscent of the days when they were dating. Of all the times he had smirked while telling her how worthless she was and berated her into believing that no one would want her. He was wrong, she reminded herself. She wasn't worthless. She'd worked hard to regain her confidence and like the person she saw in the mirror. She knew that the lies that he spewed at her then were a tool to control her.

Her eyes fell on the flowers on the table between them. Anaiah had wanted her despite what Cole had said. Anaiah's eyes flashed through her mind as she remembered his words. "What kind of men made you believe that... You don't deserve a guy like that." Something in her chest cracked at the thought. She felt her rage rising. Cole was dead already. He was a ghost. He couldn't hurt her. He didn't own her, not anymore. And she wasn't going to tolerate his bullshit any longer.

"Why are you here?" She snapped as her eyes snapped back to his face. "What do you want?"

He took a step forward and closed the distance between them. She refused to back down. He put his hand to her cheek. "Can't I just want to see you? For old times' sake?" She would not break. She would not let him see her cower in fear again. He lowered his face next to hers and ran his hand down her side possessively. His lips were less than an inch from hers. His touch was warm and real, not a cold haze like that of a spirit.

She forced herself to take a single step back and put a shaking hand on his chest. "That is over, Cole. Done." Her confidence built with each word. "I am seeing someone else. And even if I wasn't, I have no interest in fucking you for old times' sake." Her voice tried to shake on her, but she bit down on it and said it with all the venom she could muster. She still had no inkling of what was happening, why he seemed to be corporeal, in her house and not an apparition. She set her jaw and stared him down. She would be damned if some undead asshole was going to feel her up. *I left him once, and I can say no to him again. He can't hurt me.* She set her mind to match her body language.

Faster than her vision could recognize, his hands moved. She didn't realize what was happening until she was pinned to the wall with her feet dangling off the ground. His hand clamped around her throat as the other bit into the flesh of her upper arm, lifting her up. His fingers crushed into her, almost tearing at the bruising skin where he squeezed with such force. She choked and gasped for air, but none came. Only a garbled choking sound as she struggled.

"If that was all I wanted, I could take it." He growled at her. "If I wanted to fuck you, I would fuck you." He shook her slightly for emphasis. "You have as much say in that as before. I take what I want, and I do as I please. You are nothing but a toy for me to play with. And believe me, babe. Once I get tired of playing with you, I can just as easily break you." His eyes were a storm of rage and hate as his grip tightened on her throat.

Her lungs burned for air as her head throbbed. She knew that her face had turned purple. The pressure she felt there at the cut off supply of blood was immense. A combination of absolute terror and anger rang through her. She kicked and flailed, but it only increased the agony ripping into her. Hot tears rolled down her face as she tried to beg him to put her down. Her hands grappled with his arm, like an iron vice on her, completely unmovable. No voice could choke out of her mouth. The seconds felt like an eternity with the burning hard pressure in her face as her vision filled with black patches. She tried to keep staring him down, and her eyes pleaded for her life as she mouthed the word "please".

As she felt the world begin to fade, he released her, setting her down on her feet roughly. She coughed and gasped. Shuttering breaths wrung in and out of her in jagged heavy sobs. She bent over double as the tears flowed harder down her face. She had lost the towel in the commotion; it was out of her reach. She sobbed with each inhale and exhale, pain lancing through her throat.

"I am here to help you." His casual calm voice was a shock. As if nothing had happened. As if he hadn't just nearly choked the life from her.

She looked up incredulously. "What?" She croaked. He reached over to the towel and handed it to her. She forced herself to stand upright and wrap it around herself while still breathing raggedly.

"You are clueless. And because you...fascinate me, I've come to help you. I can't directly help you; that's not in my nature, but I can point you in the right direction." He pulled a card out of his pocket and placed it in her palm. He leveled his stare at her and got back into her face. "I don't need to harm you, but if you insist on behaving like a bitch, I can end this." He paused for her acknowledgement of his threat. She gave a slight nod to let him know she understood. "Go see the cambion, she will fill you in on some details. I'll return after. Do not disobey me on this. It will be worse next time." With that last threatening glare, he transformed into a black smoke that dissipated quickly with a popping sound.

Eden stared in disbelief for a few moments before she looked down at the card. It was a business card for a bakery called Selah's Sweets. Located in a town about thirty miles from here. The owner's name was Selah McGrath.

Eden made the decision to postpone her shower and try to get some insight as to what the fuck just happened. Eden grabbed her robe and wrapped it around herself. She cleared her aching throat and grabbed a glass of warm water to help soothe it.

Upon her first internet search, she looked up what the hell a cambion was. It yielded a listing for some electronics company, a book of mythology about half-demons, and some dungeons and dragons' websites also claiming cambions were the result of a human and demon getting it on. *That sounds delightful, let's take a trip to the half demon's bakery.* She rolled her eyes.

A search of Selah McGrath's name resulted in a search engine cluster-fuck that had nothing of value to offer her. Searching the name with the word cambion following it brought even more nonsense. The internet had failed to solve her problems. She would just have to go to Selah's Sweets and check it out later. Her neck and arm continuously throbbed with pain; she rubbed them as she headed to the bathroom to finally shower. Out of the corner of her eye, she caught a glimpse of herself in the mirror. She turned in horror. *HOLY SHIT! My neck and arm are fucking purple!* The area around her eyes was peppered with hundreds of tiny red dots from straining to breathe. Her eyes were bloodshot, and her under eyes were already darkening with a deep blue. It was April in north Texas; how the hell was she going to hide these bruises? She couldn't possibly use her clumsiness as an excuse for this. No one would buy that. Old patterns of thought began to snake through her mind: how to cover it, how to lie about it and make it believable. *What the hell am I going to do? Not to mention that talking and clearing my throat is like swallowing a fireball.*

She tried and failed to think of excuses while she showered. *I got mugged? Nope, the paramedic boyfriend would have heard about it. I got mugged and didn't report it? That just sounds stupid.* She could see the outline of his fingers in the bruises. She realized that nothing she came up with was going to be reasonable. *My dead ex-boyfriend showed up inside my house and strangled me with superhuman strength, all the while cryptically claiming to help me?* Even the truth sounded ridiculous.

As she dried herself off, she settled on the decision that this was just going to be one of those moments, like so many in her life, in which she would just have to tell the people who trusted her that she couldn't explain what happened. She dressed herself and got into bed. What would she say to Anaiah? The truth? *Do I want Anaiah to know about what I can see? Will he still want to be with me?* She was clueless. Cole had been right about that. Her throat burned as she tried to fight the tears that threatened to fall as she drifted finally into sleep.

In her dreams, Eden watched as the events of the night she met Cole unfolded. She had been waiting tables in Oklahoma City. She was a shameless flirt with all the guys when she waited tables to get better tips. When Cole came in at the end of the lunch rush, she did her same flirty routine. He flirted back like most customers. He was charming, handsome even. His blonde hair was swept back and longer on top. The underside was shaved down. Strong jaw with a clean-shaven face. He had dimples that she adored at first but grew to hate. A tall golden god, straight from Greek mythos had begun complimenting her, not just for her beauty and how grown up and mature she seemed. Like the young naive idiot she was, she ate it up.

Her shift ended as he was leaving so he offered to walk her to her car. She admitted that she didn't have one, so he offered to take her home. At the time, she had been so charmed by this gesture of goodwill. He was looking out for her, the streets could be dangerous he had said.

They had been hitting it off well on the ride to her co-worker's house where she had been renting a room. He asked her out. She was flattered and they agreed he would pick her up to go to another restaurant that night.

The entire night he kept touching her lightly in a way that made her want him to touch her more. He had the kind of smile that made you feel rewarded for getting to see it. By the end of dinner, they were making out and he suggested they go back to his place. She wanted to scream at the young girl in her dream. To tell the younger Eden to run. Of course, then, she'd been Evie to all she knew.

Just like it had happened in her past, Eden had slept with him on the first date. The reason she decided to never do that again. Never to attach herself so quickly to someone who could hurt her. In her dream, she watched all of it happen from outside of herself. Hovering above them on the bed. As she watched, she noticed he was saying things in a low gravelly voice that she couldn't quite understand. His body moved in an unnatural way that she couldn't pinpoint. Her eyes had been closed for most of it when it happened, but here she could see it all. The pained expression on her face when it began and how her tension eventually faded, and she enjoyed it. She watched the way he gripped her. Not with the gentle, yet passionate way Anaiah did. Cole grabbed her body with rough possession.

Eden felt sick. This was her first lover. Her introduction to intimacy. After the deed was done, she watched herself cradle herself against him and sleep in Cole's arms. As if he was some sort of knight in shining armor.

After her breathing evened out, Cole's eyes opened, and he rose from the bed. His shape transformed with sickening bone popping sounds from that of a normal man to more of a thin monstrous creature. Taller, with broader shoulders, his reptilian looking skin stretched thin over his body and wings of shadow and sinew emerged from his back. His mouth was a gaping maw of massive, jagged teeth. His glowing red eyes turned slowly and looked directly at Eden as she watched the dream play out. A low grating voice rose from that monster, "Now that you've seen my true form. Do as I have instructed." The implied threat was there. She would meet this monster beneath his skin if she failed to follow his instructions.

CHAPTER EIGHTEEN

E den woke drenched in sweat, despite the chill in her room. Her long messy curls stuck to her clammy skin. She glanced at the clock. It was only three in the afternoon, but there was no chance of more sleep after that nightmare. Five hours of rest, if you could call it that, would have to suffice. She pushed her aching body from the bed and stripped off her sweat drenched clothes. She dressed for work in a blue polo and denim pants. She managed to do something resembling a bun with her hair while trying to use her left arm as little as possible. She regretted raising it over her head immediately. Her makeup mostly covered the damage done around her eyes and face. She applied a coat of makeup over her neck. She surveyed her work, it was better, but she still looked like hell. She grabbed a three-quarter length sleeved shirt to cover the other bruise and added it to her outfit under her polo.

She decided to head over to Selah's Sweets. Might as well claim the demon destiny Cole wanted for her, she guessed. Better than being face to face with whatever he was. She grabbed her phone and purse and headed out the door.

She swore quietly at the glaring hot sun. Her voice was a mess. Pain was nothing new to Eden but hearing her rasping voice made her nervous for work. She drove the thirty-minute trip to the bakery in silence, stewing over the dream and the events from that morning.

She located Selah's bakery easily. It was a little shop front on the town square around the courthouse. As she opened the door to the bakery, she sensed an odd presence. She had felt something like it before but was unsure of where it came from. Ghost felt like an extra person in the room that didn't fit in. Sometimes they felt like nothing at all. But this. This gave her a queasy sort of feeling in her gut. A young woman with blonde hair looked at her anxiously from behind the counter.

"Selah, you should come out here." The small woman said. Through the swinging saloon style doors strode a middle-aged woman. She was around Eden's height and build. Just over five feet tall. Not skinny, but not rotund either, with some curves. The woman looked very motherly. Her frilly apron added to this image, along with her warm smile and chin length chestnut colored hair. Her skin was brown, Eden wondered if she was Latino by her features.

She caught sight of Eden and said, "C'mon back to the office." She turned to the blonde woman. "I'll be a little while. Don't disturb us." The woman nodded.

Nervously, Eden headed back to the kitchen and around a corner to a small office. There were two chairs in front of a computer desk against a wall.

'Have a seat." Selah motioned to the two identical office chairs. Eden sat in one. She took the other. "Who sent you?" Selah's tone was light.

"Cole Sparks." Eden said flatly. By the way Selah acted, Eden thought she had already known.

She nodded with recognition, "Honey, that's not his real name." She took out a piece of paper. "Don't say it out loud. There's power in the names of demons." She scrawled a name on the paper. "There, that's his name. Only use it if you wish to address him. To summon him." She sounded more like a mother telling her daughter how to make a casserole than delivering the news that Eden's ex-boyfriend was a demon. The name on the paper was written in all capital letters. AZAZEL.

"He's a demon?" Eden's mind raced with questions when she had seen that thing he had turned into. It was monstrous, but a demon? *Holy hell.*

"Yes, one of the eldest. Cast out of heaven with the other rebellious angels." Her smile was near cloying. So at odds with the news, she delivered.

"How do you know him?" Eden demanded.

"Well, dear. He is my father. He is father to a great many of us." Her grin had faded away into a more grave, sympathetic expression as she spoke.

"You mean the cambions?" Eden asked bluntly, trying to gain some sort of control over this situation. Over herself. *Cole was a demon. That explained a lot. And he had half demon children. Gross.*

"What is your name, honey?" Her soft gaze over Eden's troubled face did nothing to help with the turmoil inside her.

"Eden." Eden responded flatly.

"Eden, when I say he is father to most of us, I mean OUR kind. You and I are both cambions. Can't you feel that sickly pull in your stomach? That connection we feel. It's because we are of two worlds. We feel things others don't, see things others don't, are able to do things others can't. Sometimes, when you are of two worlds and you meet another, like us, you feel that sickly pull. Others have more of a magnetic effect." She gave Eden's hand a reassuring pat.

"I'm half demon?" Eden asked incredulously. "I can't be... I had two very religious parents. They would have never...with a demon." She shook her head and her voice started rising. The tears forming in her eyes threatened to fall. *What the hell am I? I had always felt different, but not human? My parents said I was demon possessed but this. A child of hell? It would explain why I'm different. Why I see the things I see...right? Being the child of a demon would explain it. Was I HIS child? Jesus Christ, I slept with him!*

"Eden, please calm down." Her voice was a calm but authoritative one. She patted Eden's hand again. "Now, listen. You are what you are. We can't change that. As far as your lineage, let me ask you a question. Do you have any unusual scars on you?"

"I have a lot of scars," She searched her memories for any scars that could be considered unusual, even for her. "There is one that is an odd shape, like a brand or something, just below my hairline on my neck. Why?" She failed to hold the tears back. She tried to think back to the day when protective services first questioned her about all her scars. She had felt it there on her neck before. When she was shown a picture of it at the hospital, it was the first time she had seen it. They said it looked like it had purposefully been carved into her. They wanted her to describe how she had gotten it. Eden didn't know. She had always been able to trace its outline with her finger as far back in her childhood as she recalled. She'd even been self-conscious about it because it was one of the few visible scars she had when she was fully clothed and wore her hair up.

"This is the sign of my father's children. The goat's head." She showed Eden her small scar on her wrist. "May I?" She motioned toward Eden's neck. She turned so Selah could see. "No. You are not one of my many sisters." Eden breathed a small breath of relief. She wiped her eyes. Selah offered her a tissue.

"Can you tell me who my father is?" Eden took the tissue and dried her eyes though she knew her make-up was a smeared mess.

"Eden, there is so much to tell you." She sighed. "You are already so overwhelmed. Too much at once can really be hard to take on emotionally. There are things you must learn about what you can do. When you are of two dimensions, things like magic, prophecy, and the like are open to us. I want you to come back next week. Around the time the bakery closes on Wednesday." She reached over and penciled in Eden's name on her calendar. "I can tell you more. Even start to teach you." She rubbed Eden's shoulder reassuringly. "I will research your scar before then. Take this, read through it. It will help you understand some background." She handed Eden a book from the desk.

Eden wanted to demand information, but Selah held all the cards right at this moment, and she wouldn't dare upset her. She felt so lost. She walked out past the counter and the shop assistant moved quickly in the other direction. Selah gave her a reproachful glare and then handed Eden a cupcake from the display. As if this was a completely normal thing to do. Comfort the demon spawn with a cupcake.

On the drive home, Eden contemplated running into the catholic church and scooping up a cup full of holy water to ward off Azazel. She had an empty Styrofoam cup in her car. Would it keep him at bay? Burn him? Would that burn her as well? Better to not risk it.

She ate the cupcake Selah gave her. The entire concept of that maternal woman who bakes cakes for a living being hell spawn just blew her mind. She wondered for a moment if Selah was someone's mother? Could half demons have kids? She mentally added the subject of half demon procreation to her list of questions to ask her new demon "fairy" godmother.

She was consumed with questions and lost in thought as she walked up to her front door. As she pulled her keys from her purse, she noticed her front door was ajar. She halted and surveyed the area. The door jamb was splintered; someone had kicked the door in. *Shit!* She lifted her phone and contemplated calling the local police. On the one hand, if she called them, they may dig up things on her that she would like to leave alone; this was a small town and rumors about her past were not something she wanted floating around. Her hesitance also stemmed from doubt about what a local police officer was going to do about this exactly. They would simply take down a report of what was missing, and nothing would probably come of it. The only valuable things she owned were in her purse right now, including her little laptop.

She leaned closer to the doorway and pushed the door open with her foot, careful to not touch or disturb anything. The door hung on by hunks of torn wood. From the doorway she noted that her living room was ransacked. Her couch cushions all over the place and they were even unzipped. Like someone was looking inside them for hidden treasure. Slowly, cautiously, she tiptoed through the house, from room to room. Every room was torn apart. All her belongings were strewn about the house. Some piled in odd collections, others seemingly flung about. Even her kitchen was a mess of broken dishes and emptied cabinets. In the middle of her bed was a bowl filled with odd items. Some sticks, a wad of some sort of herb or grass or something, some water, and like a giant "fuck you" candle on top of a shit cake was a used condom. *Fuckin' gross.* Around it was some random items that belonged to her. This was beyond fucked up. She was shaking with anger, frustration, and fear.

Deciding that the police would be able to give her validity when she had to call in so she could clean up this mess, she found the non-emergency police department's number online and dialed it.

A bored sounding operator answered it on the second ring. "Angelina Police Department, how may I help you?"

"Hello, my home has been broken into." Her gravely rasp grated searing pain down her throat.

'What is your name and address?" The dispatcher asked.

She gave them her information and sat on her porch steps to wait. She ran her hands over her face and growled in frustration. The last twenty-four hours had managed to block out the happiness she had felt for the last several days. Somewhere in the mess of her house, was the vase and flowers that Anaiah had dropped off earlier that morning. *Was it really just this morning?* As if thinking of Anaiah had summoned him, her phone rang loudly in her hand, startling her.

"Hey." Her voice croaked. Holding back more tears was taking an extra toll.

"Are you okay?" His voice was panicked.

"I'm having a shitty day." Admitting it aloud threatened to unleash the tears building in her eyes. That pissed her off even more. She had been crying off and on all day. Realization dawned on her, "So I'm guessing someone recognized my name and called you?"

"Yeah, my friend Sean's a cop. He sent me a text to give me a heads up. Were you sleeping when they broke in? Did you see anyone?" His voice dropped from his concerned but apologetic tone to a deeper one with a dangerous edge to it. Her chest tightened and she sat up a little straighter without meaning to.

"No. Actually, I wasn't even home." She took in a deep breath.

"I'm glad you weren't there, but what were you doing up, sugar?" His voice softened into his lovable drawl. She eased a bit at the calmer tone.

She sighed while deciding what she could tell him. "I had another nightmare. A pretty bad one. I couldn't sleep and I had an errand to run out of town. I came home to this mess." She opened her eyes again and blew out a frustrated breath.

"I hate that you had a bad day, but I am so relieved you weren't home." Anaiah said.

"You know, I am amazed that you aren't running screaming from me. I seem to attract the worst sort of chaos," She took a breath. "I'm calling in to work tonight. I'm going to try to get this mess cleaned up." She sighed.

Anaiah laughed a little. "Honey, I won't back down from a challenge. It took months of flirting to get a date out of you; I'm not giving up now." He was an angel. How on earth did she land a guy so sweet and wonderful? "I'm almost there." She looked up to see the police car turn the corner and Anaiah's car tailing it.

"Oh, I didn't know you were coming..." Anxiety poured over her. *What am I going to say about my neck?*

"See you in a sec..." Anaiah hung up as the cars parked in front of her house. Anaiah hopped out of his car first and strode toward her. "Hey sweet...HOLY HELL! What happened to you?" He ran over to her and crouched in front of her on the steps. Her tears fell and she swore under her breath. He looked her over. Her outburst at Selah's had removed or smeared most of her makeup. Her eyes probably looked worse than before. Anaiah reached out and gently touched her cheek.

"Eden, who did this?" He searched her face for answers. She had none. Nothing to say that would take that look from his face. The truth would probably send him running. She couldn't bear that. Not today. Not after everything she had learned.

"I can't tell you." she whispered and wished for what was probably the hundredth time that the pain of talking would go away. She couldn't even look at him. The sympathy and sorrow in his eyes were too much. It was going to make the crying worse.

"Why? You said you weren't here. Was it the same person who broke in?" His voice took on that same dark edge to it she had heard before. "Eden, tell me. I won't let them hurt you again." She flinched at his tone. She felt the sob that she tried to choke back rip through her. The more she cried, the angrier she became with herself. As always, her rage brought on more tears. She felt his hand tense against her cheek in response to her reaction.

"Ma'am, can you tell me anything about the break in, or the assault?" the officer said from behind Anaiah. She looked up at him, slightly thankful for anything to look at beside the sadness and menace building on Anaiah's face. The officer was wearing a navy-colored police uniform. He was a few inches shorter than Anaiah but had a similar build. He wore no hat on his dark blonde head. He held up a small clipboard and pen, expectantly waiting for her to answer.

"They aren't related." So painfully, Eden forced the words out loud enough for him to hear.

"Are you certain?" the officer asked. He eyed her curiously.

"Yes." She stared at the officer, determined not to see the look on Anaiah's face.

"Do you know the person who assaulted you?" the officer continued taking down notes.

"Yes." She saw Anaiah's jaw clench a little out of the corner of her eye. She couldn't help but look at him as he stared back furiously at her.

"Regarding the assault, ma'am, do you want to press charges?" The officer looked up at her expectantly.

"Of course, she fucking does, Sean." Anaiah snapped. The fury behind his eyes sent shivers of panic down her spine. His head dropped down when he noticed her eyes go wide with terror in reaction.

"No. I don't." She studied her hands in her lap. She knew the look of disappointment she would see if she looked back at Anaiah. She'd seen it on others' faces when she stuck things out time and time again with Cole. When she made excuses for him and accepted that it was the cost of his love. She couldn't bear to see it on him. "Sir, can we have a minute? Please." She looked up at Officer Sean. His eyes softened as he nodded.

"Sure. I'll head inside and inspect the damage." He walked past her while she stared down at her nails to avoid the look on her boyfriend's face.

"Anaiah, I will explain this," As she looked up, she made a sweeping motion with her hand in a circle around her face, "later. I need to deal with this," and she made another sweeping motion toward the house, "now. Like I said, I have had a shitty day." She said with a bit of a choked back sob.

"Baby, who hurt you?" The quiet of his voice made her heart ache. The anger in his eyes had faded and he just looked so sad.

"Please..." She leaned forward and kissed his forehead. "Later. Just stay here for me. Okay?" She stood up and went into the house. She could only hope that his patience with her would hold out. She walked through the house with Sean and gave him all the information she could. She called her landlord and he sent over a handyman to replace the front door. The dayshift manager at work hadn't been excited at the prospect of her calling in but she explained that the police were still there investigating, he had relented, pending her turning in a copy of the report as proof. Officer Sean and Anaiah talked on the lawn while the handyman made quick work of replacing the framing of the door and installed a new metal framed storm door.

She considered texting Journey but thought better of it. Eden would have to sort through what she was going to say. What she could reveal to her without weirding her out too much. She'd hung with her through knowing most of Eden's baggage, but would finding out that Eden was part demon be just a little too far for her to stretch their friendship? She stared out the front window at Anaiah and Sean as the handyman told her he would return the next day to paint the door frame.

What was she going to tell Anaiah? She had no clue, but she began bracing herself for the worst. It may not be tonight, but the closer he got to her, to truly knowing her, the more it was going to hurt when the other shoe dropped, and he decided to leave. As Sean pulled away and Anaiah walked up the steps to the porch, she stepped out of the new front door and asked him what time he had to be at work.

"I switched shifts." He stepped up to her and carefully folded her into his arms. "Can you tell me what happened, any of it?" He kissed the top of her head. "I lov...look, I care about you, Eden."

"What if I told you something that sounds too crazy to be true?" She looked up at him despite the pain. "Would you want to be with me if you thought I was crazy?" He gave her a confused look. "Look, I don't want to get dumped today. I don't think I could take it." She had to look away from the way he was gazing at her. Like he wanted to tell her that it was impossible for her to make him want to leave.

"I need a drink." She pulled away and went through the house to the kitchen. Anaiah followed silently. She found that only one of her wine glasses was unbroken, still sitting on the shelf. She pulled out a cheap bottle of Moscato from the fridge and poured a glass. She handed the glass to Anaiah and took a long pull directly off the wine bottle. He took a drink from the glass, watching her carefully. She took another pull from the bottle.

They started straightening up in the living room. He helped her get her couches back where they belonged. Anaiah flipped the coffee table back over to its position and carefully picked up the shards of glass from the broken vase. Eden picked up the roses, attempting to salvage them, but they were crushed and fell apart in her hands. Tears fell silently as she threw them into the trash can she carried around with her. She turned away from Anaiah and continued to work on throwing away broken knick-knacks from her end tables. They worked in silence only broken by his occasional asking her where to put something or if she wanted to talk about it. She didn't want to talk about it.

"You don't have to stay if you don't want to." She said in her quiet strained voice. "I'm okay. I mean, I'll be okay." She amended. She was far from okay.

"I'm not going anywhere, sweetheart. I'm making sure you're safe tonight." He said quietly.

"Thank you for the help." She stepped past him and moved to the bedroom.

He stilled before the bed. "What do you think this is all about?" He eyed her with a mix of caution and confusion.

"Your guess is as good as mine. Looks almost ritualistic compared to the rest of this." She shrugged. She picked it up and tossed the whole thing, bowl and all in the trash bag he'd been using. She stared for a moment at the completely shattered antique lamp. She'd glued it back together once before, but now it just seemed so utterly ruined. She felt it was symbolic of how well she'd been handling her new life. Something beautiful and new, smashed and shattered as soon as she started to enjoy it. She bent down with her dustpan and brush and swept the pretty little shards into the trash. She replaced her empty wine bottle with another from the fridge and drank.

They folded and separated clothes to hang back up in her closet. She needed more hangers as most of hers were broken. The more they worked, the more she drank. Thirsty and emotional, it seemed, was a poor combination for Eden. Somewhere in the middle of her third bottle, she tripped over something on the floor, and considered that she was a little drunk.

"Eden, here, honey, you're spilling that wine. Hand it to me." Anaiah said patiently. She complied. He set down a mostly empty bottle of wine on her nightstand. He helped her get up off the floor. He had his concerned face on again. She looked down and realized that the thing she had tripped over on the floor had been her own damn foot. Definitely drunk, then.

"I like you..." She whispered as she booped his nose with her finger. He half smiled at her. "I do. I don't deserve someone nice like you." His expression only changed slightly. "I am a bad person. A liar. And I am evil by nature..." She rambled. Her tongue loosened by too much wine and emotion.

"Eden, what have you lied to me about?" He soothed her with calming tones. He tucked a few loose locks of hair that had fallen from her bun behind her ear.

"Doesn't matter, I lie to everyone. I'm a liar and no one knows who I really am." She stared up sadly at his perfect face. It was better to do this drunk, she reasoned. Maybe it would hurt her less.

"Baby, calm down. You haven't lied to me. You are a good person. I know you." He stroked her cheek with his thumb.

"But...I lied." She said loudly. She noticed his jaw tightening ever so slightly. Anaiah was getting annoyed.

"Fine, you lied. Wanna tell me what you lied to me about?" He said sweetly despite his tense posture.

"My age." Her eyes filled up with tears ready to fall again. She was going to lose him too. She deserved it; she knew. It was better to push him away now with the truth than for him to really get to see the mess she was deep down.

"What?" he asked with genuine surprise.

"I'm eighteen." She gritted her teeth. Fighting against the sob that wanted out of her. She was the worst sort of moody drunk.

"I saw your license, you're twenty-one." he tried to be reasonable.

"That's just it. I LIED." She nodded to emphasize the word. It started pouring out of her then. The things she hated that he would know. "My parents are crazy cultists, so I didn't have a birth tercificate until months ago." She drunkenly butchered her words. "They didn't even bother filing for one. They didn't really even care that I was born. The cops asked me for my birthdate when I was found. So, I lied, because I ran away. I couldn't go back.

I couldn't just...marry some old man...Anaiah, they hate me!" She had begun fully sobbing now.

"Are you serious?" His face aghast. His arms still cradled her against him as she stared down at her.

"Yes." She said through the tears. She waited for him to get mad. She waited for him to leave. "What are you doing?" She demanded when he continued to hold her. "Why aren't you leaving? I'm a fake." *You're a big mess pretending she has it all together. Just wait until they all find out what a terrible person you are. Until they all realize how much they hate you.* She wanted him to run, so she wouldn't have to see his face when he realized what a shitty person she was.

"I'm taking care of you tonight. I'm making sure you are safe. I'll decide how I feel about the age thing later, Eden. I just want you to be okay." He said, too quiet. Anaiah set her down on her bed. He picked up the wine bottle, walked into the kitchen and dumped its half full contents in the kitchen sink. He brought back a glass of water. "Here, drink this." he said in a defeated tone.

Eden took it and looked up to see herself in the mirror. She looked like hell. Her face was blotchy from crying, still swollen and bruised from the events earlier in the day, and her neck was multiple shades of black and blue. She had dark circles under both eyes which were red and bloodshot. She wondered what would be the breaking point: *when will he decide I am too crazy to want? I am half hoping he will stay, half hoping he will run for his life from me.*

"Can I tell you some really crazy truths?" She asked. She might as well just give it all to him. Let him decide that it was too much now so she didn't keep giving him little bits of crazy and wait for him to run. *Just rip the Band-Aid off quick. Get it over with.*

"I'm all ears." He said with an annoyed but concerned look.

"Anaiah, I see things. Like, supernatural stuff. Ghosts and spirits and demons. I always have. My parents hated me because they thought I was the spawn of Satan. AND... It turns out they were close. This," she pointed to her neck, "my ex-boyfriend did that this morning. Cole Sparks came back from the dead to kick my ass once again. AND... apparently, he's a fucking demon. I met a very nice lady today that told me that I'm a half demon too. I have a mark on my neck that is supposed to prove it. Oh, and I've been seeing the ghost of my dead boss everywhere. She wants me to figure some shit out." She made wild animated motions with each sentence. He just silently sat down and pulled her into his lap. "Do you believe me? Do you think I am crazy?" She rambled on.

He sat stony faced and silently held her in his lap attempting to soothe her with gentle strokes with his hands down her back. She couldn't take this. She started to cry again. She pushed out of his lap and lay on her bed weeping into the pillow. *Why do I have to screw this up?*

"I think you are drunk, sweetie. We can talk about all of this later." He rubbed her back patiently. "You had a rough day and I think you should just go to bed." He covered her with a blanket and laid down next to her. He wrapped his arms around her. Sleep tugged her under its dark embrace as Anaiah held her close.

When she opened her eyes, it was still dark out. Her bedside lamp was on. A noise from the kitchen had her frozen in fear before she realized it was probably Anaiah. Her head was hammering a pounding beat along with her pulse. Her mouth felt bone dry; she swallowed, and pain shot down her throat like swallowing shards of glass. She needed water. She rose off the bed and went into her now clean kitchen. She found Anaiah standing in front of her coffee maker.

"Hey." she said quietly. He turned around and offered her a small smile.

"Feeling better?" he asked while pouring himself a cup of coffee.

"Not really. Now I'm hungover and my... everything hurts. What time is it?" She looked around.

"It's nine-thirty." He grabbed her a mug.

"What? It can't be. I went to bed at around five in the morning...It's still dark out." she rasped.

"It's nine thirty at night on Thursday. You slept all day. I called work for you. Told them you were sick." He shrugged.

"Thanks. They let you call in for me?" Her eyebrows furrowed.

"I said I was a paramedic and that you were unconscious. It was mostly true." He laughed and shrugged. "I figured you needed a few days to sort things out."

"I'm sorry about last night. Emotions and alcohol don't mix well for me." She said avoiding eye contact while pouring coffee in the cup he handed her.

"Yeah, I had a hard time controlling my emotions when I first started drinking too." He smirked at her.

"Aren't you mad at me? You know, lying about my age." She looked at him incredulously. He looked entirely too understanding.

"I called my friend, Sean, from the PD. He looked your family up for me after what you told me. They found your CPS case. I know I was prying, but I needed to know." He sighed and sat down his mug. "Eden, I understand why you did it. They did horrible things to you." He gave her his sad puppy dog eyes that told her that he heard some of the more horrible things her parents did to her. "Just...do me a favor, okay? Lay off the drinkin' a bit. I mean, legally, you're twenty-one, but your body is still eighteen. You still need those brain cells." He slowly wrapped her in a hug. He kissed the top of her head.

He breathed deeply like he was bracing for something. "I also know about the year in the psych hospital," he said quietly. "Are you on any meds, honey?"

"No." She breathed slowly and told him the truth. "They made things worse, so I quit taking them and just lied about being better." She suddenly feared that his sweet embrace was going to turn into some sort of restraint like they had used at the hospital. She looked up at him, knowing what she would see there. "I promise I am not crazy." He didn't look convinced.

"Okay." he sighed. He let her go and walked out of the room. *This is it. He's done. Or worse, he thinks I should go back to the mental hospital.* He came back into the room with two pills. "Here, it's for the hangover. It's just ibuprofen."

She took them with her coffee and said slowly, "What about the other stuff I said? It is the truth." She asked, waiting for the shoe to drop. "Please...I can show you." She reached out for his hand.

He stepped back. "About that... how about this: give me some time, show me you aren't... maybe... you could see a doctor. I have seen some weird shit. I can believe that what you tell me is the truth, as you believe it to be. So, let's take that a little slow." His face bore the same pitying look she'd seen on doctors and nurses faces. It was the 'okay, tell me the crazy version of what happened' face. She felt a new pain icing its way through her chest. She resolved to not cry.

"So, the guy who died? He was demon possessed?" He was attempting to get her story straight in his head. Goddamn, that look on his face stung. More than she thought it should, but she decided that he could either accept the truth or run screaming.

"I guess so. He appeared here, but it wasn't like a normal ghost. I see those a lot. He was different, but I didn't quite realize it. He picked me up by my neck and my arm. Threatened me, then he said he was here to help me. He told me to go talk to this lady. She said she was like me. Said we are both half demons." Eden watched out of the corner of her eye as he shook his head. She turned her head to face him and winced at the pain that shot through her neck. At that hiss of pain, he instantly closed the gap between them.

"Here, let me look at you." Anaiah looked at her neck. She pulled her arm out of her sleeve and showed him. His face fell when he saw it. He compared the marks to his own hands. Anaiah had massive hands, but these fingers were at least two inches longer than his. "Someone did this to you. Choked you and grabbed you like that...I want to believe what you are telling me. I just..." he let out an exasperated sigh and dipped his head between them.

Eden tried to tiptoe slightly and lean in to kiss him on the lips, but he was holding back.

"Isn't that sweet?" Came the voice she loathed from behind her. It was Cole...No. Azazel. Anaiah's head popped up. She turned around to look.

Azazel leaned casually against the frame of the doorway to the kitchen. Was he taller?

"Who are you? And how the hell did you get in here?" Anaiah stepped in front of Eden protectively.

"Oh, just checking in on my Evie… Oh wait, that's right it's Eden. She was Cole's Evie." His smirk never slipped as he said, "Calm down, boy. She and I go way back." Azazel's voice was entirely too casual for her comfort.

"Do you know him?" Anaiah glanced back at her. He looked ready to fight.

"Yeah." She said, annoyed. "Didn't summon him, or whatever I am supposed to do, so I wasn't expecting him, yet." She glared at the demonic son of a bitch. She should be cowering with fear, but his bullshit was probably going to cost her this relationship and maybe result in her having to uproot everything all over again. She was pissed.

Anaiah pieced together what she was saying. "He's the guy who did that to you?" Anaiah looked at her, his eyes full of rage and violence. Her mouth went dry, she felt her body freeze into place.

"My handiwork. Though, to be fair, she was being a bit of a bitch." Azazel said from across the room grinning.

"I'm going to rip your fucking head off and shove…" Anaiah turned away from her and Azazel's expression turned from amusement to violence, in a flash. Eden's panic over what this demon could do to her boyfriend seized her, and she ran to get between them.

"Stop!" She yelled as loud as she could, pain searing through her throat. "Anaiah, please stop." she said quieter with her hand on his chest. Confusion was plain on Anaiah's face. He looked down at her hand as she turned to Azazel. "I went to see Selah. I will be seeing her again in a week. Did you want anything else?"

"You did as instructed," he looked disappointed. "No need for a reminder then. Do as she says, and I'll see you soon." He shot Anaiah a look that was just daring him to try something. Anaiah leaned forward against her hand, his jaw clenched, and his fists balled at his sides. Azazel disappeared into smoke with a small pop.

"What the hell was that?" Anaiah looked adequately befuddled. He blinked and looked at her for an answer.

"Demon ex-boyfriend." She rubbed her temples against the pounding in her head and swallowed hard. "Is this the part where you run screaming?"

"Not a chance." he looked at her as if hurt by such an accusation.

"So, you believe me that I am not insane?" She asked. "Because a few minutes ago, I thought you were going to send me on a grippy sock vacation back to the psych ward."

"Well..." He paused to consider.

"If you're crazy... so am I. We both saw that man vanish into thin air." He wrapped his arms around her. "I believe you sweetheart, but it may take me a while to really understand." He breathed in a calming breath and let out a sigh. "And I really don't like that asshole putting his hands on any girl, especially when she's mine. I'd love to teach him some manners."

"Look, you can't kick a demon's ass, okay?" She arched a brow at him. "No, stop thinking about it. You CANNOT kick a demon's ass right now. And until I figure out how we can get rid of him, I don't want to piss him off." She laid her head against his chest.

"I could try, you know. I'm stronger than you'd expect." He kissed the top of her head.

"Please don't." She giggled and looked back up at him, ignoring the pain in her neck. "So do you still like me even though my life is filled with supernatural bullshit?"

"Yes." He kissed her and smiled against her lips. "I like you..." he gave her another peck. "a lot. Demon ex-boyfriends be damned; I'm sticking around for you." He kissed her again and she sucked gently on his bottom lip as he pulled back. She pulled him in for another kiss and slid her hand up his back pulling him close to her. Realizing that she was of sound mind had apparently meant he was okay with touching her after all. He picked her up gently and carried her to the bed. She flipped the light switch off as they went by.

Anaiah was careful and caressing. He covered her face with soft little kisses as he sat her on the bed. She tugged his shirt up to remove it. He held her hand with his own, stopping her.

"You're hurt." He whispered.

"Distract me from it." She said playfully.

"Eden...I don't want to cause you any more pain." His voice sounded a little strained.

"You won't hurt me. You've never hurt me." She whispered and kissed his lips softly.

He sighed. "Let's take things slow, then." He gave her another warm, slowly burning kiss. She pulled his shirt over his head when he came up for air. He gingerly pulled her clothes off along with his and joined her, kneeling on the bed. In the dark, he felt his way up her side with his hand. He used the light touches of his fingertips to feel from her breast to her chin, lifting it slightly to meet his lips. His hand rested on her neck naturally and a sharp pain shot through her. She tried to stifle it, but she inhaled sharply and let out a sad little sound. He froze.

"This just kills me." He whispered to her, still as a statue kneeling next to her on the bed.

"I'm fine. I really am. I'm more than fine, now that you know I'm not insane." She took his hand in hers. "You know, when I asked you out, I didn't think we'd be like this. I didn't know you would be like you are." She said quietly.

"What do you mean, like I am?" He asked, confused. She was a little distracted by the way he says 'am' with that country boy charm.

"You barely know me. Yet, you are willing to take on a hell spawn to defend me. I wonder if you are half angel." She kissed his hand with it still entwined with hers.

"I wouldn't really know," he sighed.

"What do you mean?" She asked.

"I don't know my dad. My mom was no saint. They hooked up one night. She got pregnant and having me ruined her life. She didn't really want me. She just didn't want to go to hell for...not having me." His deep voice steady in the dark room. The truth hung there. They both had issues.

"I'm sorry." She said quietly. "Guess we both lost the parental lottery."

"Yeah." His breath was heavy in the dark. "She ended up with the kind of scum that beat women...and kids. An' she blamed me when they left her." He paused and took a breath. "I mean, I wanted them gone, and I loved my mom despite everything. But it didn't matter what I wanted. After I..."

She reached up and touched his face in the dark. Eden caressed his cheek in her palm. He'd listened to her. She wanted to comfort him and listen to his story as well. He leaned his head into her touch. "Go on. I'm listening." she said.

"After I left when I was seventeen, my stepdad... killed her." His voice cracked. "That's why it's so hard to see you like this. I wish I could have been here to protect you. Maybe if I stuck around for you the way I should have for her, this wouldn't have happened." She felt his weight shift as he moved away from her and laid on his back.

"Honey. No, it's not your fault." She slid herself up against his side. The strain on her neck caused another unexpected wince and sudden inhalation. She felt him tense again and heard him breathing slow determined breaths, as if trying to calm himself.

"Hey." She put her hand on his chest. "We can't change anything in the past. What matters is that we are here, now. And right now, I am here, happy, and safe with you. I honestly thought I was going to lose all of that. It's why I was so upset last night. But you believe me. You listened to me. You cannot imagine how much that means to me." She gently guided his face to hers. She gave him a little kiss. "Now, why don't you help me think about something else." She whispered against his lips. "You can make me feel good for a while."

"Yes ma'am," he sighed, "but if I hurt you or do anything you don't want, you stop me." He kissed her again. "Please, Eden."

"Okay. I will." She said quietly as she laid all the way back on the bed. He covered her with his body. He started by tracing her jawline with little pecks. He shifted his weight to one side and used his other hand to move her face to the side. He kissed just below her earlobe and trailed down to her shoulder. She shivered and her skin covered itself in goosebumps. His finger traced the outline of her nipple while he gave her short sweet little kisses on the lips. Anaiah moved his mouth down to her nipple and repeated the outline with his tongue. She breathed in deeply.

"Ahh" was all she could say as he took the nipple in his mouth and barely touched her hip with the tips of his fingers. As he moved to the other side, his fingers moved between her thighs. He parted her lower lips with his fingertips. She sighed with anticipation. As he took her nipple in his mouth, he gently massaged her there at the apex. She cried out with pleasure. He paused.

"Don't stop. It feels good," whispered Eden. Once he was satisfied that she was not suffering, he released her nipple and kissed between her breasts. He softly traced a line of kisses down the middle of her abdomen then below her belly button, while positioning himself between her legs. He gently rubbed again, before kissing the same spot with his lush lips. When he kissed her there, he sucked gently on her, the effect was both divine and maddening. He glanced up at her, she could barely see his face in the darkness, but she could see that grin. She brushed his hair out of his face.

"You like that, baby?" She could hear the smile in his voice.

She made a noise that resembled 'mmhmm.'

He leaned back down to his task and used his tongue, while he took two fingers and slid them carefully inside her. His fingers started making a come-hither gesture inside her while he licked her on the outside. The combination of two pleasures at the same time almost put her over the top immediately. He rubbed his other hand over her hip as she writhed with pleasure, but he didn't stop. He worked her into a frenzy with his fingers and mouth. Her body clenched around his fingers as the spasms rocked through her. He slowed for a moment, as she breathed raggedly and as her body came back to rest after the spasms of joy, then he sped up again. This time as she started to build toward a climax, he smiled up at her and said, "That's it, baby." He went back to work with his mouth with renewed fervor and she put her hands in his hair. She was so close to coming again, and she almost yelled as much at him. Once he started to suck on her clit as she came, she couldn't believe it or help it, but she pulled his face into her harder. Her fist grabbed a handful of his black hair. Her hips started rocking against his lips of their own accord. He kept on with the come-hither motions with his fingers and firmly grabbed her ass with the other hand pulling himself into her as well. The excitement inside her built again like bubbling lava boiling over the top of a volcano. In an explosion of ecstasy, she had the most powerful orgasm she'd ever experienced. Screaming with pleasure, she begged for him to enter her. He sat up and grabbed a condom from his wallet. While still throbbing from the orgasm, he gently turned her over. He swiped the tip of himself over her wetness between her legs.

"Yes. Anaiah. Please." She moaned. She felt him press himself to her entrance. She leaned back into him, sliding him in just a bit. He gave slow, sweet thrusts to start with, rubbed his hands along her back and told her how amazing she was, how beautiful, how sexy she was as he slowly seated himself into her. As he drove himself into her fully, she breathed out. "God, yes." She panted his name like a prayer on her tongue. He increased his pace and she rocked back into him, meeting his thrusts until he built into a steady deep rhythm.

She begged for him to keep going, deeper, harder, faster. She wanted every inch of him. He gave her wishes, with each thrust, he sent a ripple of pleasure through her. She let out moans of pleasure.

"I'm not hurting you, am I baby?" he asked, slowing down. His hands rubbed over her hips and up her back. One ventured around the front and he massaged her left breast. In doing so, he leaned his body over her, pushing him deeper inside her. She inhaled sharply as the intense pleasure. "Eden, are you hurt?" He whispered. And kissed her down her spine.

"No, sweetie." She rotated her hips a bit and let out a gasp of pure pleasure. He moaned as well. She rocked back and forth until he was thrusting in her again.

"Yes, baby, faster. Mmm, yeah, harder, yes. Like that. Oh my god." She encouraged. Within a few minutes, she felt his thrust speed up and become shallower. She could tell from the way his breath was catching, he was about to finish for her. She cried out to him. "Yes, Anaiah, come for me sweetie. Yes." She tilted her hips up to him and let him drive her over the top with him.

In the afterglow, they held each other for a long time. Anaiah traced his fingers along her arms as she laid with her head resting against his chest. She watched the corded muscles of his forearms move with the little motions. A sheen of sweat shone across the lines of his tattoos. He was quiet and contemplative. She wondered what he might be thinking. She disentangled herself after a while and cleaned herself up in the shower. After she dressed, she walked into the bedroom to find him sitting on the bed with his head in his hands.

"Are you okay?" She asked quietly. She wondered to herself when he had last slept. Had he rested when she did earlier that day? He'd cleaned her kitchen by himself while she rested. Maybe he hadn't slept at all.

"Eden. I really like you." He was still staring at the floor. "I'm just struggling a bit with some things. What does it say about me, that I still want you, knowing you're younger than I thought you were?" Eden was sure it meant he was overthinking it.

"I've been living as if I was an adult for the last three years. You didn't do anything wrong. I AM an adult. And I wanted it...wanted you. And I loved every minute of it. I really like you too. Can we please not have a moral dilemma about my age?" She asked softly.

"Can I ask you something?" He looked up at her with his jaw set. His eyes had that dangerous glint to them. He didn't wait for her to respond. "How long ago did you date Cole?" Her heart had begun to beat faster in her chest. She instinctively went still. Her face went flatly blank.

She knew these questions. She knew why he was asking. She turned her voice as soothing as she could as she answered. "We broke up over a year ago. We were only together for like eight months. Why?" She said softly.

His jaw was tense as he asked the next question, "Did you sleep with him?" He didn't even look at her face. She'd answered these sorts of questions with Cole. The answers were never to his liking. He would either accuse her of not confessing to what she had done or berate her for what she had.

"Do you really want to know?" she asked weakly. She hadn't taken him for the jealous type. If anyone had looked at her the wrong way, flirted with her too much, Cole had been on her about it. Anaiah, though, he seemed different.

"Yes. Did you?" He said too quietly. His low voice sounded deadly.

"Yes." She said in nearly a whisper. "I... I didn't think you cared about that sort of thing." She silently inched backward.

He was staring straight ahead of himself, not looking at her. Eyes that were just hours ago filled with compassion and kindness, were now hard and unyielding. He let out a slow breath and flexed his right hand open and curled it back into a fist. She was still inching back to the wall into the corner. Her heart was racing in her chest. Was she stupid? Of course, she was, no one was that perfect. *No one.*

"You were only sixteen? And he was older than me. That's just so..." He was getting really worked up. "And we don't know how old he really is... he's not even human and he slept with you. It's just sick." The malice behind his eyes grew deadly. Eden could feel the tension, the anger, the hate rolling from him in threatening waves.

"Why does that matter now?" She tried to plead softly. Tears started to spring up in her eyes. She flinched when he spoke.

"Because he had to fucking know! He took advantage of you! And am I any better than that?" As his voice got louder, she curled up in the corner, in an effort to make herself small. She covered her head with her arms trying to quiet the sobs building in her chest. Her dream of a good decent man shattering with her control over her tears. She listened for him to move and waited for the hammer to fall. When his hand gently touched her arm, she jerked away.

"Oh no. God no. Eden, no." He said softly. "I'm not mad at you. Oh baby, no, please don't be scared. I will never hurt you." he sat next to her, rubbing her back. He laid his head against hers. The sobs still came, terror still had her in its grasp. She looked up at him and saw the tears in his eyes. His face was full of regret.

"You don't want me." She sobbed quietly. "I'm too young. Too broken. I'm damaged goods. I'm just..." she sucked in air, "I'm just not someone that you could love. You found your out, take it." She wanted to run. She wanted to scream. "Please, just go. You don't need this. This isn't NORMAL. No one wants this." She shook as she spoke. He pulled her into his lap.

"No, baby, I'm here. I want you, and I'm staying. I'm so sorry I made you feel this way. I got so upset about him hurting you. God. I'm so sorry." He was soothing her with small strokes of his hands down her arm. "I let my anger get the best of me, but I promise, I would never take it out on you." She was relieved he wasn't running from her, but she wouldn't blame him if he ran and never looked back.

"You still want me? I'm a mess. I mean, who does this? Who reacts this way to someone getting upset?" She was still crying. She felt she was in a constant state of tears and self-loathing lately.

"Someone who's been abused. We both have baggage, baby. I worry too much. Because I just don't want to be that guy, you know. Our first date, I was worried that I was taking advantage of you. Fuck, I was so worried about that and now, look at me. Then when things started to get going, I was worried about getting you pregnant. Saddlin' you with a kid, like my dad did my mom. I didn't have protection then, I wasn't ready. I was worried that I was just your rebound after Cole. I thought you still had feelings for him. I mean, I know better now. Tonight, I think what bothered me most, was that I am here trying to take care of you, trying to be careful with you when you are hurt, and I just got so overwhelmed by what I was feeling, that I was done before I realized, I really could have hurt you. I lost control. My body just took off to get what I wanted, and I didn't think. I thought about what kind of jerk would do that. You're always sayin' I am so good to you, and you seem surprised when I go slow." He kissed her forehead. "And think about makin' you feel good. Who treats a woman like that? Just does what he likes and doesn't care if it's what she likes or...God, if it hurts her." His voice lowered to a whisper. "Then, I realized what kind of man does that, the kind who fucks a teenage girl and doesn't bat an eye at it. I was disgusted with myself. I shouldn't have let you see how much that bothered me." He hung his head in shame. Tears rolled down his cheek.

"Jesus, baby. We both definitely have baggage." She reached up and touched his cheek, wiping his tears away. "But you're wrong about being that kind of jerk. I wanted all of you. You told me to let you know if you hurt me, and I didn't stop you. I told you what I wanted. You have to trust me too.

Anaiah, neither one of us is perfect, you don't have to be perfect for me." She turned his face to hers. "Hey, we can be broken together. My broken pieces fit right with yours."

He rested his head against hers and said with his eyes still closed. "You just make all my self-control go away. It's a bit unnerving for me. I'm cool, calm and levelheaded in the worst situations, but you come along and I'm just undone."

"I guess it's good we are getting our crazy out of the way now, instead of it slamming us in the face a few months down the line." She laughed humorlessly.

"Can I ask you another Cole question?" He said quietly.

"Yeah." She sighed.

"What ended it?" He kissed her head again.

"It's kind of obvious, isn't it?"

He brushed her mess of curls out of her face. "So... he hurt you like this before?"

She steadied herself for his reaction. "Yes." She felt the ever present need to justify it. She set him off. She couldn't calm him down. All her normal excuses. "It wasn't bad at first. Just harsh words. Followed by him being sweet and gaslighting me into believing it was all my fault. I mean, I know that now. I know what it was now, looking back. But I still catch myself doing things... calming people. Defusing the threat. Or even mirroring his behavior with my friends, with people I trust and blowing up at them. It started slow. He was charming and wonderful in the beginning. Then we would fight, and he'd tell me how worthless I was. Then he'd make it up to me. Then he got jealous of guys I waited on at work and gave me a black eye and I lost my job as a waitress."

"Is that when you left?" He asked quietly.

"No." She hid her face in his chest, ashamed.

"I don't understand why..." He started quietly as if to himself.

"I thought that deep down, all men were like that. That it was my job to keep the peace. My parents didn't exactly set the example of a loving family. I thought it was part of being with someone. You are the first one to prove that wrong. Plus, he put up with the weird shit that seemed to happen around me. I thought that if I left him, no one else would love me. Cole shrugged like it was no big deal when I called it off. I expected a fight, but he told me that I was nothing and that losing me was losing nothing. I knew he didn't love me at all after that. I realized in that moment, that in all my life, no one had really truly loved me. And if they said they did, they said it after they'd hurt me to try and make it okay. I thought that I could handle some pain if it meant I was loved." Her voice was small, it felt as fragile as she felt saying it aloud. Anaiah was staring at her in disbelief.

"Who wouldn't love you, honey?" He breathed out. "You are smart and funny, not to mention beautiful. Look at all you've survived, Eden. You are so incredibly strong. Hell, even with all the crazy shit, I think I've fallen for you." He said in a rush of words.

"Really?!" Her shock visibly stung him.

"Yeah." He said quietly.

"No, I mean, did you really just tell me, basically, 'despite your crazy. I think I love you'?" She smiled.

"Oh darlin', I think I love you more because of it." He smiled back. "Never a dull moment, huh?"

"You might be insane, sticking with me," She laughed. "Not sure who's crazier, but I'm pretty sure I'm falling for you too." She kissed him softly. His stomach growled loudly.

"Hungry?" she asked. "Who am I talking to here, of course, you are. Waffle Casa?"

"Maybe…I'll go pick up food?" He traced his finger along her collarbone. She remembered she looked like a domestic assault victim and thought better of it.

"Yeah. Maybe we just order take-out." She agreed.

Elle E. Evans

CHAPTER NINETEEN

The next day was spent repairing and cleaning up her broken belongings. Anaiah made a trip to the store to replace some essentials for her. They also spent a good portion of the day in bed, some of the time was even spent sleeping. Anaiah was by her side the entire time. It was Friday again, and Anaiah suggested that they spend the night at his place to give her some distance from the disaster that was her house and the emotions attached to it. She agreed and packed an overnight bag.

As Anaiah buckled himself into the driver's seat of his car, she plugged her phone into his charger. Hers was lost to the disaster that was her home. Her phone had died the day before. It lit up with messages from Journey. She read through them.

'*Where are you?*' Her first message. '*Are you dead?*' The next one was in all caps. '*YOU BETTER NOT BE DEAD, BITCH!*' The last one read, '*Are you in the hospital? CALL ME!*'

"Gotta call Journey really quick, I have a bunch of frantic messages from her." Eden said to Anaiah as he backed the car out of her driveway. He nodded and drove towards his house, reaching over and placing his hand on her knee.

"Hey, you aren't dead!" Answered Journey. She sounded out of breath.

"No. Not dead. Tired. Pissed off, but not dead." She answered back.

"Did he drug you?" Journey said back sharply. "He called in and said you were unconscious. I'll stab him in his balls if he..."

In the background Eden heard Jayse as he said something that sounded like "Needlessly graphic."

"No…No. Anaiah's been great. Tell Jayse I said hi, by the way." Eden rolled her eyes.

"I'd prefer you didn't talk to my boyfriend while he's naked." Journey whispered. "It's awkward." Eden burst out laughing, almost choking from the sudden pain in her throat. She cleared it.

"Were you two…ya know…when I called?" Eden giggled. "Why'd you answer?"

"I needed to find out if I had to stop what I was doing and stab your man." She said simply, as if Eden should expect no less than that from her.

"As much as I appreciate the offer, it's not needed. I'll fill you in later. Call me on your lunch break tonight." She said with a smile.

"Gonna get back to this then." Journey said and hung up her phone.

"That sounded…interesting…" Humor lit Anaiah's eyes.

"Be forewarned, Anaiah Parker. If you ever wrong me, Journey is prepared to climb off her boyfriend and stab you in your balls." She giggled.

"Good GOD!" He declared. "Let's not ever go down that road." His horrified expression only made Eden chuckle more.

As her giggles died down, he grinned at her. "I was going to say you need better friends, but no, darlin'…you need a best friend who is willing to maim a man in the worst way if things go south." He squeezed her knee. "She's feisty. I like it."

After they arrived at his place, Anaiah prepared her coffee with just enough creamer and plopped down on the couch next to her. She sipped from it and picked up the book she brought back from Selah as he turned on some sort of sports on the television.

"You sure you don't wanna watch something?" He asked.

"I have a book." She kissed him on his cheek. She set the coffee on the table and leaned against him.

"It won't bother you for me to watch a game?" He sounded doubtful.

"No, I have a book and you as a pillow. I'm good." She wiggled her back into him for emphasis. He squeezed her close with his arm.

"As long as you don't care." He kissed the top of her head.

"You are a noisy pillow." She said without looking up at him. She cracked the smallest smile and opened Selah's book about demonology.

He startled her once or twice when he suddenly moved or gave a restrained "yes!" during the game. He made up for it with kisses and by refilling her coffee. She quietly read, laying against his torso, with her bare feet on the couch and his arm wrapped around her. She learned about the princes of hell. Azazel was among those demons mentioned. It didn't seem useful yet, but it was interesting. If she was going to do research, she preferred to do it this way.

Eventually, she felt Anaiah relax and heard him softly snoring. She knew he hadn't slept well at her place since the break in. Anaiah likely felt the need to be alert, ready to defend her at a moment's notice. She leaned her head against him and savored the rhythmic rise and fall of his breathing as she went back to reading.

She awoke to a strange noise. She must have nodded off. The book was open across her chest, and her head rested in Anaiah's lap. She glanced around the room. A baseball game was replaying on the television. Anaiah still snored softly with his hand resting on her stomach. A loud gurgle from his stomach resounded and Eden laughed out loud.

Anaiah stirred. "Hey. Sorry, I dozed off." He said as she sat up.

"Me too. Let me guess, starving again?" She grinned as his stomach bellowed again.

He put his hand over his noisy stomach. "I have frozen pizza," he shrugged.

She worked the soreness out of her neck with a small popping sound as it rolled. The pain was much better. "I could go for waffles. People are going to see me eventually. It's not too terrible with make-up on." She winced. "But you are the one who will get the dirty looks if we go out. So, it's up to you."

"No, you're the boss. Let's get waffles." He smiled at her.

The midnight crowd was sparse but most of the patrons of the Waffle Casa were giving Anaiah the stink eye. She felt bad for him, but he ignored them without comment.

The waitress was so bold to say, "Anaiah Parker, did you put your hands on that lady?" He started to respond to her and defend himself, but Eden spoke before she could think.

"Only in ways I want him too." She smiled as he blushed slightly. His embarrassment only encouraged her loose lips. "Our safe word is butter pecan. Speaking of which, do you have any for the table?" The waitress's eyes went wide as her jaw dropped. She walked away slowly mouthing the word "WOW."

Anaiah sighed, "Now she is going to tell the whole town, 'Anaiah Parker choked that girl while he screwed her until she said butter pecan. Then he took her out for waffles to show off her bruises and oh my, she asked for butter pecan. I wonder if it was a cry for help. Did I do the right thing?'" he said in a high-pitched voice as Eden's sides began to hurt from trying to stifle her laughter. His voice dropped to his normal baritone. "Lord, she's going to tell her mother." His expression shifted to serious, before he asked in a low voice, "So, safe words, were those a thing for you? With him?"

She looked at the table. "Anaiah, I..."

"You don't have to tell me." He sighed. "I don't want you to feel bad about what he did. My mind just runs wild with the worst-case scenario." He sighed. "I fucking hate that he hurt you."

"I'm sorry you are making yourself suffer over it." She hesitated, but she'd rather he knew than to think worse had happened. "Anaiah, we didn't play those sorts of games. My understanding with that sort of thing is that it requires mutual trust and respect. That wasn't the case with us. The sex...wasn't always terrible for me, but I didn't always enjoy it either. If it had always been bad, do you think I would have been so keen to jump into bed with you?" He looked slightly horrified. "You have to face the facts that my life, up until recently, when I met you, has been awful. I still have some issues...okay, a lot of issues, but emotionally I am done with shedding tears over that chapter of my life," she said.

"Just like that?" he said with his brows raised.

"I'll tell you what you want to know. If you want details, then I will share them, but I don't want you constantly trying to make up for his mistakes. Or looking at me with pity in your eyes. I really don't want that," Eden scrambled for another topic of conversation. "We've talked about my ex, what about you? You certainly weren't a virgin the first time we were together." She smiled at the memory.

"That's true. You aren't my first." He sipped his coffee. "Truth be told, you are actually my...fifth." He sort-of coughed over the words.

"Your what?" She pretended to not hear him.

"Fifth. Okay, there were four before you." He sincerely looked ashamed.

"Don't be embarrassed, sweetie. Tell me about it." She said with a soft encouraging tone.

"Do I have to?" He was avoiding eye contact.

"Turnabout is fair play." Eden said. She lowered her voice. "Only if you want to."

"No, fair is fair. I know your story; you should know mine. My first was..." He paused and winced. "This sounds so redneck and trashy...my stepsister." he hung his head, ashamed. "Mom was married four times, all jerks. The last one," He paused and sipped his coffee, "had a daughter who was around my age. When her dad would get drunk, she would come hang out with me until he passed out. He got hands-y when he was wasted. Yeah, like that with his own daughter. I know, it's fucking terrible. He left her alone if she was with me." He said in response to the face she made. "Well, one night, she came in and got in bed with me. And it just sort of happened," he looked all sorts of unsettled.

"Was that the only time?" she asked.

He let out a huff. "Yeah. I wasn't around after that." He pushed his hair back out of his face. "The second one was a girl I dated in high school. Her name was Tonya. We were young and stupid. She broke up with me before prom, her parents never liked me anyway." From the way he was shifting in his seat, Eden suspected there was more to the story. Eden held out her hand. He automatically placed his hand in hers. A dirty trick, but if he thought about Tonya, Eden might get a small flash of memory or feeling. She concentrated on his feelings.

"What was so horrible about Tonya and her parents? Why do you dislike them so much?" Eden grasped at that thread of feeling and memory.

"I didn't say anything was horrible. How did you..." His eyes narrowed and he dropped his voice. "Wait, can you, like, read what's going on in my head if you touch me?"

"Only feelings, sometimes little memories." She winked at him. "You are smarter than the rest, you know that? Nobody ever picks up on the psychic girlfriend. What was so bad about her parents?"

"Racists." He said quietly. "I know. We live in the south, it happens. But they were very overt about it. They said to my face that they couldn't tell WHAT I was exactly except not right for their daughter."

"Oh, no. That's terrible." Her eyebrows furrowed with concern.

"I'm native American and Mexican, by the way. If the tats don't give that away." He held up his fully covered right arm. "At least, that's what I got from Mom. She said my dad was white." He pointed out the tattoo on his left upper arm with a small smile, pulling his dark t-shirt sleeve up. "This one's for her. Her name was Rosalinda, but everyone called her Rosie." A beautiful but sorrowful looking woman in calavera makeup surrounded by red and black roses was inked on his upper arm. "I didn't have these then, but I wasn't ashamed of where I came from then. And I definitely am not now."

"We don't have to keep doing this if it's hard for you." She said sympathetically.

"Where's our waitress?" he asked, not addressing the conversation topic.

"Eh, probably putting in the police report on you brutally fucking me. Erm, sorry." She winced at the face he made.

"Next, I..." He started.

"Really?" She was surprised he continued. He shrugged as if to say, 'might as well get on with it."

"I dated a girl named Amy for a while. We were in school together to get our paramedic certs. We broke up after the class was over and she moved to Dallas."

"Why'd you break up?" She asked curiously.

"I was going to move to Dallas with her, but I had just started here. I told her to give me six months then I'd move. We tried to make it work, but it was just too hard. And then I met someone else."

"For shame!" She whispered. She giggled, delighted by his moral struggles. Maybe Mr. Perfect wasn't so perfect. "So, you broke it off to be with this other girl. Who was she?"

"Not exactly. Amy and I were done before I started dating my last girlfriend." Anaiah sighed. "Eden, I don't mess around like that. I have to feel something first. I don't do the casual sex thing or cheating." Eden felt the familiar ick of religious shame wash over her. Anaiah gave her an assessing look. "I don't judge people who do. I'm just not wired like that. I'm demisexual."

"Demisexual… you have to fall for someone first?" Eden thought over the last several weeks of dating.

"Not necessarily fall in love… but there has to be a connection. Romantic, emotional…" Anaiah shrugged. "Otherwise, I'm not into it."

"You seemed pretty into me since the first date, though." Eden said without thinking.

"I'd had some romantic feelings for you for a while… but we've gotten off track. You wanted to know about the girls before you." Eden could tell he was deflecting but didn't push him. Anaiah went on, "My last girlfriend before I dated you...I don't think you are going to laugh this time. I think you might be a little embarrassed." He gave her a half smile.

"Really?" She raised her eyebrows.

"Yeah." He crossed his arms.

"Now I have to know." She stared at him expectantly.

"Our waitress...her name is Reesa." He started slowly.

"No… you're trying to mess with me." she laughed. He raised his eyebrows, pursed his lips, and shook his head slightly.

"Reesa has a birthmark about the size of a quarter on her left hip." He held up his hand and made a circle with his thumb and forefinger. He took in a deep breath. "A little over a year ago, Reesa James was going to be Mrs. Anaiah Parker, before the wedding was called off."

"Yeah, right." She said, but he wasn't breaking.

He looked her straight in the eyes, all humor gone from his face and said, "I didn't really want to be her husband…" He licked his lips, looking down and then back up to her. "But I didn't want to leave her by herself with the baby." She could see the earnestness in his eyes. Was he playing some sort of game with her? He held his hand out in front of her. "Don't believe me? Go ahead, check."

"Do you have a kid that you haven't told me about?" She whispered. She took his hand. She felt the shame, the regret, the resentment pulsing through him.

"No, I thought I was going to be a dad. Reesa and I dated for a few months. When she told me she was pregnant, I tried to do right by her. She agreed to marry me but wanted to wait until after the baby was born. We rented a house, started buying baby stuff, and I really was hoping it would work out. I didn't want our baby to grow up with parents that hated each other. A few months before the baby was born, I caught her with another guy. Turns out, it'd been going on the whole time. She didn't know which of us got her pregnant." He shook his head.

"I moved into the nursery. We broke up. Waited it out as roommates. After all that, the baby was his. He moved in, I moved out, and they're a happy little family now." Anaiah let out a disappointed sigh. She could feel the echoes of those emotional wounds in his touch.

"Did you love her?" Her heart ached for him.

"No. I think I was just in love with the idea that I could have a family. I mean, I'm not ready to find a wife and pop out some kids right this second, but when it was offered to me, I kinda wanted it." He gave a half grin.

"I'm not sure I'm ready to...." Eden struggled to find the right words to tell him that she was just trying to figure her life out. She didn't even know where a husband and kids fit in the whole scheme of her life. She spent the last three years just surviving and never hoping for anything beyond making it by and maybe having another person to love her, eventually.

"I know. I'm not there either. Not anymore." He picked up on her internal conflict, seeing the panic in her eyes. "I have you, right now. Things are new, but good. That's enough. I mean, I haven't really dated in the last year. It messed me up for a while." He squeezed her hand.

"You do have some baggage." She winked and hoped to break the tension. Anaiah's stomach growled again as if on cue. "Where is that cheating bitch anyway? I'm hungry."

"No clue...I'll get up in a minute and check. Is that enough of my history?" He pulled his hand back to pick up his coffee cup. "We done digging there? What about you...you told me about Cole, but did you date before that, or after?" He took a big sip of coffee.

"I dated a guy when I was in the state hospital. We rounded some bases...you know. The sort of stuff that lost you movie night privileges." She wiggled her eyebrows.

"Oh Lord, how old were you guys?" He snickered.

"I was fifteen. I was going through a rebellious phase. I'd never had a boyfriend. He asked for "head" and had to explain what he wanted to me because I'd never heard of it." She smirked at the memory. Anaiah choked on his coffee as he laughed. "I haven't dated anyone since Cole. Well, at least, not until now. I sort of avoided that for a..."

"SOMEONE CALL NINE-ONE-ONE!" The cook bolted into the dining area screaming. He spotted them, "Anaiah, come quick, it's Reesa. Oh God, it's bad."

Anaiah was on his feet in an instant and Eden ran after him out the backdoor. She followed him as he turned toward the dumpsters and stopped dead in her tracks when she beheld the sight before her. The pole that held the signs to the restaurant next door had snapped in half. The pole was twisted at an odd angle and the end drove through the dumpster, pinning Reesa against it. It was like a scene from a horror film. The sign had broken into a thousand pieces on the back lot and the jagged metal pole had impaled Reesa through her midsection. She hung limply giving no sign of life. Anaiah stepped into the dark pool of blood around her without hesitation, checking her over. Eden felt her stomach clench at the sight.

Anaiah called out, "No pulse. She probably bled out quickly. This is all the way through and through." Anaiah leaned in to check for a heartbeat by holding his head against her chest. Eden didn't fail to note that her chest didn't rise or fall. She felt her own tightening in response.

Eden needed air. She needed to lie down. Her head swam. She walked around the corner and began retching on the pavement. Anaiah whipped out his phone and called into the station.

As Eden tilted her head up and wiped her hand across her mouth, she saw a glass bowl, with a few sticks and herbs in it. Around it, she saw the underwear she had worn the night at the cabin with Anaiah. There was a piece of some sort of small medical tool, it looked like a clamp. She also spotted a toothbrush, a receipt of some kind, and dammit, there was a used black condom, just like the one Anaiah worn the night before. *SHIT.*

"Anaiah, honey, can you come here for a minute." She called out, still bent over with her hands on her knees. He hung up his phone and walked over and rubbed her back.

"You okay?" He asked in a soft voice. In response, she just pointed at the mystical trash bowl. "What the fuck? That's like the one in your house, isn't it? This is bad." He whispered.

"You think?' She said in a hushed voice.

"Well, your house got broken into, and my ex just got impaled, and both have these things. Yeah, this is fucking bad, honey." His low voice sounded exasperated.

"Yes, yes it is." She whispered back.

"Ugh, not to mention your ex and your boss died in a weird accident...shit, this looks bad. Are you sure your demonic ex-boyfriend isn't doing this?" Anaiah kept his voice hushed but was clearly getting pissy about this whole situation. Eden straightened up next to him.

"Are you mad at me because I dated a demon?" She eyed him suspiciously.

"No. Mad at the situation. Mad that we don't know if this and that are connected." He motioned to the bowl and back toward where Reesa's body was. They both looked to the side as they noticed flashing lights pull up around the corner, casting odd shadows around them.

"You go talk to them, and don't tell them about this. I'm going to pick this up and put it in the car. Maybe Selah can help us." She whispered.

"You want to take evidence from a crime scene and take it to a half demon baker?" He looked at her like she'd grown a third eye.

"Yes, what does it do but tie us to this? It doesn't prove he's connected to it! And I'm pretty sure that's our DNA in that bowl." She said in a hushed but terse tone as she pointed out the condom.

He sighed, "Shit. You're right. Okay, I'll buy you time." He rubbed her back again before walking off. Once he was back around the corner and talking to the cops, she hurried to gather all the items in the bowl and walked quickly to the car. She grabbed an empty plastic bag from the back floorboard of Anaiah's car and shoved everything inside. As she shoved the contents into the bag, one of the sticks poked through the bag, scraping her wrist.

Her vision blasted white with the flash of a vision. She recognized Jayse and Journey as they were walking into the twin's house. The door closed behind them. Suddenly, there was a loud explosion. The door her friends had just stepped through flew off the hinges as the interior of the house exploded outward and the flames shot out the windows and door.

As her vision cleared, Eden stood next to the car, stunned. What had she seen? Was that the future? A vision of something to come? She heard Kyle's eerie voice in her mind again. *"Promise me you will protect her. Do not let the fire consume her."* Fuck! Had it been a warning? Pastor Joseph? Kyle? Even Loretta...warning me of the darkness coming.

She snapped back to herself, shaking as she breathed in deeply. She told herself that this was not the time to lose her shit. She tied the bag closed and plopped it on the floor of the back seat. Anaiah's backseat was the opposite of his apartment. The bag blended in with discarded fast-food bags. She rinsed her mouth out with a bottle of water she had left in the cup holder and grabbed a piece of gum from his center console to help with the vomit breath. This mystical bullshit was wearing her out. She quickly pulled up Journey's contact in her phone and hit the call button; she would be working, but Eden hoped she would answer.

"Hey, I'm stocking pets, make it quick." Journey answered.

"Are you going to Jayse's after work?" She asked in a rushed voice.

"Yeah, why?" Journey's tone changed to more concerned based on Eden's inflection.

"I saw something. Weird shit is happening. Just do me a favor, don't go over there, take him to your place or something." She rambled.

"What did you see? And what do you mean you saw something? Are you telling me you see the future now?" She sounded annoyed and confused.

"I don't know, Journ. Weird shit is going down, okay?" She took a deep breath. "Look, Anaiah's ex just got impaled by a fucking taqueria sign behind Waffle Casa. I have to go. You and Jayse go to your house tonight. DON'T GO TO HIS HOUSE. I don't think it's safe." She pleaded with her.

"Alright. Are you sure you're, okay?" Journey conceded.

"I'll be okay, just stay safe, okay?" Eden said.

"I'll do my best." She said as Eden hung up. She grabbed the gym bag in the backseat of Anaiah's car, suddenly remembering that he had stood in a puddle of Reesa's blood in his boots. She pulled the large blue and black sneakers from his bag.

She walked back around to the dumpsters where Anaiah was talking with a cop. When he saw her, he gave her a small reassuring smile. "You okay, sugar?" He asked sweetly.

"Yeah, that's just a lot of blood. Just turned my stomach. I'm okay now that I grabbed a piece of gum." She held up his sneakers. "Thought you might need these."

"Shit. These were my favorite boots." He toed the heels of his boots off and slipped the sneakers on. It certainly made the jeans and t-shirt look more casual. He looked down at the boots. "Evidence, I guess?" And shrugged to the officer.

"EMS crews will have biohazard bags. This was clearly a freak accident, man. We aren't collecting evidence." The officer said back. "We'll toss em for you."

Eden tucked herself under Anaiah's left arm, wrapping her own arm around him, and faced the officer. He looked like a typical small-town cop: brown hair in a simple haircut, mustache, and dad bod. Eden was glad to know that not every public servant in their town looked like Anaiah and Sean. She almost laughed then remembered a dead body was less than thirty feet from her.

"Bobby, this is Eden, my girlfriend." Bobby looked her over for a second. She watched him piece together what he was likely told at the station and why she looked like hell warmed over. She felt the urge to apologize for looking like she did but shoved that thought down. She needed to apologize less for things she could not control. Her life already felt like it was spiraling out of her control. She needed to control anything she could.

"Hey Eden. Sorry we had to meet this way. I heard you met Sean. You folks are having all the bad luck this week." Bobby shook her hand.

"Yeah, it's been an off week for me." Eden said simply as an ambulance pulled up without flashing lights along with a firetruck. Anaiah waved a hand at his coworkers.

"Eden, if you can just verify Parker's statement. Then y'all can get back to your date." Bobby nodded at her.

"Sure, we came here from his place. Reesa had been gone for a long time and that man came out and yelled for someone to call nine-one-one. He saw us and asked Anaiah to come help. We came out here, saw her like that. Anaiah said she had no pulse. I got sick and I went around the corner to throw up. Watch out for that. I went out to the car to get a piece of gum and shoes for him from his gym bag. And now...I'm talking to you."

"Alright," He wrote down a note. "Last name's Grace, right?" Eden tried not to cringe at what it implied. All Anaiah's friends likely knew who her family was. She nodded.

"Okay, you folks try to enjoy the rest of your night." He shook Anaiah's hand.

"Thanks, Bobby." Anaiah said. Anaiah's hand again rested on the small of her back as he led her back to their table. She grabbed her purse from the booth and Anaiah dropped a twenty on the table. "Let's go somewhere else, sugar."

"Okay, but I'm not sure I am hungry anymore." She said quietly.

"Frozen pizza at my place, then." His expression was wary as he led her out to the car by the hand. When they got to the car, he stopped and turned to her. Placing both hands on her face, he pulled her in for a slow kiss.

As she closed her eyes, white light flashed, and she caught a glimpse of a bright light shining over a young dark haired woman. A booming authoritative voice full of unearthly power said to the woman, "My son." Then in a flash, the vision was gone. Eden had gone limp while Anaiah kissed her. Her arms dropped to the side. He stopped and stared at her.

"Everything okay? No, of course it isn't. I'm sorry. I just thought, 'what if something happened to Eden,' then I just wanted to..." He shook his head at himself like he'd done something wrong. She raised her hand up and moved the dark lock of hair out of his face. She rested her hand on his cheek and traced his lips lightly with her thumb. He kissed it. He really was like heaven on earth.

"No, It's not you. I'm catching odd little visions of things. It's not usually this active when I am awake. I usually have visions when I dream." She shook her head.

"What did you see?" He looked at her seriously.

"I'm not sure. Some woman being talked to by a bright light. I saw Jayse's house explode earlier. I called Journey and told them to stay away."

"What? You saw an explosion? You felt no need to tell me?" He laughed.

"Not used to having a partner in crime." She shrugged and laughed.

"Ok, partner, let's go. I'm still starving." He opened her car door for her, and she slid in. He drove them back to his place to watch movies and eat his junk food. He ate most of the pizza and she drank a beer and had a slice. She nodded off while laying against his chest on the couch. If the world was going to fall apart around her, at least he was there to help shoulder the pieces.

CHAPTER TWENTY

E
den's eyes flew open at the sound of her ringtone blaring from her
phone. It took her a moment to realize that Anaiah had moved her to
the bed while she was sleeping. She'd fallen asleep laying against him
on his couch. Her phone continued to ring from her purse on the
nightstand. She fished it out and peeked over at Anaiah. He was still sleeping
soundly, snoring softly next to her.

"Hello?" Eden croaked groggily.

"Where are you?!" Journey shouted through the phone.

"At Anaiah's. Why?" She kept her voice low. She tiptoed out of the room
and shut the door behind her.

"I came to your house, and you weren't here. I need to talk to you. It's not
the sort of thing you say over the phone." Eden's heart dropped. Journey was
crying.

Eden gave her directions to Anaiah's apartment. She'd left her car at her
house and Anaiah was out cold; no chance of him driving her home right now.
She hung up and realized wasn't wearing her jeans. She was still wearing her t-
shirt and all her undergarments, but now, she had to locate her pants. How she
had slept through him, not only moving her from one room to another, but
also removing uncomfortable sleep attire, she had no clue. She glared at the
time on her phone. It was only one in the afternoon. *Coffee, then pants.* She
prioritized.

As she walked through the kitchen, she spotted her jeans over the back of
the couch in the living room. She grabbed them and slid them on. She turned
back to the kitchen on a mission. After she located a mug, she fiddled with his
coffee maker, and added cream to her cup.

Nursing her cup of joe, she surveyed the kitchen. She hadn't spent much time in this room. She spotted some pictures of Anaiah and his friends on his fridge. She recognized officer Sean in a lot of them. She examined them closer. *Damn, Anaiah is a good-looking guy. Aw, there's a few pictures of him as a kid. Same crooked grin, same tawny brown eyes.* Her eyes fell on the face of a woman in the photo with him. She recognized that face. It was the woman from her vision with the light and the overpowering voice. Was that Anaiah's mom? She bore a striking resemblance with the tattoo on his arm as well. The artist must have been very good.

The sudden knock on the door snapped her out of her thoughts. She set the mug down and hurried to open the door. Journey was standing in the doorway with tear-streaked cheeks, her glasses pushed up on her head as she wiped her eyes. She rushed past her into the apartment.

"Kris is in the hospital. They're not sure if he'll make it. He's burned really bad. There was a gas leak in the house. They said something must have kicked on. And it ignited as he came into the house." She was crying again, staring at the floor. She wiped her face and said, "I told him what you said about not going to their house. He said you were messing with us and went home anyway." The breath went out of Eden for a moment. *Kris was hurt. He may die. I didn't do enough to stop it.*

"How's Jayse taking this?" Eden pushed her own emotions down. She broke Journey's no touching policy in an attempt to comfort her. She laid a hand on Journey's back and a single sideways look from Journey had her dropping her hand.

"Not well. He's upset, obviously. He's really freaked out that you knew it was going to happen." She gave Eden an apologetic look. "I told him about all the strange shit you see all the time. It helped him understand why it was important to me that we stay at my place. What the fuck is going on? Why didn't you tell me you saw an explosion?" The twins knew her secrets. It seemed so insignificant with Kris' life in the balance.

"I don't know what's going on. My place got broken into, and Anaiah's ex-fiancé got impaled. There were these bowls at both places filled with some mystical crap, but also like disgusting sex related things. I saw the house blow up when I touched something from the bowl." Frustrated, she threw her hands in the air. "I'm so fucking clueless."

Journey dried her face on her shirt, pulled her glasses down from on top of her head and looked up at Eden. "Hey, at least you tried to help... Jesus Tap Dancing Christ, what the fuck happened to you?!" She yelled when she finally got a good look at Eden's face and neck. "I thought you said he was a good guy?! I'm not even kidding when I say I will cut him. No, Eden!" She yelled as Eden held up pleading hands. "I will end that big-ass son of a bitch!"

"Calm down. Shh." Eden tried to keep Journey from waking Anaiah. "He has to go to work tonight. Calm the fuck down." She felt her new status quo would be trying to convince people to chill the fuck out while freaking out on the inside herself.

"Hey. What's going on out here?" A very confused, half naked Anaiah stood in the bedroom doorway.

"I didn't want to wake you. The explosion..." Eden turned to explain.

Journey stormed past Eden and slapped Anaiah so hard across his face that his head swung to the side with the impact. "Piece of shit!" She balled up her fist and swung again, but Anaiah was able to catch her arm.

"What the fuck?" He yelled, while catching her other arm as she swung it. Eden sprang into action.

"Journey, he didn't hurt me. It's not him. Stop." Eden tried to force herself between the two to separate them.

"What the fuck is going on, E?" She shot venomous eyes at Anaiah as she took a step back and he released her hands.

"Sit down!" Eden said forcefully and pointed at a barstool at the kitchen island. "I'll get you coffee and fill you in. Go on. Sit!" She turned to Anaiah. "You!" She commanded with a bossy tone. "Go back to bed." She softened her tone as she touched his reddened cheek. "You have work tonight."

His serious face broke into a small grin. "I'm awake now. I'll put on a shirt. Pour me a cup, too?" He grabbed her chin a little less gently than usual and tipped it up to a quick kiss. "I like you bossy." He whispered and walked off.

She poured two more cups of coffee. She added creamer to Journey's and left Anaiah's black. She sat down and explained about Cole, careful not to use his real name. She told Journey what Selah said to her and filled her in on the bowls at the break-in and at the Waffle Casa.

"So, you're a demon?" She asked. "And your ex is too?"

"According to Selah, I'm half demon, the child of a demon and my mom. And yeah, Cole is a full-on demon." She corrected.

"You're a little on the tiny side to be the spawn of Satan." Journey observed.

"Well, I guess I got the dark lord's recessive short gene from his mother's side." Eden rolled her eyes.

Anaiah walked in and accepted his cup of coffee from Eden.

Journey took a long sip from her coffee and said, "Sorry about your face."

Anaiah nodded at her apology and said, "You throw hands like an inmate gone blind on jailhouse hooch. And I mean that in the nicest way possible."

"Uh, thanks. I guess." She shrugged and began to tell them about the explosion. The twins lived in the middle of nowhere about fifteen miles outside of town, by the time the ambulance got there Kris was in bad shape. A neighbor heard it from a mile away and called the cops. They thought that the guys had a meth lab at first with all the homebrew stuff in the garage and questioned Jayse about it. Jayse was pissed. He asked Journey to go see Eden and have her 'work her voodoo' to see if Kris would be okay.

"I don't know." She looked at them helplessly. "I can't see the future. Well, at least not on purpose. The best I can do is usually tell you what someone feels when I touch them, maybe get a few thoughts or memories." Eden thought for a moment. "Selah. I'm supposed to see her Wednesday at five. Maybe she can tell me how this works, how I can help. Maybe she knows what is in those bowls."

"Could you ask your ghost friends? Like do a seance or something?" Journey asked.

"They don't really come when I call them...and they never give me straight answers. It's like something about being beyond the vale means they can only cryptically say vague shit." Eden shook her head. "Loretta told me to help you and Jayse weeks ago...but I didn't know what to help you with."

"So, she was warning you? Has anything else happened? Any other ghosts?" Journey asked.

Eden thought back. "Yeah, the day Tessa got transferred...the head of the cult appeared to me. He had just died a few days earlier. He said...shit. I can't remember...he kept calling me devil's child and told me the devil's spawn had killed him or something. What the hell do you think that means?" *Have I just been missing some big picture?* Everything was falling around her and all she could do was just stand there, oblivious.

"Didn't you say you usually have visions in dreams, darlin'." Anaiah offered.

"Yeah. Haven't really had many since I moved here though." Eden bit her lip worriedly.

"What about that first night I was with you? Was that a nightmare, or..." Anaiah looked at her desperately. Like he could will her to piece this all together somehow.

"I don't know...it was me. But it wasn't anything I had done before. Might be me foreseeing the future. I was running away from someone. Someone I knew. I was trying to get to the hospital since it was the closest to where I was. Which means it wasn't far from my house. I don't know who or what was after me, but I was scared." She looked at him wide eyed. She felt so useless. "If I'm the expert on this, we are screwed."

Journey and Eden formulated a plan to go out to the twin's house later, after dark, but before work. Eden volunteered to go into work to make up for missing the night of the break-in and the night after since they were short-staffed with the twins at the hospital.

Currently, the Angelina Police and Fire Departments were still investigating the house, but they hoped by sundown, they would be gone. The women were going to check around for another 'voodoo bowl' as Journey had started calling it. Anaiah suggested that he could check to see if anything was checked into the evidence log before he went into work. If the police found a bowl, it could be connected with the one at her house and the cops would be looking into Eden again, especially since she was there during Reesa's accident. As it stood, the town was small enough that people just knew each other, and terrible things had happened.

"Do you think Cole is doing this?" Journey asked. "He could have taken out Loretta by running head on into her."

"I don't think so. He said he's here to help me. I don't have any reason to believe him, but he's the only one to offer a place to get answers." Eden shook her head. "Seems so fucking backwards."

"I don't trust him. I think he is trying to play you." Anaiah added while he poured himself more coffee and leaned back against the kitchen counter. Eden had sat down across the kitchen island from him, next to Journey on a stool.

"Well, do we trust anything Selah says then? Are we back to square one? This is not a coincidence that these things happened. And I think if Cole wanted to cause all this to happen, there would be easier ways. He's not human, so he doesn't have to worry about being arrested. He could just kill people. Why make it look like an accident? And why contact me?" She ran her hands down her face in frustration. Then a thought occurred to her, "Wait, did they recover anything weird like those bowls at Loretta's accident scene?" She asked Anaiah.

"No." He considered, "We were focused on clearing the highway. It was out on highway 287. The debris was cleared but nothing like that would have drawn attention, especially if it was off to the side like the one last night. We could go look around that area. Do it now while we wait for it to get dark." Anaiah said as he straightened up. "I'll go put on my jeans and boots." He walked into the bedroom. Eden finished her cup of coffee.

"You coming?" She asked Journey. She looked a little shell shocked.

"I guess so. I should probably go check on Jayse after." She stood up, walked across the kitchen, and set her mug in the sink. "It may make me a terrible friend, but I can't help but think, what if you had just moved on to another town. Would this still be happening, just somewhere else?" Journey sighed, "I know that's not fair. I know this isn't your fault. I know you aren't causing it. I'm glad you're my friend. I'm glad you are here...I just don't want Kris to die. I...I don't want to die because I know you." She stared down at the floor, unwilling to look Eden in the eye.

"I wish every damn day that I could have just been born normal." She said quietly. "But then again, if I was normal...I'd be married off to some old man in a cult." It came out in a near whisper. She cleared her throat. "Guess I would rather be out here trying to sort this shit out than back there. I don't want anyone to die. I just wanted to live. I'm sorry that I brought whatever this is on all of you."

"Okay, let's head out." Anaiah walked out of the bedroom and handed Eden's shoes to her. They walked in silence to Anaiah's car. It wasn't her fault, but she still felt somewhat responsible. It was frustrating to know that her presence was enough of a catalyst to allow disaster. What could she do to stop it? Every time she opened her mouth to talk, she felt the burn of tears in her eyes and anger rising like acid in her throat. She wasn't hurting her friends. Someone else was. She was doing all she could to help, but she knew it wasn't enough. She wanted to say something to cut the tension, but she knew she would either scream or burst into tears, so she sat in silence with her mouth clamped shut.

When they pulled over to the side of the road several minutes later, Anaiah broke the silence by pointing out which direction each vehicle had come from. He showed them where the point of impact was and the areas where they found debris.

"Alright, I will head up that way." Eden pointed away from the car.

"I'll cover this end." Journey pointed, still obviously upset with Eden.

Anaiah came around to Eden as she walked through chest high weeds in the ditch on the side of the road, praying there would be no rattlesnakes. "What's that about?" he nodded his head toward Journey.

"She blames me. She knows she shouldn't, but she does. And I can't help but agree. If I hadn't come here, she wouldn't have narrowly escaped death only to have our friend get hurt. She lived her life just fine before I came along." Eden used a random stick to search through the tall grass while she moved back and forth in the ditch.

She felt Anaiah's hand rest on her shoulder. He squeezed gently and before he started to speak, she knew what he would say and all the venom she had pushed down in the car ride started boiling up.

"It's not your fault, sweet…."

"I KNOW! I know…I know it's not my fault that this is happening. I KNOW that I was too busy thinking about how to hide for the last three years to even think about picking up a book or trying to find someone who might be able to help me figure ME out. I was busy being a victim my whole life…I've heard 'it's not your fault' so many damn times. My dumb ass really thought running and hiding was overcoming it. Nope! Still the victim! Still cowering in corners waiting for someone else to save me. None of this is my fault, bad things just happen to me." She hissed at him. "I'm just tired of the pity, tired of the never-ending shit storm that is my life. I want to DO SOMETHING to fix it. I want to punch life in the throat for once. So please, stop telling me it's not my fault and stop treating me like I am going to shatter into a thousand tiny pieces if you don't hold me together, and let me DO SOMETHING." She yelled at Anaiah. The shock of her words hit him as hard as Journey had earlier. The rush of anger was gone. It was instantly replaced with regret that threatened to break her and a familiar panic she knew came from fighting back in the past. "Anaiah, I'm sorry. I didn't mean to yell at you. I..." She held her hands up in front of her, pleading for forgiveness.

"I just want to help you." He said quietly as a determined grin appeared on his face. "If you want to learn to become the next Buffy the Vampire slayer? Then, fine. Baby, I don't think you are some fragile delicate angel, waiting to fall apart. You've been through hell. You say you're the victim, but you're wrong. You're a survivor. That takes strength. Life has tried to kick the shit out of you for eighteen years. You're not made of glass; you're fire tested steel. You're a fighter, and it makes you sexy as hell. So, hell yeah, let's figure this shit out! Let's punch life in the throat!" He closed the distance between them, brushed the hair out of her face, and lifted her chin. He kissed her hard. When he pulled back, she felt a little lightheaded. She stared at him in amazement.

"Find anything?" Journey yelled back at them.

"Not yet." Anaiah yelled back as they returned to their quest. They walked a quarter of a mile down the side of the highway and found nothing. They doubled back to recheck.

Eden closed her eyes, focusing on Loretta. Focused her will on pulling Loretta here to help them somehow. "Loretta, help me." She said out loud. She heard Anaiah still.

"What am I doing here?" Loretta called out in front of her. Eden opened her eyes and grinned. It had worked.

"We are trying to find something. We think it might have something to do with your accident." She focused on Loretta, the way she focused on people's emotions. Like a tether. Anaiah looked around, unable to see the ghost.

"My accident? He killed me," said Loretta.

Eden replied, "Who? Loretta, who killed you?"

"He was a dark man. He is coming for you." She wavered for a moment; Eden pulled the thread she now felt between them. Loretta became clear again.

"Loretta, was there anything that you can tell me about him, or what happened to you?" Eden begged of the ghost. She felt tension building in her neck from the mental strain of holding the tether.

"All I saw was the dark man." Loretta shrugged. "After your friend left my mind. He watched you, told me what to say to you. Wanted me to get close to you. Wanted your friends away from you."

"What?" Eden asked. Loretta struggled against Eden's hold on her.

"The dark man was there." Loretta looked at her like she was afraid but pointed to a field on the other side of a barbed wire fence.

"Who wanted my friends away from me?" Eden asked.

"Find the dark man, Eden. There are worse things than death." Loretta said gravely and burst into thousands of wispy shards before she dissipated on the wind. Eden pulled on the tether, mentally, but grasped at nothing. It was gone. Why did Eden feel like she had just seen a ghost be killed? She turned toward the field where Loretta had pointed. Desperate for some sort of answer.

"Over here." Eden motioned for Anaiah and Journey. Anaiah made it to the fence first by several hundred yards. He stepped his boot on the lower middle wire and grabbed the one above it. He pushed his foot down and pulled the one in his hands, making a space for her to get through. Eden slipped through and turned to do the same for him, but he just hopped over the fence. He followed her on a painfully slow walk as they dodged small trees, scrub grasses, and trudged through thick brush.

As she rounded another squat dense tree, she tripped and fell into a cleared-out circle, about five feet wide. Anaiah almost tripped over her. Eden pushed herself to stand up and brushed herself off. She looked around the circle. The clearing looked burned or seared into the ground in a perfect circle with dry half scorched grass coated in a brownish rusty color. In the middle was a large wooden bowl and an assortment of what looked like more herbs and twigs as well as some random items. She peered closer. There was a cheap dangly earring that she recognized as one that she couldn't find the match to when she moved from Duncan. She hadn't exactly cleaned the place up to get her deposit back; her landlord was going to jail at the time. Next to it was a paper coffee cup with lipstick on it. The logo was the local coffee shop in Duncan and that was the lipstick she used before switching to lip stains and liquid lipsticks. Under everything else was some golden-brown hair. There were drops of what she could only assume was dry blood dripped over it all. She looked down at the brown color of the dead grass, it looked eerily similar.

"Is this blood? Dry blood?" Eden felt the color drain from her face. She tried to shake off the look of horror she knew was stamped on her face as she looked up at Anaiah.

"Looks like." He squatted down and pulled up a patch of the scorched grass. "It's soaked into the dirt. There had to be a lot." He swallowed hard.

"Who's blood?" Eden asked no one in particular.

"What about blood?" Journey climbed the brush to get into the circle.

"This." Eden pointed at rusty colored grass. "We think it's blood."

"How in the hell did you find this?" She raised an eyebrow.

"Loretta. I figured out how to get her to help me. She told me the dark man was over here when she died." Eden shrugged.

"And you were like 'hell yeah, let's go find the dark man and his hideout?' Bold move, E. Very badass. Ooh, there's our voodoo bowl. Any sex trash in there?" She surveyed the bowl.

"No, this one was made during my dry spell, apparently." She attempted a smile, trying to break the tension. "I think this might be a cup I used on the drive here. That is one of my earrings from my apartment in Duncan. I don't know whose hair that is though. Or who's blood we are standing on." She offered to Journey.

"It's the same color as the demon's, right?" Anaiah said with anger simmering in his gaze. "That's his hair."

"Hadn't realized you paid attention to details like that." Journey said, cocking an eyebrow. "You're a regular Sherlock Holmes."

"I assess people and situations for a living. Just trying to piece this shit together." There was danger building in his eyes.

"Relax." Eden placed a hand on his shoulder and gave him a small smile. "If she gives you shit, it means she likes you. We're cool, then?" She threw a smile at Journey.

"Yeah, we don't have to hug it out." She waved a dismissive hand at her. "Think he's right?" She nodded back to the bowl.

"It's possible. Wait," She squatted down in front of the bowl. "There's nothing here to connect Loretta unless this cup is hers. So, if that's Cole's hair...he might have been the target of this...spell or whatever that caused the accident. Loretta might have just been in the wrong place." She connected the dots a bit. "This bowl, it connected me to the last guy I was with. The next one connected me to Anaiah, but no one died there. My place just got trashed. The next one, the last person Anaiah was with before me was killed. This can't just be a coincidence, right?"

"Your guess is as good as mine, hon." Anaiah shrugged.

"Makes more sense than someone killing your least favorite manager." Journey raised her eyebrows. "Hey, Mr. Police connections, any chance you can get someone to run that blood for a match?" Journey looked at Anaiah.

"Doesn't really work that way. We don't have a lab here; it'd have to be sent off to be tested and then they'd run it in a database of criminals and samples from victims of violent crimes. I couldn't just ask a buddy to run it." He said in a bit of a disappointed huff.

"Wait..." Eden stood up and touched the blood on the grass in Anaiah's hand. Nothing. She noticed the scratch on her arm. The stick didn't give her a vision until it broke the skin. Anaiah gave her a confused look. She broke off a piece of crusty grass, shrugged and hoped for the best, as she tossed in her mouth. Anaiah's eyes went wide.

"What the..." Anaiah started.

A bright light pulsed, then Eden was cast into pitch black. For a moment she worried that nothing came of it, but then she heard a stirring in the darkness.

"Please, I'll do anything. Don't hurt her." Eden heard a familiar voice. Her mother's voice was crying in pitch black. Eden strained to focus to see anything. A light slowly glowed and in the darkness, she saw a little girl, about two or three years old. She looked like Eden had as a child. *Was this a vision of my past? I don't remember my mother ever trying to stop my dad from hurting me.* The little girl was held with her back to a dark figure. She was crying and trembling and the dark figure was crouched behind her with its arm around her chest.

"Mommy, make the bad man go away." She whimpered as tears slid down her face.

"It's okay, Sarah. Don't be scared. Mommy is here." Eden's mother attempted to soothe her from somewhere in the darkness. Panic slipped into her voice as she pleaded, "Please, we've lost two children already. She is a good girl. Please, we love her so much. Please don't hurt her." Her mother began to sob. The vision started to fade. Eden fought to stay. She tried to reach the girl. The darkness fell again as Eden heard a muffled cry of pain and a sick gurgling sound. Her mother's screams rang through her head as she was slammed back into reality with a blinding flash of white across her vision.

Eden collapsed onto the ground in front of her. She spat the grass out of her mouth and fought the bile rising in her throat. She wiped at her mouth and noticed her wet cheeks. She was crying.

"Eden, honey." Anaiah was at her side instantly. His large hand rubbed soothing circles on her lower back.

"What did you see?" Journey asked a little impatiently. "You zoned out for a few minutes. You had a vision, right?"

For a moment she couldn't speak. "I had a sister. She was just..." Eden sobbed. "She was good...she wasn't like me." Eden took in slow deep breaths. Trying to force herself to be calm by sheer force of will. To be strong. "My mother loved her. This is her blood."

"No," Anaiah shook his head. "I looked it up, CPS only took you. You didn't have any siblings on your case."

"Now, I know why they didn't fight to get me back when I ran. They had another one on the way." Eden flexed her shaking hands into fists.

"How old?" Journey added quietly.

"Around two." Eden looked up at Anaiah. His eyes softened with understanding.

"Just a baby." he said softly. He stared into her eyes with concern. Puzzling out how to soothe her hurting heart.

"Jesus." Journey blew out a breath.

"How do we report this? How can I get the law involved without hanging us all up in the middle of this?" Anaiah asked no one in particular.

"I don't think the person who did this is going to be easy to arrest." Journey said flatly.

"I wonder if they even reported it." Eden pushed herself up to her feet. She brushed bits of blood-crusted grass off herself. Anaiah rose with her.

"What do you mean, their baby was murdered, 'course they reported it." Anaiah's face screwed up with confusion, his voice rising slightly with anger.

"Anaiah, they didn't even document my birth. Do you think if I had died, that they would have told anyone? It would just draw bad attention to the church. I'd have been buried in the graveyard on the compound's grounds. I've seen it. Graves marked with rocks or little stick crosses. She's been thrown in a hole in the ground." She balled up her fists. "Maybe not. My mom said she was good. She said she loved her. It should make me feel better that they loved her...but I'm just so sad."

"You o...." Anaiah started to say but stopped himself when he saw the irritation flash across her face.

"Stop. You know damn well I'm not. Kris is hanging on by a thread, and I just listened to my baby sister get murdered. I am not okay. I'm just not. You can't fix that. I love you, but you can't." She placed a hand on his chest. "Let's take this crap out of here and get ready to see what kind of mess is in the woods out at Jayse's. We should swing by the hospital and see how they are doing. Maybe I can see if I see something there too." She picked up the bowl.

"You gonna have to put some of Kris in your mouth too?" A smile crept across Journey's face as she cracked the tension. A small laugh escaped Eden.

"God, I hope not. My boyfriend might beat him up in a jealous fit." She grinned, placing her free hand in his.

"I'd give him a pass until he was back to full health." Anaiah joked. The dark cloud over her heart lifted. He took the bowl from her with his free hand.

"I'm sure he appreciates your generosity, honey." She laughed.

CHAPTER TWENTY-ONE

I t was late afternoon when they arrived at North Texas Memorial Hospital. Journey wasted no time, hopping out as soon as the car stopped. As Eden followed, Anaiah tugged her hand slightly to keep her behind. Eden gave Journey a glance to indicate she should go on ahead without them. Journey rolled her eyes as she walked on.

"Hey." He gave her the half smile that undid her nerves. "You said something back there." He brushed her hair back out of her face.

"I'm sorry if I've been on edge today." The apology tumbled out. Her old habits rose to the surface and her fear crept in. He noted the unease in her eyes, as she tried to look away. He gently lifted her chin to look him in the eyes.

"Not that. You're right. It's not my job to fix you. It's my job to be here for you if you need me." His thumb brushed her cheek and she leaned into it. "What I was talking about was the part where you said you loved me." His smile lit up his whole face.

"I thought we covered that the other night when I melted down." She gave a small, embarrassed smile.

"No, I confessed I was falling for you, and you said you thought you might be too. Today, you just said it outright. Like you'd been saying it for years. You love me." He kissed her cheek softly. His face hovered inches from hers as he breathed her in. She let out a soft sigh of contentment.

"Yes, I love you." She kissed his lips softly as she closed her eyes.

"I love you, too, beautiful." He said against her lips before he returned her soft gentle kiss with a slow, deep, and claiming kiss.

"We should head in." Eden said reluctantly as she finally pulled back. She steadied herself. She didn't want to face Jayse or Kris. She wanted to stay in this bubble with her boyfriend and just be content for a few more seconds.

"You've got this." He said quietly. She nodded.

They located the intensive care unit and waited to be called back. There was a two-visitor limit and Jayse refused to leave Kris' side. Eden waited for Journey to swap places for her in the waiting room. When Journey walked into the waiting area, her face was a stony mask.

"He's a little more stable. They are having to give him a lot of fluids and medications to keep him sedated." Her mask slipped slightly, and Eden could tell she was fighting back emotion she didn't want to feel.

"He's better, though?" Eden asked.

"A little." Journey slumped into a chair. "Go on. Voodoo." She motioned to the door.

Eden pushed through the double doors down sterile white looking hallways. The nurse at the desk pointed her to a room filled with the quiet whirring of machines. Her eyes traced over the poles filled with bags of medications, the little glowing machines attached to them, and tubes that ran to the bed. So many tubes. The rhythmic whoosh of the machine closest to the bed directed her sight to the tubes connected to his mouth. They were breathing for him.

There were other machines; all sorts of monitors and wires attached to him. A large monitor displayed his blood pressure, pulse, and other vital information they were tracking. She stared down at him in the bed. She wondered where they could possibly have put a blood pressure cuff. His body was one giant wound. Her heart broke for her friend. His face was burned and swollen and barely resembled the one that usually grinned at her stupid jokes.

"Hi." Jayse muttered from the chair by the door.

"Hey. I'm so sorry, Jayse." She closed the door behind her.

"You tried...I guess. I mean, I don't really know what it is that you do." He sounded exhausted.

"Can I...can I hold his hand or something?" Eden asked weakly.

"Jesus," He sat up straighter. "I guess so. You acted like he didn't exist before." He cast his annoyed gaze on her.

"What do you mean? I'm his friend. I'm YOUR friend. I meant what I said about you two being like brothers to me." She said in a harsh hushed voice.

"He liked you. Don't say you didn't notice. As soon as you got a boyfriend, you just paraded him around and let Kris know that you were off the market." He stared her down.

"Look, Jayse. I get that you are upset, but I can't help that I feel the same way he did. You want to take it out on someone, but I'm not the one to blame here." She said quietly. "You've been in love with Journey for a while. What if I professed my love for you? No matter what I felt, you wouldn't owe it to me to feel it back. Do you want me to try to help or not?"

"Go ahead, read his palm. Whatever the fuck it is that you do." His voice was quiet but sharp. He crossed his arms and sat back looking doubtful. Eden realized that in addition to this trauma of seeing his brother like this, Jayse's anger at her secrets may be seeping out too.

Eden crossed to the other side of the room, searching to find a piece of skin without bandage or burn. She reached down carefully and held his hand searching mentally. *Come on psychic powers...help me out here. Kris if you are in there, talk to me.*

Eden? She heard Kris' voice in her head. As he spoke, her mind's eye shifted the view to her and Kris holding hands in a blank white space.

Kris? She thought back.

What's happening? Am I dead? It hurts. It hurts so much. Where am I? His voice echoed in her head.

You are in the hospital. They are keeping you sedated. As she conveyed this, his subconscious changed the setting to a room like his hospital room.

So, I'm not dreaming about this? He looked around.

Yeah, I'm here talking to you. You might be dreaming a bit too. You are on some very strong drugs. Eden hoped to relieve his confusion about having this strange mental conversation.

The house? What happened? He asked her expectantly.

There was a gas leak when you came home, something clicked on, and it blew up.

Yeah, I remember. After that, someone was there, I was afraid they were hurt too. Some guy. Eden tried to see what he was remembering, hoping for a glimpse of a memory. It was there, but it was so blurry. Some shape of a person stood over him, his palms glowing. Was that fire?

"You're the wrong one." A cold deep voice said matter-of-factly. Eden couldn't place the voice. Almost like she'd heard it before but couldn't recall where.

Kris, everyone is here. We want you to get better. You gotta be strong. Your little family needs you. We love you, brother. She told Kris, hoping to soothe him. She wanted to give him this little bit of peace.

I'll try. I love you too, little sister. His smile was weak, but genuine. *I think I'm going to sleep. I'm so tired.* He added.

It's *okay. Rest. We can talk later.* Eden squeezed his hand gently before she pulled back her hand. She wiped the tears from her eyes.

"Anything?" Jayse said looking hopeful despite his anger.

"Yeah. I sort of talked to him. He remembers the explosion, saw someone there. A guy. I couldn't make out his face. It was weird, he had fire coming out of his palms." She knew she sounded crazy. "He's still strong...in there...mentally. The smoke inhalation didn't do a bunch of damage, you know, to his brain." Eden realized she was failing at being the comforting friend Jayse needed. His face fell. She shifted on her feet nervously.

"You're fucking crazy. Just leave." He leaned forward and placed his head in his hands. *He can be mad at me, that's fine. He's struggling. I can take it.*

"Jayse." Eden paused at the door. "You can be pissed at me all you want. Push me out. That's fine. But Journey loves you. She has for years. You pushing her away is going to destroy her. She looks tough, but you are her soft spot. Please, don't hurt her."

"Just go..." He pointed to the door, but she saw his silver lined eyes. Her heart felt like it was being ripped apart. She wanted to console Jayse and help Journey with the feelings she was avoiding. What could she do for Kris? She was failing her friends.

Eden walked back out to Journey. She wanted to hug Journey and tell her it was all going to be okay. Journey would hate that. Eden gave a brief description of what she could do with Kris.

"You just did some telepathy?" Journey cocked her head to the side.

"Maybe the drugs affected him, so his subconscious is more open to me. I get feelings and memories from normal people. Maybe that's all subconscious. And the drugs made it work?" Eden guessed.

"Sounds plausible. Sounds like bullshit too." Journey shrugged. Journey must be more on edge because of Jayse taking his feelings out on everyone.

"Don't let him push you away. He knows he's being an ass." Eden gave her what she hoped was a reassuring look of determination.

"He's allowed to be an ass right now." Journey's eyes softened and she looked younger, more fragile.

"No, he isn't. He's allowed to feel whatever he wants, but what he does is entirely on him. He can be mad at me. He can be mad at God. He can be mad at anyone else but you." Eden looked back at her with compassion. "Don't let him hurt you because he's hurting." Eden wished she could go back and give that advice to herself years ago.

"Okay. I won't." She took a deep breath. "Ready to go trudging around the woods?" Eden let Journey's obvious subject change slide. It was a hard day.

"Okay, but first, I have to feed the man. He's been so patient and has not complained of starving once today. He's always hungry." Eden shifted her tone for a lighter mood.

Eden found Anaiah staring at the vending machine, cash in hand. *Ha! I knew it!* At least she was getting this one thing right.

"Babe, let's get real food." She patted him on the shoulder.

"Yes, ma'am. I'm starving." His drawl threatened to melt her, but she looked at Journey and gave her a knowing wink. They headed to the local Tex-Mex place. Over dinner, Eden quietly told them what Kris saw.

"Do you think it's the same guy that you saw, you know, in the field?" Journey fumbled around for some tact. At least she was trying. Eden was honestly surprised that she didn't just say "the sister killer" in her usual direct way.

"Unless there is more than one of them working to destroy everything around me, it's probably the same guy." Eden shrugged and took another bite of her fajitas.

"And his hands were actually on fire?" Anaiah asked skeptically. He casually picked food off Eden's unfinished plate. He had devoured his like a man who hadn't eaten in days when it arrived. She never finished the huge pile of fajita toppings, so she was okay with it.

"So that's where you draw the line?" Journey deadpanned. Anaiah swallowed and regarded Journey with annoyance. "Flaming hands? You've gone along with everything else and the fire in his hands is your line in the sand?"

"What? Am I not allowed to be surprised anymore?" He huffed. "I got a hot psychic girlfriend and suddenly I have to just be unimpressed with the world?" Anaiah was cranky from sleep deprivation.

"Dude, calm your tits. I'm just messing with you." Journey shot back. Her thin veil of cool unaffected badass was starting to fray around the edges.

"You need to learn that everything she says is a sarcastic joke to avoid real feelings." Eden added and winked at her. In response, Journey pushed her glasses up by the bridge with her middle finger.

"If we find another voodoo bowl out at Jayse and Kris' place, how does that connect?" Eden wondered out loud as she pushed her half-eaten plate towards Anaiah for him to finish. "I mean, we have my ex, my boyfriend, his ex and what? My best friends?" Eden raised up an eyebrow.

Anaiah swallowed a mouth full of fajita meat and shrugged. "I don't know. Until we fill in some holes, I'm not sure how it works."

"That's what she said." Journey giggled to herself.

"Walked into that one." He chuckled.

"Nice." Eden said to Journey. "I guess, one connection was that Kris liked me. I don't know…I don't want to believe it's all about me. But it all points back to me. I'm the common denominator." Eden rubbed her hands over her face.

"Well, until we find out what's going on, it's all connected to you." Anaiah added. "And Kris liked you?" He raised his eyebrows, pretending to be jealous.

"Yeah, but I didn't like him like that. I knew what I wanted the minute I saw you." Eden beamed coyly at him.

"Same, gorgeous" Anaiah leaned over and kissed her temple.

"Your adorable adoration is making me ill." Journey pulled out cash for her part of the ticket. Anaiah waved her off and settled the bill before they headed to Anaiah's apartment. Anaiah's shift began a few hours earlier than Eden's, so he needed to get ready.

"You two be careful. And call me if you need me, I'll bring my rig and all." He called out as they walked to Journey's car, leaving him at the apartment.

"And the other guys on the rig? Are they coming out too?" Journey pointed out.

"Just be careful." He turned up the stairs to grab a shower and get dressed for work.

Journey backed out of the parking spot and pulled out onto the street. They passed the city limits sign just after the sun had set. After several minutes of driving in silence, Journey turned and began winding down the dirt roads to the twin's house. Eden had only been there a few times for brew days and after work hangouts.

The small farmhouse was their grandparents' home when they were still alive. Eden had found the house to be charming if a little cramped. There was a small amount of acreage behind the house and a small barn that they used as part hobby shop, part brew pub. The twins didn't talk much about their parents, but their grandfather was their hero. He'd brought them up in the art of brewing and gardening. They still tended the small garden he had kept in honor of their grandmother. Eden recalled the small angel statue in the garden with a concrete bench in front of it. "Ariel's Garden" was etched into the seat of the bench. The twins had told her how their grandfather never referred to her by name. Only as his angel. Kris had expressed his want for a love like theirs someday. The thought tightened something in her chest.

She set her determination on positive thoughts. If she had anything to do with it, Kris would get through this thing. She would help find whoever did this to him and when he recovered, she would help take vengeance for him. She resolved to stand by his side as his friend and help him reach that day when he found a love like his grandparents. There had to be a future for all of them beyond all this mess they were in. That hope had to drive her forward or she risked breaking down and never getting back up.

Eden hopped out and held up the yellow caution tape as Journey drove her small car under it and parked between the detached garage and the little barn to hide the car from the road. They pulled out the small flashlights Anaiah had supplied and started walking the perimeter of the house. Eden squatted down to check under the house, but Journey wanted to be more thorough. Journey shimmied through the door into the crawl space and checked every corner under the house. As Eden held her flashlight steady to help light up the dark space, she considered the need to bake Journey a cake for her assistance in supernatural inspection.

The barn and area around it were also a dead end. The trek through the acreage behind the barn wasn't as bad as the field they had walked through at the crash site earlier that day. They fanned out to walk about twenty feet apart, picking their way through the field.

"We should be able to walk the whole field in less than an hour. I hope we stumble on it soon, so we don't have to check the woods on both sides." Eden broke the silence.

"Yeah, this is going quickly. That," Journey glared at the dark woods in an almost accusatory tone, "most definitely won't be." Journey said it as if the woods should know how inconvenienced she would be if she had to trek through them.

Thirty minutes later, they ducked into the woods next to the house. They had found nothing, and Eden felt like they were figuratively stumbling in the dark as well as literally stumbling through these dark woods. They had to keep a tighter formation between the two of them than walking through the pasture. Eventually, they reached the fence line and worked their way around. It was getting late. They still needed time to shower and get dressed for work. They walked through the remains of the incinerated house carefully. Nothing remained but the debris that was blown from the house. Shards of glass from the exploded windows, the twisted metal of the steel front door and the like littered the ground.

"Wait a second." She muttered. Kris had touched that doorknob seconds before the explosion. She bent down and touched the doorknob and was disappointed to get nothing.

"You gonna lick it?" Journey's tone was mostly serious.

"No. I don't think licking magic is the key here." She looked up at her weary friend. Eden desperately wanted to find something, anything here. She thought for a moment, then pulled her box knife from the back pocket of her jeans. She carefully sliced a shallow cut in her thumb. She pressed the blood down over a fingerprint pressed into the metal on the outside edge of the knob.

As soon as her finger made contact, her vision flashed white, and she found herself standing in the morning sunlight, walking into the house. Her body turned and closed the door behind her. *I must be watching from Kris's point of view.* She braced for the explosion mentally, but it didn't come. She moved into the kitchen. She watched as large hands covered in black work gloves pulled the stove out enough to expose the bendable extension pipe. The hands pulled out a knife, made a hole in the pipe and pushed the stove back. *Oh shit... This isn't Kris' memory. This is the memory of the guy doing all of this!*

Eden watched from his perspective as they headed to a bedroom, Jayse's bedroom, in the back of the house. He closed the door and placed a towel at the bottom of the door. He opened a window. She tried to catch a reflection to see his face. *Walk by a mirror!* She mentally strained to make herself turn when he passed one. The body she was trapped in continued to open windows. He sat down on the bed, facing an open window. A few minutes later, she could smell the gas seeping in despite the open windows and the towel on the floor.

She heard the car pull into the driveway. He got up and closed all but one window. She heard the front door, and footsteps into the living room.

"What's that smell?" Kris wondered out loud. Her host removed his gloves and the towel from the door. He cracked the door open slowly and reached a hand around it. Eden heard his vaguely familiar male voice chanting something, but she couldn't make sense of it. His hands spontaneously ignited in flames. As the gas sparked, Eden felt the man crouch behind the door. Her ears rang from the concussive blast, but the person in this body was impatient to see his handiwork. The house was engulfed in roaring flames as he ran out of the room, down the hall and into the living room. He stood over Kris with his hands glowing with fire.

"No. You're the wrong one." She heard him say in an angry tone. She fought to probe the mind of this psycho and it hit a solid wall in his mind. As the killer stepped out the front door, Eden was pushed back into her body. The flash of brightness followed by sudden nightfall had Eden stumbling over as soon as she was back into her own mind.

Eden was trembling. She tried to steady her shaking hands. She was vaguely aware of Journey shouting something, but Eden couldn't hear her over the ringing in her ears. Eden cradled her aching head in her hands. She tried to say, 'there's no bowl,' to Journey but it was muffled and garbled in her ears."

Journey walked over and pulled Eden to her feet; she gave her a bit of a shake. Eden's ears started to pop and clear but her head pounded out a painful pulse.

"There's no bowl." Eden repeated.

"You're sure?" Journey asked.

"He just cut the pipe and sparked it with the fire in his hands." Eden nodded. She felt nauseated from the movement.

"Did you see him? Like Kris saw him?" Journey spoke at a volume that Eden's throbbing head barely tolerated.

"No. Journey, I was him. I was in his memory, but I couldn't hear his thoughts. I was just there seeing from his eyes. I tried to turn him to a mirror or something. Jesus, my head is fucking killing me." Eden massaged her temples.

"I've got some Excedrin in my bag. And! Some glass cleaning wipes with alcohol, for the blood. You know in case they come back to recheck. See, all those true crime shows weren't for nothing." She jogged off to the car. Eden sat in the grass and tried not to vomit from the throbbing agony splitting through her skull.

Journey popped back around the corner, wipes in hand. She wiped the doorknob, then pulled Eden up by her hand. She handed her two white pills. Eden popped them back and swallowed them dry. She could walk, every step brought a steady throb with it.

"Let's go get cleaned up for our paying job. That's going to blow." Eden walked to the car.

Journey sighed. "Yeah. It's going to be extra sucky because everyone will want to talk... about your face... about Kris."

"Oh, fuck me! Do I need a job?" Eden declared.

"I imagine that boyfriend of yours would support you." She cracked her wicked grin.

"He seems the type to volunteer to do that...but I can't abandon my friend in need." She said with very little enthusiasm as she buckled herself in.

"Damn right you can't." Journey backed out of the driveway.

When they arrived at Eden's house, Journey reached into the backseat and grabbed an overnight bag. "From my romantic sleepover at the hospital. Mind if I just get ready here?"

"Nah. Mi crime scene es su crime scene." Eden motioned toward the house.

"Super boyfriend really helped you clean this up after it got trashed? Even called out of work so he could stay?" Journey said as they walked up the steps. The new door stood out in stark contrast to the older paint.

"Yeah. Then I got drunk and told him everything. Freaked him right out. He had his cop buddy pull up my files while I slept it off. Found out I was in a mental hospital for a while when I was a teenager." Eden shook her head in disbelief that only a few days had passed. Everything had changed so quickly after that night. She could hardly believe she'd only been dating Anaiah for a little over three weeks.

"Shit...mental hospital? For the ghosts?" Journey walked through the front doorway.

"No, for my shitty teenage attitude. Yes, the ghosts." Eden walked into her closet to pull out her work clothes. She offered Journey the shower since she was muddy from crawling under the burned-out house. While Journey showered, Eden called Anaiah to catch him up.

Eden could tell from the 'uh-huh' and the 'that's interesting,' every so often that he was out in the ambulance with his coworkers. "Okay, call me on your lunch break. An' maybe I can swing out there to grab something to eat. Love you, sugar."

"Love you too." She grinned at the butterflies she felt. Journey strode out of the bathroom showered and dressed. She headed for the mirror to fix her hair while Eden stepped into the bathroom to get ready. Eden attempted to cover her bruises with makeup, which was minimally helpful as some were still deep blue. A few were yellowing. She finally threw down the concealer in frustration. With a few of her favorite curse words, she declared she was ready to grab a coffee before they went to work.

CHAPTER TWENTY-TWO

T he drive home from work was quiet. Eden and Journey had exhausted all the energy they had left at work. They had stocked entirely too many products, accepted condolences, told people to mind their own business, and theorized throughout the night. Eden didn't care if the devil himself was standing in her living room, she was headed straight for bed. Journey still had to stop by the hospital before she headed home. Eden didn't know how she was still standing. As they turned onto her street, Eden noticed Anaiah's car in the drive next to hers.

"Are we sure he's, like, an actual human?" Journey said with mock disgust.

"He's just…protective. He's got issues…his mom was a human punching bag." Eden noted Journey's sidelong look. "I think he's sweet." She shrugged.

"Well, have fun with your emotional support puppy of a boyfriend. I'm going to go see Sir Broods-a lot." She smiled sarcastically as Eden stepped out of the car.

"You're the emotional support puppy for him right now, boo." Eden gave a small smile.

"True. Text me later, girl." Journey called out as Eden closed the car door.

Eden walked up to the steps, smiling at what she saw on her porch. Anaiah snored softly with his head propped against the railing of her front steps. An overnight bag laid between his feet. Instead of having lunch with her last night, he had gone out on nonstop medical calls and texted her to say he couldn't make it. Poor guy.

"Anaiah?" Eden wiggled his shoulder. "Sweetie, I'm home."

His eyes slowly opened. They went wide as he realized that he dozed off on her porch. "Oh, hey. I was just waiting for you. Care if I sleep over?" He smiled sweetly.

"Yeah, if you need to play bodyguard so you can sleep, I'll share my bed. If I must." She feigned an exaggerated huff.

"Not fooling you, huh?" He stood up and kissed her forehead. He walked with her as she unlocked the door.

"If you weren't so dead tired, you could have played the horny boyfriend who wants to fool around card...but we both know we are probably just going to crash the minute we get in bed." She kicked the door shut and locked it. "Should I shower then sleep or sleep then shower?" She asked.

"I say we strip 'n sleep. You can shower with me later." He threw a sleepy if not mischievous glance her way. He'd already kicked his boots off and was working on untucking his shirt. *Sleep, Eden...you need it more than you need to peel the rest of his clothes off.* She reminded herself as she took in his muscled abs while he took off his belt.

"Mmm. That sounds good." She gave a coy smile. She pulled her shirt over her head, peeled off her jeans, and tossed them into her hamper. She stepped into her closet to grab a night gown as she unhooked her bra and let it fall to the floor. She stared down at it for a second, and decided it was future Eden's problem. She reached over to the shelf and grabbed a ponytail holder. She threw her hair up in a very messy curly bun.

"God, you're beautiful." Anaiah said from the doorway behind her. As she started to turn to say something about how she looked like complete trash, he walked up behind her and hugged her from behind. His bare chest was warm against her bare back. She leaned into him as he leaned down and kissed her neck lightly. She closed her eyes and melted into him more. His hand flattened across her stomach and held her fast against him. The other hand slid up from her waist and roved over her chest.

"Thought you were tired." She moaned.

"I am. But I can't help myself." He whispered onto her neck. She tilted her head to the side to let him kiss up and down her neck. She winced a little from the stiffness in her neck. He asked softly. "Did that hurt?"

"My neck is just sore. Between work and hiking all over Jayse's property, I'm just kind of sore all over." Eden sighed.

He released her carefully as he stepped away from her. Eden was about to tell him for the hundredth time, she was fine, when his large hands started massaging her shoulders and neck. She leaned forward in the closet and braced her hands on a shelf to keep from falling forward. His hands ran over the ridges of scars on her back. She expected a comment about them. Anaiah leaned over and kissed them softly.

His hands delivered just enough pressure. She relished the small ache of each knotted muscle as slowly, each gave way to his massage. As he reached her lower back, he wrapped an arm around her stomach and braced her as she leaned into his hand. Using one very large hand, he released the tension in the small of her back. She felt her body relax more and more into his arm's embrace until he gently leaned her back against his chest. Both arms wrapped around her waist. She closed her eyes and sighed in contentment as he kissed the top of her head.

"Let's go to bed, baby." He whispered in her ear. At that point, she was pretty sure she'd do anything he said. She grabbed a nightgown and slipped it over her head.

Eden snuggled into his warm embrace. As she tilted her head up and kissed him goodnight, her vision flashed white with the tell-tale signs of another vision. She saw Anaiah holding her as he slept next to her. She recognized the disaster around her as her house on the night of the break-in. Anaiah whispered something intently. As Eden slipped from the vision back to herself, she heard his familiar deep, but tired and husky voice say "amen."

Her eyes flew open. She'd bared her truth to him, but in the process, had forgotten the fear that his prayer in the cabin had instilled in her.

"Anaiah." She said softly.

"Everything okay?" His soft sleepy voice murmured.

Her heart thundered in her chest. Asking about this felt like a confrontation: like starting a fight. It felt like if she pulled at this one thread, she would unravel everything they were building. She knew it was foolish to feel that way. He wasn't like that, she had to remind herself. She steeled her nerves and said, "I need to ask you about something I saw." It came out barely a whisper.

Anaiah sat up abruptly. "Was it a vision? Did someone get hurt?"

"No." Eden sat up next to him. "I know this is silly of me to be concerned. But...I had a vision of you praying with me in your arms the other night, after I told you everything. And...I saw you praying in the cabin. I didn't mean to spy on you or anything. I was just looking for you. It shouldn't matter, but you know my history with religion. It's messy." She put her hand on his arm.

He let out a breath. "I told you on our first date that I believed. I didn't mean to keep it a secret." He turned to look at her.

"But you did." Tears threatened to fall from her silver-lined eyes.

"Yeah." He shook his head. "At first, I didn't think it would matter a lot, as we got closer, I thought I would bring it up and see where we stood with our faith. What you believed, what I believed and what not. But on the night that I found out about your parents...what they did. I was praying for a way to keep you from hating me for what I believed." He touched her face softly.

Anaiah continued, "I was praying to keep you safe when I couldn't. And I was praying for the strength to not drive to Houston and beat the living shit out of your father." She could see the danger behind his words in his eyes. He was looking at her, earnestly pleading for her to understand his heart, but his eyes held onto the violence promised to her father if he ever crossed his path.

"I look at this," he laid a soft touch to her neck, "and I want to end Cole. And it eats me up inside. I shouldn't want to do that. I shouldn't...crave that." He closed his eyes and shook his head. When he opened them, they were silver-lined. His deep voice was soft and brittle as he said, "When I read your file...the account they took down about the scars, the cuts, the bruises..." He inhaled on each of those words like they dealt a blow to him each time he said them. "You know they had the radiology report from the hospital? Do you know how many healed fractures you had?" Tears welled up in his eyes. "Baby, I don't just want to kill that man. I want to...hurt...Him. I want to take him apart piece by piece, so he feels everything you ever felt and more." His hands shook. He clenched them as a tear rolled down his face. "So, I prayed that God would keep me here, with you so I could help you heal, so I could love you like they never had. But mostly to keep me from becoming a monster too." His low voice shook as he breathed out, "They didn't just break your body and emotionally abuse you, though. They had to use the one thing in my life that has held me steady. They had to break your faith, your spirit, and leave you without a hope of trusting anyone, especially not God."

She didn't know what to say. She pulled herself into his lap and wrapped her arms around him. He returned her embrace and for a few moments, they just held each other and let their tears fall. She finally cleared her throat, voice husky with emotion.

"The first time I hung out with friends, Kris asked me questions about my life before. If it made me lose my faith. I didn't lie to you about that. I believe there's something...someone. There's been too many things that just worked out. The way I was able to stay safe when I ran. The way I always found another job, another place to stay, a ride to another town without getting hurt, kidnapped, or raped. It made me think that someone was looking out for me. I've doubted in the harder times. I've not been faithful in prayer, or worship or any of that, but I always felt some force there, helping. And now, when all this horrible chaotic mess is going on around me, I find myself able to get through it because I have you. A man who's heart breaks for me. Who wants to fight for me and with me. Who, despite knowing how hard it is for me to believe, talks to his God for me. You tried to have faith for both of us. You don't have to hide it from me. Yes, I will always question the motivation behind religious people, behind churches and ritual, but when I look at you and what I have found with you, how can I not believe there has to be a heavenly father taking care of me?" She placed her forehead against his. "Keep praying for me. For us. Maybe someday I will get back there too, but I don't want to be the thing that makes you hide any part of you. I want all of you." She kissed him gently.

"And you say I'm the good one?" He sighed and cracked a small smile. "I didn't mean to fall apart on you like this." The tears were still running down his cheeks.

"I think it makes it more fair, if anything. So far, I have had most of the emotional breakdowns. Maybe we can work out a schedule or something for who's turn it is?" She pushed his hair back with a hand and looked into his beautiful brown eyes. "I love you. I want to know all about you. Not just the best of you."

"I want to talk to you about all of this. Tell you everything about me, but we don't have to do that all today. I'm a big mess, darlin' and we both need to sleep. Are you okay with us putting a big ol' pin in this and taking it down to talk about when things are a little calmer, maybe?" His exhaustion poured into his voice.

"Of course." She said, "We haven't even unpacked all my baggage yet, no need to keep us up to drag yours out. We don't have to rush into trying to scare each other off." She giggled. "Let's go to sleep. Say your prayers." She smiled at him and laid down on her bed. She patted the spot next to her and he cuddled up beside her. She closed her eyes as he spoke his prayer in a hushed whisper over them both. He prayed for her to receive wisdom and peace as she was tumbling off into a blessed dreamless sleep.

CHAPTER TWENTY-THREE

In the afternoon, Eden's alarm blared at them. She sleepily untangled herself from Anaiah's arms. After heading to the bathroom, she returned to Anaiah making coffee. They drank coffee in a comfortable silence, with Eden leaning against his shoulder as he leaned back on the counter.

After his cup was empty, she sat it in the sink with hers and took him by the hand. Eden pulled him behind her as they headed into the shower. They didn't talk about ghosts, demons, or anything on earth. Once they got the essentials clean, their focus turned to exploring each other's bodies. He picked her up with one hand under her legs and used the other to brace them against the wall of her shower. Anaiah kissed her deeply while sending waves of pleasure through her again and again with each thrust. He drove her over her peak twice, each time slowing his thrusts to gently kiss along the nape of her neck as she cried out in ecstasy. As he neared his end, Eden disentangled herself and dropped to her knees. She intentionally took her time, teasing him with her tongue at first. Then she slowly slid him, inch by glorious inch into her mouth, relaxing her throat, and teasing with her tongue until the beast was nearly swallowed. He let out a low approving moan. She swallowed again and looked up at him with a satisfied gleam in her eye.

"Oh fuck." He growled as his eyes met with hers. She drew back and forth slowly, swallowing. His pleasure was evident in the throb she felt rippling through him. She set a torturously slow pace at first, but his every moan drove her onward to her task. Within moments, he was ready to climax. Eden withdrew him and grasped him firmly in her hand, stroking him until he released with a shudder onto the shower floor.

He lifted her up by her hand to him and held her close to his chest.

"My God, I love you." He breathed into the hair on the top of her head. His heart was racing, and his breathing was still unsteady.

"I love you too." She tipped her head up to him and grinned. Soon the hot water ran out and they dried themselves off.

"I've got to go see Selah today." She pulled a blue polo over her head.

"I want to go with you, but I have a safety meeting before work tonight." He gave her an apologetic look.

"It's fine. I'm not expecting a lot. Just going to take the bowls in the car. Ask her about them and see if she can give me some insight as to what I'm doing, but she may not really have that much information. I'm trying to keep my expectations low." Eden scrunched her curls with conditioning cream. She pulled the front of her hair back with bobby pins to keep it out of her face. As Anaiah dressed in his clean uniform, she couldn't decide if she liked him better in it or out of it. He brushed his hair back out of his face.

"Need to put it up?" She held up a ponytail holder. He looked up as she flung it at him. He flinched slightly when it hit him in the chest.

"Thanks." He grinned as he bent over to pick it up. "I need to get it trimmed. They let me keep it longer as long as I can fit the fire helmet over the bun. A lot of the guys have their hair short because we do both firefighting and paramedicine. I like my hair a little longer. For a while it was longer than yours." He grinned as he sat on the couch to tie his boots.

"I'd like to see pictures of that." Eden's eyes lit up. "I love your hair." She crossed the small living room and sat in his lap, straddling him. She ran her hands through his hair. "I couldn't wait to get my hands in it and kiss these lips. They looked so inviting." She leaned in and kissed him.

"Let's not start something I don't have time to finish properly, baby." He whispered.

Eden let out a very theatrical sigh. "Fine! You...and that uniform..." She paused and gave him a coy smile. "Should probably go then. Just one more." As she kissed him, he stood up, carrying her with him. He leaned her against the wall, kissing her passionately, taking her breath away. He set her down on her feet gently as he broke the kiss.

"I gotta go, sugar. Before you distract me too much." He winked at her, threw his hair up in a bun, and headed out the door. She stared after him, breathless.

She checked her watch. It was time for her to leave as well. Anaiah had moved the two bowls they had found to her car. She gathered her messenger bag and headed out the door. She daydreamed a bit as she drove for the next half hour, choosing to think over the nice parts of the last few weeks instead of using this time to stress about what she didn't know. As she pulled up to Selah's Sweets, she saw Selah flip the sign over to "closed". Eden hurried out of the car. Selah unlocked the door and let her in.

"You look rushed." Selah cast her look of pure matronly concern over Eden.

"I just want some answers. Have you had any luck finding out anything about my mark? Finding who my father is?" Eden blurted out.

"No. I've not had time to uncover that so far. You have a lot of questions, I see." Her pleasant expression was hiding some underlying weariness. Eden could feel it.

"Yes. This is all new to me. It's been a long week. My house was broken into. There was this bowl with twigs and junk in it. I was hoping you could help." Eden rambled out.

"What sort of things were in this bowl?" Selah's interest was suddenly piqued.

Eden told her about the bowl at her house. After, she described the one from outside the restaurant. She explained how the waitress was killed. She told her about the connection between Anaiah and Reesa. As Eden talked, Selah's face began to fall. Her expression slowly changed from alarmed, to horrified and finally to a fierce disapproval.

"That is magic from infernal texts. The most abhorrent kind. Most likely using the power of a fallen angel to fuel it. I do not know what they would want, but you seem to be involved. I...I don't...I can't..." She stuttered, "I can't teach you. I don't want to get mixed up in this."

"You're a half demon, isn't this sort of what you guys do?"

"I do a lot of things because I am half demon. Mostly, I serve my father. I keep him happy to keep myself comfortable, to keep me from the notice of other demons. Those sort of spells...they twist you. Breaks you. Fractures you emotionally, mentally, the mortal soul really cannot handle it. I may be half demon, but I still have a mortal soul. I have yet to trade that away. I don't plan to. I can't be associated with you if you are in the middle of this mess." She pulled a cupcake out of the display case and shoved it into Eden's pleading hands, as if this was somehow a consolation. "Sorry, dear."

"Can you give me another book...anything that can help me? I mean, I have these bowls in the car...I need to figure this out." Eden begged.

"You have the bowls here? With you?"

"Yes."

"You've been carrying them around with you?" She looked horrified.

"Well, I didn't know what to do with them." Eden shrugged.

"Whoever cast those spells is still tied to the elements of his spell. You need to get them away from you. The spell caster could track you very easily with them." Her panic rose. She began to guide Eden to the door.

"Could I use them to track him?" Eden held onto some hope.

"He's using a demonic force to kill people, why on earth would you want to find him?" She gave Eden a look she was familiar with. One that said Eden was completely out of her mind.

"To stop him. He is leaving a trail of dead bodies that lead to me and my boyfriend. And he tried to murder my friends. HE MURDERED A CHILD." Eden snapped.

"What makes you think you can stop him?" She said quietly with wide eyes. "I can't help you. You need to leave." She gripped Eden's arm and pushed her toward the door.

"You can't even tell me where to look any of this up?" Eden pleaded with her.

"Try Google." She said hatefully as she locked the door behind Eden.

Well, thanks for nothing! As Eden drove away, she wondered if a search engine could help her at all. *Guess it's all I have.* She thought in frustration. She pulled into the parking lot of a coffee shop and pulled her laptop out of her bag. She turned it on and connected it to the coffee shop Wi-Fi. She closed her eyes and focused for a minute on what key phrases might yield real results and not just give the plot to crappy TV series or movies.

After a few cracks at it, the results seemed a little more based in reality. She found a link to a university website and a professor who studied the occult and the cultural aspects of satanic and demonic worship. She downloaded scanned pages of an old text with demonic rituals detailed on them. She perused what she could read from them and tried to search some of the Latin phrases on them.

She typed in "Sanguinem innocentem" and it popped back with "The blood of the innocent." Her heart skipped a beat. She searched the title at the top of the page, "Inveni de Filiis Caelo" and it translated, "Find the Children of Heaven." She translated more from the page. It seemed to be broken instructions. Some of it made sense and other things were just bonkers or nonsense. Something here about 'breaking the discarded ones.' A disturbingly large amount of blood of the innocent was mentioned. At least, it was a lead of sorts. She bookmarked the page.

She searched for tracking spells. The results were disappointingly dismal. She went through three pages of search results before she wanted to toss her laptop out the window. Instead, she went inside to purchase herself and Anaiah two very large coffees with extra shots. She dropped his coffee off at the firehouse and prepared herself for a night of retail stocking. She wished that being a supernatural detective was a legitimate job that would pay her bills.

Work that night had been much the same as the night before. Too many people talked to her about things she didn't want to talk about, and it was only broken up by occasional Anaiah texts when he got time to message her.

The only good news of the night had been that he had somehow arranged to move his days off to the same as hers. As she headed to her car, her phone rang in her pocket. She pulled it out, hoping it was Anaiah. She looked at the screen but didn't recognize the number. Afraid it was a call from the hospital room from Jayce, she hit 'accept'.

"Hello?" She answered and hoped that for once, someone wanted to reach her about her car's fictional extended warranty.

"Eden?" Selah's voice picked up.

"Yes." Eden said in surprise.

"I know I said I was staying out of this, but here's the thing. I need to warn you. I know my father is more involved in all this than he is letting on. He could be the one the sorcerer is using as a power source." She said in a rush.

"Why do you think that?" Eden asked.

"I went to the site you told me about and did a detection ritual. The ritual uses the blood of the innocent, it powers up the sorcerer so he can locate the children of angels. I think he is trying to get a weapon; one that can be used to cut down heaven's armies."

"What weapon?" Eden asked incredulously. This sounded crazy to her. But then again, she was the daughter of an unknown demon, so there was that.

Selah waited for a moment to speak but said quietly, "The angelus blade."

"The what? I don't know what any of this is." Eden said, exasperated.

"The angelus blade was a blade formed from the bones of the first fallen archangel after Lucifer. It was forged with pure gold and heavenly fire. It was intended to be used to purge the heavens of Lucifer's followers."

"Why would he need it? Wait, it's a blade that could kill a demon, right?" She asked, then realized that this blade might be useful to her.

"It can be used on all angels. Demons are fallen angels after all." She responded.

"So, he's after angels? Why?" Eden felt like her head was spinning, unable to keep up.

"Heaven and hell are always at war. Been that way since the beginning of time." Selah responded as if Eden should have just pieced that together. "I'm taking off. I am not getting caught up in the middle of this. You should do the same. Just get the hell out."

"I can't really do that." Eden said. "Whoever did that ritual, obviously has a connection to me. They killed my little sister. She's the innocent whose blood was spilled. Did you happen to figure out who that might be?" Eden added.

"No. He's powerful though. That spell would put me down for a day or two if I cast it." Selah said. "I'm going to ditch my phone, so don't try to call me."

"Do you really think that's going to keep you hidden from your dad?"

"No, but the spell I cast after I hang up will keep him off my trail for a while. Not going to give him an easy way to track me in the natural when his supernatural ways fail." Selah said.

"I wish I had time for you to teach me how to do these friggin' spells." Eden said in exasperation.

"I've taught enough of your kind." Selah said sadly. "You won't find your father in my books, girl. I shouldn't tell you...he's going to kill me."

"Shouldn't tell me what?" When she didn't respond, Eden's voice rose. "Selah! What shouldn't you tell me?"

"I can't." Selah said softly as the line went dead. Eden tried calling back and it went to voicemail. She tried a few more times. She felt like throwing her phone but realized it wouldn't help anything, so she screamed in frustration. She tried to think through what she gained from this call. *Cole is using me...to do what? I can't help anyone apparently, and he's sent me to find this person who tells me to run away? Why the hell do I have to get caught up in a fight between heaven and hell?*

As Eden contemplated all the events of the last few weeks, she pulled her car in the drive next to Anaiah's. He sat at the top of the steps on her porch, phone in hand. His smile was like warm sunshine on a frigid winter day. It soothed the anxiety that had built up in her in the last hour.

"I did some research last night. And I think I found something based on what you told me after talking with Selah." He had a serious look on his face for once.

"Yeah, she just called me again. I got to fill you in on what she said." Eden said as she reached the bottom of the steps.

"Oh?" He perked up.

"Yeah, she thinks that Cole is more involved than he's letting on. Demon energy was used to do all these rituals, but he's not the one doing it directly, but she said he's involved. Also, whoever is doing this is looking for a weapon called the angelus blade." As Eden told him, he stood up in front of her. She was giving him terrible news and he was practically beaming. What had he found?

"I found something about angels too. Basically, I was looking into that scar on your neck. Thing is, Selah couldn't find it because it's not a demonic symbol...It's enochian. That's the language of the angels. Your scar is a symbol tied to an angel. Baby, I don't think you're part demon, I think you are part angel. That's why she couldn't figure out what demon was your dad. She was looking in the wrong place." He looked at Eden's doubtful face and continued, "I know you worried about it. You thought you were bad or something because of it." He brushed her hair back and cupped her cheek. "I knew it couldn't be true. You're a good person."

"Selah said I wouldn't find my father in her books. How did you find that?" She said incredulously, not meeting his stare. She couldn't dare to hope this would be true.

"I took a picture of it while you were sleeping, as a reference. Then, I did a reverse image search online. I found one that matched an old manuscript on the ancient languages of religious texts. Your dad isn't some lowly demon, baby." He showed her an image on his phone. "This symbol is the one for the angel of death, which I guess explains how you see the dead all the time. Here, look." He handed Eden his phone.

"His name is Azrael." As Eden spoke, a loud roll of thunder clapped in the distance. The clear skies suddenly darkened, and flashes of lightning filled the clouds. Suddenly, a blindingly bright flash of lightning struck in the grass. Anaiah and Eden stumbled backward on the porch. Anaiah wrapped her up in his arms protectively. As her vision cleared, his grip loosened, and Eden sat up from the top step to see what just happened.

In the middle of her lawn, the earth was scorched black, leaving a clearing in the grass about three feet wide. In the center of the scorched spot was an ancient looking book of parchment bound in worn leather. Slowly, Eden approached the center of the blackened earth. She gazed up to the sky which had returned to a normal blue color with a few fluffy clouds scattered around. She reached down and picked up the book. As her hand closed around it, her vision flashed white. With a deafening crack, a commanding voice not of this world spoke to her.

"Daughter of heaven, the book of Seraphi will guide you. Use its words, make them your own. They are holy and divine. Set apart, as you are set apart. You and the other nephilim will defeat the armies of hell and save mankind. You have the power of heaven within you and at your side."

The powerful voice set her spine straight. The command of authority was both terrifying but somehow reassuring. It felt like a voice she had forgotten was familiar to her ears. Something within her recognized this as a part of herself. She remembered hearing a voice like it weeks ago in a vision. Powerful. Commanding. The way it had said "Daughter of heaven" with reverence. She'd heard a voice just like that. A voice that would shake the heavens as it demanded justice and truth.

Suddenly as it went, her vision cleared. She peered around her neighborhood. Anaiah was sprawled on the porch, propped up on his elbows, and looking completely flabbergasted. Nothing on the street looked amiss. No cars stopped in the streets staring. A neighbor down the street continued to mow his lawn.

"Did you hear that?" Eden asked too loudly, her ears still ringing.

"The lightning? Or did you have another vision? Eden, honey...are you okay?" Anaiah was staring at her in disbelief. "You're kinda glowing."

Eden could still hear the reverberation of the voice of what she realized was the angel's voice in her head. The voice was so similar to the one she had heard in the vision of Anaiah's mother. No one else on the street had seen the lightning or heard anything amiss. Anaiah had. Hadn't she said he was too good to be true? That he was part angel? Hadn't she been drawn to him immediately, but around Selah, she felt a sick twist in her stomach. Because he was like her. Could this be real?

"Anaiah, do you have any scars?" She said, still doubting her thoughts, walking toward him with determination.

His brow furrowed. "What?"

"I had a vision, just now. My father…an angel, sent this book to us." She held it up in front of her. "But the way he spoke…I had a vision when we kissed, after Reesa died. It was a voice speaking to your mother about his son, it was very similar. Not the same voice, but like it. I can't describe it. I know it sounds crazy, but…"

Anaiah's concerned, confused face seemed to smooth out as understanding took hold. "Eden, I…" He hung his head. "I didn't think it meant anything. It's just a little white line with some crosses through it." He untucked his shirt, pulling up the back of his shirt. Was that fear she saw in his face as he turned and showed her a small scar on his left shoulder blade.

How she hadn't noticed it, she didn't know. She realized as she snapped a picture with her phone, that every time she had seen him shirtless, she was terribly distracted by his chest and tattoos. His back seemed like a blank canvas compared to the front of him. She outlined the scar with the doodle feature on her photos app to make it stand out. She pulled up the search engine on her phone as he turned back to her.

A quick reverse image search later, Eden found herself staring at a Wikipedia article for an archangel who was named after the righteousness of God. He was the angel of justice and benevolence.

"Anaiah," Eden handed him her phone. "Could we really both be children of angels?" Her voice was low. Anaiah stared down at her phone, his face strangely blank. Eden went on, "I mean, I always wondered why I was different. But you don't see things or have visions or dreams. Right?" Eden stared at him bewildered.

He let out a sigh and handed her the phone. "I have dreams sometimes." He sat down on the step and placed his head in his hands.

"Why didn't you tell me?" She barely whispered, afraid of what the answer could mean. *What else could he be hiding from me?*

"I wanted to. The night we saw Azaz…your ex. After you told me about your dreams, about what you see. I wanted to tell you that I have dreams like that." He cleared his throat. "Eden, I wanted to tell you that I saw you in a dream right before I met you. That dream was what made me come again the next time to see you at work. But I was afraid that if I did, you would think I was either lying to you, or trying to trick you like Cole did. I thought my dreams came from God, not from being some…half-breed angel thing." He swallowed hard. "There's something else you should know." He looked at her pleadingly. "I don't want to scare you."

Eden was torn between stepping closer to him to soothe that anxious look of fear on his face and stepping away from him because of the fear she felt herself. She made her feet stand their ground. He hadn't backed away from her. She would hear him out.

Anaiah looked around the yard for a moment. He stood up and strode quickly toward some large landscaping stones a neighbor had left on the curb across the street. Eden backed to the porch, and sat down, suddenly feeling very weary. She watched him in stunned silence.

He picked up a large stone, carried it back with ease and sat next to Eden. "I should have told you sooner." He said in a low voice. "I wanted to show you this…so you would understand. You know how I am always so careful when I am with you, and I worry about hurting you or losing control? This…this is why." Anaiah snapped the thick stone in two and crushed the edges in his hands to pebbles and dust.

Involuntarily, Eden gasped and pulled away, standing up suddenly. She found herself backing into the yard. She placed a hand over her mouth, afraid to speak.

"I would never hurt you." Hurt flashed momentarily across his face and then his expression shifted. His eyes softened and he regarded her like she was a spooked horse, trying to calm her. "You can see why I didn't want to tell you. This…isn't normal. And I didn't have some reason why, like you did. I didn't have an explanation other than the one I had told myself since I was a child. I assumed it came from God. It was all mixed up in my faith…you know how worried I was about you leaving me over that. I believed that God gave me strength and dreams to help people. It's why I do what I do for a living. To help people. Please, don't look at me like that. Like I'm some sort of monster." He hung his head.

"No. Anaiah, I know you aren't a monster. I just needed a minute to process." Eden breathed and calmed her thundering heart. "You caught me off guard, that's all." She approached him slowly as he sat perfectly still like a statue. "I wish I would have known." she said, reaching her hand out to him.

"I didn't know how to tell you. I've never told anyone. And then, there's just never been a good moment to drop this on you. I am so sor…"

"No, Anaiah. I don't mean…I wish I would have known that there's someone, anyone, out there in the world like me." She slid her hand under his chin, raising his eyes to meet hers. "I've felt so alone for so long. Being with you, it's been like a dream. Like my whole life has been this horrible trainwreck, but you are this breath of fresh air. I am always waiting for the other shoe to drop, because it always does. And then this...this is the other shoe dropping. Only, it's not bad. I hid this thing about me. I have hidden it for years. It wasn't until I came here that I let people in and told them what I could see. I can't be mad at you for doing the same thing." She saw the tension in his shoulders ease. She stood between his knees as he sat on the porch, eyes level with hers. He saw her, all of her and loved her for it. She stared into his eyes and hoped he knew that she saw him too. She saw all of him and loved him even more.

He wrapped his hand around hers and said, "So this isn't the part where you run screaming?" He let out a small laugh. He was her mirror. Her equal. Her match.

"Not a chance." She sighed. "You have dreams about me, huh?" She flashed a half smile.

"Oh, I wish they had been dreams like that." He chuckled. His expression darkened. "Baby, I dreamed of you sittin' on these steps with your eyes full of tears, with your neck bruised. Like you had been choked half to death." She tried to smooth away the sadness in his expression with her hand on his cheek. "The way you looked at me, like you were ashamed to have me see you that way. Well, I know now, you didn't know how to explain what happened. But in my dream, I felt like it was my fault. Like I should've been there. Done something. I felt like I might as well have been the one to do that to you." His eyes shifted to his feet, somberly looking away from her.

"You didn't know." She consoled him.

"I knew it was coming. I didn't know when, but I should have been here. I was supposed to protect you." He pulled her closer into his arms.

"That's why you are with me? To protect me?" She asked defensively.

"No." He quickly snipped back. "Hell, no. Eden, when I had that dream, I didn't know you. I met you. Then I kept an eye on you because of it, but, sugar, I fell in love with you before you even asked me out. Weeks went by, and the dream hadn't come true. I had sorta hoped it wouldn't. I was afraid of asking you out, for fear that if we did date, it would set it off somehow. After we went out though, I talked myself into thinkin' that you being with me had somehow changed things, so you wouldn't get hurt."

"We both kind of suck at this, you know. We see things but are clueless to stop them. We have these visions of things to come and no way of knowing what to do to avoid them. And everyone we know gets hurt." Eden thought sorrowfully of Kris. Anaiah rubbed his hand on her lower back reassuringly.

He looked away briefly, as if considering. "I dreamed about the night my mom died." Anaiah stared past her, out into the yard, his face stoic. She could tell he was trying not to tear up. "I dreamed that my stepdad and I got into a fight. I dreamed I lost control and after, I wasn't sure if he was still breathing.

I woke up feeling sick. Disgusted with myself. I mean, I hated the guy, but I never wanted to kill him. So, I just packed up my stuff and left. But that didn't fix a thing. A few days later, instead of pickin' a fight with me, my mom got into it with him. And she was the one who..." Despite his efforts, a tear rolled down his cheek. "Yeah, I'd say we suck at this, baby." Eden wiped his tear away with her hand softly.

"Maybe we can get better at this. Maybe that's why we were meant to find each other." She tilted his eyes back up to hers. "Maybe I was meant to find you all along." She watched his silver lined brown eyes for a moment. She leaned in and kissed him lightly on the lips.

"I think I was meant to love you all along." He whispered as she pulled back.

"So, I'm the daughter of death, and you're the son of righteousness, huh?" She grinned.

"Angels are some deadbeat dads." He sighed, giving her a half smile. "Haven't gotten a single birthday card or child support check from...who was it?" He picked up her phone. "The hell sort of name is Raguel?"

A flash of lightning struck again in the circle of ash. Anaiah pulled her against him protectively.

"Surely that's not going to happen every time we say these names, right?" Eden said as they stood up and looked back at the blackened spot on the lawn. Spidering wavy lines like veins or roots reached out to the edge from the center of it in all directions. They walked together toward it. Where the book had been before, now lay a scroll of parchment.

Anaiah reached for it. He unrolled it and revealed black script on the page. Eden tried to read it but was struck with a sudden ache behind her eyes.

"What do you think it is?" Eden looked up at him expectantly.

"It's a spell." He said unflinchingly, staring at the page.

"You can read it?" She looked back at the dark squiggles on the parchment.

"No, my father just told me. It will take us to the blade." He said slowly, like he was trying to believe what he was saying. "We have to look in the book of Seraphi to figure out how to read it. That's the book there?" He pointed to the leatherbound book in the crook of her arm.

"Let's go inside. Before all this holy lightning causes my neighbors to freak out." She scanned the neighborhood in disbelief that life seemed to be carrying on as usual. She pulled Anaiah inside the house.

CHAPTER TWENTY-FOUR

H ow's Kris?" Eden asked Journey over the phone. Eden surveyed the bowls, bottles, books, and papers scattered around her living room. It had been over a week since they received the book and scroll. Anaiah and Eden had poured over them between work and sleep. Parts of the book were completely unreadable. They had spent the better part of today sleeping, exhaustion finally winning out. Anaiah spent half the time he normally slept by hunting down herbs and ingredients that they needed for a spell in the book for the last week.

"He's stable. They're keeping him sedated while he still needs the breathing tube. He tried to pull it out when they backed the medication off. Anything new? Any leads?" Journey's exhaustion seeped into her voice.

"We're working on it." Eden sighed. She had convinced Anaiah to sleep first and then get the rest of what was needed for this spell after. She had even considered turning off their alarms but thought better of it. The spell was supposed to give them vision. It looked like a bad recipe for the world's worst soup. Journey cleared her throat, indicating that Eden had spaced out.

"I'll let you know as soon as we figure anything out. How's Jayce?" Eden asked.

"He's better. He apologized for being an ass. He knew he was being one but didn't mean to be an ass to me. He's at my place showering and grabbing a change of clothes. I'm with Kris. Jayce's supposed to be back anytime." In the background, Eden could faintly hear a voice of an overhead page saying something about a code-something to room number two thirty-two as well as the gentle whooshing sounds of Kris's ventilator. Journey sighed, "just wanted to check in and see if you found anything."

"Sorry, nothing yet. I'm trying. Maybe soon. I'll text you later." Eden hung up and rubbed her hands frustratedly over her face. She wished she had answers. Everything felt like it was on the verge of breaking open and revealing things to her. She thought this book would just open up and give her answers. That things would make sense for once.

She heard tires rolling on gravel. She peeked through the blinds and watched Anaiah pull up as the sun was setting behind him. She opened the front door and watched him walk up the lawn.

"Got it!" he called out triumphantly. He held up a small paper bag for her to see. He had driven to an herbalist in Dallas while Eden stayed here, setting everything else up.

"That's it then?" Eden stared at the bag with a mixture of excitement and apprehension. Now that they had all the ingredients, they could attempt to cast a spell in her living room. She couldn't decide if it was the worst idea she had ever had. She knew it probably wasn't her best. She had declared that Anaiah's apartment should remain ritual-free as a safe space should things go badly. She wondered if she should give him a key to her place, and possibly ask for one to his. The speed at which they had dove headfirst into a serious relationship was a little frightening at times, but then again, they were far from normal. They hadn't slept apart from one another since the break in over two weeks ago.

"This is it. You ready?" He picked her up into his arms and carried her into the house. He shut the door behind him deftly with one foot. He planted a quick kiss on her lips and set her down beside him. He seemed excited that he didn't have to hide his strength from her anymore. In hindsight, Eden knew she should have noticed how easily he carried her before. To be fair, she was distracted by hormones and his muscles.

"I'm as ready as I'll ever be." She grabbed the bowl that Journey had dubbed 'magic potpourri' with the various twigs, herbs and bark in it. "Kiss me again, for luck." She smiled as he bent down and brushed his lips over hers.

Anaiah picked up the book from the table. He read the words and pronounced them with a little difficulty. They looked to be Latin but their attempts to translate them online had failed. He picked up a vial of oil and uncorked it, pouring it over the magic potpourri bowl. He took the bowl from her and handed her the book. Following instructions they could understand, she read the next part, stumbling over words occasionally. She picked up a little bowl she had prepared in advance with ground herbs in it. She read the instructions and in a counterclockwise motion, sprinkled them over the top of the larger bowl.

They exchanged the bowl and book again. He pulled the gnarled root from the bag and set the book on the table. With his large hands, he crushed the root, twisting it to bits. *Guess that's one way to do it.* He read the next part of the incantation and sprinkled the root into the bowl. He took out a scalpel he had grabbed from work and an alcohol prep sponge. He opened both. Eden held out her left hand, keeping the bowl in the other. He scrubbed down her hand with the alcohol sponge stick.

He hesitated before she gave him a stern nod. Anaiah cut a slit into her palm following the specified angle per the book. He held up the book for her to read as she sprinkled her blood over the bowl. He set the book down for a moment, wiped down his own hand before slicing into it. He repeated the line from the incantation as he poured his own blood in the bowl. He picked the book back up and they read the last part together. Eden placed the bowl down on the table.

Smoke rose in twisting tendrils from the bowl. The trails of smoke twisted and curled up in a purposeful fashion. Two separate wisps of smoke spun mid-air and drifted toward them. Eden wanted to back away or close her eyes, but she made herself stand steady. The smoke grew darker and thicker and suddenly lurched forward into their mouths and noses. Eden's vision blurred and she heard Anaiah suck in a sharp breath. Her head grew heavy and dizzy with her vision clouded. She grabbed Anaiah's hand beside her and squeezed. The jolt of pain through the cut in her hand shocked her enough to snap her to attention when she felt herself falling backward. The fog began to clear from her eyes, the pressure in her head eased and Eden stared at the now empty bowl on her coffee table. Eden turned to see Anaiah staring back at her with a similarly bewildered expression. *Did it work? Why is the bowl clean now? What's wet on my foot?* Eden looked down to find the top of her bare foot was covered in her blood, and a small puddle had formed beneath her foot. Blood dripped from the open cut in her hand as she held his right hand. There was blood on the floor by Anaiah too. The pain from the cut flooded in behind the clearing of her mind. She clenched her teeth.

Anaiah dropped her hand to grab his bag. *Of course, he was prepared to do first aid.* He wrapped his own hand with a roll of gauze and some red stretchy wrap that stuck to itself. Then he took her hand in his and washed it with saline. He blotted the wound with some squares of gauze.

He swore in frustration. "I cut too deep. You need stitches. Dammit!" He began to wrap her hand up.

"Then do it." Eden said. He looked up at her with his kind sad eyes. Eden set her jaw. "Don't look at me like that. You have the stuff, just do it. I am sick of explaining away my injuries to medical professionals. Do it." He stared at her for a moment before he reluctantly nodded. He guided her to sit next to him on the couch. He pulled out a tube of gel.

"This is lidocaine. It will numb you...but I don't have the stuff to inject down below the skin...You're still going to feel some of this. You sure you don't want to go to the hospital?" His eyes begged her to reconsider.

"Quit asking...just do it. What about you? How's your hand?" Eden tried to ignore the throbbing ache in her hand.

"It's fine. I'll super glue it." He shrugged. He used a swab to apply the lidocaine to her hand. He pushed the hair out of his face while they waited for the numbing to start. "Wonder if it did anything?" He picked up the scroll and unrolled it. He shook his head.

"What about the book?" Eden nodded her head toward it. He pulled the book over toward them on the table. When it was close enough, she tried to read the spell page. The words rearranged themselves on the page. Once the page was still again, she could read the entire ritual. Some instructions were in clear English before the ritual, but the entire incantation had been in a foreign language. Now, it was all clear. She read one of the lines from the incantation. "My blood poured out to see and seek, to follow the path of the blood of my father. Give my eyes your blessing and my mind your understanding." As she said it aloud, she could hear her voice speaking clearly in enochian.

Anaiah's wide eyes met hers. He looked back at the book and flipped the page to one of the ones they couldn't read at all before. "Sight of Daemonium," The enochian words come out of Anaiah's mouth. Then he spoke to her in English. "This is what we need to read the scroll. It's how to read daemonic."

"Well, what do we need for it?" She asked excitedly, and he pulled the book over where they could both read the smaller print. The list was extensive. There are some ingredients they had before, but some of it they were going to have to look up to find. "Well, I guess that's on our next to-do list." She sighed. "I had hoped this would help more with finding out who's doing all of this. Or why Cole is involved. Or even how we can stop anyone else from getting hurt. This is cool and all, but I still feel like we are groping around in the dark." She let out an exasperated breath. "I think it's numb now. It hurts a lot less." She motioned to her hand.

"I know how you feel. Feels like we are spinning our wheels." He pulled out a suture kit with some little clamp things and some small scissors. He had her put her hand on top of a paper pad sheet, then he opened a package of gloves, and put them on in the way she had seen on surgery shows. "Tryin' to create some sort of sterile field here and keep you from getting an infection. The guys would laugh at me for being so careful." He poked her hand a bit with the little clamp plier looking things. "Does that hurt?"

"No. It's numb there." She said.

"Okay. Guess I'm starting then." He swiped her cut with a swab of disinfectant. Then, he picked up the small, curved needle with a string attached to it with the clamp tool. She did her best to hold her hand steady as the needle pierced her skin.

OH shit. It's not numb there. FUCK! That hurts. She steeled herself, taking slow, even breaths as the needle passed through the other side of the cut and he tied little knots in it. He snipped it with a little pair of scissors and went for a second one.

"You doing okay?" He didn't look up. Eden was certain he knew she was white knuckling it and he'd have to stop if he looked up and saw her hurting.

"I'll be fine." Eden managed to speak in an even tone. She used her other hand to pick up one of the pillows on the couch and hugged it to her chest. "Four more, maybe? Or more?"

"Yeah, probably four more." He started on the second one and she leaned her face into the pillow. She willed herself to not flinch or scream. She reminded herself that she had been through worse. *I am stronger than this.*

"That's two. Need a break?" His eyes were still fixed on her hand.

"No. Just get it over with." She lifted her face from the pillow. She braced herself for the third. He finished it quickly and started immediately on the fourth stitch.

"One more." He said as he stuck the needle in the last time and pulled it through the other side. "There, all done. Let me dress it." He placed some antibiotic cream and gauze over the five little stitches. Then he wrapped some of the stretchy wrap around it. When he finished, he pulled her hand up to his lips and kissed it gently.

"That part of the standard procedure with field sutures? Kissing it better?" She smiled.

"You bet. It's the best part. Patient's love when I kiss their owies." He winked at her.

She reached over and took his left hand in hers. "Okay, walk me through fixing yours with the glue." She looked at him determinedly.

"I'll be okay." He shrugged.

"Let me help you, please. I love you. Let me do this." She stared into his brown eyes and his expression softened. When she unwrapped his hand, the gauze was saturated with blood. "This looks worse than mine." She looked up at him with a stern expression.

"Okay, it's not a competition. It's still just flesh deep, no tendons cut. Wash it out with saline. Yeah, over the top of the chucks pad. Yeah, that green one. It'll absorb the blood and saline." He walked her through cleaning it out. "Now, take the lidocaine and put it on there. Ouch, damn. Yeah, get in there with it." He winced as the cotton swab brushed over his wound with the lidocaine. "Shit, that stings. Alright, while we give it a minute, how well can you sew? 'Cause if you can't, I can stitch that an' you can help me tie it."

"I made my own cultist attire since I was a kid, I think I can sew." She shot him a sassy half smile.

"Secret skills, huh?" He raised an eyebrow.

"Oh yeah. I learned to sew. I learned to crochet. Could barely read on a second-grade level when I left at fifteen, but I could sew a simple, modest dress." She rolled her eyes.

"Can you knit?" He kept the mood lighthearted, but she saw the tension in his shoulders.

"No. Too dangerous to give me big metal needles." She chuckled.

"I'm sure you were a menace with a crochet hook too." He grinned then turned more serious, "Did you see how far I went out on the edges on yours?" He pointed to his hand. "Don't go too close to the wound bed. It'll tear, also, don't pull it too tight to tie. I kinda wish we had some whiskey for this. God, I'm nervous. Sorry." He gave her an embarrassed smirk.

Anaiah spent several minutes with his explanation of how to hold the suture needle with the tool he informed her was called "forceps" or "needle driver". After going through the technique of tying knots for the second time, he affirmed his readiness to get this over with. Eden held the forceps in her right hand and started to insert the needle where he instructed.

"Oh Jesus, that lidocaine don't work for shit. Yep, now pull it up and make your knots. Yep, snip. Okay. Do the next one. Ouch! Shit! Jesus Christ! How the hell did you let me put five of these in you without screaming or cryin'?" After she finished the stitch, she noticed he was staring at her expectantly.

"Oh, you want an actual answer?" She raised her eyebrows. "I knew if I did, you'd stop. You would drag me to the ER to wait, and then have to explain why we're both bleeding, just so they can stick me with a few needles to numb it up some more. I mean, it's not the worst pain I've ever had." She wiggled her nose. "Pierced this myself in a bathroom while I was making my big escape. That hurt about as much as one of those stitches did." She shrugged. "Now, let's get this done. You're going to need six at least. Or do you need a break?" She gave a big smart-ass smile.

"You're kind of amazing, you know that? Little bit stubborn an' crazy, but mostly amazing." He said with one eyebrow raised. "Alright, go on then. I'll try to reign in my bitchin'." He motioned with his good hand.

Eden resumed the task of stitching up his hand while he breathed through the process, attempting to handle it as well as she had. In the end, he needed seven stitches. Eden copied his dressing technique and wrapped his hand up. She leaned down and gave it a gentle kiss.

"You're a natural, baby. What do you say, we go out to the lake and gather up some of these things? We can get the willow bark and a couple other things out there." He looked over the book again.

"Sure. Let me wash the blood off my foot and put on some shoes. Do you think that's going to come out of the rug, or are we going to end up trashing it?" She motioned to the living room floor. Her grey and blue rug now had a few maroon puddles.

"Yeah, I'll get you a new rug, sugar." He said as he lifted her foot in his hand and used the rest of the saline to rinse her foot over the green pad. He dried her foot with a bit of leftover gauze. As he bagged up the medical waste, Eden went to put on socks and shoes. She hadn't bothered with dressing up today. She'd woken up to her period starting, so leggings and soft t-shirts it was.

She glanced at the mirror as she passed it. Her hair was in a messy bun and her bruises were yellowing around the edges. The dark purples and blues had faded to a lighter green. She grabbed her socks from the drawer and threw them on. She slipped her feet into her tennis shoes and walked to the kitchen where she had left the bottle of ibuprofen she had taken earlier for her hellacious cramps. She took a few and carried the bottle and the glass of water to the living room.

"Here," she said and tossed the bottle once Anaiah looked up.

He caught it deftly with his right hand and popped it open. He tossed a few pills in his mouth and took the glass from her to wash them down.

"I'm ready when you are." She said setting the glass and the ibuprofen on the table. Knowing her cycle, she'd need more later. Anaiah's phone interrupted as it played the ringtone for his job from his pocket.

"Well, shit." His disappointment was written all over his face. He pulled the phone out to answer. "This is Parker." He let out a sigh, "Yeah, I can be there in less than five." He hung up and let out a sigh. "Baby, I'm sorry. I know it's my night off, but there's a huge structure fire at an apartment complex. They need everyone they can get. All the ambulances are out there already, I'm riding in with some volunteer fire guys on their rig. I gotta go."

"It's okay. Go." She walked with him toward the door. He stopped and kissed her deeply. "Come back to me when you can." she said breathlessly when he pulled back. "And be careful."

"You too." He said.

She laughed. *He's running off to a fire and he's the one wanting me to be careful.* "I will try to behave." She winked.

She picked up her laptop and started searching for the ingredients on the list. One of the listed items was grave dirt from a murderer's grave. Her search history was either hilarious or horrifying. She wasn't sure which. She researched local murders who were buried nearby. She found grave locating to be particularly tedious. She tracked down each individual item and where she could find them. Some would require walking around the lake or hiking at the grasslands to find the plants. She saved pictures as references to send to her phone.

By the time she had finished her list, it was pitch black outside. She checked her phone and fought with disappointment when there were no messages from Anaiah. She worried for him despite knowing that running into burning buildings and saving people was what he loved to do. He was strong but not indestructible. She perused her list and thought, *nothing like the cover of night for stealing grave dirt.*

She picked up her bag and gathered her supplies. She'd picked up a small gardening kit for clipping herbs, snipping branches cleanly off trees and the like. She threw a box of resealable plastic bags into her backpack and headed to her car.

She cursed the makers of women's clothing for not providing adequate pockets as she threw her phone in the bag on her way down the steps. *You would store spell ingredients in pockets if they gave you pockets. They had to keep the witches at bay.* She giggled to herself. Her internal monologue had been mostly worrying about her friends with Kris in the hospital, concern for Anaiah fighting fire, and stress about not knowing what the hell was going on. Her momentary laughter had lightened the dark cloud over her slightly, but not enough to be safely left alone with her thoughts. She turned on the radio to drown them out.

She pulled into the back entrance of the cemetery, off a smaller side street. She had hoped it would look less conspicuous than driving off the main road straight into the big front gate of the cemetery. She picked her way through the winding roads through the rural cemetery until she came to the older part of the cemetery at its heart. Here, old overgrown oak trees lined the road. She parked next to them and grabbed her bag. It took her several minutes of trying to reorient herself and find the markers that noted the sections of the cemetery.

She finally came across a moss-covered headstone labeled only with the name "William Briars" and the years 1912-1937. She had to search through a ton of old stories online from her town's historical society to find out that this man had been hung for murdering his own brother.

She set her bag down and pulled out a gardening shovel and a couple of plastic bags. She scooped out dirt from the center of the grave, unsure how close to the edge of the grave might be considered 'not grave dirt'. She didn't want to take chances.

She filled two quart-sized bags and sealed them. Still kneeling in the dirt, she stuffed them in her bag, then rose to dust herself off. She suddenly felt sick to her stomach. Had she stood up too quickly? She placed a hand on her stomach and took a deep breath, as if she could mentally overcome the nausea. A shadow moved out of the corner of her eye. Nausea be damned, she spun towards the movement near her car. A dark figure leaned casually against her car.

"You look different." A cold dark voice said. Her heart hammered in her chest. She knew that voice. After the visions of her sister's murder and the attack on Kris, she'd heard it in her nightmares.

She willed her voice to be steady as she said, "Different than what? Than you imagined?" She wanted to see his face, to see who had been doing all of this to her.

"You were always small for your age. Guess I thought you would be taller, stronger or something. But you don't need that when you always have your guard dog with you. Do you?" He said as he stood up straight. His hooded jacket made it impossible for her to discern any features in the moonless night.

"Do we know each other?" Eden asked while she slowly bent down to pick up her bag, keeping her eyes trained on him. She wanted answers, but something told her to run.

"Don't recognize me? You were still so small when I left. Skittish little thing too. Just as scared of me as you were of Father." He moved slowly toward her. She stepped back and as realization hit her, she was stunned.

"Adam?" She breathed, not believing it.

"Baby sister Eden. Now you remember me." Her brother said as he walked out of the tree cover and into the dim light cast by nearby streetlamps. The planes of his face were similar to her own, but rougher. She hadn't recalled that edge of cruelty to his features. His face was more aged than she imagined it should be with salt and pepper stubble along his jaw.

"Adam, I haven't seen you in over ten years...why find me now? Why are you doing this?" She backed away, nearly tripping over a headstone.

"We were both given special gifts, weren't we?" He sneered. "I was born seeing demons and imagining hellfire. Our father tried to rid me of it, but it never worked. I couldn't change what I was. And to balance it out, heaven stepped in and MADE YOU." He growled.

"I didn't exactly have it easy." She said defensively. "But that didn't mean I had to start murdering people because my parents abused me."

"Awfully bold of you to speak to me that way without your big strong man around to defend you." Anger flickered across his face as he took another step toward her. She was shaking with fear and reluctantly admitted to herself that she wished Anaiah were here to defend her.

"Hurt me, and he will fucking kill you." Was it anger or fear that made her voice tremble? Eden didn't know.

"I sent your angel boy on an errand. He loves to be the hero, doesn't he?" He spat at her. "It's just you and me, little sister. You're coming with me. I have someone for you to meet." He stepped closer.

Eden needed a weapon. She needed to run. She would not let him take her. She dodged the large headstone behind her as she backed away. With her eyes locked on him, she reached blindly into her bag for anything to use against him. He suddenly bolted forward and snatched at her. He knocked the bag from her hand, but she gripped the handle of one of her garden tools. She swung the small rake wildly at him and caught him in the face.

He stumbled. His hands went to his face with a loud curse. She didn't wait for him to react. She bolted to her left, running over the tops of graves and heading for the first small road to take her out of the cemetery. Rows of headstones and her brother had been between her and her car. Her keys were likely in the bottom of her bag anyway, so she ran instead. She reached the small winding road and bolted toward the main road. She heard him yelling after her to stop. She had gotten a good lead on him, but he was bigger and probably faster, so she pushed herself harder.

She darted out the front gate and continued up the empty street. Her heart hammered. Her legs burned. She needed help. She needed a plan. She couldn't think straight. She turned on the next street, toward her house. *FUCK! No keys! No phone!* Going home wouldn't keep her safe. She turned, suddenly remembering her dream. She ran between two houses, cutting between their open lawns. She remembered where she was, remembered the large open concrete lined drainage ditch that ran through that part of town, how it curved back toward the hospital. It would be the only place guaranteed to have people in it at midnight that might help her. She jumped down into the drainage culvert and fell to her knees. It was deeper than she judged. She had no time to spare for the ache in her knees or ankles, so she pushed herself up and bolted down the ditch. She ran as hard as she could push herself, passing under the small bridge that was under a main street. She heard his shoes hit the concrete somewhere behind her. Her footfalls and his echoed through the tunnel. She thought of Anaiah as she prayed, tears streaming down her face. *Please, GOD, please, help me.* Her lungs burned. Her throat was raw and dry from her heavy breathing. She kept pushing herself, pumping her legs forward.

She saw her destination as she took the sharp slope up the side of the ditch with burning aching legs. She pulled herself out of the ditch and over the fence around it. As she descended the chain link fence, she spotted him about a hundred feet back, barreling toward her with his hands ablaze. She didn't pause. Her feet touched down on the earth and in the same instant, she was turning, pushing herself toward the hospital.

She saw the ambulance in the bay as she ran toward the emergency room door. She spared a moment to look in the cab and found it unoccupied. She dashed to the back and threw the doors open. She found no one inside. She turned and bolted through the automatic doors. She took in the vacant waiting room, just like in her dream. Not a soul at the little window to check in. She hurried to the double doors that lead inside the hospital and fought against locked doors. She panicked as she banged on the door and called out breathlessly for help. She could feel that Adam was close.

One of the doors she pounded on cracked open by a few inches. A familiar police officer looked out at her from the opening. She nearly sobbed in relief.

"Sean…my brother…he's after me. He's going to kill me." She said between gulps of air. Officer Sean immediately pushed the door open and helped her into a chair in the hallway behind him. As the door swung back closed, she watched as Adam approached the glass automatic doors. Blood ran down his fury filled face. The door clicked closed behind Sean. She realized he was speaking to her, but she hadn't heard him over her heart pounding in her ears. She turned her face up to him. He placed a hand on her shoulder with a kind look on his face.

"You're safe. Breathe with me. In…and out…" Sean instructed her. "Breathe with me. There you go. Again. In. Out. Again. In. Out. You're safe here. In. Out. Now, can you tell me what happened?" Eden shook her head and focused on her breathing. She closed her eyes. She forced herself to remember to use grounding techniques she had learned from therapy, so many years ago.

She could feel Sean's hand on her shoulder. She listened for things she could hear. She heard commotion in a room across the hall, a nurse counting out loud, the beeping of a machine. She opened her eyes and looked up. *I can see the tan curtain in the next room.* She noted how busy the room was as she heard a voice that she instantly knew and melted her panic like a healing balm.

"Tube is in, we have a color change, it's good. Vent is attached. RT, you got a bite block, or want me to tape it?" She heard Anaiah's voice call out.

"Eden, talk to me." Sean pulled her attention back.

She drew in a ragged breath. "I was being chased. It was my brother. He's the one who broke into my house." She looked up at him. "Adam Grace."

He pulled a pen and pad out of his shirt pocket. "Can you describe him?"

"Yeah… he's like six feet, maybe? a little shorter. Wearing a black hoodie, black jeans and boots. Brown hair, black and grey stubble." She smiled a bit when she remembered a detail. "He has some bad cuts on his face. I hit him with a…" She held up her hand with three fingers bent like the small rake, "little metal garden tool thing, like a rake. It was the first thing I could grab when he tried to grab me." She realized that she had no explanation for what they would find when they looked for her car, for her bag. She said "he's probably still out there. I ran here from my house, down the storm drainage ditch."

Sean looked at her with suspicion for a moment. Then he nodded and spoke into his radio, giving a brief description of the circumstances to dispatch. "You said he threatened you? And was trying to abduct you?"

"Yes, he said I was going with him, and he tried to grab me, chased me the whole way here." As she spoke, Sean continued to relay information to dispatch. Motion in the other room caught her eye as Anaiah stepped out from behind the curtain, pulled gloves off his hands, and threw them in the trash. He grabbed the nozzle on the wall for hand sanitizer. As he rubbed his hands together, he looked out the door and saw her. His eyes locked on hers.

"What happened?" He moved quickly toward her; his face was serious, dangerous.

Sean looked up. "Hey, Anaiah, stay with her. I am going to have a look around the hospital. She said she was chased here. Suspect was trying to abduct her." Sean stepped away as his radio called back Adam's description to the other patrol units in the area.

"Talk to me," Anaiah's face was smudged with soot. He had a stern look on his face, but his eyes softened. "Who? Was it Cole?"

"No. I went to the cemetery to get grave dirt." She coughed, her throat was dry from running and being out of breath. Her voice felt strained again. "My older brother, Adam, was there. He's the one doing all of this." She lowered her voice as she remembered that other people might overhear.

"He tried to hurt you?" His eyes darkened.

"He tried to take me. He said he had someone for me to meet. I got away. I didn't have my keys or my phone, so I ran here for help."

"He followed you?" He asked. She nodded. "Stay here." His voice commanded while he turned toward the door.

"Anaiah, please, don't leave me alone." Her voice cracked. He stopped and turned back toward the room full of people.

"Carla!" he called out.

"Yeah, boss." A tall thin lady in an EMS uniform called out.

"Take care of her for a minute. Needs water. Check her over and make sure she's not in shock. I'm gonna go help Sean look for this suspect outside for a few. Don't let her out of your sight. Anyone comes but me to get her, tell them to wait for me." It was the harshest she had ever heard him speak.

"On it." Carla gave Anaiah a confused look. He pushed the door open and stormed outside.

"Let me look you over. Dang, those are some rough looking bruises. They look old though. Looks like someone already bandaged you up there." She pointed at Eden's hand. Carla looked her over and assessed her for any other damage.

"Yeah, the month of April has been especially shitty." Eden sighed. She hadn't realized her hand had started throbbing again until now. She flexed her hand and moved her fingers around.

"Let me get you some water." She walked into a room down the hall and came back with a bottle of water.

"Parker is pissed. What happened, girl?" She said as Eden took a drink of water.

"My brother keeps trying to kill me...Anaiah's not a fan." Eden took another gulp.

"Oh, you know Parker pretty well?" She asked.

"Yeah, I'm his hot mess girlfriend." Eden finished the water bottle. "Can I have another?" She held the empty bottle up.

Carla raised her eyebrows. "Sure thing." She grabbed another bottle and cleared her throat as she handed it over. "None of my business, but Parker's one of the sweetest guys we have at the station. He's a catch for sure. He works codes the hardest, last one to call it off when a patient's not gonna make it, first one jumping in at a scene. But..." she swallowed, "over the last month, he changed a bit. Seemed more stressed. He and the guys work on hobbies and stuff in their down time, but he's just been off. Like something bothers him. It's none of my business, but the kid is like a little brother to me. I don't wanna see him get hurt." She crossed her arms.

Eden resisted the urge to roll her eyes. "He's tougher than he looks." She said quietly and sipped her water. Carla looked her over and determined that she was fine.

Sean and Anaiah walked through the doors together. Eden looked up at Anaiah. His expression was cold, calculating fury. From it, she gleaned that Adam was now on the list of the men Anaiah wanted to punish for hurting her.

"Alright, we are filing an official report. Anaiah tells me that your brother may be responsible for those bruises as well as the break in. Right now, he's suspected of the break in and the reported abduction attempt. You want to add assault and battery to that, and we issue a warrant?" All three of them looked to Eden and Anaiah gave her a small nod.

"Yeah. It was him." Eden lied.

"Are you hurt?" Sean asked.

"Nothing new, just sore as hell from running hard." Eden shrugged.

"She said she got him good in the face with a garden tool when he tried to grab her." Sean gave Anaiah a subtle smile.

"Good girl." Anaiah's face remained cold and hard, but his eyes gleamed with pride. He was no doubt beating himself up for not being there to defend her. "Carla, Eden's gonna ride with us back to the station. Then I'll take off if things have calmed down over at Terrace Ridge."

"Sounds good, boss." Carla said before she returned to the other room and loaded bags onto a stretcher.

"Give us a minute." Anaiah said to Eden. He walked in after Carla. "How's the patient?" Anaiah asked a nurse in black scrubs.

"Stabilized. Lungs look trashed from smoke inhalation on the chest x-ray, but he's not too badly burned. Thanks for the assist, Parker. You too, Carla."

"It's what we do." Carla called out as they loaded their equipment back on the stretcher and wheeled it out into the hallway.

"How many patients from the fire?" Anaiah asked Sean before they rolled out.

"Shit...we flew two to Parkland. One D.O.A. that we were gonna fly out, and including your last one, that's four here. They just called the building all clear. Haven't found anyone else." Sean said.

"Too many." Anaiah shook his head.

"You're not wrong. Parker, bit of advice," Sean looked Eden over as she stood to follow Anaiah out. "That piece of shit shows up at either of your residences? Make sure he makes it over the threshold, and you take care of it. Castle rights and all."

"Right." Anaiah's eyes were dark and serious.

"I don't pity that asshole when you get your hands on him." Sean patted Anaiah's back.

"You should." He said in a low voice as he turned to leave.

Eden followed him out. Carla hopped up front to drive and Anaiah held out a hand to help her step up into the back of the rig. She sat in one of the chairs with a seat belt and fastened it. He closed the doors and sat next to her on the bench seat. He didn't meet her eyes as she looked at him. He just silently took her hand in his and stared out the back windows of the ambulance.

He hadn't spoken to her since they left the hospital. Anaiah had checked in with the supervisor and cleaned himself up a little while she waited in the station house. Then he silently walked her to his car. Despite his stony silence, he held her hand in his, and drove her back to the cemetery. His face was unreadable, his eyes were cold and hard. Her nerves were fraying at the edges when he parked the car behind hers and he finally said, "Stay close to me. Show me where it happened. We will get your bag if he hasn't taken it, check your car over, then we will drop it at your house. You are coming home with me tonight."

"You haven't said anything...you haven't asked questions or anything..." She said softly.

He rubbed his hands over his face. "If we talk through this right now. If I don't keep this inside me...Please. Eden." She heard the anger in his voice.

"Okay." She said quietly. "Let's go." They walked to the grave she had taken the dirt from earlier. She saw her bag laying on the ground nearby.

Anaiah squatted down and checked the bag over, taking everything out of it. He shook it out. He put all her items back in it and handed her cellphone and keys over to her. He shouldered the backpack. She pointed out where everything happened. He inspected the area, using a plastic bag from her backpack to pick up the rake and closed the bag without cleaning it off. In case they needed evidence, she realized. He walked to her car and checked underneath it, inside the car, and in the trunk. He popped the hood and checked for anything suspicious there.

When he was satisfied, he held out his hand and said, "keys." She handed them to him without a word. He started the car up but stood back up and let her get into the car. He got in his car and followed her to her house.

After dropping off her car, Anaiah drove them to his apartment in silence. Still holding her hand. Still shuttered behind his steely look of anger and frustration.

After he closed and locked the door behind him, he turned to her. She could see the emotions churning behind his eyes. He pulled her close to him and wrapped his arms around her, laying his head atop hers. She closed her eyes and listened to his heartbeat against her ear. He gently lifted her into his arms, and she wrapped herself around him. He carried her without a word to his bed and sat her down on it. He dropped to his knees in front of her and laid his head in her lap. She stroked his hair gently.

"I love you." She said softly. "Talk to me."

"I am afraid that if I do, I'm going to come undone." He said without looking up at her. His voice was low. It still held that dangerous edge in it. The one that skittered over her nerves when she first heard it.

"I've seen you cry." She said quietly, still running her hand over his hair.

"I'm not going to cry, hon. I could give two shits about crying in front of you. I'm going to yell. Scream until I lose my fucking voice." His low voice shook. "I want to tear that bastard apart. Tear his fucking throat out with my own bare hands." He grabbed the blankets on both sides of her and balled his hands into fists. "This rage I got inside me right now scares the shit out of me. I don't want you to see it. I don't want you near it, but right now I am too scared of anything happening to you to let you out of my sight. I feel like a fuckin' hand grenade. The pin is pulled and holding onto you is the only thing keeping the lever held down…but one wrong move…one misstep. I am going to fuckin' detonate, and you are going to get hurt in the process." He said through clenched teeth. He did not meet her eyes.

Eden held his face in her hands and looked into his eyes. "Look at me. We are fighting together, remember." She said slowly, "We are going to punch life in the throat. Sometimes it fights back. I'm mad too. I'm pissed. I want to hurt him too. The only difference is that you can seriously fuck him up. I just got lucky with tiny ass lawn tools…" Her joke fell flat as he stared through her, rage simmering behind his eyes. "Anaiah, don't shut me out because you think I will be scared of what I see." She leaned in and kissed his forehead. He closed his eyes and breathed in deeply.

After several minutes, he said in a low voice, "Tell me what happened."

"Adam started that fire tonight. To get you away from me. To draw me out in the open and I just went out there and nearly got my ass kidnapped. I'm pissed at myself for that too. I should have been more careful." Eden ran her hand down Anaiah's cheek.

"Well, we can add one more kid to his death toll." Anaiah's harsh low voice almost growled. "And anyone else that doesn't make it back after tonight." He paused, giving himself a few slow deliberate breaths. "Fires are hard for us when it's adults, but that complex had a lot of kids. When you came in tonight, I was intubating a fifteen-year-old kid. He inhaled smoke while getting some smaller kids out. I was so pissed at myself, because when I saw you, my first thought was 'I should have been with her instead of here'."

"You can't be everywhere at once. You can't save us all. You helped him. You did a good job, baby. And I am okay. Stupid, but okay." She kissed him.

"You were more than okay. You were smart. You ran where you knew help was. And you stabbed him in his face. I'm proud of you for fightin' him." He gave her an approving nod as he stared into her eyes.

"He's scared of you." She spoke softly. "Called you my attack dog. He knows what we are, both of us. I think that he hasn't attacked me directly yet, because he's afraid of you."

His eyes darkened, "Good. If I get my hands on him, I am putting a stop to all of it. Prison won't hold him. I'll send him back to hell where he belongs."

"You could live with that?" She asked, knowing his heart. Knowing that he hated being the cause of pain for others.

He dropped his head back in her lap and breathed in slowly. "I think so. I know that we don't have much choice." He said in a quiet but determined voice. "Why would God make me like this...why make me able to..." He swallowed hard, "If I'm not supposed to be the punisher of unjust people who won't face man's judgment? I help people, I stop suffering, but what if sometimes I have to help by hurting evil people. Does that make me just as bad?" He looked at her for an answer, for some justification for his righteous anger.

"No. You're right. We are this way for a reason." She said thoughtfully. "Adam said that heaven created me to balance things out. Like I was born to be his undoing. Stop him from doing these terrible things."

"You didn't know it was him in the visions?" Anaiah asked quietly.

"No. I was eight when he left. And before that..." She tried to think back to her childhood. So much of it had been blacked out of her memory, her brain compartmentalizing it, forgetting it to protect itself. She remembered being scared of him. She remembered trying to hide from him in their home when he was alone with her. She had tried to stay out of sight most of the time, if she was busy with chores, making something, being productive, her parents let her be.

"Adam was more difficult than I was. I tried to hide what I saw and tried to be the good kid. He fought back, but it was more than that. My parents thought I was evil, but able to be saved. They knew he was evil. I was afraid of everyone as a kid, but I think I knew he had something wrong with him, even then. We weren't close. He's ten years older than me." She thought out loud, "he's smaller than I remember him being, but I was a little kid. His face looked so aged. It's like whatever he's been doing, it's taken a toll. He still sort of looks like my mom, though. It just didn't click. He's been gone so long; it was like I didn't have a brother. I mean, I don't really even feel like I have parents."

"When he left, they just let 'em go?" He asked.

"Yeah...he and my dad fought a lot. Really, he'd try to stand up to my dad and it would get violent. Weird stuff happened too. I know now it was probably like something demonic. Before he turned eighteen, my parents sat him down in the living room with the church leaders. They had a big 'responsibility of a man' talk. I didn't see him the next day. It took me a few days to realize he was gone. I asked where he was and was punished and told to never speak about him again. I always assumed he found his way out and left without looking back. The older I got, the more jealous of him I was. Without him around, they shifted all their demon kid focus to me. Part of me feels like he just couldn't help what he became."

"No. He could." Anaiah shook his head. "You and I both went through horrible shit as kids. You didn't turn into a psychopath. Neither did I. Even as a half demon...Selah didn't hurt people. She baked fuckin' cupcakes. No matter the shit that led up to being how he is now, he made choices to be that way." Anaiah said bitterly.

"You're right." She sighed. She brushed his hair back out of his eyes, assessing him. He seemed calmer. His eyes had lost that murderous gleam to them. His jaw had relaxed under her touch. "Are you feeling less..." she tried to think of the right word.

"Explosive?" He cocked an eyebrow. "Pissed?"

"I was gonna say 'grenade-y'." She smiled.

"Yeah." He laughed. "You defused the landmine. I'm still mad. Mostly at him, some at myself, and a little at you for going out alone and not even texting me so I would know to check on you." He flicked her nose, "I can't be there all the time. I know I can't keep you safe from everything. And until we catch him, as much I would love to keep you locked in a safe room...I won't.

So, I'm gonna teach you some stuff." He pulled open the drawer in the bottom of the nightstand. Inside was a rectangular black box with a keypad on the top of it. He punched in a code and told her the numbers out loud. "4-0-6-7-8 Pound. I need you to remember that." He repeated it and opened the box. Inside the box were three handguns, some magazines, and boxes of ammunition. "This one was always a little small for my hand. It's a nine-millimeter" He pulled out a handgun and laid it on the bed beside her.

"Why do you have guns in your bedroom?" She looked at him confused. "You can physically destroy anyone who breaks in. And you are the least violent guy I know. What do you need guns for?"

"Baby, this is Texas, an' I ain't bullet proof." He let out a huff of laughter. "Honey, I'm friends with all the cops in this town. Went to high school with half of 'em. We go shooting for fun. Hell, we throw axes in Sean's backyard while we drink beers."

"How many guns do you have?" She asked as he pulled out a full magazine and laid it on the bed.

"There's three here. Two in the other nightstand and a safe in the closet with a few hunting rifles and my big handgun." He shrugged. "Code is the same for all of them. 4-0-6-7-8 Pound."

"You have a 'big handgun'?" She raised her eyebrows.

"I have big hands." He said simply turning back to her with his smile fading and turning his face serious. "This one is gonna to be yours. I'm gonna to teach you how to use it. You can't kill a demon with it, but you can shoot your asshole brother in the kneecap if need be. Can't chase you without a knee." He placed the gun in her hand and left the magazine on the bed beside her. "Always assume it's loaded. Never point it at something you don't want to destroy. Never put your finger on the trigger unless you are ready to fire." He turned it over in her hands. "This is the safety. It's on. Repeat it back to me."

"Always assume it's loaded." She said in disbelief that he was arming her. "Never point it at anything you don't want to destroy. Don't put your finger on the trigger until you are ready to fire. Safety. On." She repeated back.

He showed her how to turn the safety off. He walked her through all the parts of the gun. He gave her all the safety points. He had her repeat it back to him. He showed her how to load it, how to unload it, and how to switch out the magazine. He showed her the different types of ammo and how to load the magazine. He told her about extra magazines and ammo in the big safe in the closet. He ran her through an entire gun safety class in his bedroom. He made her repeat it all back to him, made her demonstrate loading, unloading, taking the safety on and off, pulling the slide back to check for a round in the chamber. When he was satisfied that she had it down he pulled out a gun bag from the big safe and placed the gun and two magazines inside. He told her to put it in the front pocket of her backpack. She did as he instructed.

"I'll take you to the range tomorrow. Teach you to shoot." He said as she returned to him in the bedroom.

"I can't believe you put a gun in my hand and told me how to use it." She shook her head, smiling.

"Why? I told you I'd help you learn to be a demon slayer. I can't protect you all the time, so you have to. I figured a gun was better than a garden fork." He grinned as he pulled her close. She leaned into him and breathed deep.

"Oof. Baby, don't take this wrong, but you smell like someone set a bag of dirty gym clothes on fire." She looked up at him with her nose wrinkled.

"Well, come on. Let's get a shower." His mischievous grin broke across his face.

"Anaiah, I'm... on my... monthly..." She said, feeling a little embarrassed.

"If you're uncomfortable, you don't have to. There's stuff in the bottom drawer of the bathroom for you if you need it. Might not be what you usually use." He kissed the top of her head. "You can still join me if you want to."

"You aren't grossed out? Boys don't like that sort of stuff." She asked.

"Baby, boys get grossed out by that. Men grow the fuck up and don't give a shit. It's natural and I'm not squeamish about blood." He backed towards the bathroom while still watching her and pulled his shirt over his head. "It's up to you."

"You can't just take off your shirt like that and not expect me to follow. That isn't fair." Eden grinned and moved toward him.

He reached up and placed his hands on the frame of the door and leaned out toward her slightly. His muscles flexed and he gave a flirty grin, knowing damn well what he was doing. "You're a grown ass woman. You can do what you want." He teased in a low voice and bit his lower lip.

She felt her cheeks heat but smirked back at him. "You know what I want to do?"

"Me?" He looked at her through the curtain of his hair falling in his eyes and let out a low chuckle.

"Fuck you. You are too good at that." She pulled off her shirt and threw it at him. As she stepped closer, he reached out and grabbed her by the wrist. With a quick tug, he pulled her into his arms and kissed her deeply.

"Mmm, yes. Fuck me, sugar." He whispered with a grin just a breath away from her lips. She let him pull her the rest of the way into the shower. She found her solace in him; she felt his need to be just as distracted as she needed to be from the never-ending barrage of her fears. She felt his need to feel her body close to his. To know just feeling her in his arms that she was safe, she was alive, and she was happy. She found she needed it too. It was a visceral need deep in her to have nothing to separate them as they became one and focused entirely on each other. His desires melted into hers and hers became his. Nothing in the world mattered in that moment.

CHAPTER TWENTY-FIVE

S ometime in the morning, Eden felt the bed shift as Anaiah got up. Her body was sore, and her head felt heavy, so she rolled over into the large warm spot he left in his absence and fell back to sleep. A little while later she heard his phone ringing. As he answered it, he closed the bedroom door, likely to let her sleep, but she knew that ringtone. Work was calling him. Her mind buzzed with worries. Did Adam set another fire? Would he do something worse? Would she just need to stay locked in Anaiah's apartment if he had to leave? What if Adam came here and started a fire to burn her out? *OH, SHUT UP!* She scolded her own brain. *Whatever it is, we will get through it. You are stronger than this. This will not be the thing that breaks you.*

She threw the blankets off and popped up out of bed. She walked to the door and slowly opened it. Anaiah was cooking breakfast while talking on the phone. She decided to be conspicuous about being awake and present. Snooping around hadn't helped her before and Anaiah had been open and honest with her. She stepped out of the room.

She rubbed her hand on Anaiah's bare back as she reached up to grab a mug from the kitchen cabinet next to him. He turned and smiled at her. His pajama pants hung from his hips in a way that made her want to rub her hands over other areas. She reminded herself that coffee was next on the agenda, no matter the emergency waiting for him, or how great he looked half dressed, barefoot, and cooking her breakfast. As she made her cup of coffee, she listened to his conversation, waiting for the 'I'll be in soon' she knew she would inevitably hear.

"Well, I know I haven't been out there in a while, but I've been a little busy, chief." Anaiah rolled his eyes. "I think it's a little early for that. Don't want to scare her off or nothin'." He added eggs to the breakfast skillet filled with diced onions, peppers, tomatoes, and diced bacon. Anaiah's cooking skills impressed her most of the time, but his joy in watching her enjoying what he prepared was really the best part. Just one of the many perks of the last few weeks of sleeping over with each other. "Yeah, chief, hold on one sec," he said.

He set the phone on the counter and whispered to her, "Mornin' beautiful. Didn't mean to wake you. Talking with my fire chief for a minute." He leaned in and gave her a quick peck on the cheek. Then he reached over to turn the speakerphone on.

"Had to switch you to speakerphone, I'm making breakfast." He said. She set her coffee down on the counter and lifted herself up to sit on the countertop next to him. She sipped her coffee and wanted to roll her eyes back in her head. He bought the best coffee stuff for her.

"Well, you can wait a while to ease her into it, but Darlene wants you to bring her to dinner. You know, meet all the guys." The chief said.

"We'll see. She's already met some of 'em. She does need to have some of Darlene's chicken n dumplin's...oh, and her cobbler." Anaiah scrambled the eggs while he talked.

"How are you holdin' up after last night? Carla said the scene was rough. She also said you had some extra problems and left the station looking more pissed off than she'd ever seen you." The chief sounded wary.

"I know she means well, but she could do well to mind her own." Anaiah continued to stir the eggs.

"We all know that, but you are dodging the real question. How are you?" He asked pointedly. Eden thought she might like the chief. She smiled as she sipped her coffee.

"I'm alright now. Was pretty shook-up last night but got through it. You probably heard that Eden has a brother who is hellbent on coming after her. That didn't help my mental state, I admit. But she held her own with him and ran like hell. So, we are just hoping that our boys in blue are on it and find him." Anaiah sighed. "I talked it through with my girl. It calmed me down. Are you happy with that?"

"Glad to hear it. You know I like to check in with you after a tough call." The chief said. "Call me if you need to talk. My door's always open, Parker."

"Will do. Give Darlene my love." Anaiah replied. He reached over to hang up the phone. He turned the burner off and set the pan on a cool burner.

"Morning." She said after another drink of her coffee.

"Excuse me, ma'am." He gave her a playful smile, "but who said you could put your adorable ass on my countertop?" He moved to stand between her legs attempting the fakest stern face she had ever seen.

"I believe you gave me permission last week." She sipped again.

"Oh, did I?" He took the mug from her hand and drank. "Jesus, that's sweet." He sat the mug down on the counter. He leaned over her, bracing his hands on each side of her hips.

"You sat my bare ass up here last week," she ran her hand down from his shoulder to his wrist. "When you couldn't wait to get me to the bedroom."

"I did, didn't I?" He leaned further in until he was nose to nose. "Fine. You're allowed, I guess."

She kissed him and asked, "are we going to do this all day? Or do we need to save the world? I kinda vote for this." She wrapped her legs around his waist and slid her arms around his neck.

"If only..." He said with a bit of a sour face. He flicked her nose ring playfully. "We got a full day. Gotta get in some range time. Then, we are gonna go through some basics of self-defense. After that, we gotta gather the rest of the stuff we need for the scroll. Maybe do a ritual or two." Anaiah reached up and took her hands down. "You gotta keep your hands to yourself for a day." He said with a wink.

"Boo." She stuck out her tongue. "When did you get so bossy?"

"I've always been bossy, baby. Why do you think Carla calls me 'boss?' It's a big joke at the station." He grinned. "Eggs are gonna get cold. You want tortillas?"

She pretended to pout. "Yes."

He moved to grab the tortillas off the counter and turned on a burner. She watched as he warmed each one over the fire, grabbing the edge and flipping it without getting burned. He threw them on a plate and moved all the food to the bar on his kitchen island. Eden hopped down and grabbed her coffee.

"So, they call you 'boss' as a joke?" She asked, filling her tortillas with cheese and scooped the scramble on top. She added a very small amount of the salsa that Anaiah added liberally to his breakfast taco. She learned the hard way that it was too hot for her. He had made it himself, with extra serrano peppers.

"Carla and Allen do. Every now and then, one of my superiors does too. Carla, Allen and I are all the same rank. Carla and I are the two main lieutenants on the night shift. All the probies, EMT's and firefighters either call me Lieutenant Parker or Boss. Now, the boys in blue, they call me all sorts of names that are uncouth to say over breakfast and in front of a lady." He smiled and took a bite.

"Which of the things that I call you do you like best? Hmm?" She took a bite.

He wiped his mouth with a napkin and swallowed. "Hmm. I am particularly partial to the times when you forget how to talk and can't say my name, just those little whimpers." He nudged her foot with his.

"I like when you call me 'sugar'. I think I would hate being called it by anyone else, but when you say it…" She shrugged.

"I'll keep that in mind, but really, I don't have a preference. Anaiah, baby, honey, sweetie, whatever you want, as long as you call me yours." She reached over her left hand, freshly bandaged from the night before and squeezed his hand.

"I'd kiss you, but I don't want to stop eating." She said between bites. "You lured me in with your sex appeal and kept me with your prowess in the kitchen." She sighed and took another bite.

"That's how it's done." He smiled. "Love at first empanada. Speaking of food, Chief Davidson and his wife Darlene would love to have us over for family dinner on Sunday. Darlene cooks a big meal every Sunday and it's an open invite to all the crew. She's our mama bear. And since I haven't been to dinner all month, she's worried. He told her that it's because I have been spending time with my girlfriend and she told him to call and invite you too. Most of my coworkers…my friends will be there."

"If you want me to go, I will. It would be nice to see your friends when I haven't had to file a police report." She said and Anaiah nodded with his mouth full. "So, the chief checks up on you after calls? To make sure you're okay?"

"When it's a bad scene, yeah. He knows how I get. He started doing it after a horrible domestic scene. Kids were injured. The mom was half dead. You can see where I might have taken that call a little personally. Apparently, it's unprofessional to throw the abuser out the front door when he tries to re-enter the scene." He rolled his eyes.

"Did he get hurt?" Her brows rose.

"Just some scrapes and bruises. But I got a suspension and anger management classes. So, he checks in. That was years ago. He's one of the few people I am open with." He finished his plate. "Him and Sean."

"They have no idea how much you held back," she wondered out loud.

He picked up his plate and started clearing his dishes. "No, they don't." He said quietly. He carried them to the sink and turned to look at her. "I thank God for you." he said in a low voice. "I'm so thankful that I have someone who doesn't just know this thing about me but understands it."

"Love you." She beamed at him. "I feel the same way about you."

He watched her for a moment longer as she took her last bite and drank her coffee. He swallowed hard. "I'm gonna go shave and get dressed."

"Aww. I was digging the stubble. Added to the whole 'ruggedly handsome' thing you have going on." She said as he walked around the island and picked up her dishes.

"If I keep it, your face will get road rash and my chief will tell me it's a fire hazard." He laughed. He rinsed the dishes and placed them in the dishwasher.

"Okay, shave if you must. I still like your face that way too, I guess." She said with an overly dramatic sigh.

"You're sassy today." He winked at her and walked through his room into the bathroom. She trailed behind him. He picked up his electric shaver and she brushed her teeth. She got dressed in black leggings and a shirt from her bag. She had never really shaken the habit of carrying extra clothes. She knew she didn't have to have a bug out bag logically, but her mind rested easier knowing it was there.

She grabbed her make up bag and walked back into the bathroom. He had moved on to teeth brushing. She went through her makeup routine: moisturizer, followed by foundation, a bit of bronzer to define her cheek bones, followed by blush and highlight. She pulled out her favorite nude pallet and began applying it to her lids using various browns, golds and shimmering mauves. She added her favorite part, a small, winged eyeliner with an eye pen, followed by a few swipes of mascara. She met Anaiah's eyes in the mirror as he brushed out his hair. She applied her lip stain lipstick and blew him a kiss. He gave her his mischievous look.

"You said we had stuff to do." She shot back with a wicked grin.

"I'm just thinking of later. About where I am gonna find that lipstick on me." His eyebrow raised and his grin widened.

"Here I thought I was dating a good Christian boy...and I got a dirty one instead." She turned and smiled up at him.

"I was good...then I met you. And every ounce of self-control was just ripped right out of me." He stared down at her with a half-smile.

She frowned. She had similar worries over the last couple of weeks. She had made him happy, but at what cost for him? Anaiah had to shoulder the burden of her emotional baggage and all this mystical bullshit that she had dragged him headfirst into. He had to lie to people he cared about and put his job at risk for lying about what happened at multiple crime scenes. He slept so much less than he needed to spend time helping her investigate things, find materials for spells, and find out more about what they were. She'd carried him along with her into a fight between heaven and hell. Anaiah felt he had to be always her protector, now. He never hung out with his friends. Had she compromised a part of him to tempt him into betraying what he believed? Caused him to have some sort of moral failing that he had to struggle with?

"Eden?" He said quietly. "What's wrong?"

"I..." How could she explain what she was thinking? How could she explain that it worried her that he had somehow traded out these little bits of happiness with her for his entire life and she worried that he made a poor bargain. He took her into his arms. And held her silently, allowing her the time to process and speak when she was ready. He explained to her the night before that he often stayed silent to let her do that. Sometimes, like last night, he stayed silent to keep his own emotions in check. She had to explain to him her misinterpretation of it being directed at her. She often internalized the emotions of others as being done to her.

"Can I just sort of dump my possibly crazy thoughts out on you? And I want you to be honest with me about them." She stared up into his tawny brown eyes.

"Of course." He said looking at her like it was a ridiculous question.

"I worry that you aren't joking about that. That you were better before me, and you have had to make choices that compromise what you believe because of me. I worry that you had a life before me that you probably miss, before you had to be my de facto bodyguard and help me with some sort of supernatural war. I'm worried that someday soon, you are going to realize everything you have set aside to be with me, and every little bit of compromise you let slip because of me. And you are going to regret the shit end of the stick that you chose by choosing me."

"Why would you think that?" He looked down at her with sadness in his eyes.

"You have spent every moment you aren't working with me for the last several weeks. You haven't been able to see your friends or go to dinner with the chief and his wife, or any of the things you normally do and it's all because you can't leave me alone or something might happen. And the first time you do, something terrible happens. I'm worried that you have to be someone you don't want to be with me." She broke his intense stare. Had she just unraveled everything by opening her mouth?

"Baby, look at me." He said softly. "I am a better man because of you. You keep me from coming apart when I want to tear the world apart. You make me want to be better, to do better. You are the best thing to ever happen to me. When I think back on the last couple of weeks, I don't think about the pile of bullshit we've been dealt. I think about the fact that I get to come home and hold the one person who really knows me. The woman who sees me, the good, the bad, and the broken parts of me and loves me. You act like I'm getting some raw deal here. You act like you aren't the most miraculous, strong, funny, beautiful woman I've ever met. Baby, I found everything I ever wanted when I got you."

Tears welled up in her eyes. "I'm sorry. I..."

"No, don't be sorry. I want you to tell me what you feel." He reached over and grabbed a tissue from the box on the counter and dried her eyes. "You just worked so hard to put all that on. Don't ruin it now." He cracked a smile. "You've been hurt, it's why you think that way. But don't be ashamed of it. I can handle it too. You can put it on me." He kissed the top of her head.

"I'm not actually some evil temptress taking away your virtue then?" She laughed after hearing how ridiculous she had sounded.

"Oh, for sure, but I'm into it." He winked at her. "Sugar, I wasn't an angel before you came along. Now I'm halfway there."

"You know what I mean." She smiled despite herself. "Even if I'm not on the same page with you and your faith. I don't want to mess it up for you. If that makes sense."

"Honey, I see the glory of God when I am with you. I'm the man I am meant to be when I take you in my arms. I believe that God brought us together. Don't worry about breaking what I have going with the Lord. It's not that fragile." His voice was gentle.

"So, what about your friends then?" She asked, needing to soothe every worry.

He rolled his eyes. "You mean the jackasses I see at work every day?"

"You have to have other friends." She said in disbelief.

"Not really. Sean and I have been friends since we were in high school. He's my best friend. He's missed me online, playing games with him, but I told him I'd rather be with you. Gave him a lot of shit for not finding someone too." He laughed. "Might have rubbed it in a bit."

"That's a little mean." She cracked a smile.

"Oh, he threw it in my face not three months ago that he didn't show up to hang out with the guys, at HIS house I might add, because he was busy hooking up with a lady I said was pretty once in high school." He defended himself.

"Wait…have you told him about us? Is that what you told him you'd rather be doing?" Her cheeks flushed. She buried her face in his chest from embarrassment when he looked at her guiltily.

"I mean, we talk. Guys talk sometimes, I'm sure you told Journey about it." He chuckled.

"Sean has only seen me at the WORST times and knows about my sex life now. How am I supposed to hang out with your best friend now? How am I supposed to sit down to family dinner and not wonder what you told them about us?" She hid her flaming hot cheeks again in his chest.

He laughed. "Are you ashamed of taking me into your bed, sugar?" he asked, barely able to keep the laugh from bubbling through as he talked.

"No. I've just always been private. I kept to myself. Didn't have close friends. Cole was the closest thing I had to being close with someone. I'm just not used to everyone knowing such…intimate things about me. It took me a while to open up to Journey. She was the first person I talked to about any of my weird shit. And you…God, I've only known you a few months and you are the only person who knows me like this. It's just going to take some adjustment for me, okay?"

"You don't have to discuss it with them at dinner. No one is going to ask about that cute little noise you make when you are about to..."

"No..." She gasped. "You didn't tell anyone about that! I get embarrassed that you hear those things sometimes."

"It's goddamn adorable...and hot at the same time. And no, I didn't tell anyone about that. I might've bragged about some of my favorite features." He looked at her with a guilty pleading look in her eyes that said, 'please don't be mad'.

"Which are?" She kept her mouth tight and scowled at him.

"You do have gorgeous breasts, sugar. And..."

"And?" She kept up her scowl. In answer, he reached down with one hand and grabbed an ass cheek.

"You kill me in those leggings every damn time." He smiled.

"Is that all?" She looked up at him, defiant despite the light mood she now felt.

"I might have also told Sean that you were very...let's say, talented, with your mouth. And the best I've ever had, period."

"Best at giving head? Or sex?" She asked, confused by him dancing around the subject.

"Both." He suddenly looked a little embarrassed.

"You can talk about me sucking you off...with Sean. You can tell me it's good, but you get embarrassed telling me that you told Sean that I am the best? That's a little funny." She smiled.

"Well, it can be a little crass the way us guys talk."

"Thank you for considering my delicate feminine sensibilities."

"You were blushing not five minutes ago. Don't give me that shit." He lightly smacked her on her ass where his hand had been grabbing a moment before.

"Oh..." Her eyes went wide as she felt a little thrill go through her.

"Did I hurt..."

"Nope. No. Um... didn't know I liked that. Now, I do." She cleared her throat. "Making a mental note to circle back to that later, when we are done with our busy day. Speaking of which, are you going to wear PJ pants to go shooting, or..." She trailed off.

He let go of her with a huff and went to his closet to get clothes. A few minutes later as she was slipping on her sneakers, she heard him unlock the gun safe in his closet. He came out a moment later with a duffle bag in his hand. He walked to the nightstand and opened the gun box. He pulled out a couple of pistols and boxes of ammo and magazines. He secured them each in a gun bag that he put into the duffle bag.

She braided her hair and tied the elastic band at the end. "I'm ready for badass bootcamp."

"Badass with winged eyeliner, even." He smiled. "Let's go, gorgeous."

CHAPTER TWENTY-SIX

A s they climbed the four little steps up to her porch, Eden tried not to notice the ache in her legs. She lifted her arm to unlock the door and felt the ache in her sore arms and across her shoulders which helped her forget the ache in her legs for a few seconds. She rolled her neck and shoulders after she opened the door.

Pleasantly surprised that Adam hadn't come to tear apart her home, she pulled the gun from the holster on her hip as Anaiah had trained her to do. She walked in with him coming in behind her with his gun drawn and pointed at an angle toward the floor. She held hers in the same fashion. Together, they walked through and swept the house. He had walked her through how they would do a tactile sweep of the house, room by room. They took turns as they covered each other as they opened doors and made sure that the house had no unexpected visitors either in the form of relatives or demons. What good the guns would do against demons, she didn't know but it made Anaiah feel better, so she went along with it.

She secretly hoped to find Adam hiding somewhere so she could shoot him in the foot or something. She grinned at the thought until the very real possibility of seeing Anaiah end Adam's life crossed her mind. She realized that she wouldn't want to see it. She could do it herself, if need be. Pull the trigger and be the one to end him if he dared attack her again. The thought of seeing Anaiah do it, witnessing the emotional aftermath of what taking a life might do to him, felt physically painful to her. *Is it wrong that I am more comfortable with watching my own brother die than I am seeing Anaiah in emotional pain? Probably.* She told herself.

"House is clear," he said after checking the shower as she stood guard by the door. She wondered if Adam knew about the book or the scroll that she carried with her now. "Alright, let's set this up." He pulled off his backpack and pulled out assorted ingredients. Eden took the bowl from the last spell and washed it out in the kitchen, unsure if dawn dish soap would take off any sort of magical residue. She rinsed and dried it.

"After we do these, we should grab a bite." He said as she came back into the room.

"We just ate before we went to the grasslands." She grinned.

"That was three hours ago." He said, "after this, I'll be starving."

"Does your heavenly power run on tacos?" She sassed with a smile.

"Don't be racist, I like taters too." He joked. "But yeah, let's go get the good street style ones at that taqueria. They have the best tortillas."

"Am I going to need extra tortillas because they are too spicy?" She made a face.

"Probably. I have ice cream at home for after." He grinned.

"I LIKE spicy food. You're the weirdo that only likes food that sets your whole face on fire." She stuck her tongue out at him. "If it doesn't make your taste buds numb after, you think it's mild salsa."

She pulled the book from her bag, flipping back through the pages they had looked at earlier. There were a few spells in the back that they could read. They looked like minor incantations that required a few herbs. She opened to the one titled "Warding of protection". The plan was to cast the spell over the house. The instructions specified an area and the amount of herbs needed. It reminded Eden of pancake mix instructions. The more you needed to protect, the more herbs needed. It was insanely simple as well. They only needed to mix the herbs, then walk the four corners of the house, and sprinkle the herbs there while saying the incantation. She measured them carefully. Salt, dill, lavender, oregano, and parsley, all measured out by tablespoons into a dish. She stirred them with her fingers.

Before they left her house, they planned to make a tea of lavender, dill, oregano, parsley, and add rosemary and thyme. This tea was meant to be the same protection but when ingested, it would protect their bodies for a while. The rosemary and thyme were added to the mix to repel nightmares. The book explained that the herbs would clear up doubt in the nephilim, also called children of angels. Their dreams would be prophetic, and not out of their own fears and traumas. They planned to also take a bowl of herbs and walk to the outside corners of Anaiah's apartment complex to protect the building as well.

Eden had initially felt silly buying these herbs in bulk at the local wholesale store, but they were used often in this book. The last spell of the evening at her house would show them how to understand daemonic, or the language of hell. Several spells in her book were at least partially written in daemonic.

She and Anaiah made quick work of protecting the house. They sprinkled the herbs and when they spoke the last part of the incantation, the herbs transformed into a white fog that hung throughout the house. It smelled like ozone. For a moment, Eden wondered if they should be breathing in this smokey herb fog, then realized they would be drinking something similar soon. Anaiah pulled out a box of empty tea bags for loose leaf tea. He walked into the kitchen to start on the project of mixing and making protective tea. Eden followed.

Anaiah had gone thrift store shopping with her to replace her glassware, plates and bowls that had been broken when Adam trashed her place. She smiled at the memory of him sleepily carrying boxes of dishes in the house and insisting on helping her wash them before they went to bed. She tiptoed to reach the kettle on top of her fridge where she stored it along with other various kitchen items that her cabinets had no space for. It was just slightly out of her reach. Without a word, Anaiah reached over her and grabbed it, handing it to her.

"I would have gotten there eventually." She smiled playfully.

"You would have climbed the cabinets again. Is that what I have to look forward to when you move in with me? Scuffed up cabinet doors and shoe marks from you climbing in the kitchen?" He laughed. "You even have a step stool." He pointed out.

"Takes too long to get it out." She lifted her arms to stretch her sore back and shoulders. "Wait, you said 'when I move in with you'. When were you planning to tell me about that?" She shot him an accusatory glare and moved to fill the kettle with water.

"We pretty much already do. We just bounce back and forth. It'd be nice just to have one spot to lay our heads and quit toting bags back and forth." He shrugged. She felt an initial panic at being tied to his apartment, but that soon fell away as she realized that she didn't want to sleep in her bed without him. They were moving so fast, but with all they had been through the last few weeks, it felt normal. What the hell was normal, anyway?

She sighed. "It feels like moving forward with any sort of normal life stuff has to wait until we get this all sorted, you know?" She placed the kettle on the stove and lit the burner. "Maybe we keep my place as a backup. Use it to do rituals and spells somewhere where we don't sleep."

"Don't gotta rush into it if you don't want to." Anaiah filled the tea bags with the herb mixture, tied them off and placed them in two coffee cups. "Ain't never been too big on hot tea. 'Course, mom's sweet tea was the sweetest I've ever had."

"Hmm, I've never been big on sweet tea. Tastes like an excuse to drink syrup. I like hot tea. Lady Grey is my favorite. It's Earl Grey with citrus. Peppermint tea, with a good book, curled up with a blanket on the couch. That's just a good way to spend a lazy day off." She smiled.

"I'll have to give it another try. I've only ever had plain black tea. You know I love a good cup o' joe without all the frills you like." He smiled. "Think we should start mixing up stuff for the daemonic one?"

"We can lay it all out, but I want to get this done first. Just something in my gut telling me that once we get that one done, it's going to set off the next wild goose chase. Here, let's get it all out on the table." She walked back into the living room, soreness dogging her every step. "You know, I don't know if my body appreciates the new workout routine."

"Sore?" He asked, trailing behind her.

"Yeah, I feel like I ran a marathon yesterday. Then you had me shoot, draw, and reload for two hours. Not to mention you and Sean throwing me around on the mat and teaching me how to punch and kick. And the hiking trail in the grasslands." She noticed his smirk and a thought occurred to her. "No...don't tell me that you don't get sore! Because of the super muscles, you don't feel like crap after going to the gym?"

"Have you seen me go to the gym much?" He winked. His secret was out.

"You eat like you have a tapeworm, you don't have to work out, you don't get sore, and you just get to look like that, all the time?" She imagined her jaw hitting the floor like a cartoon with the realization. He shrugged. She smacked his arm. "UNFAIR! I see ghosts, but it doesn't let me walk through walls and stuff!"

"Maybe you should have gotten a better dad." He joked and then realized what he said. As he remembered her entire childhood in an instant, his face fell.

She burst out laughing. "I have been saying that this whole time! I get a second crack at it, and what do I get? Lamest abilities ever. Getting woken up by my manager from beyond the vale!" She nearly doubled over laughing then winced. "Ow. My abs are sore too." She laid out spell components as Anaiah handed them to her. They had most of them laid out when the kettle started whistling.

"I got it." He said and walked to the kitchen to pour the water into the mugs.

She finished laying everything out. She looked down at the hand that was still bandaged. She wondered to herself why she had to cut her hand in just the right direction and pour out her blood as a cost for learning enochian, but not for daemonic. It seemed backwards to her. Like the demon language should be harder to learn, but then again, she wouldn't have been able to decipher the spell without learning enochian first. She looked up as Anaiah walked into the room carrying two steaming mugs.

"How's your hand?" She asked.

"It smarts every now and then, but it's nothing too terrible." He said, handing a mug to her. "Careful, it's hot." She gingerly took it by the handle in his hand. "Yours bothering you?"

"No more than anything else. Just a little ache." She wiggled her fingers. She sat her hot mug down on a side table next to the couch. "I want to sit for a minute." She plopped herself down on the couch and immediately regretted it. She knew when the time came to get back up, she would not want to move. She should have stayed on her feet if she wasn't going to give into taking a nap or refusing to leave the couch without Anaiah carrying her.

"Alright, turn around." He said plopping down next to her. "You just look so sad."

She turned on the couch to face away from him. He worked his fingers and thumb down her neck from the base of her skull to her shoulders. She felt the tension loosening.

"You did good today." He said softly. "Your shooting was better'n I expected. Sean was impressed too. And you can fight, by God. You pack a mean punch for weighing a little more than a buck fifty." He chuckled, "I know you are worn out, but today was fun for me. Got to do some stuff I like to do shootin', hikin', hangin' out with Sean. It made me real happy to see you two joking around." He worked his hands down her shoulders to her mid back.

"I had a lot of fun. I like Sean. He's a genuinely good guy, despite his mouth. I can tell. And I see why you two are so close. Two boy scouts sticking together." She giggled. "On the one hand, I wish things could be normal, you know. We just get to go on dates, get to meet each other's friends and not have all this…weird shit in the middle of it. But on the other hand, I really love what's happening with us. Things may be moving at breakneck speed, but it feels good. Hanging with Sean today felt like a normal thing until you take into account that the reason, we did that was to use his range, and train in his gym. I'd love to go hiking when we aren't on a mystical quest. You know."

He sighed. "Yeah, I know. But we ain't normal. Never gonna be. At least if we've got some sort of divine purpose, we have it together." He moved his hands to her lower back and worked out the tension there.

"That's true. Who would give me back rubs when I don't want to keep going if I was doing this alone?" She turned and gave him a peck on the cheek.

"Glad to be of service, sugar." He winked.

She reached over and grabbed her cup. It smelled more like a vegetable broth with seasonings than tea. "You ready for this part?"

"Let's drink our magic potion then, I guess." He grabbed his mug and flipped open the book. He began reading the enochian phrases of protection over her. She began sipping her tea. To her surprise, it wasn't terrible to drink.

She took a drink at the end of each phrase. Nothing seemed to happen until after he spoke the last part, which roughly translated into "heaven protect with the power of the father." She expected mist or smoke to rise from her empty cup, instead she felt a strong gurgling in her stomach. Her stomach clenched. *Oh god... am I going to puke this up?* This was not something they had considered. She doubled over as the churning became more rapid and violent within her.

"What's wrong?" Anaiah's voice rose with his rising panic as she gripped her stomach.

She gritted her teeth against the cramping in her gut. "I don't know." She didn't dare look at him and see the worry in his face. Then she felt it rising in her throat, like hot burning bile. She sat up quickly, feeling nauseated. Then sudden wonderful relief as she heard the near ground shaking burp came out of her mouth with a large plume of white smoke. She sat still for a moment, unsure of what she should feel: relief? embarrassment? Until she heard Anaiah's bellowing laugh next to her. She looked over, and he was doubled over in laughter. She found herself laughing too.

"That was priceless..." He said between his continuing bouts of laughter. "Reminds me of when the guys all tried to see who could chug those sparkling water cans fastest. Bobby puked. And Sean let out the biggest longest burp I ever heard." He wiped the tears from the corners of his eyes.

"Well, now that you know that's coming, try to recite the alphabet or something. I got to be the heavenly protection burp guinea pig." She laughed as she took the book from his hands and started reciting the words of protection over him. He quickly tried to compose himself and sip his tea. He made an assessing 'not bad' face after his first taste. She continued. When it was done, she waited to see his reaction to the stomach cramps she had endured. He placed a hand over his stomach and squinted one eye. Then he let out a thundering burp that put her's to shame. The cloud of white that came with it dissipated into the room.

"Thought I was going to throw up for a second. Felt like the time I had really sketchy tacos with Sean, and we got food poisoning." He grinned. "Don't tell him I told you, but he totally shat his pants."

"And you didn't?" She raised her eyebrows making a disbelieving face.

"Oh, I totally did. But you didn't have to call me out like that." He laughed. "Ok. Protection spells done. Let's get hooked on daemonics."

"Hooked on daemonics worked for me?" She was pretty sure she got his joke. He winked at her before he turned to the correct page and started reading. He added the grave dirt to the large glass bowl. They read the spell the same way that they had the first one, with pre-selected sections for each to read so they wouldn't mess it up after reading too much. They added their ingredients: various plants, chicken bones, a jawbone of an ass, which Anaiah had ordered online from a taxidermy shop, and purified water.

That water had been like the world's dumbest recipe. They had to boil the water under a new moon, add salt, boil until halved, and then speak the cleansing enochian words over it once it was cooled. They stored it in a mason jar and hoped nothing they did around it would make it impure again. They finally added the purified water as instructed and waited hopefully. Anaiah sat the bowl down on the coffee table as the wet ingredients suddenly burst into flame as if instead of water, they had dowsed the little twigs, dirt, herbs and bones in lighter fluid. Eden instinctively took a step back as the flames rose to over a few feet high.

Two licks of flame shot toward them and struck them in the chest. Eden grabbed Anaiah's hand and braced herself against the heat and pain searing through her chest. She felt like her very heart was on fire. Her pulse pounded in her ears. It burned like a branding iron through her heart and started to spread outward. She gritted her teeth against the pain. Was she incinerating from the inside out? Anaiah's hand slid from her grasp, and she fell to her knees next to him. Her vision went white as the searing pain reached her head. She held on as long as she could as her whole body burned but could no longer take the pain and screamed out. The last thing she remembered was hearing Anaiah's scream next to her on the floor as she slipped into darkness.

CHAPTER TWENTY-SEVEN

The incessant pounding in her head was the first thing Eden registered when she stirred. As she turned onto her back, she noted every aching muscle in her chest, arms, and back. Her heart hurt and not in an emotional sense. One of the worst physical pains Eden had ever felt was throbbing in her chest. She draped her arm across her face blocking out the bright overhead light of her living room. Silently, she swore at herself to get up off the floor and make some sort of plan for their next steps. However, the ache in her chest made it difficult to breathe. Pulling herself into a sitting position seemed to be her Everest at the moment.

She stretched a hand to the apex of her pain, just to the left of her sternum. What she felt startled her into a sitting position despite feeling like hot garbage. The flames had seared a fist-sized hole in her shirt. Through that hole, enochian symbols whirled in a stark black pattern on her pale skin. She rubbed her hand over the raised and irritated pattern.

As her eyes fell on Anaiah's unmoving body sprawled out on the floor next to her couch, she lurched into action. Anaiah had fallen through the coffee table. It now lay broken; its contents scattered on the floor. As she moved toward him, she breathed a sigh of relief at the sight of his chest rising and falling. She shook his shoulder and called his name. He didn't budge. Her second attempt was more forceful but yielded nothing. She stood straight, kicking the debris of her coffee table out of the way. She attempted to roll him over on his back. He barely moved. Eden squatted down, wrapping both arms around his upper arm, grabbing onto his chest. She pulled on him and pushed with her legs with all her strength.

"Why do you have to be so fucking big?" She grunted in frustration as she flipped him on to his back. "Wake up, Anaiah!" She smacked at his cheek. "Wake up."

His eyes fluttered open. "Did you yell at me for being too big?" He asked sleepily.

"You're fucking enormous. It took all my strength to flip you over." She laughed deliriously. "If you need to be carried or dragged to safety, you are screwed if you are dependent on my tiny ass." She looked him over. "Does your chest hurt, like you got stomp kicked right over your heart? Or are you immune to that too?" She squinted at him suspiciously.

"Oh, I feel like I got the shit kicked out of me." He sat up with a grunt. "What the hell is that?" He pointed at the scorched hole in her shirt.

"I could ask you the same." She pointed at his matching burn mark and new enochian tattoo. He looked down at his shirt and touched the raised black marks.

"Oh, geez. That feels like a fresh tat. But deeper. Like its inside too." He eyed her as she reached over and grabbed the book of Seraphi out of the coffee table rubble. "Oh, did I break that when I fell?" He noticed the pile of crushed furniture.

"Figured it was part of your plot to get us under one roof." She grinned as she scrolled down the page with her finger. "Oh, that's fun. It's written in daemonic so you can't read it 'til after you do the spell." She pointed to the bottom of the last page of the ritual. "Let not mercy and truth forsake thee; bind them about thy neck, write them upon the tablet of thine heart. Wait, isn't that in the bible too? It's from proverbs. Do you think this is written on our hearts too?"

"The way this feels, I'd say so. I need a drink. Or some morphine." He rubbed at his chest. "Didn't I leave a shirt here the other day?" He pulled his ruined shirt over his head. Eden spied the small white scars immediately; they twisted up his arms and around his neck. She grabbed his hand and turned it over in hers seeing the enochian symbols raised like healed scars ending in a loop across the palm and back of their hands. She had them too.

She flexed her hand against the snug bandages binding her incision. She no longer felt its insistent ache, likely muted from the other pain she felt. The only sensation was the tug of the stitches under the dressing. They felt too tight. She unwrapped it curiously and gawked at her now healed hand in awe. The incision hadn't left a mark. Under the sutures, her palm was now scarred in enochian. Anaiah mirrored her reaction, unwrapping his hand after seeing her palm. She looked up at him, speechless.

"Guess we don't need the sutures anymore." Then he asked, "Got a small pair of scissors and tweezers?"

Eden stared at him, mouth agape. "That's your takeaway?"

"Baby, I don't know if you have noticed but I'm a do-er. I take in a situation and find something to do. Nothing I can do about getting some

tattoos, but I can take out useless stitches before the skin grows over them."
He shrugged.

She shook her head. "Your shirt is in the closet, hanging on the end. It's the one that's three times bigger than mine. I'll get my cuticle trimmers and tweezers. I have wine. No hard liquor. Do you just want ibuprofen instead?"

"I'll take both." He stood up. "Want a glass?"

"I think I deserve it. Got my first tattoo and didn't even get to pick the design." She knew her voice took on a pissy edge, but she didn't care. She stalked into the bathroom, grabbing what she needed from the top drawer. She discarded her damaged shirt, tossing it into the trash. She slathered vitamin E lotion over the new marks. She'd used it on scars and knew it helped. The lotion soothed the burning. She strode for the closet to find a shirt. Anaiah met her there with two glasses in one massive hand and a bottle of ibuprofen in the other.

"Let me see what we are working with here." He motioned toward her chest. She lifted her chin for him to see the chain-like links of the words etched on her skin, from her heart up to her collar bones, winding around her neck and down her arms. "Justice, peace, protection, mercy, vengeance, grace, nature, life, death... It's all the angels, isn't it? These are all the things the angels represent."

"This helps with burn." She held up the lotion. She tucked the little tools in her back pocket and squirted the cream into her hand. She rubbed it on his marks. Anaiah stood in front of her closet with his hands full, helpless to take over the task for her. She could tell he was itching to take over. "You don't like depending on others much, do you?"

He let out a huff. "No. Do you want to take this from me so I can apply some on you?"

"Already did it myself. But here." She took the bottle of medicine from him. She opened it and threw a few pills in her mouth. Taking a glass from his hand, she smiled at him before washing them down with the whole glass. She took out a few tabs for him and handed them to him. The nearest t-shirt was as good as any, so she threw it over her head.

She returned the ibuprofen to the kitchen, refilled her glass of wine and grabbed a paper towel. She returned to Anaiah in the living room. She sat her glass down on the end table and pulled the little tools from her back pocket. She handed them to Anaiah and placed the paper towel in her right hand, palm up, ready to receive the discarded stitches.

"Patient and assistant, nice." He sat his half empty glass down next to hers and turned his attention to his task. "Hold still. This won't hurt, just pull a little."

"I am fully acquainted with home stitch removal." She said quietly.

"Why would you be... oh, yeah." He sighed. "Sorry, I forgot."

"You just woke up from a small coma, I'll forgive you. Shit, what time is it anyways?" She wondered.

"Looks like we lost a couple of hours. Sun's set, but it's not dark yet." He removed the stitches quickly without any fuss or pain. "You seem upset."

"Trade me." She handed him the paper towel in his right hand before taking the little scissors. He handed over the tweezers. She rolled her shoulders and neck. "I have a lot of scars that I didn't have any say in getting. Most are easy to hide. It would have been nice to decide what the first tattoo I put on myself would be. It seems silly, but I might be a little annoyed with my heavenly dad. I feel like he's making choices for me that I want for myself." She sighed. "But they aren't bad. And looking at the book, they do more than just let us read daemonic. It's like they link us to heaven, open our eyes. Maybe it will be more helpful than just new tats in trade for reading hell's language."

"I get it." He nodded. "Maybe I can take you to get one that you pick." She looked up at his encouraging smile.

"I'd like that." She grinned back. "Let's plan what's next while I do this."

"Guess we need to check the scroll in my bag, see what it needs. Flip through the book and see what all we can read there; what may be useful. Plan that out. Then, I say we mix up the herbs for the apartment and throw 'em in a bag. Head to get tacos and go do that before we go back ho... I mean to my apartment."

"You can say home. I'm cool with it." She turned her concentration on getting a stuck knot loose from his skin with the tweezers.

"Don't sound too excited, sugar." He said in a low voice.

"No, really. I'm tired as fuck and all I want to do is eat tacos with you and pass out next to you in our bed. If you can help me, I'll even pack a suitcase with my clothes. I'm feeling spent though." She sighed and smiled up at him. "You know, just before we did the spell, I was thinking how stupid it was that the first one required us to cut ourselves and sacrifice blood, and how this one seemed too easy. Now I know better." She finished pulling the last stitch. "There."

He let out a chuckle. She looked up at him confused. He laughed again. "It's just...we talked about how we were brought together an' stuff. How it feels like it was meant to be? And we have a serious talk about moving in together and things going fast... an' our dad's go and give us matching tattoos." His grin spread wide across his face.

"A little warning would have been nice. What if I didn't want to get matching tattoos?" She said sarcastically. She set the little tools down on the end table and picked up her glass. She took a hefty drink.

"Slow down, little miss wino...I remember how you get when you have a little too much." He winked at her while picking up his own glass and finishing it off. "We need beer. Or shots. Or both."

"We are going to have to tell your friends that we got matching tattoos across our entire chest and arms." She realized. "I can tell my friends about this. Journey knows what's up. But there's no way you could tell Sean." She said quietly.

"We might be able to cross that road someday." He said somberly. "But today, we just gotta lie our way through it." He laughed. "You know, I let him out bench press me in high school a couple of times to keep him from getting suspicious?"

"Powerlifting?" She laughed.

"State champ, baby." He grinned proudly. "I know it wasn't fair, but it explained why I was so strong. And why I'm built like this." Eden looked over at Anaiah to appreciate his build.

She picked up the book as Anaiah grabbed the scroll from his bag. Some rituals looked helpful. The healing spell seemed helpful. It was like a potion that you could store for later. She made a mental note of the herbs they would need to throw it together. They had most of them already.

"Well, shit." Anaiah swore softly as he read the scroll. "We got a lot of the spell ingredients, but we need blood. Specifically, we need the blood of four different children of heaven."

"We count for two of those, right?" She walked over to look at the scroll.

"Yeah, but how do we find two more of us? The closest thing we have is that spell you found online and that required a lot of the blood of the innocent. I don't want that on our hands." He cursed again under his breath.

"But Adam did the spell. He did the spell to gather the children of heaven. Shouldn't they be gathering? I mean, we came together, but we already knew each other before he cast that. Wouldn't we feel some pull to him? Or does it just show him who we are?" She pulled out her phone and pulled up the document. The script she couldn't read before was definitely daemonic and enochian. "He can 'see them for what they are' according to this. And...he feels a pull toward them. Well, shit. He can track us. That's how he knew what you were."

"We need to find some other way. We ain't killin' anyone and we need two more nephilim to get the blade." Anaiah said.

"Do we need the blade? Or do we just need to take Adam out? He's obviously just as human as us. He's not impervious to physical harm. He didn't handle getting stabbed in the face any better than most people would."

"What about Cole?" Anaiah's voice took on a dark violent edge. "How else do we kill a demon? I've looked into it an' I want him dead."

"He hasn't shown up in weeks, and he did claim he was helping me. Maybe Adam is working with him, maybe not. He's a wild card." She put her hand on his chest, trying to be reassuring.

"We can't just let him live and hope that he doesn't come back to bite us in the ass." Anaiah said a little harshly. He took in a calming breath. "He will always be a threat to you, as far as I am concerned." He put his hand over hers. She felt his chest rise and fall with his deliberate breaths. She knew he was trying to defuse the building anger within himself.

"Ok. We research. That's what we do. We look for another way to find the other nephilim. We make healing potions; we prepare to fight them while we look for answers." She said in a calm rational tone.

"We can do that." He cocked a half smile. "That gives me an idea."

"Hmm?" She looked up at his thoughtful stare.

"Just an idea...I'll work on it with the boys at work this week."

"Okay..."

"I think it'll be a pleasant surprise for you if it works out." He leaned in and kissed her forehead. "Don't worry. It won't set off any alarm bells with the guys."

She pulled him close and snuggled herself into his chest. She sighed contentedly. They may not have all the answers, but somehow, she knew that it would be okay as long as she could always go back to this place, her place, in his arms.

"I know this is usually your line..." She looked up at his adoring smile, "but I'm starving. Rituals are hungry work."

"Let's gather this stuff up and get my baby some tacos then." He kissed her deep and true. She wished they could live in this moment forever. Wished that there was no danger to them, no celestial battles to fight, no friends on life support, no evil big brothers to run from. She wished for a moment that they could just be a boy and a girl in love, taking steps forward to building a life together. As she had that thought, her mind's eye flashed white to a vision.

Anaiah laid unmoving at Azazel's feet. Azazel stepped over him, wiping blood, Anaiah's blood, from his taloned hand with the shredded remains of Anaiah's shirt. Eden couldn't breathe. She wanted to scream, to cry. She wanted to burn the fucking world to the ground around her. She tried to shake herself from this vision. She didn't want to see this. This was not the end she knew in her heart would come to pass every time she stepped into Anaiah's arms. Hadn't she known without a doubt that they would win? Hadn't she felt his heart drummed out a beat in rhythm with hers like it was meant to go on that way for all time? She had been so sure. She had felt promised, owed somehow, this one thing. This one thing in exchange for the life she had lived, for the person she must become. As Azazel stepped toward her, she saw the blade in her hand. She knew what she had to do. No matter what, she would end him. End the entire world as punishment for making her live in it without Anaiah.

Eden was not trained in sword fighting. All she knew was that she would put this blade through Azazel's heart. She would tear his heart from his body the way he had torn hers out when Anaiah fell to the floor lifeless. She opened her mouth as a scream ripped from her along with a crackling spark along her arms. She raised the sword toward his heart and felt the power within her flowing out in an arc with blinding silvery light. As the lightning flashed, she returned to herself.

Anaiah or Eden, she didn't know which, had broken the kiss and they were staring at each other with looks of horror mirrored on their faces. "What did you see?" She asked him quietly at first. He said nothing. "What did you see?" She asked again more insistently. "Tell me, please." Her voice broke.

"I saw you...Journey, Jayse and Adam were there too. I swear Sean was too. I saw you try to fight Adam for the gun in his hands. And you..." She saw the pleading in his eyes. "Don't make me say it."

"Where were we?" She asked him calmly, patiently. Trying to be rational. "We can prevent this. I changed my vision before, with Adam...with Journey and Jayse. We can fix this."

"I didn't recognize the place. It was like a big metal barn type building, grey walls, concrete floor, red painted iron beams. I was there...but I couldn't get to you in time."

Eden forced herself to try to recall the details in her vision. She closed her eyes. She recalled the room, the area around them. "I think this is two different possible futures, in the same place." She replayed the vision in her head. She thought back to when Azazel stood up, what was it behind him she saw? She tried to focus. There was something laying behind him. A black pile of something. Or someone. Adam.

Adam was laying behind him on the ground. Anaiah was wearing a blue shirt and jeans. She tried hard to focus on the little details but his body in her memory, laying limp and lifeless, brought tears to her eyes. She tried to remember; did she see anyone else in the room with her? Did she hear anyone else? She couldn't remember.

"In mine," she started. "Adam was on the ground behind...Cole...in his demon form." She caught herself from saying his name. "You were on the ground, bleeding," She swallowed. "I think you were dead. He had your blood on his...claw. I had the sword. It was in my hand. He was coming toward me. I raised it and screamed. Something like lightning came out of me, through the sword, and was headed at him before it was over."

"How do we stop that from happening?" He asked quietly. "I can't..." his voice broke as a tear rolled down his cheek. "I can't watch the life leave your eyes again." He held her face in his hands.

"We must find the sword. Kill them both before they kill us. If I can do what I saw myself do with it. We can win." She stared into his eyes. "We have to win. I won't live without you."

"Don't say that." He said quietly. "If something happens to me, you have to go on. You have to finish it."

"If something happens to you, I won't be me anymore." She felt the sob rise in her throat. "I didn't care about heaven or hell, good or evil. In that moment, I didn't care if it took out everyone else on earth with me, I wanted to burn the whole world down for spite because you were taken away from me. And I felt powerful enough to do it." Her voice shook.

He looked at her with surprise. "I thought the same thing. I was going to kill them all. Angels, Demons, and the whole goddamn world so they wouldn't have a damn thing to fight over anymore."

"We have to win this." She said again.

"We will, baby. We will." He pulled her against him. She let his warmth wrap around her, soothing the icy feeling in her heart. She heard his heartbeat in his chest, and she knew beyond a shadow of a doubt that it beat in time with hers. She felt the surety in her heart that they would prevail. And she prayed to her heavenly father that this was his sign to her and not just some delusion of hope.

CHAPTER TWENTY-EIGHT

Eden barely slept. The vision of Anaiah's death kept replaying in her head. She struggled to think through ways to keep this horrible nightmare from becoming a reality. At one point, she went to the couch to cry, afraid her sobs would wake Anaiah. A few minutes later, he had wrapped his arms around her and carried her back to bed, holding her, and telling her that they would figure this out together. She fell asleep at last with her head on his chest, listening to the sound of his heart beating as Anaiah gently stroked her hair.

The alarm was set for eleven in the morning, but it felt too soon when it finally went off. Sunday had come, and they were going to have family dinner with the fire chief and his wife. Anaiah had confirmed their planned attendance the day before. Now, most of his friends and coworkers were going to try to be there to meet her. Anaiah rolled over after turning off the alarm and gently stroked her arm.

"Hey sugar." His deep voice was soft. "We have plenty of time if you wanna sleep a little more, but I just wanted to see if you wanna hop in the shower with me." He kissed her bare shoulder. She had worn a tank top to bed to keep the new tattoo irritation to a minimum. His voice dropped a little lower as he slid his arm around her. "I could distract you for a bit." She wiggled her body back against him, burrowing into his warmth.

"I'm so tired. Everything hurts." *And I am scared to death of getting up and going on with life, knowing our pending doom awaits us.* Her thoughts made her heart ache.

"I know, baby. We don't have to go anywhere today. You can sleep. I'll text them and let them know you need to rest before work tonight. They'll understand." Anaiah said softly. She could hear the slight disappointment in his voice, but he would be understanding if she really didn't want to go. *But I do!* She argued with herself.

"No. I want to go. I'm not sleepy. I'm tired. Just fucking tired. Tired of trying to keep my world from falling apart. Tired of crying. Tired of seeing people get hurt because they happen to be collateral damage to the fuckery that is my life." She sighed.

"I know." He whispered. "I wish I could make it better for you."

"You do. You make it so much better, but last night. It shook me because when I look at you, I know that I can get through this. When you hold me, I know that I have a purpose and you will help me achieve it. And it felt like every ounce of hope was bled from me when I saw you laying there. I was in disbelief because I believed that you and I could do anything. That we may be stumbling into this blind with one hand tied behind our backs, but we would be unstoppable together." She whispered her fears to him in the dark bedroom.

"Oh?" He whispered.

"I wasn't just losing you. I was losing the entire hope for a future, a life after all this mess. I was losing the one person I wanted to do all of this with. And it just seems impossible without you." She let the words fade into the dark. "I don't want a future without you in it."

"I am not going to leave you if I have a choice." His voice was husky with emotion. "But remember, I saw you die too. You are so sure that we can prevent that, but you're terrified that I am going to die. Why is that?"

"Are you kidding?" She rolled over and stared into his eyes. "You run into burning buildings for a living. You are the first to jump in and do something heroic to save everyone but yourself. It's easy for me, don't fight Adam for the gun. But you won't miss an opportunity to take Cole out. He will bait you into that fight. I am so scared that he has some sort of demon advantage on you, and I am going to lose you."

"Don't fight Adam for the gun...the gun pointed at Journey's head? You are just going to sit back and watch him shoot her? No...I don't think that's my Eden." He placed his hand on her face. "We know what we are up against, but we don't know enough to stop it. What if what I saw, was before what you saw. What if, you don't go for the gun and somehow, we take Adam down? Then what? I don't fight that bastard bare handed. I fight with the sword. You throw some lightning at him if we can figure that out. You are smart as hell. We will figure this out. You figured out how to live a whole secret life like a damn con man as a teenager for Christ's sake. We will get through this. I am not letting you go without a fight, and I swear to God, I will kick your father's feathered ass if he tries to take either of us to the other side. We ain't dying. Deal?" He searched her eyes for some semblance of agreement. She nodded and closed her eyes. *I will make a deal with my father if I have to.* She decided. They would make it through this.

He kissed her softly on the lips. She slid her fingers into his hair and opened her mouth to him. He claimed her mouth with his as she slid her body closer to his. Anaiah wrapped his arm around her, grabbing her ass and pulling her closer to him. She made a soft moaning noise. He seemed encouraged by that sound and squeezed it again. She let out another small noise of pleasure. To her surprise, he gave her ass cheek a small smack. The thrill that shot through her had her climbing on top of him. She kissed him deeper as his hands slid over her. She felt her desire pulsing between her legs, begging for him. She pulled back breathlessly and jerked her tank top over her head. Her hands roamed over the warm soft skin over his rock-hard muscled chest as she moved her hips against him. He hardened beneath her. His boxer briefs and her leggings were a thin barrier between them. She ran her finger over the tattoo on the right side of his chest, tracing the outline of the Maltese cross with her finger. Then she traced the star of life within it. Both a symbol of who he was, the strength, the passion, the mercy, and care that he used to make the world better. She moved her fingers down his arm. He took her hand in his. He held it to his mouth and kissed it. He looked her in the eyes as he bit down gently on her thumb. He began kissing his way up her arm and he slowly pulled her back down to him. He kissed and sucked on her neck and whispered softly into her ear with his low delicious voice.

"My gorgeous Eden. Sugar, I love you so much. How do you want me to prove it to you?" His breath was hot on her neck. She felt the throbbing need between her legs grow stronger. Pulsing with his every word.

"I just want you. All of you. And my God. I want it now." She said breathlessly as he gently sucked on her nipple. He deftly turned them over in a quick movement and dove straight into a passionate kiss, his tongue dancing with hers. When he backed away to remove the last of their clothing, she longed for his mouth on hers desperately. He quickly pulled away her leggings and the panties beneath. She expected him to climb back over the top of her and give her exactly what she wished for, all his considerable length. Instead, he slid his head between her thighs and kissed the soft skin there. He worshiped her with his mouth. She moaned his name loudly and felt him smile against her skin. He worked his tongue over her again and again, stopping only to suck gently on that magic little bud at the apex. After nearly taking her over the edge, he slowly slid two fingers inside her, and began to drive her again towards her climax. He returned his mouth to her and together with his hand and his tongue, he plunged her into ecstasy. She cried out as she came. Her legs shook with the little spasms within her. He rose onto his knees in the bed, pushing his hair back out of his face. He watched her as she rode out the little shock waves following her climax. She looked down between her legs and saw his full length bare for her, in all its glory. She licked her lips in anticipation.

He gave her an approving mischievous grin as he smoothed his hand over her body, looking at her for confirmation that she was ready. She smiled a wicked grin. "Come here, baby. Show me how much you love me." She bit her lower lip. His smile grew nearly feral as he lowered himself over her, sliding himself in with each shallow thrust inside her. She opened like a blossoming flower to him until he filled her completely. He withdrew slowly, building that wonderful ache within her. Then, just as slow and deliberate, he slid his entire throbbing member in her. She felt that delicious full feeling where they fit together so perfectly. She bucked her hips against him, and he let out a low moan. She felt him throb with pleasure inside her. She smirked up at him. "You like that?" She ground her hips against him again.

"If you wanted to be on top, you could have said so…" He closed his eyes and inhaled sharply as she repeated the motion. "Fuck… that's hot."

"I did climb on you first." She giggled.

He gave her another mischievous smirk, "you're right, baby. What was I thinking?" He leaned down over her again, giving her a small kiss before placing his hands under her hips and shoulders. In a smooth motion, he lifted her off the bed. She threw her arms around him and held tight as he repositioned them on the bed with her on top. His large hands settled back on her hips. "There, sugar, do what you want with me." He said in his low deep voice. "I'm all yours."

"All mine?" She smiled. "I like that." She began to move her hips again, feeling him glide smoothly within her. "Say it again for me." She whispered.

"I'm yours." His deep voice reverberated against the hands she had braced on his chest. She picked up her pace.

"And I'm yours?" She gasped.

"You are mine." His voice was a low reverent near whisper.

"You're mine." She said leaning in to kiss him, keeping her pace. "And I'm yours."

"You're mine, sugar. All mine. And my God, I was made to be yours." His hands moved over her body as she rode him. He let out a deep delicious moan. He watched her as she writhed against him, as if she was the most beautiful seductress he had ever seen. His hands groping her breast, then roaming to squeeze her ass, then tracing the line of her hip bone, but letting her set the pace and take full control. He was hers. He was completely hers in a way that threatened to break her into a million pieces, but all the while made her feel a more complete person than she had ever been. And she was his. She blushed slightly at the thought. He wanted her in a way she never dreamed was possible. She looked over him in adoration. She felt her pleasure's zenith approaching. She let out a moan. Small breathy noises escaped her as she ground against him, sending rippling tidal waves of rapture through her. She cried out to him. He held her against him as she caught her breath, kissing the top of her head and whispering little phrases of love and adoration to her.

"You are the most amazing woman... I love you." He whispered into her hair. "You are so beautiful, my love." He kissed her again and again. "I want to give you everything you want, baby."

She whispered to him, "Everything I want?" She tilted her head up to his smiling face.

"Of course." He rubbed his hand down her back. "Tell me what you want, sugar."

She grinned at the thought of what she wanted at that moment. "I want you to lift me up in your arms, let me wrap myself around you, and have you take me against that wall, until you come." She whispered as she pointed the way. "You only ever do that in the shower...and it's my favorite." She said quietly, feeling suddenly shy about expressing her wants.

"Mmm. Damn that's hot." He growled.

"What?" She looked up at him.

"You telling me what you want me to do to you. It's so sexy. I like it when you are a little bossy." His hands continued to stroke down her spine.

"Only a little bossy?" She raised her brow.

"You haven't really shown me 'really bossy.' That might be too much. I'd finish too soon." He chuckled.

"Anaiah?" She sat up and looked him in the eyes. This was going to be too fun.

"Yes, sugar?" He grinned.

"Get your ass up and pound me against that wall. Now. Make. Me. Scream." She commanded.

"Oh fuck." He growled and kissed her hard before he lifted her with him off the bed. She wrapped her arms around his neck and her legs around his hips. He carried her to the wall next to the bed and leaned over her, bracing her against the cool wall. She nearly climaxed as he deftly slid himself back inside her. *Oh god, he's so fucking hard.* His slow deep thrusts made her breath catch before he sped up, going deeper, harder. She felt the slap of his thighs against the bottom of her bare ass with her hips tilted toward him.

She moaned loudly. "Faster baby. Mmm." She felt the fullness in her lower belly growing. The dam filling before it burst. Her eyes rolled back in her head, and she let her head thump back against the wall. "Yes...Yes..." She moaned. He kissed her playfully at first. Then his kisses became greedier, hungrier. She gripped him tighter, as he drove her over the edge with a muffled scream against his mouth.

He slowed only for a moment, to let her recover. Then his rhythm ticked up faster than before. Deeper. She cried out in bliss. "Yes, like that. Oh my

God." He pounded out a rapid, hard pace and she felt the heat rising in her again. She kissed him hard. "Come with me, baby. You've got me so close." She didn't believe it was possible, but he went faster, harder, and she knew she wouldn't be able to hold on much longer. *Holy shit. Has he been holding back? I'm going to fucking explode.* She let out unintelligible noises of pure joy and bliss. His deep moan against her bare throat seemed to reverberate through her whole body. She felt the cascade begin over the peak. She cried out his name as she came with force she had never felt before. He roared as he reached his release with her. She felt as though electricity crackled through her in a shocking spasm, her chest squeezed as if her heart had reacted to the sensation as well. She clung to him as she shook in his arms.

"Woah..." His voice was full of awe.

"Yeah, that was really good." She panted as she opened her eyes and met his awestruck face.

She saw flickering light reflected in his dark eyes in the dim room before she caught the flicker of light from her arm. She turned them over with her palms up looking at them. Little arcs of silver and black crackling light flickered along her enochian scars. She looked back up at him, concerned. He just smiled his little half grin.

"Lightning..." He reverently. "You never cease to amaze me."

CHAPTER TWENTY-NINE

When they pulled up to the chief's countryside Victorian home, Eden tried to hide how nervous she was. She thought she was doing a decent job of hiding how fidgety she felt, but apparently, she failed. Anaiah squeezed her hand.

"Baby, they aren't going to bite." He moved a curly strand of hair from her face.

"I know. It's just that this is your family. Or the closest thing you have to it. Unless you are hiding some secret grandparents from me." She crossed her arms.

"No secret Abuela's here. She passed when I was young." He leaned in and kissed her forehead.

"I want them to like me." She said softly.

"They will. Don't worry. They might give me hell, but they will love you. Trust me." He cupped her chin with his hand and gave her a quick kiss. "Besides, if we are lucky, Bobby brought his girlfriend, and it will be a show." He smiled. She gave him a confused look. "She's a bit of a bit...let's say drama queen."

"You were going to call her a bitch." She laughed.

"Yeah, I was, but if I don't watch my mouth, Darlene will be all over me." He smirked.

"Okay, let's do this." She huffed as Sean pulled up beside them. She waved at him. Sean was dressed in a light blue button-down short-sleeved shirt that matched his eye color with black slacks. He still wore his silver aviator sunglasses, which Eden had decided must be standard issue for the local police. They all wore them.

"You clean up nice." Eden said as Sean exited his car next to her.

"Better than Parker, too." Sean smirked and removed his sunglasses. "Well, you look beautiful."

"Thank you." She smoothed her hands over her dress. It was a green retro dress with a collar and black buttons down the front of the top. It was a 1950's style swing dress that hung just to her knee. She had paired it with her black swing style pumps with a five-inch heel. Anaiah had told her that any broken ankles would be on her for wearing them. High heels were her own secret rebellion. She'd loved them since they were forbidden by her parents' cult. She had learned to walk in them quite well but had never had cause to own more than a single pair before she settled here. Anaiah walked up behind her and took her hand in his.

"With those shoes you are almost to his shoulder too." Sean let out a little chuckle.

"Where's your date, O'Brien?" Anaiah taunted Sean.

"Well, I would say something inappropriate about somebody's mommy...or daddy," He shrugged, "but it's the Lord's Day and we are in the company of a lovely lady. So, I think I will refrain." Sean laughed.

"Such a gentleman." Anaiah rolled his eyes. "C'mon, sugar, let's introduce you to everybody." She looked at him from the corner of her eye as they walked up the brick front walkway of the house. Anaiah had dressed a dark green button-down shirt with long sleeves with his slate-colored slacks and black dress shoes. She assumed he wasn't ready for questions about the markings on his arms, hence the long sleeves. Eden hoped no one commented on hers. She hadn't thought up a convincing lie. Then again, thanks to the break-in, most of them probably knew her history with her parents and out of politeness might not ask. Anaiah's dark hair hung down nearly to his shoulders now and the open top two buttons on his shirt were distracting. For a moment, she marveled at her gorgeous boyfriend as they walked. Just for an afternoon, they would playact at being a normal couple.

The chief lived outside of town in a large Victorian home with a wraparound porch. On the right side of the porch was a whitewashed wooden swing, hanging by chains. On the left sat two tall-backed rocking chairs with a small metal table between them. This was the sort of home that she had never really allowed herself to dream of. Something that tickled the little wants in her heart that she kept buried during years of surviving. *Isn't that what we are doing now? Surviving? We just have another enemy to run from. But I have Anaiah...a partner in this. Never dreamed I would have that before either.* She glanced over at him as he silently held her hand and strode alongside her. He looked over at her out of the corner of his eye.

"What's on your mind, sugar?" Anaiah asked quietly. She looked pointedly at Sean walking up the brick path in front of them.

"Maybe later." She whispered. He squeezed her hand. "I love this house." She whispered to him as they walked up the steps to the porch.

Anaiah smiled. "Always wanted something like this...someday." She squeezed his hand. He looked down at her.

She said, so quietly that she wasn't even sure he could hear her, "Someday." It was as much a promise to herself as it was to him. Sean reached the door before them and turned to Eden for a moment before he knocked.

"Did he warn you?" Sean said, looking serious for a moment.

"We ain't playing today." Anaiah gave Sean a threatening glare.

"It's not a real family dinner without it, now, is it?" Sean grinned.

"C'mon...don't fuck this up for her." He said in a low whisper.

"See, already starting. Let her in on it. I want to see her rattle you." Sean nodded his head toward Eden.

"What is happening?" Eden looked between them. Anaiah let out a frustrated sigh.

"Afraid you'll lose for once?" Sean whispered to Anaiah. He turned an excited grin to Eden, "It's a game we play. Darlene is a real stickler for her rules. The chief enforces them. No foul language. No inappropriate talk. No crass jokes. That sort of thing. We mess with each other and see who can get the others in trouble. And Parker...is stone cold. He doesn't break, never loses his cool. He can make us all crack. He can have the whole room giggling and piss off the chief, but he's never lost. Help me fuck with him. Team up with me, Eden."

A slow devious smile spread across Eden's face. Anaiah hung his head in defeat and whispered, "fuckin' shoot me now." Sean gave Eden a quick, unexpected hug, lifting her up off her feet.

"Best. Dinner. Ever." Sean said in hushed tones as he set her back down on her feet and turned to knock on the door. "Good luck, brother."

"Fuck off, traitor." Anaiah whispered.

"She's the traitor...did you see how quick she moved to my team? Watch out, Parker. I might steal your girl." Sean teased.

"Oh, I doubt that." Anaiah said in a low voice that sent shivers up Eden's spine.

"I doubt he can do that thing I like..." She made a breathy sigh, "with your tongue." Eden whispered just loud enough for the three of them to hear as the door opened. Sean's ears turned a dark shade of pink. Eden felt Anaiah tense beside her. She smiled and held out her hand to shake the chief's outstretched hand. "Thank you for having me over. So sweet of you." She'd had years of playing the perfect part so as not to be suspicious to anyone around her. She could play this game.

"Glad Anaiah decided to quit keeping you all to himself. He says the nicest things about you." Darlene held her arms open for a hug. *You want them to like you. They love him.* She stepped forward and loosely wrapped her empty hand around Darlene's shoulder and let herself be hugged. She expected to be uncomfortable. She expected awkwardness and to want to break away as soon as possible. She was surprised by the warmth, the genuine care and love she felt emanating from Darlene. She felt herself melt a little into the hug and then pulled back, smiling.

"He said sweet things about you too." She said as Anaiah leaned in to hug Darlene. Darlene was shorter than Eden was without high heels. She had to be less than five feet tall. She was a plump woman with silver curly hair. She looked like a typical grandmother in her floral-patterned dress and her red apron with frilled edges. Next to her stood the near perfect complement to this woman. Chief Davidson had dark skin and black curly hair with greying edges. He stood around Sean's height. Anaiah towered over them both by half a foot. Davidson had a thick comb mustache and a kind smile.

"Good to have you back too." Darlene squeezed Anaiah.

"C'mon boys, set the table." Chief Davidson directed them into the foyer. Anaiah led her by the hand into the dining room. He let her hand drop as he picked up a stack of plates sitting on the table.

"Grab those place mats and napkins, sugar. Sean can get the silverware." He strode out of the room. She followed him to the back of the house. French doors opened to an expansive patio with lights strung overhead. The table had at least thirty chairs around it. It stretched the length of the patio with a long off-white lace tablecloth covering it. Eden placed the mats and cloth napkins at each spot. Anaiah followed behind, placing a plate on each. Sean trailed behind, placing silverware at each place setting. The chief walked out the back door carrying a wooden crate filled with drinking glasses. He sat them on the table without a word and walked back into the house. The men took the glasses out and began placing them in the corners of the place settings.

"He has you all trained." She whispered with a grin.

"No. He's trained too. Darlene's the mastermind." Sean laughed. He looked over his shoulder toward the house.

"Like your dress by the way. Very classy." Sean looked at Anaiah. Anaiah's face hardened and his eyes narrowed. "You should ask Anaiah how he likes it."

"She's gorgeous, as always." Anaiah said simply.

"What are you not saying?" She whispered to him.

"Later." He shut her down and walked back into the house with the empty crate.

"Oh, this is going to be too much fun. All his feathers getting ruffled." Sean laughed. "The dress really does look nice. And I mean that in a nice friendly way. Not a 'hitting on my brother's girl way.'"

"He's really like a brother to you?" She followed him to the house.

"He is. Hey, all games aside." He stopped and lowered his voice. "So, I know that you have a...let's say complicated, past. And things have been rough with your brother." He paused and gazed into the house for a moment.

Shit. I thought he liked me...thought he approved of us. Now he's going to tell me that I'm dragging his best friend into my personal shit. Dammit. She forced her face to remain blank and not give away her thoughts. She felt like she was just starting to find a groove with him and develop a friendship with him beyond just being Anaiah's girlfriend. She felt a little heart broken.

"I've got your back too." He said quietly. "Parker would kick my ass if he knew I was saying all this. He hates not being able to handle it all by himself. He's crazy about you. I've never seen him like this with anyone. Not even Reesa... when she was... you know." He held a hand over his stomach. "If you are going to be with my brother, that makes you my little sister too. I got your six. If he's not around and you need me, call me." He said in a hushed voice. She felt the tears building in her eyes. She didn't know what to say. She threw her arms around him and hugged him. He hugged her back. "Welcome to the family." He whispered as he patted her back. "We are a hodgepodge of bastards, but we will be there for you like Anaiah would be."

"Thank you." She pulled back and wiped at her eyes. "Did I mess up my makeup?"

"Nah. Now, quit crying or I'll end up with a black eye." He smiled. "We still gotta finish helping. It's the hazard of showing up first."

They finished setting the table while they made small talk. Anaiah told Sean he had a little project he was going to work on at the station with Trevor, one of the newer firefighters, if they had time this week. Eden had no clue what they were talking about. Sean poured himself a glass of sweet tea and continued the conversation with Anaiah about his next build on the range. Eden pulled her phone out of her pocket to shoot a text to Journey to check on the twins, remembering that she needed to be a good friend to her little found family too.

'Kris is the same.' Journey's text read. Eden responded by asking how she and Jayse were holding up. *'Jayse is better, I think. He's going to come back to work on Tuesday night with me. He's out of sick time.'*

'That's BS. Maybe it will be a decent distraction?' Eden texted back.

'Our corporate overlords demand it. Thanks for trying to find a silver lining, dude. Things have been fucking bleak.' Journey messaged back.

'I know you don't always want to talk shit out but call me later or swing by the apartment before work if you want to.' Eden typed back.

'The apartment? Not HIS apartment anymore?' Trust Journey to turn the attention off her feelings and focus on Eden's drama.

'Yeah, I kinda moved in with him. My lease isn't up for another couple of months. My rent was paid up through then. But we moved my essentials over last night.' Eden sighed.

'Moving things right along with Super Boyfriend.' Came Journey's reply.

'Well, tragedy has forced both our asses into cohabitation with our boyfriends. I'm sure this is a completely healthy step in any relationship. Dodge a murderer and then move in together.' Eden grinned.

'We are the poster children for positive mental health, girl.' Journey texted back.

'For sure. I'll call you later.' Eden sent her text and put her phone back in her pocket. She looked up to see what the boys were talking about now.

"How's Journey?" Anaiah glanced her way.

"How do you know it was her and not my other boyfriend?" She teased.

Anaiah lowered his voice, "Tell him to pick up the slack so I can get more sleep, then." And gave her a wink with his half grin.

"You were the one who woke me up this morning, begging for a shower together." She shot back. Sean choked on the sweet tea he was sipping on.

"See, this is the problem with bringing her in on this." Anaiah glared at Sean. "She looks sweet an' innocent. But that mouth..." Then he stopped, realizing what he said when humor lit Eden's eyes.

"You said you liked the dirty things I do with my mouth." She whispered with a wicked grin. "At least, that's what those noises you make usually mean."

"Goddamn." Sean cursed under his breath. "You might not win today, buddy, but I am sure as shit going to lose."

"Oh, you brought this on us both, brother." Anaiah clapped him on the back. "I'm going to make myself useful, so I stay out of trouble." He turned and headed back inside the house.

"How's your friend doing?" Sean asked as they followed Anaiah inside.

"About the same. They said he's in for a long recovery. Right now, his lungs are too damaged to come off the ventilator. So, they are keeping him sedated." She sighed. "His brother isn't handling it well. And HIS girlfriend is my best friend. She avoids talking much if it makes her too emotional. I'm not sure how she's holding up. It sucks."

"Yeah, been a hell of a month." Sean said. He didn't know the half of it. As they walked into the kitchen, Anaiah washed his hands at the sink and Eden followed suit, unsure what sort of job he was volunteering them for. The kitchen, much like the rest of the house was all dark woods with white accents.

The countertops were covered in eggshell-colored tiles with rose accents on them.

"Miss Darlene, you want me to take these rolls out for you?" Anaiah said as he opened the oven. He grabbed oven mitts off the countertop and took out the trays of fresh baked rolls.

"Mmm hmm. Eden, if you wouldn't mind" Darlene looked up from the bowl of potatoes she was adding butter and cream to. "The blender behind you, with the strawberry puree? Can you add it to that pitcher of lemonade, there?" She pointed to the counter behind Eden.

"Yes, ma'am." Eden mirrored Anaiah's good southern manners. She turned and set herself to her task, following Darlene's instructions before taking it to the table. When she returned to the kitchen, she saw others arriving. Anaiah was transferring hot rolls to cloth lined baskets.

"Carla, you've met Eden." Anaiah looked up with a smile. "Wasn't the best day to meet." He shrugged. "Introduce her to your wife, would ya?"

Carla looked younger with her hair down and make-up on. She was wearing a loose black blouse with leggings. Next to her was a tall woman with umber skin in a gorgeous floral dress with bright vibrant colors. Her midnight black hair was in braids down to her waist with metallic accents throughout.

"This is my wife, Mina." Carla was practically beaming with pride. "Mina, this is Parker's girlfriend, Eden."

"Nice to meet you." Eden said.

"The pleasure is mine." Mina said with a rich accent. Her smile spread wide across her beautiful face.

"Mina's a nurse. Originally from Cameroon in Africa. Carla dragged her out of Dallas to our little neck of the woods a few years ago. She works in the ER here." Anaiah handed Eden a basket full of rolls. "We'll take the rolls to the table, Darlene." He picked up two other full baskets. "Ladies." He nodded to Carla and Mina as he led Eden past them.

"Carla's wife is drop-dead gorgeous." Eden whispered to him as they exited the house.

Anaiah snorted, "Yeah, Carla lost her mind and acted like a lovesick puppy when Mina showed up as a travel nurse in our ER. I'd never seen her look at anyone like that. Suddenly, she wanted all the quick runs to the ER from the nursing home during Mina's shifts. You know I gave her hell. Well, she's been doing the same to me since I met you." He said to Eden in his hushed voice. "Carla can be a bit rough around the edges, but Mina balances it out."

Eden looked up at the table and recognized Bobby, the police officer from the night Reesa died. Next to him was a short, skinny blonde woman who radiated unhappiness. Bobby was laughing, conversing with the chief and Sean. A few other people were gathered around the table. Eden expected a whole round of introductions.

"Oh, Darlene is not going to like this." Anaiah said softly. "I'll introduce you, but Lila hates all of us. Just FYI." As they approached the table, Eden felt her stomach start to turn slightly. She knew that feeling...Lila was a cambion. Eden looked over to Anaiah who gave her an odd, confused expression. She was tempted to stop and whisper what she knew to him, but he continued walking so she kept pace with him. *She could be harmless.*

"Hey, Bobby. You remember Eden, right?" Anaiah said as he set a basket on one end of the table. Eden placed hers near the middle and Anaiah walked over to set his other one down at the opposite end. Bobby and Lila stood directly across from Eden with the table between them.

"Sure do. How are you?" He leaned across the table to shake her hand.

"I'm good. Thanks." Eden smiled politely. She did not feel good. This felt foreboding. Like there was something evil lurking under Lila's skin waiting to jump out at her. A feeling washed over Eden like Azazel had reached out and touched her, unbidden. She shook off the chill that ran down her spine.

"This lovely lady is Lila." Bobby turned back to a scowling Lila. "Honey, meet Anaiah's sweetheart, Eden." Eden held out her hand to Lila. As Lila took it, Eden felt as though the chain of her tattoos tightened around her neck and in her chest. A slight jolt went through her and into Lila's hand.

Lila jerked back. "Motherfucking bitch." She hissed at Eden. Eden stared at her wide eyed. Everyone's eyes turned on Lila. Everyone except Anaiah. He stood pin straight at the end of the table, jaw clenched, staring at Eden. Eden looked at him out of the corner of her eye. Had no one else seen it? Not from the way they all stared at Lila. No one else saw the little sparks that flared down her arm. Just Anaiah. Eden stood frozen with her mouth agape. She noted Sean looking over at her with concern in his eyes.

"We will not be having any of that, young lady." The chief's brusque tone broke the silence. "I don't know what your dealings are with Ms. Grace, but you can bury the hatchet now, or you can leave." A couple of the other men at the table stood up as if waiting for the chief to give them the signal to bounce Lila from the party.

"What's going on out here?" Darlene called out from the porch, hands on her hips. "I need some of you boys to carry dinner out to the table." The men Eden hadn't been introduced to walked toward the house to help Darlene.

Lila stared straight at Eden. "Just wait...you'll get what's coming to you." She sneered at Eden. Eden took a small step back and folded her arms across her chest. Afraid of what the tattoos might do if Lila came closer.

"I don't know what you're talking about." Eden stepped back. Lila took a step closer. Sean placed a hand on Lila's arm, just firm enough to stop her from coming closer. The venom in her eyes gave Eden the impression that Lila was about to pounce over the table to claw her face off. Eden clenched her jaw.

"You better get her out of here, Bobby." Sean said in a low voice.

"I'll walk you all out." Anaiah walked toward Bobby, who seemed stunned into silence. He snapped out of it suddenly.

"Let's go, Lila." Bobby took her arm and steered her away from them. Anaiah trailed behind them.

Eden turned, eager for something to do, and hoped no one would turn their attention to her. She headed into the house. As she entered the hallway headed toward the kitchen, a hand closed around her wrist. She turned her head suddenly, ready to fight and pulled her arm out of the grasp holding her. Sean stepped back with his hands up and in a hushed voice said, "Sorry. Should have said something. Come here, let's talk."

She stared at him for a moment suspiciously then followed him into what must have been a guest bedroom. She shut the door behind her. The room was a continuation of the theme of the house: simple country decor, rustic touches, and lots of dark wood.

"Is Lila a friend of yours?" He asked, keeping his voice down. He stood near the foot of the bed.

"No. I've never seen her before." Eden replied.

"She seemed to know you." He crossed his arms.

"What happened to 'I got your six?'" Eden crossed her arms, matching his posture.

Sean seemed to notice how she was mirroring him and how this conversation sounded like an interrogation. He relaxed his shoulders and uncrossed his arms. "She's hateful and self-centered most days. But she seemed to have it out for you, and I swear I saw something." His eyes narrowed.

"What?" Eden didn't change her posture. She stared him down, arms crossed.

"When you shook her hand...I saw something happen with your arm. You wanna tell me what that's about? Because you didn't have those scars yesterday. You still had fading bruises and scrapes yesterday. They're all gone now." He pointed at her arms. "I'm trying to let things go because of how Anaiah feels about you, but I remember what was in your house. It looked like some sort of occult ritual gone wrong. Then Anaiah's ex dies in some freak accident...and the next day the guy who flirts with you at work gets blown up in an accidental explosion. Oh, and don't think I didn't read all the reports Anaiah had me pull on you and your psycho brother. Give me some sort of answer here. Something that makes any sort of sense, Eden. Are you some sort of witch or something? Anaiah's a religious guy...he should know. He should know if you're into some satanic shit." He slowly built his hushed voice into a normal volume. She wanted to shush him.

"Sean..." She shook her head. *Why does my boyfriend have to be best friends with a damn detective?* "I'm not a witch...or a satanist. And I am not hiding anything from Anaiah." She said quietly but not weakly. "We should have this conversation with him here."

"Why?" Sean asked.

She startled as the door behind her creaked open. She turned to see Anaiah step in and close the door. She sighed with relief.

"Were you listening in?" She whispered. Anaiah nodded.

"He ain't exactly quiet." Anaiah crossed his arms as she relaxed.

"What is happening, Parker?" Sean looked at Anaiah with pleading in his eyes.

"This isn't the place for this conversation." Anaiah's face was stony. He was still on alert, still assessing dangers around them. She placed a hand on his arm. "But we will talk about it, soon. Trust me." He said quietly to Sean.

"What happened with her arm? You saw it too. I saw the way you looked at her. Like you were spooked. Like she freaked you out." Sean said.

"I was scared for her, not of her. The people after her...after us," He corrected himself, "They are the ones you gotta worry about." Anaiah unbuttoned his sleeves and rolled them up. Sean shook his head trying to figure out what he was seeing. Anaiah had bared his new additions to his tattooed arms to Sean.

"This makes no sense." Sean said.

Anaiah turned to Eden. "Sugar, I'm gonna go for a walk with Sean. Stay near the house. Stay with the others. We won't go far. He needs to know. He can decide what to do with that information afterward."

"Be safe." She stared into his eyes. He was worried that Sean would push him away. That's what the fear she saw there was. She prayed that this wouldn't tear the two of them apart. Sean was upset because he cared about Anaiah. Maybe he could accept this part of him too. Anaiah leaned down and kissed her on the top of the head.

"You too." He turned to Sean, "walk with me?" Sean just gave a reluctant nod. As he walked past her, Eden grabbed his wrist to stop him.

"Please, just listen to him. Be open minded. He's your brother. Remember that." She begged him. Sean swallowed hard and nodded to her.

Eden turned back to the kitchen and went to work helping Carla, Mina, and Darlene grab the serving dishes left in the kitchen. Darlene introduced her to three of Anaiah's coworkers as they carried dishes out to the table. She met a firefighter named Matt, who was a few inches taller than Eden herself. Standing next to Matt, was a police officer named Jacob who worked the dayshift opposite of Sean. He was older than the rest of his crew, but younger looking than the chief. The third coworker was an EMT named Quintin. Quintin looked like a typical frat guy in a polo and jeans. He called Matt 'bruh' and Darlene gave him a stern look.

"Where's Parker?" Carla asked Eden as they carried two casserole dishes filled with vegetables to the table.

"He and Sean took a walk. Think the whole thing with Lila got the better of him. They are talking it out." Eden didn't feel it was a complete lie. Just an omission of the truth.

"Ah. He's so...protective of you. It'd be cute if I wasn't such a feminist." She laughed.

"Hey, I'm learning some things. He took me shooting and he and Sean are teaching me how to defend myself." She protested.

"Oh, are you packing in that cute little handbag?" She pointed at Eden's small emerald purse which contained her wallet and her gun bag.

"Yes." She laughed. "I am."

"Oh! Well, good for you." She smiled. "Gonna get your brother back if he comes for you again?" She raised her eyebrows.

"All kidding aside, yeah. Does that make me a bad person?" Eden asked as she laid her casserole dish on the table.

"No. Makes you a smart one." Carla said. "But don't talk bullets where Darlene can hear. It's off limits today."

"Why is everyone so scared of a tiny woman who cooks like Martha Stewart?"

"Oh, we don't fear making her mad. It's making her disappointed." Carla laughed. "Plus, Chief will take it out on us at work. Assign us toilet duty."

They finished setting dinner up on the table. As everyone was gathering to take their seats, Anaiah and Sean walked up, both silent as the grave.

"You boys alright?" Darlene asked.

"I'm just peachy." Sean grumbled. "Sorry, ma'am. Just fine." He perked back up as he realized who he was talking to.

"Everything okay?" Eden whispered to Anaiah as he sat down next to her.

He kissed her on the cheek and whispered into her ear. "He's pissed. I'll tell you in the car later."

"Parker, say grace for us, will you?" Chief Davidson asked.

Anaiah bowed his head and prayed over the meal, over their crews, and over the time they got to spend together. He thanked God for the family they found in one another. At the end they all said as one "Amen."

Eden shook off the chills that ran down her spine. She didn't realize the effect that one word, spoken in unison, would have on her. She feared for a moment that when she opened her eyes, instead of Anaiah's closest friends, she would be surrounded by the cultists all packed into a glorified shed with a cross hanging at the front of the room. Anaiah squeezed her hand. He knew. Somehow, he knew. He wrapped his arm around the back of her chair and ran his hand down her arm soothingly as conversation started up at the table.

The meal was filled with jokes, stories and laughter. Eden met another police officer, Daniel and his wife Julie who were seated a few seats down from her. Darlene asked Eden questions about her job, about her plans for the future. Only briefly did she feel that same pang she had felt before when she realized she had never dreamed of life beyond survival. She had never planned a future built towards finishing up some sort of formal education. Anaiah gracefully directed the conversation elsewhere. He brought up the chief's upcoming birthday in the summer and asked what sort of plans were being made. Eden squeezed his hand in thanks.

The food was delicious. Darlene had made a ton of side dishes and her husband had smoked the brisket. By the time desert was served, Eden was leaning on Anaiah's arm, listening to his coworkers try to one up each other to find a story properly embarrassing enough about him, but also fit Darlene's definition of appropriate for the dinner table. She ate her fill of chocolate pecan pie and let Anaiah finish off the last few bites for her. Anaiah made excuses for them to go nap before they had to work that evening. Darlene requested they return the following week. She gave Eden a long warm hug and wished her well.

As they walked back to the car, Sean caught up with them. "Hey, Eden. Wait up a second." She was pleasantly surprised he wasn't radiating anger anymore. He seemed calm, even.

"What's up?" She turned to him.

"I owe you an apology. I shouldn't have come at you like that. It wasn't fair. You can't help what you are, and I can't help what I am not. Anyways, I hope you can forgive me. I still have your back. I promise." Sean gave her an apologetic smile.

"Of course, I can forgive you. You were just looking out for him." She looked up at Anaiah with a smile. She lowered her voice. "Pretty ballsy too...you thought I was some sort of satanic enchantress and you confronted me to save Anaiah's honor." Anaiah stifled a laugh.

"Well, when you put it that way, I'm a hero, really." Sean smirked.

"Totally." She laughed. "Friends?" She held out her hand.

"Hell yeah." He lunged in and hugged her. As he pulled back, he playfully punched Anaiah in the arm. "Don't forget to tell her about the skirt thing." He grinned. "You're welcome in advance." He winked at Eden and slipped into his car.

"Dick..." Anaiah said under his breath and opened her car door for her.

"You said he was pissed?" She said when he got in the car.

"Yeah, pissed off that you and I are some sort of angel warrior and he's just a human cop." He said. "He accepted it all. ALL of it. But was mad that he got stuck being, in his words, 'a human sidekick.' Should have known he would pick up on all this shit. He's too damn observant."

"Isn't that how cops are supposed to be?" She laughed.

"I guess." He sighed. "Go ahead an' tell me what happened on your end with Lila. Did you do that on purpose?"

"I didn't mean to. I knew she was half demon, because of what I felt in my gut. It's what I felt at Selah's. She said it was something about being of two worlds. The tattoo reacted. It got, like, tight around my neck and in my chest and then it shocked her."

"I felt it too. My stomach felt sick. Then my chest got tighter as you reached out to her. I thought it was fear, but it pulled from my chest down my arms, and it was all I could do not to come through the table and chairs and tackle her to the ground."

"It's like the tattoo knew she was the enemy." Eden said.

"Guess it did."

They drove the rest of the way discussing Lila and Bobby's on again off again relationship. No one understood why he kept going back to her. None of them saw what he did in her. Sure, she was pretty, but her personality ruined it.

"It's like she has her claws deep in him. He shakes out of it from time to time but keeps going back." Anaiah said as they climbed the stairs to the apartment.

"Wonder if she's doing something, like magic or something to keep him tied to her." Eden wondered out loud.

"That hadn't occurred to me. If you think about it, it'd be smart to have a man on the inside if you're doing illegal or sketchy magic shit to make evidence go away...or make him look the other way." Anaiah thought for a moment. "I'll get Sean to look into it. I don't wanna get Bobby in trouble, but she could be connected to all of this. Sean can look quietly."

"She blew the shit out of her cover if she is." Eden stepped into the apartment.

"Well, she wasn't expecting it...it was...kinda shocking." He laughed at his own pun as she rolled her eyes.

"That's the last straw," She teased. "I'm leaving. That joke was terrible." She chuckled.

"Baby don't go..." He grabbed her wrist despite knowing she wasn't going anywhere.

"Tell me about the skirt thing, then." She whispered.

"Shit." he whispered back. "It's just a thing..."

"What kind of thing?" She was pretty sure she knew what kind of thing it was.

"Like a fantasy thing. Always been a thing for me. Dresses, skirts. Sean knows about it. Asked me if you modeled any cute dresses for me yet. I admitted you didn't wear them often. Only on one date so far." She cocked an eyebrow, and he went on, "I don't care, wear what you like. I love what you look like in everything. But with you in this dress, he had to screw with me."

"You mean to tell me that I could have been driving you mad with desire this entire time by wearing my dresses and heels?" She said in an exasperated voice.

"Oh, the heels were a very nice surprise." He said in a low, hungry tone.

"Lucky for you, I love wearing cute dresses and heels." She smiled up at him.

"Really?" He sounded surprised. "You live in leggings and t-shirts, honey."

"Like I'm supposed to wear this to a gun range? Or tromping through the woods to find ritual sites?" She laughed. "Take me somewhere besides the Waffle Casa and watch me dress to the nines, baby."

"Problem is, I wouldn't want to leave the house." He laughed.

"So, this," She motioned to her outfit, "has been the reason for the silent stoic behavior all day? You've been keeping yourself in check all day?" She giggled.

"Well, I didn't hold back that much this morning. When I made you scream my name." He walked forward toward her. She let him back her against the wall with only inches between them. "Did you really have to play Sean's little game?"

"Oh, I knew what that was doing to you." She smirked. "Sean thought it was embarrassment, or anger...but I knew. You like when I talk dirty to you, don't you?"

"That mouth..." He said, devouring it. He slid his hand down her side and when reached her hip, he scooped her leg up to his side. She wrapped it around him and pulled him closer. He slid his hand up under her dress. She felt him trace his fingers along her hip where a panty line should be, but he found no barrier there. He moaned.

She pulled her mouth from his. "Had a feeling. Why else would he tease you...thought it'd be a nice surprise when you got me home."

"You're good with surprises. You do keep me on my toes." He kissed her again as she made quick work of his belt buckle. She was nearly frantic with desire. His eyes were near feral, matching her need to close the space between them. She pulled him free from his pants as he hiked her leg higher, pressing her against the wall. She guided him into her, wet and waiting. She wanted to be his fantasy, his desire, his ecstasy and more. She didn't know if she could give him the future he had once hoped for, but she could give him all of herself. She could give him everything he was for her. And maybe with their broken pieces fitting perfectly together, they could build something they liked even more.

CHAPTER THIRTY

Eden had managed to make it through the last four nights of work without incident. A copy of the police report was filed with HR at work to get the one security person on night shift to be on the lookout for Adam and maybe get a cop back up in the store if he showed up. She didn't put it past him to pull another stunt while Anaiah was working to keep them all distracted. Not that he had been available to chat with her much on work nights. He'd check in every few hours to make sure she was safe. Anaiah made an appearance with Trevor in tow the previous night. They smelled of smoke, but he assured her there was no firefighting, just something they were doing at work. Eden had brought Journey and by proxy Jayse up to speed on everything. He had let go of the rest of his doubt when he saw her new scars and tattoos.

On her last work night that week, Eden rolled over to shut off her alarm. She expected to roll back over and snuggle up to Anaiah, but his side of the bed was empty. She sat up. The room was dark with little slivers of bright light peeking around the edge of the blackout curtains. Her eyes adjusted to the dim light, and she looked around the room. She checked her phone. It was four in the afternoon. No messages or missed calls. She answered nature's call first, then went to find Anaiah. As she opened the bedroom door, she considered that finding Anaiah would be easier if she had coffee first. She spotted a still warm and half full coffee pot sitting on the machine. She poured a large mug of coffee and added creamer. She walked into the living room and suddenly regretted her choice of sleepwear. She was acutely aware of how little she wore in just her black panties and a loose t-shirt as Sean, Trevor and Anaiah looked up at her in unison.

"Nice." said Trevor.

"Shut the fuck up, rookie." Anaiah said as he stood and walked toward her. "Did we wake you?" He kissed her on the cheek.

"Nah. It's four. I'm going to the hospital with Journey in a bit." She swigged a drink from her mug. "What are you guys doing?"

"Sharpening axes." Sean called from the couch.

"On our couch?" Eden yawned.

"We were gonna watch this movie and sharpen axes on my couch, but Anaiah wanted to stay here and babysit you while you sleep." Trevor said.

"What'd I say, rookie?" Anaiah glared over his shoulder.

"Shutting the fuck up, Lieutenant." He piped up.

"Be nice, baby." She winked at Anaiah.

"Not complaining at all about your fashion choices, but you may want to wear pants, and possibly a bra to the hospital, Eden." Sean said. "But totally up to you."

"Maybe in the future, someone could leave me a text to let me know the living room would be full of first responders?" Eden said.

"It's like waking up to a fireman's calendar on your couch." Sean quipped.

"Sweetie, I sleep with the fireman's calendar." She took another swig of coffee. Anaiah turned back to grab his coffee and noticed Trevor's eyes locked on Eden.

"Eden, out of concern for young Trevor, would you please put on some pants." Sean requested. Eden placed a hand on Anaiah's shoulder as he glared at Trevor. "The kid is going to either slice open his hand sharpening this axe or he is going to get murdered by his supervisor."

"He could just not stare." She shrugged.

"That's true." Anaiah turned his focus back to Eden.

"Sorry, boss. Sorry, Eden." Trevor diverted his gaze back to his axe.

"Lemme see your axe, baby." She motioned at the axe on the coffee table. He picked it up and handed her the handle while taking her coffee mug in his other hand. She understood why he freed up both hands when she took it in both hands, struggling a bit with it. He relieved the weight by taking it back in one hand and showed the axe to her while he gave her mug back. He had his smart-ass grin plastered on his face.

"Show off." She whispered. She noticed the details etched into the weapon. "Did you make this?"

"Yeah, Trevor and his dad do blacksmithing on the side. He set up a small modern forge up at the station. We all got into making stuff. And I got the idea for this from that book you got from Selah. And some other things." He tapped the spot over his heart. The axe was entirely made from iron, which had detrimental effects on demons per Selah's book. The handle was engraved with the same enochian words etched on their arms. As she read the enochian across the head of the axe, she touched it and looked up at him.

"It means 'God answers.' It's my name in Hebrew." He said quietly. "Did you see the rest?" Under his name were the enochian symbols saying, 'with vengeance and wrath.' He flipped it over and on the other side it said, 'God answers with justice and righteousness.' Symbols associated with his angelic father.

"That's awesome. Looks sharp as hell." She nodded at the shining edge of the blade side.

"I made two." He beamed. "Matching set. Sharpening the other…this one's done."

"He said he's gonna hang them in the bedroom." Sean gave her a knowing smile.

"We are gonna throw them tonight at work." Trevor added.

"Have fun with that." She laughed. "I'm gonna go get dressed. Can I borrow you a second?" She raised her brows at him.

"Be right back." He said to the guys.

"Keep it down, Trevor is young and impressionable." Sean called after them.

"How old is Trevor?" She asked quietly as they walked into the bedroom.

"Nineteen." Anaiah closed the door behind them. She gave him a look that said, 'older than me.' He nodded. "Don't remind me. I don't have to tell you to pull your head out of your ass ten times a day, though."

"Has he never seen a half-naked woman before?" She giggled.

"I doubt it." He laughed. Trevor looked younger than Eden. In fact, the first time she saw him, she thought he might be some high school kid hoping to become a firefighter. He's as tall as Sean but had a baby face and a buzz cut that made him look to be about fourteen. The fact that he was the most gullible and naive person Eden had met didn't help. "What's on your mind, darlin'? Or did you bring me in here for other reasons?" He raised an eyebrow.

"Would it be a crazy idea to take one of those healing…potions…for lack of a better word, and try to use it on Kris? He's getting worse. He has an infection from being on the ventilator for so long. I'm scared that he's never going to get better." She felt helpless to do anything for him. Jayse wanted her to visit, to pray to her father to heal him, to do anything that might help. She really wanted to help.

"He's human." He sounded disappointed to have to point it out. "The book is for nephilim, right? Would it work on humans? What would happen if Sean drank the protection tea? Would it just fizzle in him, or would it burn him from the inside out? The smoke comes from heavenly fire consuming the components. That's what the book says."

"You're right." She sighed.

"I wish I wasn't" He shook his head. "I'm praying for him. It's what I can do. We just have to hope that the medical interventions work."

She pulled her dirty shirt over her head. He cocked an eyebrow. "Don't get any ideas. I wanted to cuddle, but you were sharpening axes with your bros." She reached into the dresser drawer that he had cleared for her and pulled out a clean bra.

"Shoulda given you a heads up. I didn't want to wake you." He said as she walked past him to the closet.

"It's fine. It will give Sean an advantage on Sunday, I think." She called out from the closet. "What do we have that's quick for breakfast? Bagels?"

"I can make you something, whatcha want?" He called back.

"No, go sharpen your axe. I'll find something." She grabbed her blue polo and jeans.

"I can feed them too...I'll cook while you fix your face."

"What's wrong with my face?" She stuck her tongue out playfully at him as she strode out of the closet.

"Not a damn thing, but you like wearing all that make-up. So, go put it on and I'll cook. Breakfast tacos?"

"Perfect. Thank you." She planted a quick kiss on his lips before turning to the bathroom. She threw her hair up in a ponytail and set about her makeup routine. She sent Journey a text telling her what time she would meet her at the hospital.

When she walked into the kitchen, Anaiah, Sean and Trevor all stood at the countertop bar eating breakfast tacos over their plates. Anaiah pulled out a stool for her and passed her a plate made up the way she liked it.

"I am so spoiled." She added salsa to her food.

"He made my plate too, you ain't special." Sean winked at her.

"Sorry I stole your boyfriend, Sean." She shot back.

"Boyfriend? I thought we were married." Sean scoffed. "Was it ever real for you?"

"I never loved you, O'Brien." Anaiah shrugged.

"Liar." Eden winked at Sean before she took another bite.

Anaiah rolled his eyes. "I'm not even his type. He likes dad bods."

"Are you still making jokes or does Sean really like guys with dad bods?" Trevor looked very confused.

"Dad bods, lumberjacks with beards, girls with dummy thick thighs and ooh don't forget the goth gamer girls." Sean licked salsa from his thumb while smiling. Trevor still looked confused and a little weirded out. "Not to be confused with thick headed dummies." Sean said sarcastically as he eyed Trevor.

"He's bisexual, rookie. Stop being weird about it." Anaiah passed Sean a paper towel. "And quit spilling shit on my floor. Eat over a plate like a human." Sean accepted the paper towel and looked like he wanted to make a smart-ass retort to the 'human' comment. He wiped up the salsa and eggs he had dumped on the floor.

"So...lumberjacks?" Eden giggled. "Is that why you do the axe throwing thing?"

"Throwing axes is fun. Impressing bearded, flannel-wearing men is just a bonus." He smiled. "The goth girls usually like it too."

"He was the worst wingman when we used to go out in Denton. It's all hipsters and scene kids." Anaiah laughed. "He's like a kid in a candy shop. Can't decide what he wants, just drools uncontrollably."

"Like you were any better." Sean shot back. "You told some girl you could bench press her."

"To be fair, I was very drunk." Anaiah held up a finger while trying to make his point.

"We have to recreate this magical moment..." Eden laughed, realizing she had yet to witness drunk Anaiah.

"No," they said in unison.

"Although, I would like to see what she would be like as my wing-woman." Sean raised an eyebrow. "Probably much better than you. You can't even flirt properly."

"That's what you get for bringing a demisexual to a bar, dumbass. I don't pick up girls like that." Anaiah laughed.

"Demi?" Trevor looked scandalized.

"Parker, give him the birds and the bees talk." Sean snickered.

"Anaiah doesn't sleep around." Eden provided. "He's not sexually attracted without an emotional connection."

"Heart on before hard-on, Trev." Sean winked. "Plus, believe it or not, the big guy is shy unless he has a drink or seven."

"You know, I had to ask him out?" Eden giggled.

"I didn't wanna be a creep." Anaiah shrugged.

"Going to the store she works at on the same night every week to talk to her wasn't creepy?" Sean asked.

"Fair point. Still got the girl, though." Anaiah cleared his plate and started cleaning up.

"You know what? It's solid dating advice for Trevor." Eden sipped her coffee. "Find a girl with a lot of emotional trauma and just be the most consistent thing in her life for a few months." She smiled over at Anaiah.

"But then you have to be in a relationship with a girl with a lot of baggage. Isn't that like, hard? I want a girlfriend that doesn't have all that." Trevor looked at Eden with genuine curiosity. Eden's heart sank. Was it really that obvious that she was a trainwreck? Of course, it was. Trevor said they had to stay here to babysit her. Did Anaiah confide in them that he felt responsible to take care of her? All of her self-doubt rolled back into place. She looked down at her plate, suddenly afraid she might start crying.

"See, what'd I say Parker? He's pretty, but that head is empty." Sean sighed.

"Look, Rookie. Here's the real advice: everybody has something. Baggage, trauma, quirks, kinks... whoever ends up with you is going to have to put up with the fact that you say whatever shit pops into your head without thinking about it first. Eden puts up with my baggage too. It's called a relationship. Grow up." Anaiah walked behind Eden and put his arms around her.

"Trev, I think you might have overstayed your welcome. And I think it's time to go grab a nap before my shift. Get your shit, we are heading out." Sean gave Eden an encouraging smile. "See you Sunday, Eden. Parker, stay out of trouble tonight."

"Hope it stays nice and q..." Trevor started.

"If you say the Q word, I will throw you through that door." Anaiah threatened.

"Sorry, boss." Trevor ducked out the door as Sean shook his head.

"Pretty, but dumber than a box of rocks." Sean said as he stepped out the door.

"The Q word?" Eden asked.

"EMS, PD, fire and nurses alike will murder you for jinxing their shift by pointing out if it's been slow or quiet." Anaiah said with a grin.

"Worse than sailors with superstitions like that." She giggled.

"And we cuss like them too. You fit right in with that mouth of yours." He kissed her on mouth for emphasis.

CHAPTER THIRTY-ONE

E den relayed all the information she had obtained at the hospital to Anaiah over the phone. "Antibiotics worked well overnight. They were able to back the drugs down. He's not pulling in as much air as they want him to, so he's still on a small amount of meds to keep him comfortable, but he is starting each breath and the machine kicks in to support him. The nurse told Jayse that within a day or two, he may be able to come off it. Jayse looked like himself again for a bit when he told me." She had seen hope in his eyes for the first time in weeks. Eden had missed the joy he usually had, the jokes he cracked. She was happy to see a glimmer of it back on his face.

"That's great news, honey." He said quietly. He was already at the station and getting duties lined up for the evening before his crew arrived.

"I tried to talk to him again, but it didn't work quite the same. I think it's the drugs that make that possible. Like, I could hear his voice, but I didn't visualize anything. I know Jayse was hoping for more, but with the good news about the breathing trial thing, he wasn't super disappointed when I told him that there wasn't much that I could do. Plus, it helps for him to know that it was Adam that did it."

"Sean was happy for that tip too." While he spoke, she heard the rustle of papers in the background. "Glad you remembered where he touched the window so they could lift that print." He sounded distracted.

"Do you need to let me go?" She offered.

"No. Got a meeting with the chief in a minute. Just trying to multitask. Am I not doing a good job?" He chuckled.

"You can't be great at everything." Eden said as she pulled up to the fire station with an energy drink for him. She knew he was going to be tired in the middle of the night after waking up early to hang out with the boys. "I'm bringing this drink up for you. Might as well let me go. See you in a sec." She hung up the phone after waiting a few seconds for him to respond. *Yeah, he is going to need the caffeine.* She greeted Matt and Allen as she walked past the fire engines and into the station house. She took a moment to update them on Kris when they asked how he was. They genuinely cared if Kris was going to be okay. She realized they may have been the guys who picked him up after the explosion.

She walked to the end of the hallway and up the station house stairs. She thought about the laundry she needed to do after work tonight, about the research Anaiah was going to help her sort through, and she told herself she would not start this day out feeling already beaten down by tomorrow's tasks. When she reached the office that Anaiah was working in, she saw through the window that Carla and the chief were in there as well. The door was closed, and Anaiah looked pissed. Carla noticed Eden with raised brows. Eden held up the drink and pointed to Anaiah with it. Carla crossed the room, opened the door and stuck her head out.

"Hey, having kind of an important meeting. Can I just give it to him?" She asked.

"Yeah, looks intense, everything okay?" Eden asked.

"Shouldn't say, but..." She stepped out and closed the door. "Bobby's been suspended. Pending investigation. And that's all I can say about that. Anaiah's under question too. The stuff with your brother has them looking into anything he's been involved with but shouldn't have. We are trying to keep the heat off him. He's overstepped a little here and there, but nothing too terrible. He may face suspension or demotion if they find anything too bad. He's been open and honest so...we'll see. He's on probation. I'm taking the lead on the shift for now. We used to split it." Carla whispered.

"Are they looking into any of his other friends?" She thought of Sean. Without the reports Sean pulled, maybe they wouldn't find anything too damning against him.

"No. We've all been tight lipped with internal affairs about how close everyone is. We weren't happy about Bobby getting dragged down, but apparently Lila was bad news. Connected to some illegal operations in another county. Bobby helped her ditch evidence that tied her there. Bob said Lila took off on Sunday. He claimed he didn't remember doing any of it, but they have him on camera. We are keeping Sean out of this if possible. We don't need to lose any good cops. Bobby made his own mess here. Sean hasn't covered anything up. Your files, your brother's, all relevant to his investigation, and Sean's the one that brought up stuff about Bobby. He didn't want to, but once he saw it, he couldn't just let it slip."

"Yeah. Sean's a little too observant sometimes." Eden whispered.

Carla laughed, "He's a nosy little prick... but yeah. Makes him a good detective though. He doesn't miss much. Better get back in there." She nodded to the closed door behind her. Eden handed over the can to give Anaiah. "I'll tell him to call you later."

"Thanks Carla. See you and Mina on Sunday?"

"Wouldn't miss it. Darlene would kill me." She smiled.

As Eden drove into work, she couldn't help but wonder if this was the thing she had felt uneasy about. She often had an uneasy feeling before bad things happened. If so, why did she still feel like this? She pulled up as Journey was getting out of her car with Jayse.

"Sup?" Journey nodded her head to Eden. "You get bad news or something?"

"Some shit with Anaiah's job. He's being investigated because of stuff that happened with me." She must have looked upset. Journey somehow always knew when something was up with her.

"Are they gonna find out about all your angel magic?" Journey asked.

"Don't think so. Just hate that he's in trouble. It's more like he didn't do things according to procedure because of me, I think. Probably that night with Adam chasing me, he shouldn't have given me a ride in the ambulance. They are looking for anything out of place because of all the open investigation with my brother. Seeing if he has tampered with evidence or anything. Apparently, his friend Bobby, the cop, covered some shit up for his girlfriend. You know, the one who is half demon and sort of threatened me."

"Oh, the one you tattoo tasered?" Jayse said as they walked toward the building.

"Yeah. I feel bad for Bobby, because I think she used some sort of magic to get him to do all of that."

"Or the sex was just that good..." Jayse added.

"With her personality, I visualize it having sharp teeth or fangs..." Eden made a disgusted face at her own vivid imagery.

"Like a vampire vag?" Journey laughed.

"I'm sorry I did that to my own brain..." Eden said in a low voice. "It's a horrifying visual." She shook her head. "Can't wait for this night to be over and we haven't even started."

"Same, dude, same." Journey added as they walked into the building to clock in. The night started like any other shift. Decent sized load on their truck and not surprisingly, the grocery side would need help again. Eden didn't understand why they didn't just hire more help on the grocery side or move her permanently over to the grocery side. She expressed as much to Journey as they walked around to start on the houseware's pallets.

"Frozen and Dairy get paid an extra twenty cents an hour." Journey laughed. "For the cold conditions in the freezer and walk in. So, they only hire a few for those departments. If there's too much to do, they have us lesser paid individuals help them for free."

"Damn, I was just making an observation… but they seriously nickel and dime us." Eden said while cutting open a box.

"They do, but what other jobs are we going to find in this shitty little town?" Journey shrugged and picked up a box.

"Ugh. Questions about hopes for my future came up at dinner with Anaiah's crew. And honestly, I just couldn't think of anything. Never hoped for much besides staying out of trouble and making it by. Darlene was trying to figure out what I am passionate about; what sort of job would be my dream job, but it just kind of made me sad. I didn't even finish high school." Eden broke down the box she was holding.

"Dude. That's rough. I went to art school in Dallas, but when I came back here to help my parents out, I couldn't figure out a way to make that sustainable without having to teach. I am not a people person. I still sell pieces online, but it's not enough to be reliable. This job pays the bills so I can do my art without it having pressure on it to crank it out." Journey avoided eye contact as usual when she talked about herself.

"Well, I don't even have that. This supernatural bullshit feels like a second job. And I don't even feel like I am any good at that either. Anaiah is amazing at everything he does. He's good at his day job, loves helping people. And he's got these hobbies that he's good at. Hell, he's even incorporated the angel shit into those. I just feel like I am living life just to get by still." She vented. "The only thing I've ever really felt good at is surviving hard shit."

"Maybe that's the problem. Life's always been hard. You haven't been able to be normal enough to have hobbies that don't include escaping reality. You read like you don't want to live on planet earth, dude." Journey pointed out. "Even with Anaiah. Like, you just made him your newest escapism."

"Fuck, that's a harsh reality." Eden stood still staring at the shelf in front of her. "You don't know how hard that hits home. Even when we are dealing with the supernatural…I've asked him to distract me. He's offered to distract me. Damn." She said in a low voice. Was it really so hard being alone with her own thoughts that she used Anaiah to escape that?

"Maybe start with getting your GED?" Journey offered. "Take time to think about what you want to do. You might not be stuck in retail forever, dude."

Eden nodded. "That's a good plan. Maybe when we get this stuff with my brother sorted."

"You really think that life is going to give you a break to let you go back to school?" Journey laughed. "Nah, time is going to pass. You are gonna keep seeing spooky shit. You wanna improve yourself, you just gotta do it and not wait for it to get easier. It never will. Don't wait for it."

"When did you become so wise instead of being a wise ass?" Eden laughed.

"I gave Jayse a similar talk before he came back to work. Told him that Kris has a long road ahead. He can't put his life on pause. Thinking it's good advice for all of us since we are all in the middle of this shit and don't know when it's gonna end." Journey looked down at her feet. "I just want to move on and quit feeling this pit of anxiety in my gut like something terrible is waiting for us. I want to quit feeling like everyone around me has this black cloud over their head. I just want to numb it, and I don't know how." Journey said in a low voice. "Goddamn, I hate this." Journey wiped her hand across her eyes.

"I thought it was just me feeling that way. Sorry, Journ." Eden wanted to hug her. She knew how Journey would respond to that. Physical affection was not comforting to her. Eden wondered why. Journey had loving parents; she hadn't been abused. She just didn't like to be touched.

"Jayse feels like that too. It's why he's having a hard time going back to normal life. It's not just Kris. He said he feels like he's just waiting for the next shit storm to hit us. Dammit. Tell me something crass or make a joke because I can't take this shit all night. We need to lighten the fuck up." Journey wiped her eyes again.

"Well, if it makes you feel any better, I'm relieved to be normal for once." She lowered her voice. "You human bitches can feel that imminent doom too. It makes me relieved it's not just me being some harbinger of destruction all the time. It's just run of the mill anxiety. Fucking yea." She said with mock enthusiasm.

"Glad I can help, I guess." Journey grabbed another box. "Better get back to work or someone will come talk to me about my emotional outbursts."

"Your emotional outbursts are like a normal conversation for anyone else." Eden laughed. "I've cried more watching a movie than I have seen you cry in the last few months."

They finished up their areas around lunch and headed over to the grocery departments to help. Eden discovered that the new guy working frozen foods had left in the middle of the shift and told no one. Their inept manager had waited for her to move departments after finishing her job. He hadn't helped at all. *God, I hate this job. Maybe I do need to go back to school. How much is that going to cost me though?* Lost in her thoughts, she barely registered that someone was walking toward her out of the corner of her eye until they were a few feet away. She jumped and turned around brandishing her box knife.

"Jesus, E. It's just me." Sean held his hands up in front of him and backed up.

"You startled me, dude. Did you forget that I have an evil brother trying to kidnap me? Don't sneak up on me!" She realized she was attempting to whisper and yell at the same time.

"Yeah. That's why I am here." He looked around. "Got somewhere we can talk?"

She thought for a second. "How do you feel about having this conversation in a walk-in freezer?" She whispered. He was wearing his short-sleeved police uniform. "They have some jackets we use when we go in there to grab stock. They are huge on me, but it should work fine for you. It's insulated. No one will overhear anything."

Sean nodded, and Eden led the way to the freezer, pulling her cart of frozen boxes with her. She grabbed one of the big puffy coats and threw it on before tossing one to Sean. She pushed the sliding door open and pulled the cart in behind her. The roar of the refrigeration units always took her a second to get used to. Sean slid the door closed behind him. The freezer walls were lined with pallets of stacked frozen goods in cardboard boxes. She slid her cart of boxes in the aisle between the pallets.

"This doesn't look suspicious." He said as she turned to face him. "Okay. The reason I came by was we found Lila." His expression was pained.

"What? Where?"

"I'll get there in a second. It all started tonight at Bobby's" He took a breath. "Eden, there's no easy way to say this, but Bobby's dead. We think she killed him, but it's gruesome." Sean's face was heartbreaking for her to watch as he tried to push the emotion down to get out what he had to say. "He was gutted. His neighbors heard screaming, they went to check on him, called us, and reported some blood on the floor. they didn't go all the way in. Carla and Anaiah went out there, full lights and sirens and found him...just eviscerated. Anaiah doesn't think it was Lila though." He hesitated. "He thinks it was your ex... we can't exactly put that in an official report. They called in the police chief and some higher-ranking detectives to investigate. They knew Bobby and I were friends, so they told me to go on with my shift. Anyway." He paused, pinching the bridge of his nose as he struggled with what he was feeling. "I went by the station to check on Parker and Carla. They were shaken up to be sure. Anaiah's pissed. He was going to wait to tell you in person, but...there was a call that came through for a fire, at your house."

"Shit. My brother?" Eden sat down on a half-stacked pallet. She was dizzy with anxiety.

"No, we don't think so." He shook his head. "He's connected. Lila attempted to enter your house. There was a broken window, but she didn't make it inside. Now, that's not what the report says. Officially, it appears she fell into the window and broke it. When she tried to get in, whatever ritual shit you and Anaiah did to protect the house caught her on fire and burned her alive. Chief said he thinks she covered herself in some sort of accelerant and lit herself on fire to try to burn your place down, based on the severity of the burns on the remains and on the basis of being a crazy bitch who threatened you."

Eden couldn't breathe. They wanted to keep themselves safe, not burn people alive for fucks sake. "I didn't know…we didn't know what it would do." She was shaking.

"I'm not here to accuse you of anything." His face softened. "Just letting you know what we found. She fell out into the yard and burned to death on your lawn. The bushes out front caught fire, some damage to the porch, but that's it. The house is fine. I found her purse, with her phone. Eden, they were looking for the book."

"They?" She almost yelled. She breathed deep. She needed to calm herself down.

"Adam and Lila." He walked over and placed a hand on her shoulder. "I was the detective on the investigation. Don't worry. I got the phone out and it didn't get logged into evidence. We got ID off her license. Car she was driving was Bobby's though. Anyway, I went through the phone." He shook his head. "Your brother and Lila are together. Delila, I should say. That's her real name. They are fucking crazy too, but that's beside the point. They were trying to get the book. They found out about it, and she went to your place to get it."

"But I don't leave it laying around, Sean. It's in my backpack, locked in my locker right now." She pointed in the direction of the breakroom.

"Anaiah told me that. I told him I would come catch you up on everything and check on you. Once Adam finds out what happened to her, we're sure he's gonna pull some crazy shit. We didn't want you to be out here alone and unaware. I figured I'd tell you what's going on and see if you wanted to spend the next couple of hours at the station with me while I do paperwork. Anaiah can't guarantee he won't get called out again tonight and he's on probation. I have a shitload of paperwork to do so I won't get called out again. Also, my job requires me to have a couple of guns. I thought you might be safer with me than possibly alone at the firehouse."

"I gotta tell my manager why I am leaving. What about my friends? Journey and Jayse are here." She shook her head trying to think. "We still don't know why Kris was attacked, or how they are connected to this. Was Adam just trying to hurt me by killing one of my friends?"

"I don't know. Looking through her phone didn't give me any leads on that. I was hoping you could help me try to sort some of what they said to each other out. Some of it is written in some weird fucking language that Google translate doesn't help with." Sean patted her on the shoulder. "I don't know why he went after them, but he hasn't tried again since. And I know he's trying to kidnap you and get that book you have. They are probably safer without you here. Hell, he might have thought you were with them that day. You hung out with them a lot before you started dating Anaiah, right?"

"Yeah." She watched her breath fog up as she let out a deep breath. "Okay. First, we warn my friends before we leave. Then, we go and find my manager. You tell him that I am needed for an investigation or some shit. Something sounding official so I don't lose my damn job, okay?"

"A woman burned to death on your lawn. I think he should let you go home without a problem." Sean's face contorted with confusion.

"You've never worked in retail. They made Jayse come back after his house blew up, and his brother is still in the hospital." She stood up. "Let's get this over with."

Sean escorted her to find Journey and then track down Jayse. They quietly relayed a synopsis of what happened. Eden made them promise to be careful and on the lookout for anything weird at Journey's place. Eden told them that she and Anaiah would come out and do the protection ritual at Journey's place if she wanted her to. Journey looked horrified, but Jayse said it was probably a good idea.

They found her manager, Scott, in the office. Sean explained that there had been a death of their close friend and his fellow officer and an open investigation of an incident with the potential killer at Eden's home that both occurred tonight. He told Scott that Eden was needed at the station. Scott attempted to explain to Sean that they were short staffed and really needed Eden to finish her shift. Sean then asked why he was sitting in an office not working instead of stocking. Sean also let Scott know he was impeding an investigation by keeping Eden here. Scott then agreed that Eden could leave without consequence. Eden gathered her things and walked out with a pissed off Sean.

"You need a new job, Eden." Sean said as she buckled her seatbelt.

"I'm a high school dropout. Where else am I going to work?" She said a little defensively.

"Take the test to get your diploma and come work at dispatch." He said simply. "You don't get too freaked out by horrible shit. You'd be great." He gave her a small smile.

"I'd have to study for that test, Sean. The only official education I have took place in a psych hospital. I could barely read when I first got there." She worked to hide the shame she felt, but he noticed anyway. He always noticed her subtle changes in moods, picked up on everything. *Fucking cops.*

"So, study. Anaiah and I can help you. You aren't dumb. You were kept ignorant on purpose. You're so fucking smart that they couldn't let you get educated. You were a threat. Don't let them win. Even if you don't go to college, get that piece of paper as a big 'fuck you' to them." His face turned a little red with anger.

"Geez, Sean. Calm down." She shrugged. "Why do you care so much if I do?"

"It just hits home for me. Sorry." He started the cruiser.

"Why?" Eden eyed him with concern.

"I was a foster kid too. Parker didn't tell you?" He gave her a sideways glance. "No, guess he wouldn't. He knows I don't talk about it much. My mom was an addict and a drug dealer. I was in and out of foster care. She'd get busted, go away for a while, and then get me back. When Anaiah left his mom's place, he stayed with us. The Davidson's were my foster parents from the time I was sixteen until I aged out. That's when I started going by my middle name, cut ties with my mom, and chose the opposite road from the one she was dragging me down." He sighed. "I went to the academy because they encouraged me to. Darlene said I was constantly investigating everyone's motives all the time anyway, and said I'd make a good detective. They did the same for Anaiah."

"Why didn't he tell me that?" She asked quietly.

"Probably was waiting for me to tell him it was okay. Most of the guys at work don't know. We don't exactly go around bragging about how our mother's failed us." He pulled the car out of the parking lot and onto the road.

"I'm glad you trust me enough to tell me now." She reached over and squeezed his shoulder.

"I figured you would understand." He stared at the road ahead of them.

"Your middle name is Sean?" She raised an eyebrow. It fit him so well, she wasn't sure she could picture him as anything else. "Surely your first name isn't so bad."

"It's not bad; just reminded me too much of her. It's Thomas. And if you want to try to make a cute and call me Tommy, just fucking don't." The humor was gone from his expression. Eden could see the pain behind the stony facade he put up.

"Your mom called you that?"

"Yeah, it was her dad's name. To be honest, I hate it for a lot of reasons. I made my peace with being called O'Brien, but that doesn't mean I'm one of them. Honestly, don't you ever think about changing your name?"

"I went by other names for a while. Always something close enough that I'd answer easily to: Evelyn, Eve, Ellen. I was relieved when I could use my name again. Just be me when I came here. Not everyone makes the connection with my last name. Grace is just a name."

"Oh, I don't know about all that." He tried lightening the mood. "You could end up being Eden Parker instead."

"Shit." She shook her head. "Don't get me wrong, I love him. Like so much, it's scary. Like, I don't want to do this without him...but marriage?" She made a face.

"Oh, that's a sensitive topic then..." Sean made a hissing noise. "You danced around that worse than Anaiah and I two-step after a few too many drinks."

"We are gonna circle back to you dancing with my man..."

"Of course." Sean laughed. "He's gonna hate that."

"Marriage scares the shit out of me. Haven't been able to shake that sentiment... Sean, I would have been a child bride in the Church. The only reason I wasn't married off already was all the ghost shit. I was...defective." She cringed as she said it.

"Thank fucking God for that." Sean exclaimed.

"I guess so." She shrugged. "I love Anaiah. I do. And someday maybe we can cross that bridge, but I'm too young for that now. I mean, I don't even know what I want to be when I grow up."

"You'd probably make a good social worker for kids like us. Someone who understands what it's like to be a kid in those situations. Take your time. Think about it. By the way, the state would give you free tuition. Perks of being a foster kid."

"Didn't know that." She shrugged. "Like an official government apology for having shit parents, huh?"

"I guess." He shrugged too. "I know it sounds cliche and you'd think I'd crack jokes the whole time, but if you ever need to talk about the stuff with your parents, I'm here. I sort of picked up on the fact that you don't like laying that stuff on Anaiah. He gives you the sad boyfriend face that makes you pissy. I'd listen, maybe give you some of the advice I got from good people. I won't think less of you because of what they did to you."

"I mean, you've read the file. You know what happened." She said quietly.

"I've seen evidence. It's a completely different thing for you to talk about your experience. I went through a lot of bad shit too. Made me a really pissed off kid. I'll listen if you need to talk."

"Thanks, Sean. I think maybe when we are done with the current trauma we are living through, we can address the past." She shrugged. "My life seems like a continuous trainwreck."

"Copy that." He nodded. "Since you wanna change the subject, the phone is in that console there. Look through the text messages with Adam, see what you can figure out there."

She scrolled through the messages, making faces at some that grossed her out. There was a fair amount of sexting, not to mention pictures she could have lived without seeing.

"You could have warned me about the pictures of my brother's dick." She said as they pulled up to the station.

"Didn't get that far back..." Sean looked like he wanted to laugh at her but refrained.

"I scrolled all the way back to see where it started." She smacked his arm.

"See, you're smart. You wanna be a cop?" Sean smiled at her.

"No, y'all are all goodie two shoes. I'm too mean." She stuck her tongue out at him.

"You could be the bad cop to my good cop." He said as they unbuckled. "For real, it's an option. I imagine the psych stuff could be passed off as childhood trauma. We could get you re-evaluated. You could pass, just lie about your superpowers. No 'I see the souls of the damned' on this one."

"Hey, I was really young and didn't know any better when I said that!" She recognized her quote from the hospital interview.

"You also said that you thought you were demon possessed 'cause your dad said so. There's proof it was trauma." He shrugged. "Hey, before we go in here, everyone is really fucked up about Bobby. So even though we deal with grief like proper childhood abuse survivors by cracking jokes and laughing, they do not. Okay?"

"Okay." She wiped the grin off her face. "Hey, Sean."

"Yeah?" He said as he grabbed the door handle.

"I'm glad we're friends. I'm glad you get it." She gave him a smile.

"Me too. It's a definite plus that my brother's girlfriend is fun." He patted her shoulder. "My paperwork is not going to fill itself out. Your job is to keep me from jamming a pen in my eyeball to end it all, and to translate the shit on that phone. Let's go."

Sean was right about the mood in the station. Everyone was on edge. One of the dispatchers had to step away for a bit after breaking down. One officer threw something across the room at one point in frustration. Sean whispered to her that it was Bobby's partner. This police station was hell to be in as an empath. She could feel herself shaking from the overwhelming feelings all around her.

"Bathroom?" She asked Sean, afraid that more words would let him know just how on edge she was right at that moment.

He looked up at her with concern. "You alright?" he whispered.

She typed a message on her phone but didn't send it. She passed it to him. *'I can feel everything they are feeling. EVERYTHING! It's like they are screaming it at me. I don't know if I am going to cry, scream, or set your desk on fire. Where is the fucking bathroom so I can cry in peace?'* She had typed out. Sean took a moment to add his number to his contacts before handing it back and leading her silently down a hall to the bathroom.

"I'll be at my desk. Let me know if you need me." He pointed at the phone. Sean was taut with stress too. She felt his grief rolling off him. Of course, he was upset, his friend was murdered, and he had to see the charred remains of Lila's body. He somehow held it together to hide evidence to cover up for her and Anaiah. *Of course, he is stressed. You idiot! He's comforting you, when he's dealing with all of that on top of having to lie and risk his job for you.* She checked her phone to see if Anaiah had replied to her last message that she was with Sean and safe. Nothing. She wanted to scream at the situation. Was she going to keep hiding from her brother under the protection of Sean or Anaiah until he somehow slipped up and they caught him?

She locked herself in the bathroom stall, sat down, and ran her hands through her hair. Being out of that room bathed in emotions helped, but now she was alone with her own thoughts and feelings, which was somehow worse. All she wanted at that moment was to be pulled into Anaiah's arms and held until she felt better about everything. Then she thought of Journey's words. Did she use her boyfriend to numb the thoughts in her head? Was she a terrible person who would use him like that? *No. I love him.* Anaiah's love was like a comforting balm to her frazzled soul. His love helped fill in the gaps of the incomplete person she felt like. He had told her that she was the same for him. Was that using a person? Or was that how love was supposed to be? That other person who made you want to do better and be better? She wanted to be better. Now, everyone seemed to think she was better than some shitty retail job. That she was smart enough for a college degree or something.

She felt the anxiety building. She wanted to believe it was true, but were they all just saying that because they were her friends? Had she somehow tricked them all into thinking she was better or smarter than she was? She'd pretended and lied about who she was for so long... did they even know the real Eden? Did she?

She began hyperventilating as her tears rolled down her face. All her fears began to bubble up. What if she tried to learn more and take the test to get her diploma and failed? What if Anaiah realized that she was stupid? That she was some bumbling idiot who had lucked into figuring some of this bullshit out with his help. What if she tried to become a cop or social worker and they wouldn't let her because of her psychiatric history? What if she failed? What if her failure left her with no friends, no job, no future? She heard every single doubt bubble up in her head. Then she heard the voice of her mother from her childhood say in her mind, *"Eden, those things are for good girls. And you are not a good girl."* It rang through her like a bell.

She shook as she took a shuddering breath and sobbed. She realized then, the core of her fear. She was afraid that no matter what she did, how hard she worked, who her father actually was, that she would never be good enough. She closed her eyes and attempted to steady her breathing. Another voice bellowed in her head. A commanding voice that told her she had a purpose. A voice of power and authority that called her daughter of heaven.

"You are chosen. You are my daughter." She heard the voice speak, *"You are NOT alone. When the time comes, you all will be enough to do what must be done."* She thought she might be hallucinating. Was Azrael really in her head? Talking to her?

Eden stood and fumbled for the lock on the stall, feeling a need to move to do something to show herself she wasn't crazy. She gaped at herself in the mirror. Around the edge of her irises, they glowed silver. "Is it really you?" She whispered. "Are you really talking to me, Father?" One iris glowed silver and the other went completely black.

"I will never forsake you, my daughter. You have claimed your birthright as I have claimed you. Do not hang your head in shame. You must help the others claim theirs. I cannot stay with you long, for the heavenly fire would certainly kill you. Prepare yourself, drink of heaven's protection, protect the others." His voice thundered through her head and as it did, she saw the silver slivers of light bleeding through the markings on her skin. Was it a heavenly fire burning through her? As the color shifted back to her grey green eyes, she nearly fell to the floor feeling suddenly weak with her heart aching in her chest. She caught herself on the sink. She panted as she tried to catch her breath. Once it evened out, she attempted to wipe away the evidence of tears she had cried. Her makeup was ruined. She laughed a little deliriously at the thought. Mascara had run down her face. That was her concern? An angel had temporarily inhabited her, and she was concerned about smudged eye makeup. She fixed what she could and grabbed her backpack to walk back to the desk where Sean was filling out paperwork.

"Good cry?" He said in a low voice when he saw her face.

"The best..." She rolled her eyes. She looked at her watch. *Almost time for Anaiah to get off work.* "Can I make some tea?" She pointed at the little coffee bar area across the room.

"Knock yourself out." He didn't look up from his paperwork.

Eden pulled the premade protection tea bags from where she kept them in her backpack. They only lasted a few days, and when she felt it begin to wear off, it was like coming off a sugar high heading towards a crash. She hadn't felt that coming yet, but if her angelic dad told her to drink heaven's protection, she was going to do it. She tossed the tea bag in one of the paper cups and poured hot water over the tea bag from the little spout on the coffee machine. She refrained from giggling when she thought about the surprise Sean would get from her heavenly belch that would come after drinking it. After she let it steep a few minutes, she cooled it down by adding a little cold water from the water cooler. She whispered the incantation over the cup before she returned to Sean's desk.

"What the fuck kind of herbal tea do you have there? Smells like when Darlene is basting a turkey." Sean whispered to her.

She was about to respond when her phone buzzed. She sat the cup down and pulled the phone out of her pocket.

Anaiah had texted, *'Gotta give a handoff report to the next shift and then I will be there to pick you up. Fuck today and all its bullshit. Can't wait to kiss you. Love you.'*

She typed a reply, *'I couldn't agree more. Got stuff to tell you. Love you more.'* She hit send before Sean unleashed an enormous rumbling burp.

"Oh hell no." She gasped as Sean locked eyes with her with the cup in his hand. His eyes flashed golden for a moment then back to their light shade of blue. "No." She breathed out in disbelief. *It's not for humans.*

He registered the disbelief on her face. He whispered, "Was that some magic shit?"

"Outside...now." She whispered back. She glanced around to see if anyone else noticed. To her amazement everyone had carried on like nothing was happening. Sean stood and followed her outside. She gave another cursory glance to the street around them. "Why...why would you drink my tea?" She pulled him around the corner and into the alley next to the station.

"I was curious what it tasted like. It fucking burns, by the way. I thought my stomach was going to explode." He whispered back looking annoyed.

"How are you not burned from the inside out by heavenly fire right now?" She whispered frantically, knowing that he wouldn't have an answer. The dawning of realization washed over her. She recalled the way his eyes had glowed with fire as he was protected by the tea. She whispered intensely, "This is going to sound so stupid." She paused. "Do you have a weird unexplained scar, or birthmark. Like in a shape? Because if you do, Anaiah is going to either be livid or super fucking excited. I'm not sure."

"The fuck do you mean?" Sean stared at her like she was insane.

"A scar or birthmark? Do you have one? If you do... Sean, you might be one of us. That may be why you and Anaiah...we are drawn to each other. Like magnets. We are the only ones who are supposed to drink that tea! It's for protection from evil. The same spell was over my house. The one that burned Lila to ash." She tried desperately to keep her voice low despite what she was feeling inside her. Sean dropped the cup.

She could see the panic on his face before he moved into action, pulling her further into the alley. He started unbuttoning his shirt. "Don't get too excited, I'm showing you." He grinned.

"You are so not my type." She quipped without thinking.

"Too short. I knew it. Anaiah's six fucking six, who can compete with that?" Sean joked as he pulled his shirt open. Over his right collar bone were two small, raised scars that mirrored each other. They looked almost like an inkblot test. She pulled out her phone. "What are you doing?" He whispered.

"Magic googling. Trust me." She snapped a quick picture. "That's always been there?"

"Yes. Looks like a Rorschach test, right?" He smirked.

"Is that the ink blot thing?" She asked while tracing it on her photo app.

"Yeah. That's the name of it. What the fuck does it mean?" He stared at her.

"Wanna explain why you are undressing in an alley with my girlfriend, Sean?" Anaiah stalked toward them down the alley.

"How'd you know we were here?" She asked.

"You were trying to whisper and shout at the same time, and he was just being loud. Heard you as soon as I walked up. Maybe we can keep it down?" He lowered his voice. "What's going on?"

"I'll explain in a second." Eden reverse image searched as she remembered what happened the last time. "Closest empty field?" She looked up at them.

"There's one behind the station impound." Sean looked at her with confusion all over his face. "Trust you?" He asked with sarcasm.

"Yeah, lead the way." She motioned with her hand as Sean buttoned his shirt. He turned and led the way. Anaiah gave her a confused look before he sighed and motioned for her to follow Sean. He didn't know what she was doing, but he trusted her. She jogged after Sean. He wasn't six and a half feet tall like Anaiah, but he was over six foot which had her beat by about a foot. Anaiah caught up with them easily. They passed the impound and strode out to the empty lot.

"Now, can you both tell me what's happening." Anaiah asked.

She handed her phone to Sean. "Be prepared before you say that name, we saw lightning bolts hit the ground when we said ours."

"What do you mean?" Anaiah looked between them.

"He drank my tea and his eyes lit up. He has a scar, Anaiah. He's one of us." She proclaimed excitedly, "His father is an angel."

Sean looked between Anaiah and her phone. "This is him? The angel of wisdom and knowledge?"

"Yes! It's what makes you see everything that other people miss!" She wanted to jump up and down with joy.

"There's no way." Anaiah said under his breath while staring at Sean.

"Raziel." As Sean spoke, lightning split the sky.

Eden knew it was coming yet still stumbled backward from the force of it. She looked over at Anaiah who was staring at Sean, dumbfounded. She turned to watch Sean as he approached the scorched earth. Her breath caught as she saw another book as he lifted it from the ground.

"He's one of us, Anaiah." She tugged on his arm. As Anaiah turned his eyes to hers, a huge grin cracked across his face.

"You're a genius, baby." He scooped her up into his arms and hugged her against his chest. "Thank you, God." He whispered. She wanted to cry at the beauty of this moment, when Anaiah realized his found brother was like him. That he found another who was touched by heavenly fire and could share this burden they carried.

"What did he get?" She asked, still cradled in Anaiah's embrace. "Let me down. I want to see." He kissed her on her cheek and set her down gently.

"This," Sean proclaimed, "is the weirdest fucking welcome present ever."

"What is it?" Anaiah reached to grab it as Sean approached.

Sean dodged his grasp. "Can't read it yet, but my father said it was the "Book of Cherubi." They're the other order of angels, the inner circle. How do I fucking know that all of a sudden?" He gave Eden a look of accusation.

"I am not the one who made you a nephilim. Blame Razzie or whatever his name is." She stuck her tongue out at him.

"Ok, so when do I get my angel girlfriend?" He jokingly said to Anaiah.

"Don't think that's a guarantee. But you will feel like your stomach is turning when you're around a half demon, so that's a plus." Anaiah shrugged.

"Oh...was that what that was? Every time I was around Lila, I had this sick feeling. I thought it was just me and my inner disgust with her as a person." He burst out laughing.

"We gotta protect Journey's place, but after...we need to do the rituals we have done with him." Eden looked at Anaiah. "We gotta get him up to speed on all this stuff."

"Oh! Shit! Does this mean I am getting those tattoo scar things?" Sean looked legitimately scared.

"You scared, Sean?" Eden asked.

"Don't worry, Sean. No needles for these. Hurts like hell though." Anaiah smirked, "You wanted this, brother. Said you didn't wanna be some human sidekick."

"It seems really stupid that I gotta finish my paperwork first, doesn't it?" Sean grinned.

"Real life seems stupid now. Yeah." Anaiah agreed.

CHAPTER THIRTY-TWO

Eden and Anaiah decided to spend most of their day off educating Sean all things nephilim and assisting him to perform all the rituals they had in the last several weeks. Unsure if their physical assistance or reading of incantations would hinder the rituals, they simply gave him some coaching and watched over him in the living room of Eden's house.

Police tape still roped off the property and Anaiah had boarded up the broken window. Eden would have to call the landlord but wanted to clean up any remaining stains after the ritual before he came by. She worried about getting an eviction notice after all the property damage. That worry was eased by the fact that she had just loaded the last of her belongings into Sean's truck. Her couch was bound for his house to replace his torn one. Anaiah had lifted and moved the furniture with Sean holding one end in case neighbors saw anything.

A new worry crossed her mind. Would her landlord be burned by the ritual if he came to serve her with an eviction notice? She hoped not. Surely heavenly fire could differentiate between severity of ill will, and not dole out punishments for packages thrown too hard on her porch or a cursing repairman fixing the window. They had blessed the entire building of Anaiah's apartment complex. She expressed her concern to him as he watched Sean's chest rise and fall after the rituals were done.

"We just gotta trust heaven to sort it out." He shrugged.

Eden drank her coffee from the floor where her couch once sat. Anaiah checked on Sean for what seemed like the fourth or fifth time after he had passed out at the end of the daemonic ritual. "We don't know how long we were out after. Some time had passed when we woke up. He's breathing. He's okay." She reminded him. "I'm still a little annoyed because we gave each other stitches. He had it easy…"

"Don't be petty, sweetie. This ritual still hurts like hell." Anaiah's gaze fell on her from where he knelt at Sean's side. "Not gonna lie, if I hadn't done this one with you and had to watch you do this, I'd have lost my mind."

"Same. I'd be panicking if I didn't know that he is going to be okay. I'm just tired and hungry. And cranky. How are you holding up?"

"Starving but I'll live." He shrugged as he stood up.

"You know what I meant." She gave him a glowering look. "You've let me talk all morning. Told you about my encounter with my father and everything, but you haven't talked to me about your night. When are we going to talk about what happened with Bobby?"

"I don't know." He swallowed hard and looked down at Sean. "I'm not sure I want to talk about it. Pretty sure I want to get drunk about it. Maybe take a demon's head off about it, but talking about it? Going through those details with you? No. Don't think I want to do that." He ran his hands through his hair. "Chief and I talked. That was hard enough. Carla…she's really messed up about it." A tear rolled down his cheek. "I just can't do this right now." His voice was thick with emotion. "Don't get me wrong. I am thrilled that Sean is with us on this. I am happy that we have another nephilim to get us closer to the blade. But I am scared too. Scared something is going to happen to him. I know, he's a cop. He runs into danger too. But I'm scared something will happen to him and I won't be able to stop it. I am more scared now of losing you, because of the vision I saw. Sean was there…with us. Facing Adam with us. He was hurt. When I saw him walking back to us with the new book, I remembered him limping in my vision towards you after Adam pulled the trigger. Can't talk about Bobby, because while that fucking hurts right now, all I can think about is the two of you dying and me not being able to do anything about it."

"Anaiah," She rose and wrapped her arms around him, "we agreed that we aren't letting that future happen. No one is dying, remember? If anything, Sean will help keep you from charging in and doing something stupid. He'll do the same for me. He has our back. He can drink protection tea and healing potions. He would have our backs without being one of us. This is better. Plus, he will be able to pick up on clues we haven't. Notice things before we do. This is a good thing, babe. You've just had a very shitty day. You don't have to tell me about it. You don't have to say anything if you don't want to." She cupped his cheek. "I'm here. For whatever you need." She tiptoed up for a kiss. "We are going to make it through this. Together."

She watched the tension in his shoulders release as her words sunk in. Sean would charge into battle with them even if he wasn't a half angel. This way was safer for all of them.

"What do you want to eat after he wakes up." She smiled. "Let me distract you with the promise of food."

"I could go for some other form of distraction." He flashed a wicked grin before he playfully nibbled at her lower lip. She leaned into him and parted her lips to him.

"JESUS FUCKING CHRIST! My chest is caving in and you're trying to fuck your girlfriend right next to me? Are we in high school again?" Sean yelled. "Take your hands off her ass and tell me why my chest feels like you've been tap dancing on it."

"We're pretty sure those words are written directly on your heart, honey." Eden smiled sarcastically down at Sean. "Hurts like a bitch." She drank from her coffee cup after Anaiah released her.

"I underestimated how much it would hurt. You said it hurt really bad. I didn't believe you." Sean admitted. "I thought you were being a whiny little girl about it. My apologies."

"Tougher than I look, cupcake." She reached over and grabbed his shirt, her lotion, and the bottle of ibuprofen. She handed him the lotion and shirt as he sat up. "Vitamin E cream helps. After that, ibuprofen." She shook the bottle.

"Don't have any good drugs to help?" He looked up at Anaiah.

"Man, I'm on probation. You think I'm stealing narcs for you?" He held out a hand to help Sean out of the floor. Sean took it and hopped up.

Eden handed over the pills once he handed the lotion back. She realized she had nothing for him to drink. She offered him her coffee cup. He tossed the pills in his mouth and took a big swig from her coffee. He made a disgusted face.

"She drinks sugar and cream disguised as coffee." Anaiah laughed. Eden gave them both a foul hand gesture as she took her mug back.

"Jesus, no more sharing drinks. First one leads to me being passed out in the floor feeling like I'm being crushed to death, and this one gives me fucking diabetes." Sean shook his head.

"Are you gonna complain the entire time we save the world?" Eden scowled. Anaiah snickered.

"She's cold, man. No sympathy. Maybe she should be a medic." Sean said.

"Stop trying to pick a career for me." She threw her hands up but grinned.

"You won't do it, somebody has to." Sean grinned before he winced and placed a hand over his chest. "Did she tell you she's gonna get her GED?" Eden looked sidelong at Anaiah.

"She hasn't, but we have been busy taking you through nephilim boot camp, so it's not come up yet. Ready to eat? I'm starving. And Eden's getting meaner by the second. We gotta feed her." Anaiah ignored the look she gave him as he grabbed his medic kit. She grabbed her backpack and shut off the lights.

"We need to go by Sean's and place the protection ritual on it too." She said as they headed out the door.

"Eh, give me the ritual, I'll do it. You don't wanna see my house in its current state." Sean said as they carefully walked around the singed spots in the lawn.

"Dude, you saw my house when it was ransacked. There was a ritual with our used condom in the middle of my bed. Not sure yours could be in a worse state." She laughed.

"That wasn't your fault. His mess is all on him. He's a pig." Anaiah said, "That's one of the reasons why we aren't roommates anymore."

"Speaking of which, Sean told me about the chief and his wife taking you in when he was their foster kid. You could have told me they were like second parents to you because of that." She opened the front passenger side door of Anaiah's car.

"Hard to tell you that without telling his story. I told you that Darlene was our mama bear, and the chief is like our dad. It was close enough." He shrugged. "We can tell each other all the gory details of our pasts over the next fifty years or so, deal?" Anaiah smirked.

"Are you proposing? Because that was lame. Try again later, Parker. I won't let her accept that one." Sean made a disapproving face before he climbed into the back seat.

As they ate breakfast foods for lunch, Eden thumbed through the book of Cherubi. The spells within claimed to open the mind's eyes, give wisdom and insight, and other vague things about prophecy.

"Your branch of the angelic family tree is fucking weird. Ours is like, here, learn to speak and read these languages, protect yourself, here's some potions to brew. And yours is like angelic philosophy." Eden complained.

"Well, don't want to brag, but my daddy is the angel of the mysteries of heaven." Sean postured with false pride.

"Mine's the angel of death, so what." She rolled her eyes.

"When they run out of books to give, does the next angel bastard just get socks or a trial gym membership?" Sean asked.

"We don't even know how any of that works." Eden confessed.

"Can you two talk quieter?" Anaiah looked around the diner to see if anyone noticed their conversation. "Inside voices, please."

"I get excited." She whispered.

"I am a cop; I have no inside voice." Sean said in a hushed tone then shoved some pancakes into his mouth.

"Better," Anaiah said in a low voice. "Now, let's talk about a plan. When it was just Eden and I, we just planned things day by day, but we are going to have to talk it out a lot more now."

"You act like me joining up with y'all complicates things instead of making it easier." Sean glared at him.

"It's not like you'll be there at the end of my day for me to run down stuff that I researched at the station. She goes to work a few hours after me. She spends that time researching, making potions...we recap all that when we end the day, usually on our way to bed."

"So, call me. We can recap on speaker phone." He stated the obvious solution.

"See, gifted with solutions." Eden replied. "What's our next steps? We still need another nephilim to get the blade."

"Which of these spells do you think will get us closer to that goal?" Sean pulled the book back to look over it again.

"Maybe a wisdom one? Prophetic visions and dreams haven't been our strong suit." Eden said, "Speaking of which, do you see weird shit? Have dreams that come true?"

"I mean everyone has had those weird Deja vu dreams, right? Or are you telling me I overlooked superpowers?"

"You overlooked superpowers, dude." Anaiah rolled his eyes. "You thought we were all fools for not noticing stuff you did or remembering tiny details about everything."

"Do you ever see things like in visions? When you are awake? Or pick up on what other people are feeling?" Eden asked.

"I've never had a vision. I see emotions written all over people. Body language, little expressions or ticks. I know when I am being lied to. It's why you were so fucking suspicious to me. You're a good liar, one of the best I have met, but you have tells. I get weird intuitions like I feel like something bad is going to happen, but usually that's just me assessing a situation, right?"

"Maybe. Like we said, we are still figuring angel gifts out." Eden shrugged.

"You really thought you were part demon the day we met?" Sean asked.

"Yeah. Still haven't figured out what the deal with that is or where the hell Cole has been since then," she whispered.

"Maybe hell has been too busy to worry about stalking his ex?" Sean offered.

"Maybe he realized what my boyfriend could do to him?" She offered back.

"Maybe he's behind all of this and that's who Adam was trying to take you to?" Anaiah offered the most plausible solution. They all sat in silence for a few minutes, unsure of any real leads.

"I have to work tonight, so I gotta catch a nap." Sean said before shoving the last of his pancakes in his mouth.

"Sleep is definitely my next move." Eden yawned.

"Damn, I was hoping for some other moves first." Anaiah whispered as he stole a piece of bacon from her plate. She shrugged noncommittally. "Let's plan to meet up tomorrow after Sean sleeps…Eden's old place. We do the rituals for wisdom. We have all those ingredients anyway. Eden and I can sleep today, take tonight off from preparing for the end times, and we can start fresh tomorrow."

"You gonna translate those texts tonight, Eden?" Sean asked, remembering Lila's phone.

"Yeah, we can work on that tonight. No nights off, baby. We can take breaks though." She wiggled her eyebrows at him.

Sean pretended to bow his head in prayer. "Dear big angel daddy. Send me some hot half breed angel with a beard or thick thighs, or both. I need to get laid so these fuckers quit making me jealous. Amen." He smirked up at them.

"When he gets struck down by heaven for his bullshit, I'm taking his book." Eden sassed. Sean gave her a rude gesture in return.

CHAPTER THIRTY-THREE

After a wonderfully dreamless sleep, Eden awoke to find Anaiah sleeping soundly. He occasionally muttered to himself in his sleep. She still couldn't shake the pit of anxiety in her gut. It had quieted slightly. She threw herself into things she could handle, making coffee and food. She let Anaiah sleep.

As she sat at the bar, translating text messages, she ate a bagel with cream cheese and sipped coffee. Her phone went off in her hand, startling her. She gave her phone a confused look. It was her store's number. Was she in trouble for leaving early? She wasn't on the schedule for tonight, was she? Did someone mess up her schedule? Was she an hour late for work? She sort of hoped Scott was calling to fire her as she answered the phone. "Hello?"

Scott's irksome voice resounded on the other end, "Hi Eden, I hate to bug you on your night off, especially since the events of last night. I hope you are well. Anyway. The reason I am calling...I'm concerned that Journey and Jayse may have their schedules mixed up. You see, I heard from your coworkers that you all are quite close and spend a lot of time together. They don't happen to be with you, do they?"

"No...do you mean that they are 'no call, no show' tonight?" The pit in her stomach deepened into an abyss of anxiety as her nerves began to fray.

"I called both their phones. I called to see if they were visiting Kris and lost track of time. The hospital said they haven't seen them all day. They said Jayse comes by every day, but they haven't had a visitor except the cousin who is there now." Scott said, "I'm sure it is just a big misunderstanding, or they overslept, but if you reach them, please let them know that company policy states they have until the last hour of their shift to call and try to make this right, or they will be terminated. I hate to lose such good workers over a misunderstanding. Do you think you could swing by their place and see if they are around? I know you aren't under any obligation to check on them, but just as a friendly courtesy?" He sounded desperate. Night shift was already understaffed, and he would be two more people short.

"I'll go by and check on them." She managed to keep the panic out of her voice.

"Knew I could count on you! Enjoy your time off! See you Sunday night!" He called out before hanging up.

Eden mulled over her thoughts. Where could they be? Neither could risk their job right now by not calling in. Her body lurched into action. She got up and headed to the bedroom. She flipped the lights on and started calling Anaiah's name as she dressed in her jeans and a t-shirt. She could wear the gun belt with her jeans.

"Anaiah, get up!" She called out again while putting on the belt.

He bolted upright in bed. "What's happened? What's wrong?"

She told him about the phone call. "Get up. Get your axes. Get your guns. Get whatever you need. We are going." She said with calm authority.

"Yes, ma'am." He jumped up and slid on his jeans and boots. He loaded his belt up with a pistol on one hip and his axes in leather holders on his other. He threw extra gun bags and ammo in his backpack along with spell components, healing and strength potions and the book of Seraphi. She packed her bag in the same way. She threw Lila's phone in and texted Sean to tell him what they were up to. A police presence might not be warranted, but it could be handy.

Anaiah drove them towards the RV park. Eden called both Jayse and Journey's phones multiple times to no avail. She shoved down her useless panic. They had seen them, safe and sound at Journey's that morning when they performed the protection ritual. She wondered if the ritual was somehow to blame. If she had doomed her human friends with a spell not intended for them to use. As they pulled up to the house, Eden felt something clench in her chest. "Something's not right. Do you feel it?"

"Yeah. Can't quite place it. Something evil is here. Or was here." Anaiah said. "Just don't feel right." Journey's car was still in the driveway. Kris and Jayse's truck had been totaled in the explosion, so Journey's car was the only means of transportation. *They really should still be here.* The house was dark. It was approaching midnight. If they were in there and awake, it would have lit up her apartment.

"Let's go up and see if they're here. Maybe they overslept and we are overreacting." She drew her gun anyway. Anaiah did the same. He left the car running, the headlights lighting the way to the stairs. It was then that Eden noticed the keys dangling from the car door as she approached. Her stomach lurched. "Shit." She said under her breath and pointed it out.

"Let's sweep the perimeter first down here. Hate to say it, but this doesn't look good." Anaiah circled around the car, giving it a wide berth. He took out a small flashlight and aimed it at the perimeter of the car. Eden's chest tightened.

"Stop. Somethings up with the car. Don't get closer." She pulled out her phone and turned on the flashlight. She put her phone in her left hand and held on to her gun with her right. She shined it a few feet around the car and barely noticed the circle of salt and chalk around the car. "Anaiah, look…in front of your foot. See the circle?" He squatted down and shined his light at a lower angle. She noticed the symbols then. Each was drawn onto the driveway with little burnt piles next to each.

"A trap." Anaiah read the daemonic symbols. "Weaken, Subdue, Sleep…these are meant to knock nephilim out. What would it do to two humans for Christ's sake?" He sounded horrified.

"Let's check upstairs for good measure, but they got grabbed by Adam, right? That's what we are thinking." She didn't cry. The tears didn't even form in her eyes, but her chest ached as she felt herself shaking with rage.

"Yeah. I'm sorry, baby. We better call Sean too." He put his flashlight away and pulled out his phone.

"I texted him, but we should let him know what we found." She checked her phone for any response. She swiped open the app and her heart sank.

"I have a message from Journey. It's just a dropped pin for a location." She pulled it up on the map on her phone. It brought up a listing for a business that was now permanently closed a few miles down one of the smaller highways out of town. She clicked on the photos.

"Anaiah…" She gasped as he looked over her shoulder.

"It's the warehouse. From our visions." He said breathlessly, the shock taking the breath from him.

"That's where he took them." Hot angry tears ran unbidden down her cheeks.

"Who's this?" Anaiah nodded to a car's headlights heading up the driveway toward them. Anaiah stepped between her and the car, blocking her from view. He held his gun in front of him toward the ground. Red, blue, and white lights flickered at them from the roof of the car for a moment and then shut off. "Sean." He let out a relieved sigh.

She holstered her gun and wiped her eyes. She walked toward the approaching car right behind Anaiah. He kept his weapon out but his tense shoulders relaxed slightly. The car parked and Sean emerged.

"Tried to aim the dash cam away from you two, but maybe go ahead and put that shit away before approaching my car." Anaiah holstered his gun and pointed to the other side of his car away from the patrol car.

"We haven't checked upstairs in the apartment yet, but I'm pretty sure we ain't finding anything up there. It's secure with the spell on it. They came down for work and he trapped them." Anaiah said to Sean when he came to meet them by the car.

"What do you mean trapped?"

"With rituals in a circle around the car, meant to knock them out…Well, I think they were meant to knock us, nephilim, out. Strong enough it gives us the heebie-jeebies to be near it. You feel it?" Anaiah asked.

"Yeah, it feels like bad juju. I want to run from it." Sean looked toward the circle.

"I think that's the tea we drink. My chest got tight, like I was about to have a panic attack. Like before, when my tattoos shocked Lila. It's the spell telling us to get back." She added. "Sean, I got a text from Journey, just a location. But this place. We both had bad visions…they were at this place."

"Oh, you mean the ones where you both saw the other one die at the hands of a different psycho? He told me." Sean nodded at Anaiah. "Yeah, so that building is fucking not the place for either of you to go tonight."

"You were there." Anaiah said quietly. "You were barely able to walk, but you were there. You tried to get to her."

"You're dreaming about me and not telling me? Sexy." Sean said flatly. His joke didn't have its intended effect of lightening the mood.

"We don't know why he took them. We don't know if this is a trap, but I drug them into this. This is on me. I need to get them back." Eden looked between the two of them.

"You said when he blew up the house, that Kris wasn't his intended target. Maybe Journey was? Her parents and grandparents were some weirdo hippies. Maybe she has some weird witch blood or something that he needs for a ritual. He killed your baby sister for a ritual." Anaiah said somberly.

"He what?" Sean said. "You failed to mention a baby getting murdered?"

Eden turned to Sean with pleading eyes. "The accident with Cole and Loretta. He did a ritual in the field near it, the ground was soaked in her blood. We didn't have any solid proof that tied him to any of it for you to pursue. Besides, there's probably no record of her birth or death. There wasn't one for mine until after I was an adult."

"I looked into your parents. They have another kid, alright. Sarah. She's like two and a half. You're telling me that she's dead and they haven't reported it to anyone?" Sean looked at her incredulously.

"I had a vision. Adam killed her. Sean, we were standing on her dried blood when I saw it." She shook her head.

"Either your vision was wrong or they're hiding it." Sean stared at Eden. "I just looked into them a couple of weeks ago. That accident was like, what, two or three months ago? She'd have been dead before that. No missing child report or anything." He shook his head.

"Sean, come look around this thing with me. See what else you can pick up. Make sure we aren't going in there blind." Anaiah said.

"So, we are just walking into the death trap?" Sean said.

"Probably." Eden set her jaw. "Because I'm going after them. Anaiah will follow, and you won't let him go in after me alone. That sums it up?"

"Yeah, just about." Anaiah looked her over, seeing her determination, and began pulling out his flashlight again. They walked the perimeter of the ring. Sean noted the patterns of how they fell; Jayse and Journey's locations, based on the patterns in the dirt. He noted two different shoe patterns, so two people drug their incapacitated bodies to another car, parked on the other side of her apartment. He traced all the little tracks back to where it drove off.

"You have your spell shit on you?" Sean asked Anaiah.

"Yeah."

"Well, start grabbing it, we are gonna do a wisdom ritual before we go running in there." Sean reached into his squad car for his backpack. He pulled out the book and came back around where they were on the other side of both of their cars. Eden shone her light on it and began reading off spell components.

Anaiah made a little pile on the ground as she started the incantation. She handed it off to Sean, who read off the next section while she added components to the pile. Anaiah read the last section and Sean pulled out his pocketknife pricking his finger and squeezing a few drops over the last two components. Eden held her left hand out and he repeated it with her hand. Anaiah approached and held out his left hand, never wavering from reading the enochian script on the page. Sean added birch and hemp twine bundles with their drops of blood. They all three read in unison the final two lines of the spell. The smoke began to rise as the elements of the spell were consumed and turned to glowing gold smoke that rose in three tendrils.

"This part's my favorite," Sean said sarcastically as the tendrils lashed forward and up their noses. Eden felt hot pressure rising in her head as if the smoke boiled her brain. Her vision flashed white and then black. She rubbed her eyes trying to get her vision to clear. She couldn't see anything when she opened her eyes. She started to worry. Had they blinded themselves? Then she saw a dim glow in the distance. A figure approached in the dark, backlit by the soft glowing light. Dark billowing shapes loomed in the darkness around her.

"Our time will come, brothers." The voice sent ice skittering down her spine. *Azazel.* "I've been plotting, fighting, and fucking my way through this god forsaken world. Soon, the doors will spring wide for you to consume the earth. You were wise to follow me. You will join me in our new paradise. When the blade is mine, I will slay the children of heaven and their Gregori fathers and mothers. Then I will loose the chains of iron, of silver, and of gold; set Lucifer and Belial free. Each will take for ourselves a realm and shackle heaven's armies to be our slaves under Lucifer's command. I'll take this world, cleanse it of the human blight and rot where only our demons, cambion and nephas may live. Hell shall fall to Belial, and he will use its mechanisms on the souls we reap for him to fuel infernal fires. We are so very close. The nephilim are gathering and they are lambs for the slaughter. I've claimed as many as I can, leading them astray, binding their allegiance to myself. You may taste their souls when the time comes to bleed them dry but leave death's daughters to me. I have a special gift for them. They will be the first to bear my new children." Eden felt her blood go cold. *No, he will not touch me. Never again.* "We need only wait, for our time is near."

His voice echoed as she was cast into darkness followed by blinding light. When her vision cleared, she shivered, her skin felt cold and clammy. Her stomach turned and she retched onto the dirt. She felt Anaiah's warm hands reach down and pull her long curly hair back out of the way. She heaved over and over again until the small amount of food she had consumed was well and truly gone.

"What did you see?" Sean quietly asked Anaiah.

"The demon…talking to his followers. He's the one who came for her. Now we know why." Anaiah's voice was full of quiet fury.

"I saw the same, I think. Those words he used…" Sean said. Eden wiped her mouth with her hand and took the water bottle Anaiah offered from his backpack to rinse her mouth. She wiped her tears away before swishing the water in her mouth.

"Nephas, though?" Anaiah said.

"It means abomination in medieval Latin." Sean's eyes went wide with realization of his own knowledge.

"They are the half demon, half nephilim babies he wants me to have." Eden spat on the ground in front of them. "And I will cut off his demon dick with the angelus blade before I let him do that to me." Her stomach tried to lurch again. She stood straight, fighting it, refusing to bend to it.

"Death delivers souls to heaven and hell alike." Sean pondered. "Maybe that's why he feels like you are more…compatible with him to make abomination babies."

"If we never use the term abomination babies ever again, I would be okay with that." Eden rubbed her face. "He had plenty of opportunities to try in the eight months I was dating him as Cole. Why now?"

"I don't know the answer to that. I feel like we are skimming over something here. He said, 'death's daughters' not 'daughter.' You have sisters." Sean pointed out. "Maybe he's gathering a bunch of you. Maybe he needs the blade first for whatever reason."

"He's not getting the blade, and he's sure as hell not getting Eden. We are going to kill him." Anaiah said in a dark, dangerous voice.

"We need the blade for that." Sean said.

"Pretty sure I can hurt him with these." Anaiah placed a hand on an axe. "Iron can hurt them. This is iron carved with Enochian protection. Bet these don't tickle when I take them to his flesh."

"Ok. So, we are going in, guns blazing then?" Sean asked incredulously.

"No." Eden shook her head. "Send me in first. Make him think I came alone. Announce my arrival. While you two sneak in."

"Hate that plan." Anaiah crossed his arms.

"I like it." Sean retorted. "It's dangerous, but not any more dangerous than us all busting in at once. She may be able to distract them. Give us an advantage. Oh, shit...here. Look. Cloaking ritual for hiding from detection of both heaven and hell. We can do this one. Me and you. Leave her open for him to find. And we sneak in."

"You don't have a better plan and we are burning time here." Eden looked at Anaiah. "Trust me. Trust that I can do this. Trust that I won't make the one mistake that'll kill me."

"I trust you. It's never been a matter of trusting you." He stepped in front of her. "I can't trust what I will do if something happens to you. The lines I will cross to keep you safe." He lifted her chin and kissed her hard. When he pulled back, he stared into her eyes like it may be the last time he did so. "Fine, lets fucking do it." He sighed.

She pulled components from her bag as Sean read them out. "I don't have the raven feather." She paused.

"I do." Anaiah pulled one from his bag. "That's the last thing?"

"Besides a few strands of our hair." Sean added. Eden walked over to Sean, grabbed a small section of hair, and tugged, pulling them free. "Shit. Do you enjoy causing me pain?"

"Just trying to get on with this. We still have a twenty-minute drive." She said, "Here, put these in your bag." She pulled out a strength, far sight and health potion for him. She stuffed a small vial of each into her pocket before Anaiah pulled free several strands of his hair, handing them to her.

"Okay, let's start." Sean began to read the ritual with Eden handing him and Anaiah components as they went. She shone a flashlight on the page for them to read and on the pile to help them see where to place the components as they went. After it was done both men were coated in a fine silvery mist. As the mist melted over them, Eden felt the absence of something she hadn't realized was there all along. A pull, like gravity on her body toward the earth. A rope tethering her to Anaiah and Sean that had once been taut and solid, had suddenly gone slack. She wanted to wrap her arms around herself, over the emptiness there. She pushed the dread she felt down. *Deal with one thing at a time.*

"Let's drive." She said as she threw her pack into Anaiah's passenger seat.

CHAPTER THIRTY-FOUR

Eden approached the warehouse with her bag on her back and a gun on her hip. She swallowed down her fear as she felt woefully unprepared to face any of this. She checked the front door of the warehouse office. Finding it unlocked, she slowly cracked the door open and slid inside. Her eyes needed a moment to adjust to the dark and dusty front office before she picked her way through, weaving around desks and chairs. She crept down a narrow hall. The faint red glow of an exit sign was the only illumination to be had. She reached a door labeled with a cautionary sign that read, 'hard hat area'. She turned the handle on the door carefully and pushed gently trying to control the amount of noise coming from the door.

Immediately, light from the well-lit warehouse poured in through the opening. She peeked around the partially open door to see the nearest corner of the building and nothing more. She wedged herself through the crack in the door and shimmied through it. She noted that she and the door were mostly hidden by several stacks of empty pallets. She crept up to the first stack of pallets and peered through the wooden slats. Her heart sank as she beheld Journey on her knees before Adam. Her bloodied hands were bound behind her. She'd fought him. Despite everything, that thought brought a small smile to Eden's lips.

Adam sneered at Journey as he broke Journey's phone in half. Either Journey had sent an emergency text with her bound bloody hands or Adam had sent it in hopes of luring her here. Adam backhanded Journey hard across her face, and Eden saw that she was gagged with a cloth. Adam flung the remnants of the phone against the wall with a loud thud. Journey had sent out the SOS text, then. Eden looked for several moments but couldn't see Jayse anywhere. *Shit.* She steadied herself to follow through with her plan.

She needed to be loud, to draw attention. She planned to announce herself boldly to flaunt the proverbial hand she laid out on the table. She backed up to the door, opening it widely. Then she kicked the door shut behind her with a loud clang. She had been an actress all those years, she had forgotten. Her role as the cowering helpless girl was played all too well. She'd begun to live it. These last several weeks had shown her that. She had needed to be small and insignificant then, but now, to step into the person she needed to be, it would no longer serve her to bend to others. Her outbursts of anger and showing backbone at the most inopportune times hadn't been some moral failing, but her true self, tiring of being shoved in a box. As she stepped forward, she pulled from within and let that bold brave woman out of the cage completely.

"You got my attention, big brother. I'm here! Are you happy?" She walked forward, between the pallets with hands held wide. Adam raised a flaming hand as she closed half the distance between them with confident swaggering steps. Adam looked even more unhinged than the last time she saw him. His cheeks were more hollow, eyes sunken with dark deep circles under them. The rake marks on his face were crusted with dark dried blood above his eyes. New lines of scratches ran down his face and opened them back up, likely courtesy of Journey. Adam turned his dark bloodshot eyes on Eden.

"Throw me your gun, or I'll burn her alive." Adam lowered his hand ever so slightly toward Journey. Eden had planned on that. She slowly dropped one hand down, drawing the gun out of the holster then turning it over in her hand. She leaned over and skidded the gun toward him. His hand drew away from Journey's head. As Eden approached, Jayse came into view, laying on the ground. She took her eyes off Adam for a fraction of a second to note that Jayse's wrists were bound to his ankles behind his back. He was gagged, but he was breathing.

"Let them go. You have my gun, and you have me now. You got what you wanted." She sneered. "Let them go, Adam."

"Don't come any closer." He called out. She halted with only twenty feet remaining between them.

"Adam, just let them go. Please." Eden held out pleading hands.

"No. This one is needed by my father," He motioned toward Journey and then pointed to Jayse, "that one, well, he is more of a spare, but he serves a purpose." Adam grinned broadly. "He keeps this one docile." His unhinged gaze turned to Eden. "My father wants you too. Are you ready to be reunited?" He looked insane, but almost excited.

"They're humans Adam, what could your father possibly need with them?" Eden hoped to keep him talking – to keep him distracted.

"That's where you're wrong, little sister. You can't see it, but I can. I can see them for what they really are. This one and his brother…branded by the seal of mercy and nature," He smirked at the shocked look on Eden's face before he continued," Their grandfather and Ariel, the angel of nature, produced a daughter, Miriam. Though Miriam was already a powerful nephilim, the angel of mercy, Zadkiel chose her to bear twin sons who would share the additional power between them. Miriam's blood boiled with heavenly fire as she bore her sons. Her father, the sad human sap that he was, could not bear to lose them as well, so he raised them as humans."

"You're crazy. Jayse and Kris aren't nephilim." Eden shook her head.

"You all just came together, instant friends, without some sort of divine bond? Jayson and Kristian Puram have less human blood than you do. Even with what our mother is. I didn't know when I visited their home that I would need the blood of four children of heaven for the blade. Otherwise, I would have taken it then."

"What do you mean 'what our mother is'?" Eden stared at him in disbelief.

"You really think that a normal human woman could bear my father's child and live? Not to mention carrying death's spawn after." He laughed. "So naive, little sister. Only one other has been able to carry your father's child and it ruined her mind. Didn't your sister, Journey, tell you?" She wanted to slap the smug look off his face.

"I am the daughter of death, Adam. I don't have sisters." She lied.

"Oh, but you do. My prophetess, Delila, gave me this before when we met, her first prophecy," He pulled from his pocket a piece of parchment and read, "'Death will bring forth two daughters, one of dark temperament and one of light. The younger will be sought out by those who had died; tied forever with the imprint of death and suffering left behind. The elder to be sought by the suffering and the dying. While her sister will see the souls of the dead, and feel the emotions of the living, the eldest will feel the pain, terror, and joy of the living and the dying in their touch. Their names will be called Journey and Eden. The oldest to be the keeper of the path to death in life, her name to be given to her mother to represent that path. The youngest to be the companion of those who arrived at death but could not pass into paradise, the mediator of peace to help them cross over. Her name was given to her mother to represent the peaceful destination on the other side. The garden where life began and where in death, it would return. The youngest will know pain and suffering at the hands of those who should have loved her. The oldest will know only pain and suffering whenever she laid her hands on those she loved. Each is destined to find the other, and when their blood is shed, it will bring the dawn of the apocalypse. The raging war between heaven and hell for all the earth."

As Adam spoke, Journey looked up, turning to look at Eden, over her left shoulder. Both looked into the other's eyes, seeing in them the truth. They'd instantly been drawn to each other. Each accepting the other as they were. Journey had been the first one Eden had been drawn to. The first person who made her feel as though she belonged. Eden realized that all the physical touch Journey shied from, all the emotions she would not confront were because she felt everyone's pain as her own but thought it was in fact her own. She didn't know any better. Physical touch was almost certainly painful for her. *But Jayse.* Jayse was Mercy's son. He soothed the pain she felt without even realizing it. Fear had made Journey fight for so long to not give in to her feelings for him. It was what fueled her reaction to Eden throwing them together. It would have been devastating to feel pain at his touch. Eden blinked as she had another realization; this is why Loretta had warned her...*Help them.* Not just the explosion, but here, now. With her dark brother. *Help her sister.*

"My father is here." Adam declared as a door at the back of the warehouse opened. Eden looked up, expecting Anaiah or Sean. She took a step back at the instant recognition of who walked through the door. The pain of seeing them like a knife slicing into her heart.

Eden's mother trailed slightly behind her father, as always. Elisabeth Grace deferred to her husband with her head down. Her brown curly locks were long and unadorned. Modest hair was as important to her as her modest dress. The blue dress itself was simple, covering her from her collar down to her wrists. The pleated skirt from the loose waist continued nearly to the floor. It was the same unflattering dress pattern that Eden remembered making. Her mother, who had never struck her in her father's presence, looked like the perfect gentle wife. Her gentle mother always allowed her father to discipline her when in his presence and reserved her violence to the moments when Eden was alone with her.

Eden had never pondered what it had been like to be her mother until this moment. To be groomed from childhood to be subservient and weak. To be abused by your husband and consider it God's will. What had it done to her mother to be the surrogate of both hell and heaven alike? Had that broken her in some way that made her violent in one moment but docile and doting the next? Eden had been groomed in a similar manner, but she had fought it. Her emotions fought what she felt even now. She didn't want to pity her mother. Didn't want to consider the cost for her. Instead, she forced herself to look at the man who had raised her.

Noah Grace was a figure of pure hatred to Eden. He wasn't a tall man, standing a few inches short of six feet. In her childhood, he seemed like a hulking monster over her. He wasn't thin, but he wasn't as heavy as their pastor had been. Just enough belly to hang over his belt. Unbidden, a memory of the sound that belt made when it unfastened and slid free slithered through her thoughts. She recalled vividly the snap of his leather belt as it would strike. Recalled the hand-made tooling on it. The crosses and scripture embossed into it would leave marks on her flesh. The scripture he would quote as he doled out his punishments. Eden knew now, in reading, in studying with

Anaiah, how Noah had twisted the words of a merciful and gracious God. How he had used them like a weapon against her.

He wore his matching brown dress shoes and his pressed wrangler jeans, meant to make him more personable. He appeared as someone the other cult members could trust with information they wouldn't normally trust any leader with. Still starched and pressed to keep them formal enough to show he still kept hard lines where it counted. He wore his simple blue pearl snap shirt with no tie but had a dark blue blazer over it. Every bit of him assembled to create the persona he took on with his followers. She looked finally to his face: his receding brown hairline, swept straight back, large nose with a hooked end. His blue eyes gave a slightly handsome appearance to those that didn't know the monster that lurked beneath.

Eden had never noticed how little she looked like him. How Adam and her both resembled their mother's softer, simple features, but had none of the prominence of their father's nose, jaw, or eyes. Of course, they wouldn't, but Eden wondered how had he taken that? Children who looked nothing like him. Children who disobeyed their father, their natural leader. She stared into his eyes and saw it then. Those were not the same unyielding eyes she had seen as a child. No. His blue eyes looked at her with a mild affection, curiosity, and a dangerous lust. *Azazel!*

"Eden, this is my father." Adam said as they approached him.

"No. No, he's not." She knew it for certain. She had noted the small differences in that sick feeling in her gut. Lila and Selah had been opposite sides of the same coin. They were Azazel's children. Adam was different. Different even from the girl who worked in Selah's shop, who shrank away from Eden. Selah's helper had sensed it then. *We were not the same.*

"Oh, the body he possesses is most definitely not OUR father. Noah Grace only had one true child. Isn't that right, mother?"

Elisabeth Grace looked up for the first time. She'd been addressed by a man and thus, required to respond. She looked to her husband who just smiled mildly, taking his spot by Adam's side. "Sarah...Sarah is with the Lord now." Her voice quivered.

"Elisabeth, dear. Hand me the weapon at Adam's feet." She heard her father's stern yet charismatic voice intone. She fought the urge to tremble with fear. She told herself that she was strong enough to fight back now. She would not cower for him like a defenseless little girl anymore. She held her chin higher. Her mother reached down and gingerly took the gun in her hand before she handed it to Noah. He turned it over in his hand, placing his finger over the trigger. He released the safety and pointed the gun at Elisabeth's face, pulling the trigger. It clicked as her mother flinched.

"Oh Eden." He turned to her with a face of disappointment. "It was going to be quick for poor Elisabeth. Her burden finally ended. But now, I have to do it the other way. And it's all your fault." His hand dropped the gun, clattering to the floor before it lurched out, grabbing her mother around the throat. He raised her off the floor Eden took a step forward without thinking. Her mother's choked off sobs rang in her ears.

"What do you want from me?" Eden yelled at him. "You want me to beg you for her life? I begged her for my own. I should want her to die. But..." she breathed raggedly as tears began to fall. "I don't. Take me. Stop all of this. Take me and we can go somewhere else away from all of them...and you can do whatever you want with me." She didn't want that either. She just wanted to get Journey, Jayse, Anaiah, and Sean as far away from there as possible. She didn't want to watch her mother die. Elisabeth turned fearful eyes on Eden as she turned a horrible shade of violet red. With a jerk of his arm, his face mirrored the movement as his hand gripped tighter with a sickening crunch. Eden felt sick as her mother went limp in his grasp.

"Don't lie to me. You wouldn't go with me willingly." He spat out. Azazel dropped Elisabeth's dead body from his grip. She fell at an awkward unnatural angle on the concrete floor. Adam flinched. *So, he wasn't entirely devoid of emotion.* Sadness was replaced with a simmering rage deep within Eden as the thought of another being added to this death toll. Seeing her brother's reaction, she thought of another tactic.

"Adam, who's your father, huh? Tell me his name" She sneered.

"My father is the king of hell, Eden. You know his name. You were raised in the faith. They call him the great enemy. But what did he do, really, but question God for judging us?" His eyes took on a fanatic's gleam.

"This asshole murdered your mother with his bare hands, just now. That doesn't seem evil to you?" She inclined her head to him.

"She..." he hesitated. "She deserved to die. For the suffering of her children. Children she was trusted with." He sneered back at her with renewed fervor.

"Eden wouldn't have come alone without a plan. The others should come for her soon, Adam, we must prepare." Azazel said in Noah's commanding tone. Adam turned and walked to the far end of the building, working at each entrance. Eden noted that he was drawing a smaller version of the trap he had snared Journey and Jayse with. She tried not to panic.

Azazel said in a low voice. "Don't worry, Eden. My experiments with you failed, but you were so young. Barely even developed." His lustful expression mixed with Noah's face made her skin crawl. Even though she knew she wasn't his daughter, she was raised by this man as his child. He continued, "We don't even know if you are barren... but if so, we are blessed with another sister to bear children for me as well. I'll keep trying, for your sake." He looked down at Journey as she glared hatefully up at him.

"You will not touch her. You will not touch me. We are not your whores." Eden spat out.

"So spirited now... much more than when we were together." Azazel smirked.

"Was the real Cole even in there when you were with me?" She had wondered. Was the soft side she occasionally saw an actual man trying to be good to her, trapped in his body with a demon?

He let out a deep dark laugh. It was odd to hear Azazel's too casual tone bleeding through her father's stern voice. "You think I would permanently possess a truck driver? How fucking pathetic is that? No. I went about my business building my army. Inhabiting other forms. I did like his thoughts, depraved as they were. He knew, because I knew, that you were still just a girl. He knew that you stayed out of fear, and he delighted in it." His eyes seemed to light up with a semblance of joy when he said, "In fact, those times where you saw what looked like love or comfort in him, it was ME offering you a reprieve. So, you would stay. I tried to find others that appealed to you. But after him, you were too broken. We had failed for so long. I didn't know if you could even give me a child." He shook his head in disapproval as he said, "Like the heavenly whore that you are, you opened right up for your nephilim didn't you? Even he hasn't managed to make anything grow in the wasteland of your womb. I hope your sister is a better breeding stock. She does look sturdier." He reached affectionately toward Journey's face. Journey snapped out and bit his hand through her gag, latching on to him with a vicious force.

"Fucking cow!" He slapped her across the face with his other hand. As Journey's head reeled with the impact, Eden took another step forward.

"Here's the deal, Azazel." Eden watched as Adam moved to another doorway and began working on the trap. Time was slipping away too quickly. "I have to wrap this up. My boys will be here soon, and I can't let them have all the fun tearing you to shreds. She reached behind her back, palming the small, curved knife Anaiah had given her. Azazel reached out a hand toward Jayse.

"Keep walking forward and I'll kill the little spare we have here. I already have all his brother's blood in those jars. He pointed to the glass bottles on the floor in front of Jayse. She recognized them from the hospital. The space around Kris's lungs had filled with fluid. They had used a tube with a needle attached to pull the fluid from his lungs into the bottle. They were vacuum sealed two-liter bottles. Had Adam gone to the hospital and drained Kris's blood into them? She heard Scott's voice in her memory. *The hospital said there had been no visitors except a cousin who was there right now.*

"Kris is gone." Her voice wavered as she spoke. Eden's heart was heavy. She wanted to cry, but more than that she wanted to make him pay for hurting Jayse like this.

"Problem with nephilim twins," Azazel began, "Is that they split the power. Both are weaker even with the extra angel blood of their grandmother. And any enemy of heaven will always consider one expendable. Plus, after you took one of mine with that nasty protection spell, I had to take one of yours to settle the score."

"So, you need us for our blood? You're gonna bleed me, save my sister for breeding? Then take blood from Anaiah and Sean to get the blade. That was your plan?"

"You see the problem isn't the lack of nephilim blood. I have nephilim at my disposal. Selah took care of that for me. I entranced her to believe that they were all wayward demon children. Without a home, without a good father to claim them like she had. She took them in, had them pledge loyalty to me and thus, cut their ties from heaven. She trained them to be my unwavering disciples. Thanks to you, the spell was broken. She cleansed herself after being near you and those bowls. That's why she ran. I lost a loyal daughter and a valuable teacher for my armies. But it's no matter. I'll track her down. I'll make her see the error of her ways and she will continue to do my bidding." He sneered. "But I'm getting off subject. Nephilim must bleed to bring me a great many things I desire. This blood, though, needs to be of a claimed child of heaven. Did you notice how your power grew when you claimed your parentage? Even before you began equipping yourself with rituals, you started to grow into your power. The blood is useless for obtaining the blade until they claim their heritage."

"How did you...with Kris? He was half dead, kept alive by machines." She asked through gritted teeth.

"Through dreams. I told him what he was before I took out the tube and with his dying breaths had him claim what was his. After, I bled him dry," His evil grin sent a chill down her spine. "How do you think I got my hands on the spell?" Journey's quiet sobs shattered Eden's heart. She noted that Jayse had gone still and was staring daggers at Azazel. If looks could kill, Azazel would have been dead from Jayse alone.

"I think I've heard enough," Eden snapped.

"You speak to me with such venom these days, babe. You would catch more flies with honey," Azazel smirked arrogantly at her.

"I'd catch a great deal more with your hollowed out carcass, so what's your fucking point?" Eden sneered back.

"Fiery little bitch you turned out to be." He spat at her then smirked. "I'm going to enjoy breaking you of that." White hot anger boiled inside Eden.

She called out to her brother, "Adam! You're being played. You think THIS is your father? Azazel is the name of the demon here. He isn't your father. He's just using you to get what he wants. This prick was Lila's father and she played you too. I've got her phone to prove it." She yelled. Adam turned toward her suddenly from across the warehouse.

"It can't be true." Adam called out. "How did you get Lila's phone? Where is she?" Eden realized that Adam didn't know about Lila's death yet.

"I have her phone because the protection spell on my house killed her. Your buddy here knew that, but you didn't?" Eden called out. "Come ask him about it. Or better yet, try to call your father. Last I heard, Lucifer was in chains." The flash of recognition was momentary across Azazel's face.

"Now look what you are going to make me do." Azazel said slowly, clicking his tongue in disapproval. He turned towards a quickly approaching Adam. "What can I say? Is it really my fault that you are such a fool? So easily swayed. My daughter offered you the world on a platter and you fell for it. Believed you had earned it. Earned favor with your father? Lucifer is in chains that I made!" He said angrily to Adam. "Lila hated your weakness, but you served your purpose. She wanted to be the one to end your miserable life, but since she's gone. I'll do it myself."

Adam came rushing forward with his hands blazing. Azazel grabbed his wrists and twisted, snapping his arm. Adam burned through Azazel's sleeve before that wrist was also grabbed and just as easily broken. Azazel held fast to them as he pulled Adam forward, off balance, and stomped on the inner side of his knee, snapping it at an awkward painful angle. As Adam screamed, Eden dashed toward Journey and Jayse. She quickly cut their bonds. She whispered the name of their father into Journey's ear.

"Claim it, now!" Eden looked to Jayse. He nodded in understanding as Journey claimed Death as her father. Lightning struck through the metal roof, splitting it open, landing feet from the demon. *Close, but not close enough.* Eden sent up a silent prayer for better aim as Jayse called out Ariel's and Zadkiel's name. As he spoke the names, twin bolts of lightning struck at Azazel's feet. He dropped to the ground. A clatter rang out as a large stack of pallets fell over his body. Eden stared in disbelief. Standing over the rubble piled atop the demon, was a shimmering ghost. Tears ran down her face as Kris' spirit looked at her then to the large metal doors on the side of the room. She followed his line of sight wondering what he saw there. Suddenly, it burst inward with Sean's squad car plowing through.

"Jesus Christ!" Jayse yelled out. Eden began unpacking things from her bag and Jayse looked at her like she was crazy.

"He's down, but I haven't checked to see if he's dead." She called out as Anaiah and Sean exited the car with guns drawn. Eden pointed to where the demon had fallen. "Get the components over here, we are doing this shit now. Before he gets back up."

"What about the last nephilim?" Anaiah called out but began moving in her direction.

"Apparently, we are both fucking blind. I've been hanging out with heaven's children all along." Eden called out. Anaiah crossed the warehouse to her as Sean kept his gun trained on Azazel's unmoving body. "Journey is death's other daughter. Jayse and Kris are nephilim too," She spoke as she pulled the spell components out, looking over Anaiah's scroll. Anaiah attempted to check Journey's bleeding bruised face, but she brushed him off.

"All of your friends are part angel?" Sean called out. "That's a little weird."

"Sean, we can discuss this later. Give Journey the gun. We need you for this one. It has to be us and one of the twins." She glanced up and Kris' spirit was standing among them. He nodded to her gravely. "We will use Kris's blood. He doesn't want it to be for nothing. Give Jayse your gun." Anaiah realized what she was saying and nodded. Sean handed his gun to Journey as Jayse took Anaiah's.

"Keep your arms steady and locked if you fire that. Point it at the evil prick and squeeze the trigger." Sean began his rapid-fire gun lesson.

"I know how to use a gun." Journey scoffed.

"Your parents are hippies," Sean squinted at her.

"Hippies who don't trust the government. We all learned to shoot. I taught him." She nodded to Jayse. Jayse handled the gun like he knew what he was doing. Eden turned her attention to reading off the spell and placing cedar cuttings in a cross on the ground. She took the ground mustard and sprinkled it next as she read the next line. Anaiah took the next part, adding the femur bones of a young rat. He pulled out three different herbs and began chanting while adding them to the pile in a circular motion. Sean took over and added his ingredients and enochian chants. A shimmering ghostly hand covered Eden's as she added the fourth part which would have been his. Tears fell as she and Kris recited together. She took the knife and cut her arm next to her enochian scars. She let the blood drip over the entire pile of components, and it began to smolder. Anaiah went next, slicing his left arm as well. The smoke rose higher. Sean added his blood to the small fire. Eden grabbed a bottle from Kris's sacrifice and used the knife to pop off a cap. Anaiah read the final lines of the incantation as she poured Kris' blood on the fire, the flames growing as tall as her. She stepped back. The flames grew hotter, threatening to burn her and the others. As they backed away, the flames grew white hot before they disappeared. In its place was the bone blade. They stared at it in awe.

"Guys..." Jayse spoke up. The pallets shifted as Jayse stepped back. Journey didn't hesitate, she opened fire on the corpse that was starting to move. Sean reached down and grabbed the blade, heading toward the broken form rising on shattered limbs. With a sickening 'pop' the body of Noah Grace split apart, blood flooded around the body, and the thick billowy smoke formed into a creature of nightmares as Azazel took form. They all staggered back.

"I do love making an entrance. Oh, the screams that came from your friend Bobby when I did this to him. Delightful." Azazel's gravelly voice was like a chorus of demons singing a discordant melody as he spoke to Sean. Anaiah was already in motion, running with one axe already flying. Azazel popped out of existence for a moment and reappeared behind Sean. Sean attempted to whirl with the sword, but Azazel slashed through his shoulder with his claws. As the claws dug into his shoulder, his enochian scars flared to life. Sean yelled out as the wounds began to close behind the claws leaving his shoulder. Azazel reached for the blade, but Sean drove his bloody, rapidly healing shoulder into Azazel's chest, knocking him backward and into Anaiah's axe. Anaiah's axe swung through a black hooked wing, ripping it open as black blood poured out of it.

A howling inhuman roar ripped from Azazel's maw. He was still moving and slashing nearly faster than Eden's eyes could track. Everywhere Anaiah or Sean slashed, he was dodging in another direction, narrowly avoiding them. The three of them were a blur of movement around the warehouse, dodging and slicing at each other with sword, axe, and claws. Azazel caught Anaiah across the chest with a glancing claw strike. His tattoo flared and the claw seemed to scrape against metal, the way it shrieked at the collision. Anaiah's shirt was shredded but his skin was unmarked.

Azazel teleported with a pop again, reappearing in front of Jayse and striking his chest with a claw. Jayse crumpled to the floor, bleeding and gasping. Azazel popped again and reappeared behind Eden. She gripped her small blade and whirled. She feigned as if she had a blade in her left hand as she whirled around in a windmill motion. Azazel took the bait and raised his clawed hands. Eden finished her attack with her right hand stabbing in an upward motion just under his protruding ribs, hoping to God that the demon had a lung to puncture. He let out a howling screech as the iron blade warded with enochian protection pierced through him. She shoved the blade further in, twisting as she screamed. Black blood coated her hand. His taloned claw-hand gripped her arm as Anaiah charged toward them. Azazel jerked her hand and the knife free of his chest.

His wings flapped as he pulled his legs up and kicked her forcefully in the chest. She felt the lightning crackle within her as she flew backward, but the impact knocked the breath from her. She writhed on the floor struggling to breathe. She was sure her ribs on her right side were broken from the searing pain and tightness she felt on that side of her chest. Gasping, she fought to get the air in to open that lung. She looked up to see Sean and the beast fighting with the blade in Sean's hand. Anaiah kneeled next to her with a bag in his hand. He grabbed a large needle and told her to look away as he pulled her shirt up and felt between her ribs.

"You have a collapsed lung. Gotta re-inflate it." He slid the needle between her ribs, and she felt a small relief start to spread as she could suddenly start breathing and feel her chest expand again. Her attention was drawn to Sean as he cried out. Azazel had picked him up by his taloned claw-feet. Eden gaped helplessly as Sean was flung across the warehouse, striking a pile of pallets with a horrible crunching sound.

"Kill him. Now." She breathed raggedly at Anaiah in desperation. He hesitated, torn between helping her and running after the demon. "GO!" She yelled.

Anaiah bolted toward Azazel, axes in both hands once again. He feigned left and then brought an axe down from the right, catching the demon in his shoulder. The axe lodged there, and Anaiah struggled to try to free it for a fraction of a second before he slashed out quickly again with the other. Eden struggled to make it to her knees, trying to reach her feet. Anaiah lost the second axe, knocked from his hand as he grappled with Azazel.

Anaiah gripped the first axe with his left hand, keeping the monster close as she saw him unleash himself as if he was a feral beast. His fist pummeled the demon over and over. If Azazel were human, the demon's face would be a bloody pulp. As it stood, he looked mostly annoyed if not bloodied. Anaiah was hurting him, the sound of bone snapping and blood spurting told her that, but it wasn't enough. Azazel was still stronger. His claw grasped the axe in his shoulder. She saw the smoldering of his hand meeting the enochian etched iron. And yet, he still ripped it free. Twisting Anaiah in his arms, he gripped Anaiah against him, facing Eden.

Anaiah and Azazel struggled against each other, the axe held in both of Anaiah's hands pushing it away from his neck and Azazel slowly inching it forward. Eden fought against her still stunned body to move toward him as the blade of the axe jumped up the final few inches toward his exposed neck veins as Anaiah struggled against it.

Eden felt her chest tighten as she screamed out with a thunderous "NO!" Her voice was a shrieking thunderous nightmare that seemed to shake the foundation of the building around her. From her outstretched hand a bolt of silver black death shot toward Azazel. It seared through his left shoulder. A gaping wound oozed black blood with a greenish tinge to it. Azazel dropped both Anaiah and the axe from his grip. Eden's eyes were focused entirely on Anaiah as he fell to the ground. A sob of relief ripped through her when he tried to push himself back up. Azazel gripped his injured shoulder and stumbled toward where Sean lay, unmoving on the floor. Journey was there in an instant, blocking Azazel from Sean's lifeless form as she raised the blade.

"Not another step, cunt waffle." Journey called out. Azazel roared at her and readied to strike. Journey slashed at him wildly. Azazel dodged her swipe and slashed her arm. Journey didn't have any heavenly protection and the claws tore through her arm like a hot knife through butter. As blood poured from the gashes in Journey's arm, the blade fell from her hands. Eden screamed and attempted to throw more lightning at him, but nothing happened. She pushed herself to her feet and forced herself forward.

Azazel gripped the sword in his taloned hand, turning from Journey and heading toward Anaiah as he struggled to stand. Eden threw herself forward as Azazel stabbed the sword straight at Anaiah's back. The lightning flared to life as she flung out her arm, and shot directly at Azazel's chest, toward what she hoped was his black demon heart. Before it struck, he popped out of existence, mid-thrust. The lightning struck a pile of pallets and burst into flames. Eden spun around, looking for where he reappeared. All she saw were her friends, bleeding, broken on the ground and a now roaring pallet fire.

Anaiah looked up at her as his neck wound finished closing. She didn't drop her guard. She looked around again. Jayse lay bleeding on the floor near the police cruiser. Journey was crouched by Sean's lifeless body, wrapping her arm with her shirt trying to staunch the bleeding. Eden didn't know where to run to first.

"Go to Sean and Journey," she said to Anaiah as he pushed himself all the way to standing. She moved toward Jayse as quickly as she could, limping as she went, realizing that something felt broken in her pelvis. Jayse was lying in a small pool of his blood and trying to hold his hands over his bleeding chest. He must be in shock. His breathing was shallow and rapid in a way that terrified Eden. She pulled the healing vial from her pocket and poured it in his mouth. He sputtered a bit, but swallowed it. She pulled her shirt over her head and applied pressure to the large gash in his chest. She prayed desperately, to angels or God, she did not know, but she needed him to be okay. Within a minute, his breathing became more regular. She lifted the shirt and watched in awe as the skin knit itself back together rapidly.

"Oh, thank God." She cried.

Journey hurried toward them as her arm was stitching itself together into pink scars, calling out to Jayse. Eden looked past Journey and felt her heart shatter as Anaiah pounded out chest compressions on Sean. Eden pushed herself to dash to his side.

"Give him two breaths when I say go. Big breaths. Let the chest rise and fall, give it slow." He called out. "Now." He stopped compressions. She gave Sean two breaths into his mouth while pinching his nose closed. Anaiah checked for a pulse and resumed compressions. "He's not getting full rise with the breaths. I think he collapsed his lung like you did, but we didn't get to him fast enough, so his heart arrested. Run, get my kit!" He paused his compressions to deliver breaths to him and resumed. She shuffled to grab the kit and as she tried to run back, she silently prayed. '*Azrael, Father, Help me! Don't take him. Not yet. Please!*'

'Daughter of heaven, you do not control life and death.' She heard his voice rumble through her mind.

'No, but you do.' She pleaded. *'Don't take him! Please!'*

'Why should I grant him another chance at life when he failed his task?' Her father asked her.

'Because he died trying! He fought as hard as he could! You give us so little and want us to wage a war against demons! GIVE ME THIS! GIVE ME HIM! He will help me figure out how to stop Azazel!' She wanted to scream. She fell at Anaiah's side, grabbing out the needles he instructed her to use to decompress his lungs. She found the area between the ribs and slid the needle in. She pulled the needle, leaving the plastic catheter inside like Anaiah had done with her. Anaiah stopped and gave breaths.

"You do compressions, I am going to do this." He grabbed the other needle and inserted it as she pushed against Sean's chest with all the force she could muster. Counting out loud like Anaiah had. She watched as Anaiah pushed past the fear, dread, and grief she felt rolling off him and gave two breaths when she reached thirty. Anaiah checked Sean's pulse and cursed. Tears rolled down his face. "We got a pulse, but it's fast and thready. Keep going." She began again. Anaiah's hands trembled as he wiped his tears from his face and sobbed.

Eden pushed her arms hard and fast as she prayed, *'Please, Father. Help me!'*

She felt her tattoos sputter and sizzle with the current. The charge built inside her chest as Anaiah stared at her wide eyed.

"Stay back." She breathed out as her hair began to float up with static, crackling.

"Let it be done, in my name." Her voice mixed with her angelic father's voice reverberated through the room as the current went from her and into Sean's chest. Anaiah fell backward, covering his eyes from the brilliant light. Eden was pushed back from the force of the bolt. She scrambled forward looking at Sean as he drew in a deep shuddering breath.

"Thank you." She breathed out, "Thank you, thank you, father." As the tears streamed down her face as Sean began to come back to consciousness.

Anaiah was crying, pulling her up with him, into his arms. "You did it, baby."

"Fucking ouch." Sean muttered.

"Healing potion." Journey dropped a bottle in her hand. Eden forced Sean to drink it. Eden looked around to assess the damage. How were they going to explain all of this? A moment later, Sean sat up.

CHAPTER THIRTY-FIVE

E den surveyed the warehouse. Three dead bodies. Her mother and
brother both had suffered broken necks at the hand of Azazel in
Noah Grace's body. Noah's body lay completely eviscerated about
fifty feet from her. She was surprised to find she didn't feel nauseated
at the sight of it. Too many questions needed answering for Sean to just make
up some story of how they all ended up here. Anaiah was already on
probation. She gasped when she remembered that Kris' body was in a hospital
bed, back in town. Their blood was all over this warehouse. This would take
hours to cover up and even then, they might find something to link them to
the scene.

"How are we going to explain..." Eden wondered out loud.

"We are going to have to burn all this shit." Sean stood as he pulled off
the remainder of his ruined shirt over his head and threw it in the cruiser.

"What do you mean?" Eden gaped at him.

"Yeah. Unless Sean can think of a convincing story in which he responded
to an off the books call to Journey's house. Turned off his patrol car camera,
damaged the car by charging into a barn twenty miles away, and found all
these dead people. We gotta burn it all." Anaiah spoke up.

"Except the cruiser. That's going to be tricky, but I may be able to figure it
out. It's mostly scratches. No big damage. Could say I pursued a subject
fleeing the RV park and went through a fence. "

"That could work." Anaiah said.

"Excuse me? Are we discussing covering up the deaths of the people who
tried to murder us? Because if so, we have ideas." Jayse chimed in. Journey
pointed to the back of the warehouse.

"That's diesel." Journey pointed at a big red tank with a small pump attached to it. "Like a thousand gallons of ruby red. Also, we got a trashed RV on the back of the lot we can claim you ran into pursuing a suspect."

"There are desks and wooden chairs in the office for the fire. Anaiah?" Eden suggested.

Anaiah jogged into the office and came back with several chairs stacked together. He on the return trip, he bear hugging a giant wooden desk. Eden grinned at the site but felt woozy on her feet.

"Drink one of those potions, bitch." Journey handed her one from Eden's own bag. Journey made Eden sit back down while she drank it. Eden slowly felt her pain ease up in her pelvis and her back. Jayse helped Sean move Adam's body to the middle of the burn pile which they centered over the remains of Noah in the middle of the room. Eden looked away as they moved her mother's body. She helped Anaiah lay wooden pallets against all the walls to help the insulation inside them catch fire.

As Sean moved his patrol car, they doused the entire room in red diesel fuel. Eden was grateful for Sean's gifts and his obsession with spy movies. Sean set the old-style air-conditioning thermostat up to allow them to get a good distance away before it made a spark and created an explosion. He claimed it would work, and that was good enough for Eden.

Anaiah, Journey, and Jayse loaded up in Anaiah's car. Eden felt someone should ride with Sean since he had a recent near-death experience and jumped into his front seat.

"You got another shirt in that bag? Or are we both riding off into the night half-naked?" Sean laughed as he started the cruiser.

"We're all shirtless at this point. I'm not even wearing a cute bra." She looked down at her plain black bra and blood-stained jeans. "I'll be fine 'til I shower at home." She sighed. "What about you? You have extra clothes on you?"

"No cute bra for me either, but I do keep an extra uniform in the trunk." He pulled out of the driveway and onto the dirt road. "Surprised Parker let you ride with me. Shouldn't y'all be making out and thanking God you're both alive?"

"Oh, that will come later. Told him to get my sister home safe, and I'd make sure his brother was okay." She winked at him. "Plus, I'm giving Jayse space to mourn Kris. I'm afraid he's gonna go back to blaming me. He's going to lose it when I tell him Kris' spirit was with us during the ritual for the blade."

"You saved our asses in there. He'll come around." Sean said in a low voice. "Maybe Kris will come back around too. You can talk to him for Jayse."

"Not sure how to feel about that. I usually try to convince spirits to move on. What does it say about me that I want him to stay even if it's just some sort of spooky half-life?" She shook her head.

"That you care enough to be a little selfish about him." He cleared his throat. "Thanks for bringing me back. Glad I don't have to be part of the spooky crew with Kris."

"Anaiah told you?" She whispered, fighting the urge to cry. The adrenaline had kept her moving and without too much emotion, but she felt like the dam was about to break.

"I thought for sure I was dead. Did you have to make some deal with your dad?" *Fucking over observant Sean.*

"He helped. I might have guilt tripped an angel for you." She shrugged. "Gotta figure out how to make my superpowers work when I want them to."

"I owe you." Sean swallowed hard.

"You don't owe me shit. You're our brother. You're one of us. I already lost one friend today…a brother. I don't mean Adam. Kris was my brother, and I wasn't losing another. Fuck, I'm crying again." She wiped her eyes.

"No. None of that. My shift ends in a couple of hours. We can cry after too many drinks. Y'all get the 'we're alive' sex out of the way. I'm bringing the hard stuff." Sean gave her a grin.

"I'll do my best. We aren't exactly quick." She laughed.

"Skirt up, girl." He laughed. After chatting for a few more minutes, Sean donned his serious face and said, "I gotta call in to dispatch." Sean picked up his radio and described her brother, stating he was in pursuit near the RV park. He described the car her parents had parked near the warehouse. Near enough to get blown up as well, Eden recalled. Sean turned down some back roads and brought them out on the back side of the RV park. He drove through a bit of fence and ran into the crumbling RV that Journey had told him to hit. He called dispatch again. Asking for backup if possible due to wrecking his cruiser and the suspect was considered armed and dangerous. He got out of his cruiser, opened the trunk and pulled out a bag with extra uniform and changed. He stashed the rest in the trunk. Eden gave him a hug, told him to be safe, and to call them at the end of his shift before he came over, just in case.

She walked through the RV park with her backpack on, breathing deeply, glad to have breath in her lungs. It felt a little odd walking around an RV park at five in the morning in her bra, bloody jeans and backpack but she was beyond caring what anyone would think. Her phone rang, and Anaiah's smiling face popped up on the screen. She gave Anaiah the information about where she was in the park.

Jayse and Journey had missed several calls from work and the hospital. Anaiah told Eden that they were going to sort it out and adjust to the events of the evening on their own. Journey promised to call Eden and catch up later. After a few minutes of strolling, he pulled up next to her.

"Let's go home, sugar. You are walking around this park looking like you belong in Mad Max." He said as she got in the car. She smiled over at him.

"No idea what that is, but let's go home." She leaned against his arm as he drove them home. "I need a shower, a drink, and backrub that ends in sex."

"Can do, baby. Can we throw something to eat in the mix? 'Cause I'm starving." Anaiah said with his typical drawl.

"Of course, you are." She smiled up at him.

EPILOGUE

Sean

Sean filed the official police reports of Eden calling him to say her friend reported seeing Adam at the RV park. Chuck Atwood, the other officer who was called out to investigate an explosion half an hour after he had called in the suspect on the run, declared it murder-suicide scenario, teeth records indicated that Noah, Elisabeth, and Adam Grace all died twenty miles north of town on a property Adam was leasing. Sean handed over a concise summary of what he had gathered on Adam and Lila, including notes he had made on Eden's file regarding inconsistencies with the Noah's story and leads to follow up on to the federal investigator. He had simply omitted anything that would bring more trouble to Eden's door. He gave them plenty to investigate and all of it painted her as the victim she was. He felt momentarily guilty about it, but remembered that Eden had sassed a celestial being into saving his miserable life. He owed her everything. Sean felt no guilt whatsoever about reminding them that Sarah Grace needed to be placed with a new family. He knew the truth of the matter but couldn't just tell the agent that she was dead at Adam's hand.

The federal investigation into the whereabouts of the toddler turned into a months-long investigation into the Saints on Earth Cult where numerous unmarked graves were found containing the bodies of children and young adults who either had been reported missing or as runaways by the account of their family. Sean was not shocked to learn that foul play was now suspected in the death of lead pastor Joseph White. Eden had tipped him off on that one as well. Of course, he had to bring her in for official questioning.

Sean had stood behind the one-sided mirror as Eden was questioned by state and federal authorities. Her alibi was backed by her boyfriend who stated they had been at home, then checked on some friends who also backed their story up. The conclusion of the investigation was that Adam had been psychotic and had planned to bring Eden, along with their parents to the warehouse to kill them after he killed, Bobby who was the boyfriend of the woman Adam loved. Sean wondered if he drew the conclusions out for them a little too easily. If they would find it all too convenient and turn on Eden again.

He was protective of his new sister, but it didn't stop him from teasing the hell out of her when news stories ran about the 'Saving Grace' of Eden's near miss with a tragic murder-suicide plot. Eden refused to personally comment to reporters and Sean delighted in watching her eventually lose patience with them. She hated the attention, but he and Anaiah were helping her move on.

Sean might have felt bad for the local hospital, but they had let a murderer into the room of a patient they were supposed to protect without checking his story out with Jayse. The death of Kristian Puram led to an in-depth investigation into the sudden power failure at the hospital. The hospital temporarily lost power when it was struck by lightning. The investigation ruled that it was the fault of several alarm errors and generator failures which resulted in Kris self-extubating and passing away.

Sean knew that the malpractice insurance payout that Jayse Puram received had weighed on Jayse heavily. On the one hand, it funded the dream that Kris and Jayse had shared. He was, with the help of Journey, opening a brew pub in town and rebuilding a home on the land his grandfather owned. On the other hand, no amount of money would ever bring Kris back, and Jayse only had the comfort of Eden telling him that Kris was there with him as he cut the ribbon and opened the doors of the pub. He was living the life that Kris and Jayse had dreamed of and as happy as it made him, Sean saw the pain behind his eyes when he thought no one else was looking.

Everyone had breathed a big sigh of relief as the investigations concluded, but Sean hadn't been able to let his guard down. Every waking moment, Sean knew his breath was borrowed. He knew that out there in the world, Azazel was lying in wait. Sean had always been intrigued by mysteries, but he couldn't unravel the puzzle before him. While the end of the investigations and the demise of Eden's evil brother gave some closure, his world just felt larger than ever before now. He had too many questions he wanted answers to, and his heavenly father wasn't keen on giving him anything beyond the book of Cherubi. Why did Raziel pick his drug addict mother to bear the son of an angel? How the hell did six children of heaven end up in Angelina, Texas with a population of eight thousand people? What were their next steps to win heaven's war? Why couldn't heaven fight its own battles? Each unanswered question drove Sean forward each day and he swore he would have his answers if he had to pry them out his own father's mouth.

Anaiah

very day that he woke up next to Eden felt like a miracle. He still couldn't believe over six months later that they had not heard anything from Azazel. Anaiah knew that meant very little in the grand scheme. The demon was still out there gathering soldiers, building armies, and making as many children to follow him as possible. The hammer would fall eventually.

Anaiah marveled at her as Eden drank her creamer with a little coffee dashed in it and studied for her upcoming test. He sat across from her at the dining room table of their little farmhouse. Anaiah was supposed to be studying about medieval weapons used to fight demons that he could make in his forge in the barn. Instead, he was taking a break and watching her.

"I can't concentrate if you are staring at me." She didn't look up from her laptop.

"I'm just thinking how lucky I am." He smiled and sipped his black coffee.

"You're gonna be real lucky supporting me for another year if I don't pass this test." She grumbled. He glanced up at the framed graduate equivalency certificate on the wall in the hallway across from him. She'd studied for over a month then. She had been a nervous wreck when she took the test, but she passed it. She called it a stupid piece of paper and told him not to frame it. She said it was evidence of some shortcoming on her part in her past. Anaiah knew what it meant to her really. It was the first steppingstone for her. Proof that she could succeed when her parents had tried to use a lack of education to hold her back. He'd seen the way she looked up at it occasionally with a small smile when she was struggling.

He knew that it ate her up inside that she wasn't currently working full-time. She felt a need to earn her keep. He'd bartered a deal with her. He'd support her for a year while she made school her full-time job and they would split the bills once she started working again. He would support her for the rest of her life if that was what she wanted, but he had fought hard for a year. He smirked at the memory of her adorably angry face when she tried to fight with him about it. He loved the passion she had, the way she set her mind to do something and achieved it with everything she was. She was his warrior queen.

"I'm proud of you." He beamed at her from across the table.

"I haven't even passed my first test. I won't even be an EMT basic for the next three months. THEN, I can work part-time. Are you proud of my ability to con you into paying all my bills while I go to school?" She rolled her eyes.

"Blame Sean for that. He said your boss would have let you get murdered, so he didn't have to be short staffed." Anaiah said. "Sean insisted it would be irresponsible to let you work there and go to school at the same time."

"I blame Sean for a lot of things. That stupid video on Instagram for one thing." She made a grumpy face. Sean had reposted a video of an attempted interview with Eden regarding her family's death. Eden had made one comment and it went semi-viral on several platforms. The vlogger asked her if she wanted to make a comment on her family and her miraculous escape from them. Eden's three-word response had been, "Get fucked, Asshole!" Anaiah tried to hide his grin as he remembered it.

"Can I run through medical terms with you?" She handed him a stack of flash cards. Anaiah smiled as he flipped through them.

"O'course, baby." Anaiah began to read through the definitions and had her give the terms for them. They had gotten most of the way through the stack when they heard a knocking on their door. They'd moved out into the country. The only people who visited usually just came right in and announced their presence loudly by yelling "hello." Sean usually had other more colorful things that he yelled. Anaiah had a bad feeling about this.

He stood from the table and went to the wall in the hallway, removing a blessed enochian etched axe from a hook. Anaiah looked through the glass but didn't see anyone on the wrap-around porch. He slowly opened the door and then unlatched the screen door. He stepped out onto the porch, looking around. He spotted a box resting on the porch swing. It didn't have a mail carrier sticker on it, nor did it have any address or markings on the plain cardboard box. Anaiah shrugged and used the sharp edge of his ax to slice through the tape. Inside was some tissue paper with a note on top.

"Dear Eden,

I believe these rightfully belong to the Eldest and Youngest Daughters of Death. Please give your sister my regards and I do hope that the five of you come meet with me soon. We have much to discuss. I'll be in touch soon.

Sincerely,
The Scholar of Fire

PS. My friends call me James. "

Anaiah wasn't sure what to make of it. Someone had delivered it, but there was no trace of anyone nearby. No cars, no one walking up the path to the main road. He pulled the tissue paper up and noted that inside were two daggers carved from bone. Each had a skull carved into the handles. Anaiah walked into the house, the screen door accidentally slamming behind him.

"Who is it?" Eden called out from the dining room. He pushed the door closed with his foot with more care than was probably warranted.

"Sugar, you better come look at this package you just got and call your sister."

She came walking down the hall over the hardwood in bare feet and a sundress. He was fairly certain she wore it to drive him out of his mind while she was supposed to be studying. It was working.

"Take a look." He handed her the box. Eden smiled up at him and took a bone dagger in her hand.

"They say the war between heaven and hell has raged for an eternity." She stared into his eyes and breathed in a deep breath, clutching the dagger. One of the irises of her eye shifted to all black and the other silver. The hairs on his arms rose as silver and black arcs raced along her tattoos. Her father's voice joined hers as they spoke in unison. The sound of her small voice joined with one of such unearthly power and command sent chills down his spine.

"The time is coming. The prince of hell is drawing in his children. He has been building his army for an age. In his cunning to win this war, he has robbed heaven of its children. Take them back in my name. He wields the Angelus Blade. He is coming for blood and vengeance. He is coming for Heaven. Give him hell."

ACKNOWLEDGEMENTS

First, I would I give all thanks to my heavenly Father, without which I would not still be standing and blessed with the family, friends, and life I have. Every experience, good and bad, were worked together for my good and helped me become the person that I am now.

Secondly, I want to thank my husband for always entertaining my crazy ideas, being my sounding board and always encouraging me. Thanks for finishing a book that is so not your forte to help me grow and for the inspirations for so many scenes in this book.

An enormous thank you goes to my three children who make me immensely proud everyday and continue to have more creative ideas and wittier banter than my brain could ever cook up.

To the OG Journey: Liana. You are an amazing found sister and writer. I am so very blessed to have you in my corner. Thank you for writing nights over coffee and starting this journey with me over 15 years ago.

My Monkey, My Jen, My Birddy and My Arreyis: My amazing beta readers and copy editors: your feedback shaped this book into what it is today. You helped me grow and challenged me to dig deeper to make this world so much bigger and better. I could not have done this without you. Eden's story goes on because of you!

A special note for James: Thank you for always believing in our dreams and always encouraging me in every endeavor. Thank you for being a found brother to my husband. We miss you, dear friend. I choose to believe you are watching us from heaven, shaking your head, and chuckling in that very British way you do.

Elle E. Evans

ABOUT THE AUTHOR

Elle E. Evans is a voracious reader who has been lost in her own imagination since childhood. She grew up telling her friends the crazy fantasy plots she crafted as dreams and ideas for pretend games to play in between devouring novels and fantasy films. She has been writing short stories and novels since her teen years.

This story is especially close to the author's heart as she is an abuse survivor with mental illness and neurodivergence. Overcoming religious trauma and deconstructing what she believed lead to a lot of research and a slight hyper-fixation with angelic lore and apocryphal works of Judeo-Christian biblical works.

Elle lives in Texas with her husband, children, two dogs, and two birds. She dreams of a totally-not-haunted, Victorian-style home in the country with goats, chickens, and hours to write each day.

For more information about where to find Elle E. Evans on social media, character information, character-based playlists and more, visit her website:

www.ElleEEvansAuthor.com

Made in the USA
Monee, IL
12 August 2022

10915703R10208